THE HISTORY OF THE Science FICTION MAGAZINE

EDITED by
MICHAEL ASHLEY

VOL. 1
1926-1935

Henry Regnery Company • Chicago

THE HISTORY OF THE SCIENCE FICTION MAGAZINE
Volume 1: 1926-1935

(Introduction and Appendices), © 1974 by Mike Ashley; used by
permission of the author and the author's agent, Cosmos Literary Agency.
All rights reserved
First published in Great Britain in 1974 by
New English Library, London
First published in the United States in 1976 by
Henry Regnery Company
180 North Michigan Avenue, Chicago, Illinois 60601
Printed in the United States of America
Library of Congress Catalog Card Number: 76-015154
International Standard Book Number: 0-8092-8003-5 (cloth)
0-8092-8001-9 (paper)

To my father for lighting the fire,
and to Sam Moskowitz for feeding the flames.

Preface

Who is your favourite science fiction writer? Robert Heinlein? Arthur Clarke? John Wyndham? Isaac Asimov? Frank Herbert, Clifford Simak, Michael Moorcock . . . ??? Name any leading science fiction writer of today, and the likelihood is that he made his debut in a science fiction magazine.

Very few leading authors have broken into the field through books. True, many have risen to fame through their books, but the chances are that those very books were originally printed in a science fiction magazine.

And yet what credit has the science fiction magazine had? It is generally derided, scoffed at and abused. Today, almost too late, science fiction is gradually being afforded the recognition it deserves and is at last being regarded as adult literature. And yet, even within its field, the science fiction magazine is still regarded as juvenilia.

For what reason? For its garish covers? For its stupendous publishers' blurbs? True science fiction has been a fool to itself. Many publishers realized the potential of the juvenile audience and subsequently pandered to it. As a result *all* science fiction has become tarred with the same brush. To some extent this was the fault of the magazines, but by and large it was the treatment given to science fiction by the film industry that gave the genre its bad name in the world of literature.

The time has come to make amends. For too long science fiction has been "that Buck Rogers stuff", and adult magazines equated with juvenile comics. The science fiction magazine is the foundation of science fiction. Without it many of today's leading authors would probably be unknown scientists or straight-

forward mainstream writers. In April 1976 science fiction magazines will be fifty years old, and what better way to commemo-
rate this event than with a representative history of those
fifty years? And the book you are holding will be part of an
appraisal of those fifty amazing years.

Fortunately for science fiction historians science fiction magazine history falls into certain distinct periods. In April 1926 Hugo
Gernsback issued the first all-science fiction magazine AMAZING
STORIES. In March 1936 the last issue of Gernsback's WOND-
DER STORIES appeared and with that Gernsback departed
from science fiction magazine publishing (for a while). Consequently these first ten years are referred to as 'the Gernsback
era', and it is that era this book covers.

I have endeavoured to give a clear appraisal of the birth and
infancy of the magazines in the introduction that follows, and
then I have chosen one story from each of the ten years from
1926 to 1935 that is representative of that year. Consequently you
might not necessarily find the big names of science action here,
but you will find forgotten science fiction authors whose memory
time has obliterated, and yet who were instrumental in the growth
of the genre. Writers like Charles Willard Diffin, Francis Flagg,
and Drury D. Sharp. Here too you will find early fiction by
current day authors Clifford Simak and Edmond Hamilton.

Here you will find immortal men, sub-microscopic worlds,
intrigue on asteroids, worlds beneath the waves, and adventures in pre-history. Stories from the days when science fiction
writing was an adventure in itself, when authors vied with one
another for original ideas and themes.

It was also the period of the large 'pulp' magazine. The pulp
adventure magazine is synonymous with the early 20th century.
Big, thick issues (usually seven inches by ten inches) with rough
edges, consisting of the cheapest produced woodpulp paper that
existed and loaded with a vast variety of small ads. But all that
was the essence of the pulp magazine: detective stories, war
stories, sea stories, fight stories, everything was there. Science
fiction came late to the field, but it arrived with a bang. The time
would come when every pulp publisher would have at least one
science fiction title in his chain, often more.

Today the science fiction magazine is a rarity. As I write this
Great Britain has but one magazine to its credit. The United
States, where the animal was born, has only seven. Its heyday is
over, and the sun is setting. But AMAZING STORIES is still
struggling on against all odds. I sincerely hope it makes fifty

years, but even if it does not I can at least make this one offer in memory of what AMAZING STORIES stands for.

So let us return to that dawn of science fiction magazines, and see for ourselves the wonder of 'the Gernsback era'.

I would like to acknowledge the invaluable assistance of Messrs. Philip Harbottle and Walter Gillings in the preparation of this anthology; and also give thanks to Dot. Houghton of New English Library for giving me the opportunity to make this tribute to the under dog of literature, the science fiction magazine.

Mike Ashley
February 1974

Introduction:
An Amazing Experiment

1—PREHISTORY

When *Amazing Stories* appeared on the news-stands in America
in April 1926 it was by no means a bolt from the blue. Science
fiction readers were doubtless delighted, but they should not have
been surprised. A magazine entirely devoted to science fiction
was the next logical step in the progression of science fiction in
magazines. Gernsback himself said: ". . . the concept of *Amazing
Stories* in 1926 was not a haphazard undertaking. Its groundwork
had been well prepared for 15 years!"[1]

Fifteen years takes us back to 1911, but we can go still farther
back. As we shall see later, 1911 was the year in which Gernsback
began publishing science fiction. True it was not called science
fiction then. Gernsback would not coin that term for almost
twenty years. His term was 'scientification', but more popular
was scientific romance. However in this history I shall refer to it
as science fiction, or in its most popular abbreviation—'sf'.

The farthest our history can go back is to the start of periodical
publications. The first such periodical appeared in Paris in
January 1665 and was called *Journal Des Sçavans*. Its purpose
was to collect together articles by scientists and learned men of
Europe. It was edited by Denis De Sallo (1626-1669), the founder
of modern periodical criticism. It survived thirteen issues before
French censorship brought about its suppression. Nevertheless it
was revived the following year and lasted for many, many years.

The birth of the first general magazine in Britain came about
in 1731 with *Gentleman's Magazine*, founded by Edward Cave
1691-1754), and it was from the popularity of this periodical that
the word magazine passed generally into the English language

with that particular meaning. It was followed shortly by *London Magazine* (1732), *Scots Magazine* (1739) and *Royal Magazine* (1759). But all these publications had one thing in common—they were magazines of comment, and criticism. It was not until Scottish bookseller William Blackwood (1776-1834) founded *Blackwood's Magazine* in 1817 that fiction began to be featured as a regular part of a periodical. It also contained poems, and went to the extent of serializing novels, its most famous contributor being Marian Evans (1819-1880) better known as George Eliot, whose first work, "The Sad Fortunes of the Rev. Amos Barton" was published in *Blackwood's* in 1857.

The mid-1800's saw a boom in magazine publications. Many authors began their own periodicals, such as Charles Dickens and *Household Words*, and William Thackery with *Cornhill*. It was *Cornhill* that was the first magazine to reach a magnificent circulation of 100,000. By January 1865 there were 544 magazines being regularly published in Great Britain and Ireland.

Obviously more and more of the public were turning to magazines. Initial periodicals were more of an 'in-group' field. Authors writing for authors, politicians for politicians. But the sweeping reform in education, which began in 1815 with the start of infants' schools, and reached a peak with the 1870 Education Act, meant that more and more people could read. The expansion of the railways also meant that people spent more time on trains, and a popular way to pass the time was by reading. In 1849 William Henry Smith (1825-1891) secured the privilege of selling books and newspapers at railway stations. Obviously the magazine field had to expand to cater for the greater variety of readers.

Yet we must acknowledge *Blackwood's Magazine* as being the first to print science fiction, in the shape of future war stories. This came about from a single story "The Battle of Dorking" which appeared anonymously in the May 1871 issue. The author was George Tomkyns Chesney (1830-1895), who later became the Conservative M.P. for Oxford. The story told of the invasion of Britain by Prussian troops, and the successful defeat of our army at Dorking. Appearing within a month after the Prussian success in the Franco-Prussian War, the story evoked much reaction among *Blackwood's* readers. Countless imitations appeared, and there is no denying that "The Battle of Dorking" did much to bring about the inclusion of that type of science fiction in magazines.

The real break came in 1881. In that year George Newnes (1851-1910) started *Tit-Bits*, a pot-pourri of human interest stories. And in January 1891 came *The Strand Magazine*, the first magazine of its kind to sell for just sixpence. (*Cornhill's* for instance had been twice that price thirty years earlier). The emphasis in *Strand* was on easy-to-read stories, and a mélange of factual articles on every facet of life. *Strand* was instantly popular, due in no uncertain terms to its publication of Conan Doyle's Sherlock Holmes adventures.

Imitations flooded the market: *Pearson's Magazine, Ludgate Monthly, Pall Mall Magazine* and *The Idler* being amongst the most prominent. These publications were later to feature the science fiction of such renowned authors as H. G. Wells, George Griffiths and Arthur Conan Doyle. For instance Wells's "The War of the Worlds" was serialized in *Pearson's Magazine,* starting in the April 1897 issue. George Griffith was to be found in *Pearson's Weekly* with "Valdar the Oft-Born" which commenced in the February 2nd 1895 issue.

In fact from 1890 onwards the popular magazines of Great Britain were regular markets for science fiction as popularized by these authors. What's more, at the turn of the century advances in printing techniques resulted in better-finished copies of periodicals being produced at greater speeds.

But already Britain was behind her trans-Atlantic cousin. Popular magazines had come upon the scene just in advance of George Newnes' ideas, but even so science fiction had been a regular part of literary magazine publishing since the days of Edgar Allan Poe. Britain did not figure as a major market of science fiction for thirty years in comparison with the U.S.A.

Edgar Allan Poe (1809-1849) won a fifty-dollar prize for his science fiction story, "Ms. Found in a Bottle". The contest was sponsored by *The Baltimore Saturday Visitor,* and the story appeared in that periodical's issue dated October 19th 1833. Shortly afterwards Poe became connected with the *Southern Literary Messenger,* published in Richmond, Virginia. The March 1835 issue carried "Berenice", and within months Poe was its assistant editor. It also published his moon adventure "Hans Phaall". He left that magazine in 1837, and in 1839 became connected with *Burton's Gentleman's Magazine,* and from 1842-1843 edited *Graham's Magazine.* These were all leading American journals, and there is no doubt that Poe's influence on American readership was significant. His fiction could be found in many periodicals, not least *Godey's Lady's Book,* which had been founded in 1830 and was renowned for its coloured fashion plates. Since most of Poe's fiction was fantasy, it obviously contributed towards the inclusion of fantasy in other periodicals.

And consequently Poe's successor to the bizarre, Fitz-James O'Brien (1828-1862), found a ready market for his fiction. His most famous science fiction story, "The Diamond Lens" appeared in *Atlantic Monthly* for January 1858. The same magazine published his "The Wondersmith" (October 1859), but a major market, for such fiction as "What Was It?" was *Harper's New Monthly Magazine*, which had first appeared in 1850. Many of O'Brien's stories appeared in this magazine, which went on to regularly publish science fiction stories by the great names of literature, including Mark Twain and Edward Bellamy. Before long *Overland Monthly* (1868) appeared, then *Scribner's Monthly* (1870). These four magazines were among the leaders in American periodicals both for the high quality of their content and their wide readership.

But a force to be reckoned with was the juvenile audience. *Harper's* and *Scribner's* were aimed at the American middle and upper classes. In the 1860's Irwin Beadle had commenced *American Novels*, a cheap, regular publication that sold for a dime. The term soon was born—dime-novels. (Britain had its equivalent in the penny-dreadfuls of the Victorian era). The dime-novel entered a boom period in the 1870s, and the prominent publisher was Frank Tousey, its leading author for science fiction, Luis Senarens (1865-1939). Tousey published a regular juvenile series called *Boys Of New York*, and in its issue for February 28th 1876, began serialization of "Frank Reade and His Steam Man of the Prairies" by Harry Enton. Several more Frank Reade adventures appeared, but when Enton tired of the idea Senarens took over, with "Frank Reade Jr., and His Steam Wonder". Senarens was but fourteen at that time, although Tousey was not aware of the fact. Few readers new of Senarens' existence either since the stories appeared with the by-line 'Noname'. But New York's youngsters were agog with the Frank Reade Jr., adventures that Senarens churned out at a remarkable rate. Tousey later started another dime-novel series *Young Men Of America*, for which Senarens wrote a series around boy inventor, Jack Wright.

As is apparent, the theme for these adventures was always a new invention, and consequently they were termed 'invention stories'. So popular were they that many imitations appeared from the various publishing houses, most notable being *Good News* from Street & Smith Publishers. Street & Smith had been formed in 1855, and were formidable rivals to Tousey to start dabbling in his field. Such rivalry was no doubt a spur to Tousey to gamble, and with Frank Reade Jr., stories still guaranteeing circulation builders he took a historic plunge.

His gamble was a regular weekly publication to be devoted entirely to 'invention' stories. Entitled *Frank Reade Library* its first issue appeared on September 24th 1892. Although strictly speaking these amounted to a series of paperback books, there is no denying that it was the first regular publication of science fiction in magazine format. The issues usually contained 32 pages of demy-octavo size (about $8\frac{1}{4} \times 5\frac{1}{2}$ inches). The series was almost exclusively written by Luis Senarens, and included reprinting all the previously published Frank Reade stories. It remained weekly up until February 5th 1897 when it went semi-monthly. Its last edition appeared 192 issues later in August 1898, when Tousey decided it was best to give the series a rest. Certainly the series was popular, and it was only the hostility of many Americans, who maintained that dime novels were harming their children's education, that caused it to decline.

Nevertheless in 1902 Sinclair Tousey carried out his father's wishes and published *Frank Reade Weekly Magazine*. It was all reprint, and its first issue was dated October 31st, just over seven weeks after Frank Tousey's death. *Frank Reade Weekly* lasted until August 26th 1904, and consequently the Luis Senarens' invention stories can lay claim to not only having given birth to the first regular sf publication, but the first regular sf *reprint* publication!

But by this time the dime novel was on the decline. Before *Frank Reade Library* had appeared in 1892 we must look back to a decade earlier, and another children's magazine: *The Golden Argosy*.

Frank Andrew Munsey was born at Mercer in Maine on August 21st 1854. He moved to New York in 1882, where at the age of twenty-eight he began publication of a regular children's weekly, *The Golden Argosy*, first issue December 9th 1882. As the years passed, Munsey's interest in the children's market waned, even though the magazine was highly profitable. He consequently changed the title to *The Argosy* (December 1st 1888), and began to expand his field by starting *Munsey's Magazine* in February 1889. *The Argosy* now began to devote itself to the adult audience, and it thereby became the first adult adventure pulp magazine. It was the standard pulp magazine size (7×10 inches—super royal octavo). Science fiction became a regular part of its content, initially by reprinting such novels as "The Conquest of the Moon" by André Laurie (the nom de guerre of Paschal Grousset, a great friend of Jules Verne), which was serialized from its November 16th 1889 issue. *Argosy* became monthly in April 1894, and would remain so until September 1917. In January 1905 a companion magazine, *All-Story* appeared. Munsey would also publish *All-American Fiction, Scrap Book, Live Wire* and *Cavalier* among his titles. These in particular were the greatest repository for science fiction in the American magazine market from 1894 to 1926.

Munsey's magazines were formidable rivals to the other pulp publishers, in particular Street & Smith. They launched their own pulp adventure title, *Popular Magazine*, in 1904, but this is not remembered with the same affection and nostalgia as the Munsey titles. Only such magazines as Herman Umbstaetter's *The Black Cat*, which began in October 1895 and survived till October 1920 (by then known as *The Thriller*) and *The Clack Book* which had but twelve issues in 1896/7, evoke any such yearnings in old-time fans.

While *Argosy* reached its peak in 1907, and in general the adventure pulp magazine was at its height before World War I, *Argosy's* strength in science fiction did not really start until 1912. This is one year after Gernsback entered the field.

Brief mention should be made here of science fiction outside America and Britain, only because we must be chagrined at the fact that science fiction magazines appeared outside the English language first. It appeared in Tsarist Russia in 1903, and was called *Mirpriklusheniya* (that is *World Of Adventures*). According to the late Willy Ley ". . . the early issues consisted mainly of translations of Jules Verne, but with a sprinkling of Russian authors, one of whom was a lady specializing in interplanetary romances".[2] It appears the magazine outlasted the War and Revolutions, and was still going in 1923, but ceased sometime thereafter.

Also on the Continent, this time in the Germany of The Kaiser, another science fiction magazine appeared, *Captain Mors*. It was apparently a monthly periodical at first, starting in 1908, and later came out every other month, surviving up till 1914 and the War. At least 180 issues appeared, all of them written around the lead character Captain Mors. (One here senses the prototype of *Captain Future* and *Captain Zero*, magazines of a much later period).

Unfortunately my searches have been unable to reveal any further information on either the Russian or German magazines, and I would be fascinated with any light a good reader might be able to throw on them.

And so we come to 1911, the year Gernsback pointed to as the genesis of *Amazing Stories*. Hugo Gernsback was born in Luxembourg City on August 16th 1884. At the age of 19 he emigrated to the United States and set up in the dry cell battery business. One of Gernsback's major interests was radio, having designed the first home radio set in 1905. He subsequently issued a radio catalogue, and when the battery business failed he launched the first ever radio magazine, *Modern Electrics*, in 1908. In 1911, finding a space in the journal, Gernsback began an episode in the history of "Ralph 124C 41+". This first part appeared in the April 1911 issue, and subsequently in eleven further episodes until March 1912. Thereafter science fiction became a regular part of the contents of the magazine, particularly such series as Jacques Morgan's "Mr Foodick" stories which began in 1913, and Clemente Fezandie's yarns. *Modern Electrics* was renamed *Electrical Experimenter* that year, and it was in that periodical that Gernsback began his "Scientific Adventures of Baron Munchhausen", in May 1915. In 1919 Gernsback launched *Radio News*, and *Electrical Experimenter* later metamorphosed into *Science and Invention*.

"Ralph 124C 41+" was subtitled 'A Romance of the Year 2660', and is heavy reading these days. It is remembered as a veritable encyclopaedia of predictions, such as microfilm, tape recorders, vending machines, fluorescent lighting. It set the pattern for the fiction in Gernsback's magazine, and that was essentially a scientific article in fiction form—basic technological extrapolation.

At the other extreme was the scientific romance appearing in Munsey's magazines. Concurrent with Gernsback's "Ralph", *Cavalier* was serializing two science fiction novels, Garrett Serviss' "The Second Deluge", and George Allan England's remarkable "The Elixir of Hate". By this time Serviss was 60 years old, and had reached the peak of his career. But England, then just 34, was a rising star. Following "The Elixir of Hate", *Cavalier* began publication of "Darkness and Dawn", England's novel of a far future, degenerate Earth. Yet, hardly was the serial underway, than *All-Story* began "Under the Moons of Mars" by Norman Bean. It transpired that Bean was a certain Edgar Rice Burroughs (1875-1950), whose name appeared correctly on a second story "Tarzan of the Apes" in the October *All-Story*. A second Martian adventure, "The Gods of Mars" began in the January 1913 *All-Story*, and soon the adventures of John Carter and those of Tarzan would vie for popularity in the pulps.

The public fell head over heels for the Burroughs's adventure stories. Obviously he would be imitated, and Munsey's editors, particularly Bob Davis, looked for the best from the authors. It was as a result of this that people like John U. Giesy, Austin Hall, Homer Eon Flint, Charles B. Stilson, Junius B. Smith and others began to write scientific romances for Munsey. *All-Story*, up until now monthly, went weekly from 1914. In 1916, that one magazine would publish such stories as Austin Hall's "Almost Immortal", Burroughs's "Thuvia, Maid of Mars" and "Tarzan and the Jewels of Opar"; "Box 991" by Giesy and J. B. Smith, "Minos of Sardanes" by Charles Stilson, and "The Sea Demons" by Victor Rousseau. And in 1917 it made another scoop. The issue for November 24th carried "Through the Dragon Glass", the first story by Abraham Merritt (1884-1943). At the start of 1918, "The People of the Pit" appeared, and then in June, "The Moon Pool".

"The Moon Pool", and its sequel, "The Conquest of the Moon Pool" (which started in the February 15th 1919 *All-Story*) shot Merritt into the front of the popularity ranks. The scientific content was virtually nil. In truth the stories were fantasy, but nevertheless as works of imagination they had little equal. The effect that Merritt was to have on later science fiction writers was profound. With Merritt and Burroughs in one corner, and Gernsback in the other, science fiction would appear to be a hermaphrodite of two highly estranged parents. But surprises are always in store in the science fiction world.

The first specialist fiction magazine in the English language, outside the dime-novels, was not a science fiction magazine. It was *Detective Story Magazine*, selling for fifteen cents, and published weekly from October 5th 1915, by none other than Street & Smith. And it was Street & Smith who toyed with the idea of a science fiction magazine, even before Gernsback. It happened in 1919, when Harold Hersey was engaged as editor for just such a publication. Unfortunately when *The Thrill Book* appeared, it was only just another adventure pulp. As time is wont to distort facts, so today, over half a century since *The Thrill Book* appeared, the magazine has come to be regarded as a science fiction publication. But who better to deny that than the editor himself. As he said in his autobiography, "Pulpwood Editor" (1937):

> "It seems that I enjoy a reputation as editor and publisher in the fantasy field, far out of proportion to my just deserts. I

failed miserably with *The Thrill Book* in 1919, a pulp that included many excellent pseudo-science yarns by Murray Leinster and others in its several issues, but which was not entirely devoted to this type of story."[3]

Murray Leinster is perhaps the best remembered name from the days of *The Thrill Book*. The magazine appeared fortnightly, priced at fifteen cents, and its first issue was dated March 1st 1919. It contained a variety of fiction, from lycanthropy in Greye La Spina's "Wolf of the Steppes", to straight adventure as in "The Ivory Hunters" by W. C. Carey. Science fiction in the shape of Donovan Bayley's "The Man Who Met Himself" was not far away however. Murray Leinster did not appear until the tenth issue, dated July 15th 1919, with "A Thousand Degrees Below Zero". By that time Harold Hersey had handed over the editorship to Ronald Oliphand, and the magazine began to veer away even farther from science fiction. It contained a highly informative editorial department called "Cross-Trails" which often gave much inside information, and all in all could be viewed as a more personal magazine than many of the other adventure pulps. Certainly its letter column roared with praise, including comments from no lesser personality than Dr. John U. Giesy himself.

The Thrill Book survived sixteen issues, and died on October 15th 1919, leaving readers with a memory of what might have been.

1919 was a boom year for science fiction. Apart from *The Thrill Book*, *All-Story* and *Argosy* were overrun with excellent science fiction tales. Murray Leinster's "The Runaway Sky-scraper" had appeared in the February 22nd *Argosy*. Leinster, whose real name was William F. Jenkins (born 1896), had been selling fiction and fillers to magazines like *Smart Set* since 1915, and always sold to a diversity of markets. But in the memory of science fiction fans it all began with that time travel story in 1919. Less than a month later *All-Story* carried "The Girl in the Golden Atom" (March 15th issue), which marked the debut of Ray Cummings (1888-1957). The final issues of the year serialized George Allan England's "The Flying Legion". Then there was Max Brand's "That Receding Brow" (*All-Story*, February 15th), Philip Fisher's "The Strange Case of Lemuel Jenkins" (*All-Story*, July 26th), "The Lord of Death" and "The Queen of Life" by Homer Eon Flint (both *All-Story*, May 10th and August 16th respectively), John Giesy's "The Mouthpiece of Zitu" (serialized from July 5th to August 2nd *All-Story*), Austin Hall's "The Man Who Saved the Earth" (*Argosy*, December 13th), and his novel "Into the Infinite" (*All-Story*, April 12th to May 17th) . . . and so on and so on. Could there be any denying that the time was ripe for a magazine devoted to the genre? But still one did not materialize.

Nevertheless, the detective fiction field was booming. It attracted the interests of the Rural Publishing Corporation of Chicago, headed by Jacob C. Henneberger (1890-1969), then publishing *College Humor* and *Magazine Of Fun*. It was decided to enter the detective field, and mystery writer Edwin Baird was hired to edit *Detective Tales*. Henneberger, a great fan of Edgar Allan Poe, decided a companion magazine was in order, and so Baird also found himself responsible for *Weird Tales*, and thereby hangs a tale.

Weird Tales became not so much a magazine as an institution. Its first issue, dated March 1923, with 192 pages, and selling for the frightening price of twenty-five cents, was in no way stupendous. It carried twenty-four stories, mostly a pot-pourri of weird and straight ghost. It did however carry one important story in particular, "Ooze" by Anthony M. Rud, plus the first part of a serial "The Thing of a Thousand Shapes" by Otis Adelbert Kline. "Ooze" was illustrated on the cover, and while doubtless a horror story, the explanation of its bizarre events is completely rational and scientific. Furthermore Cranmer, one of the characters, is described by the narrator as a writer of pseudo-scientific fiction. The 'ooze' of the title is actually a giant amoeba, which had gotten out of hand. Today a very familiar theme, but "Ooze" marked its debut in the science fiction field.

Weird Tales was the first magazine to be devoted entirely to fantasy fiction. Obviously the emphasis was on horror fiction, but it attracted many science fiction stories. In this magazine, they were referred to as weird-scientific, but that does not alter the fact that *Weird Tales*, more so than *All-Story* or *Thrill Book*, soon became the major market for science fiction. Unfortunately this was not to be under Edwin Baird, even though he would first publish H. P. Lovecraft, Otis Kline, Frank Owen, Clark Ashton Smith (poetry only) amongst others. Good though *Weird Tales* was, it was not selling. Not sufficiently to recoup the expenses incurred. With its bumper anniversary issue, dated May-June-July 1924, *Weird Tales* nearly folded. It is only because of the determination of Henneberger that the magazine continued, that it survived. *Real Detective Tales* was sold, the money put into *Weird Tales*, and the title handed over to the printers, who managed to keep it going until the magazine paid off its debts.

And so Farnsworth Wright found himself editor of *Weird Tales*, the first issue under his control appearing in November 1924. Wright admitted that he was not over fond of science fiction, but there was no denying reader approval, and consequently it remained. By now, the "Ooze"-type of story was a regular feature. Basically the plot would tell of a scatter-brained scientist who had managed to create or invent a horrendous monstrosity which immediately broke free and was out of control. A perfect example of this was Otis A. Kline's "The Malignant Entity" which had appeared in the anniversary issue of *Weird Tales* in 1924. Five years later the plot would still appear, almost unaltered, in such tales as H. F. Scotten's "The Thing in the House".

Apart from H. P. Lovecraft (1890-1937), whose 'Cthulhu' Mythos was a category in its own right, only one author broke the bounds of 'laboratory-monster' science fiction in the early days of *Weird Tales*, and that was the now forgotten Nictzin Dyalhis. His first story, "When The Green Star Waned", told of the invasion of Earth by Venusians. (He later wrote a sequel, "The Oath of Hul Jok" in the September 1928 issue). This story appeared in *Weird Tales* for April 1925, and was afforded a cover illustration. It was straight, bizarre science fiction adventure, but obviously the kind readers of the magazine enjoyed. It was thus possible for the road to be open for the stories of Edmond Hamilton, who took *Weird Tales* by storm a year later, with his Martian invasion of Earth novel, "Across Space" (September to November 1926).

Before 1926 therefore, there were three types of science fiction. Firstly the scientific romance epitomized by Burroughs and Merritt that appeared in the Munsey publications. Secondly the scientific extrapolation of Gernsback, and thirdly the weird and bizarre science fiction of *Weird Tales*. These types of science fiction had not come about through authors' desire, but through the publishing policies of the magazines, something so easily overlooked today.

If you have been wondering what Gernsback was doing all this time, then wonder no more. *Radio News* and *Science & Invention* had been regular markets for science fiction for over a decade. His scientific writers were becoming more and more prolific, with the result that a backlog of fiction accumulated at

Gernsback's offices. He therefore made the August 1923 issue of *Science & Invention* a special 'scientifiction' issue, carrying six stories, plus many extrapolative articles. The issue was a success, and obviously Gernsback thought the time was right. But, in his own words:

"Several years ago when I first conceived the idea of publishing a scientification magazine, a circular letter was sent to some 25,000 people informing them that a new magazine, by the name *Scientifiction* was shortly to be launched. The response was such that the idea was given up for two years."[4]

When Gernsback finally went ahead, he did it without prior warning, and was not capable of second thoughts this time. But as I said earlier, no one was surprised when *Amazing Stories* appeared. As you can see, it was already far *overdue*.

2—Three Years Alone

Gernsback was certain not to have *Amazing Stories* overlooked on the bookstalls. All the other multitude of pulp publications, including *Weird Tales* and *All-Story* were the standard pulp size of 7 × 10 inches. *Amazing Stories* was to be large-size (8½ × 11 inches, or demy quarto), and its paper of such heavy stock that its ninety-six pages were as thick as the 192 page pulps. Strictly speaking therefore *Amazing Stories* was *not* a pulp magazine. Its paper was slightly better quality, and it was essentially a companion fiction magazine to the scientific *Science & Invention*. It cost twenty-five cents and was published on the fifth of each month, by the Experimenter Publishing Company, with offices at 53 Park Place, New York. (President of the company was Hugo, but it is often forgotten that the Treasurer was his brother, Sidney Gernsback).

The front cover was the work of forty-five year old, Austrian artist Frank R. Paul, who had originally been a cartoonist for *Jersey Journal*, before Gernsback attracted him to *Electrical Experimenter* in 1914. The cover, showing some beaming ice-skaters on a frozen world, with the great orb of Saturn seemingly inches away, depicted a scene from Jules Verne's "Off On a Comet", which was serialized in two parts.

In his editorial, Gernsback explained his intentions in publishing the magazine. First he defined science fiction:

"By 'scientifiction' I mean the Jules Verne, H. G. Wells, and Edgar Allan Poe type of story—a charming romance intermingled with scientific fact and prophetic vision." . . . "But with the ever increasing demands on us for this sort of story, and more of it, there was only one thing to do—publish a magazine in which the scientific fiction type of story will hold forth exclusively."

Gernsback had high hopes for science fiction, as later in the editorial he explains:

"Not only do these amazing tales make tremendously interesting reading—they are also always instructive. They supply knowledge that we might not otherwise obtain—and they supply it in a very palatable form. For the best of these modern writers of scientifiction have the knack of imparting knowledge, and even inspiration, without once making us aware that we are being taught."[5]

Without a doubt it was Gernsback's belief that readers would be instructed through science fiction, a belief that he always maintained. (Four years later when setting a competition for a slogan for *Science Wonder Stories* his own suggestion was 'Science Taught Through Fiction').

Unfortunately he did not back this up in the fiction he printed, the reason being that that kind of fiction was not available. It was there in small doses, but as a rule most writers did *not* have the knack of making their stories read excitingly and not like a lecture. Often in such a story the narrator would stop in the middle of a scene to explain, in text-book language, the reasons for some recent occurrence, sometime punctuated by cries of: "Why didn't I realize that!" It was the saving of *Amazing Stories* that so few of these stories appeared. For the most part the magazine was filled with wonderful adventures, and why? Because *Amazing Stories* was initially chiefly reprints. Between April 1926 and July 1928 with the first eighteen serials, all but one were reprints. (Verne and Wells had five each of these). The first two issues were entirely reprint, the first new story (Wertenbaker's "The Coming of the Ice") not appearing until the third (June) issue.

For the record that first ever issue of a science fiction magazine contained, besides the Jules Verne serial, the following fiction: "The New Accelerator" by H. G. Wells, part one of "The Man From the Atom" by G. Peyton Wertenbaker, "The Thing From

—Outside" by George Allan England, "The Man Who Saved the World" by Austin Hall and "The Facts in the Case on M. Valdemar" by Edgar Allan Poe.

It was a wise choice. There was a wide diversity of theme and style, from Wells's amusing tale of two scientists who take a drug which accelerates their rate of living, to England's psychological horror tale of alien invasion. However, one would have to delve deep and long to cull any great scientific knowledge from the contents. But there is little doubt that people enjoyed them, and *Amazing Stories* shot into the fore in circulation, within months exceeding 100,000.

Gernsback was Editor/Publisher of *Amazing Stories*, and while he wrote the editorials, decided the policy and had the last word, he did not do the donkey work. Two people in particular are worth mentioning here for their part in this prototype publication: C. A. Brandt and T. O'Conor Sloane.

Brandt was a chemist born in Germany in 1879. Gernsback learnt from a book dealer that Brandt had a fabulous library of science fiction, and that he was an ideal choice to help in the selection of great world science fiction. Brandt consequently became Literary Editor of *Amazing Stories*, and the science fiction reprints were invariably his choice. Brandt stayed with *Amazing Stories* for a considerable time, his major contribution being the regular book reviews that became a standard feature of *Amazing Stories* up until 1938. He died in 1947 before finalizing matters in connection with a new sf magazine he was intending to publish.

Thomas O'Conor Sloane was born in New York on November 24th 1851, and became the Professor of Natural Sciences at Seton Hall college in South Orange, New Jersey in 1888. A string of inventions are connected with him, mostly the self-recording photometer for determining the illuminating power of gas. In 1877 he had described a new process for determining sulphur in illuminating gas. He was also the author of several books, including "Electric Toy Making For Amateurs" (1892) and "Rapid Arithmetic" (1922). A benign, bearded old gentleman, he was seventy-four when he became Associate Editor of *Amazing Stories*. Essentially Sloane was the editor. He read the new fiction and moulded the magazine's contents, leaving the gimmickry and ideas to Gernsback. Sloane, as we shall see, would later inherit *Amazing Stories*, which he would edit until 1938. By then he was 86, and consequently the oldest science fiction editor there has ever been. He died on August 7th 1940.

Another name figured on the masthead of *Amazing Stories*, that of Wilbur C. Whitehead. In his obituary in the September 1931 issue, it was said: "In the early days he influenced the conduct of the magazine by his advice. He had an extensive knowledge of scientific fiction, which was his hobby."[6] Whitehead is better remembered as an expert on auction bridge.

Amazing Stories was scheduled as a monthly, but Gernsback put the suggestion to the readers to vote on what they thought the ideal schedule would be. The results, reported in his editorial in the September 1926 issue, were *Monthly* 498, *Semi-Monthly* 32,644. The overwhelming vote in favour of a fortnightly *Amazing Stories* resulted in Gernsback admitting he would try and attain such a schedule. It never came, but Gernsback offered something much greater. More of that in a moment.

Gernsback realized the potential of his readership. In the June 1926 editorial he remarked on his surprise at learning of the hidden army of fans in the country, "who seem to be pretty well orientated in this literature".[7] Obviously *Amazing Stories* had attracted ardent followers who had relentlessly ploughed through the Munsey magazines in search of their favourite literature, science fiction, but who now had it ready-packaged. The future of *Amazing Stories* was assured when Gernsback decided to respond to this readership, and this he did in two ways.

The first was by way of competitions. It would soon become synonymous with Gernsback and his science fiction magazines that not many months would pass without some kind of competition. The first was in the December 1926 issue. The ever capable Frank Paul had drawn a startling cover, and readers were requested to submit stories based around the cover picture. An added enticement was the $250·00 first prize. The response was beyond even Gernsback's wildest dreams. In his March editorial he declared that over *three hundred and sixty* manuscripts had been received.

His second achievement was the inclusion of a letter column in the magazine, called "Discussions". Letter columns were not new in magazines, not even in specialist magazines. Street & Smith's *Detective Story Magazine* carried one, and from its earliest days *Weird Tales* had sported "The Eyrie". But somehow "Discussions" became something different, and this is due to the science fiction fan himself. After each letter Gernsback published the name and full address of the correspondent, and this meant that readers could write to fellow fans, and even visit them.

The first "Discussions" appeared in the January 1927 issue. For the record the first named letter writer was Professor Jack Edwards of San Francisco. (I say first *named*, because two other letters were quoted from, but unfortunately the readers were ridiculed, and consequently their names were not printed. One reader had said that Jules Verne was 'a very promising writer').

In 1927 Gernsback offered a bonus to his avid readers. To celebrate *Amazing Stories'* anniversary, an *Annual* was issued. The intention here was to publish a complete novel, and the issue was padded out with shorter pieces. The *Annual* appeared in June, and the lead novel was none other than "The Master Mind of Mars", specially commissioned by Gernsback from Edgar Rice Burroughs. The rest of the issue was all reprint, made up mostly from stories that had already appeared in *Amazing Stories* during its first year. Obviously Gernsback was aiming here at the Munsey audience not yet attracted to his publication. He succeeded. Even though the *Annual* cost fifty cents, it was a complete sell-out. It carried thirty-two more pages than the monthly, and was a very heavy and hefty package. With the *Annual's* success, and repeated reader enthusiasm that *Amazing Stories* should go fortnightly, Gernsback compromised. Starting in January 1928, he issued a *Quarterly*.

Amazing Stories Quarterly was a real bonanza. 144 large size pages for fifty cents, carrying *two* novels, as well as several short stories. Although the first issue carried one reprint novel, "When the Sleeper Wakes" by H. G. Wells, it did carry a 20,000 plus word short novel by Earl L. Bell, "The Moon of Doom". (This was one of the early disaster stories of the moon falling towards the Earth and the resultant catastrophes).

Since "The Moon of Doom" was of novel length it ranks as only the third original novel that Gernsback had published in his fiction magazines. As stated previously of the first eighteen serials, only one was original. This was "Beyond The Pole" by veteran author A. Hyatt Verrill (1871-1954). However it was obvious that Gernsback was in receipt of longer material, since he was serializing Ray Cummings' novels in *Science & Invention*. What is more his choice of reprint novels was not entirely in line with his policy of learning science through fiction. For instance the most popular novel of the first two years was Merritt's "The Moon Pool" in the May, June and July 1927 issues. Merritt would have been the first to admit that this story was more fantasy than science fiction. Yet this story proved to be one of the most influential he published, many authors later pointing to this work as the inspiration for their own fiction.

When Gernsback next published an original serial in *Amazing Stories* it made history. "The Skylark of Space" began in the August 1928 issue, as a three part extravaganza. What readers did not know was that this story had been started in 1915, and in fact had been rejected by every book and magazine publisher since 1920. The authors were Edward Elmer Smith and Lee Hawkins Garby. Mrs Garby had actually only assisted Smith at the inception of the novel, which was virtually all his own work. The novel covered the search by super-scientist Richard Seaton for his betrothed, kidnapped by the villainous Dr. Marc DuQuesne. As a backcloth, Smith chose the entire universe, and the awesome space ship *Skylark* toured the cosmos encountering multifarious adventures with countless strange aliens.

Readers went berserk over Smith's novel, and if Merritt's "The Moon Pool" was the most influential novel of this period then Smith's was an exceedingly close second. With this novel superscience really got underway. Hitherto the interplanetary stories of *Amazing Stories* had been confined to the solar system. Now there were no holds barred. Ironic that it should take a story thirteen years old to create such a precedent.

Smith's novel closed in the October 1928 issue, leaving fans panting for a sequel. One was not forthcoming for two years, and by that time another author was following in Smith's footsteps, the youthful John Campbell.

In the first three years of *Amazing Stories* and its companion *Quarterly*, a considerable number of authors had made their debuts. Some are sadly forgotten today, others remembered with fond nostalgia. Among the brighter stars were the following. A. Hyatt Verrill (October 1926), Miles J. Breuer (January 1927), Bob Olsen (June 1927), Francis Flagg (November 1927), David H. Keller (February 1928), Fletcher Pratt (May 1928), Harl Vincent (June 1928), Stanton Coblentz (Summer 1928), R. F. Starzl (Summer 1928), Edward E. Smith (August 1928), Jack Williamson (December 1928) and S. P. Meek (Winter 1929). These dozen authors can all claim to be Gernsback discoveries. Of them, apart from E. E. Smith, David H. Keller was by far the most popular, and 1928 was his year. Keller's policy was to concentrate on the social implications of science, rather than the invention itself. His debut "The Revolt of the Pedestrians", portrayed a future where the automobile has taken over, and the remaining pedestrians are treated like animals. "The Psycho-phonic Nurse" predicts a future where mothers leave their children to robot nurses. Keller's fiction was a good test of the freedom of Gernsback's publishing and editorial policy. For instance, "A Biological Experiment" in the June 1928 issue, explored a future where the urge for motherhood and fatherhood still existed in a world where all men and women are sterile. Such a story was profound for its period. Even more so was "The Menace", the title given to four connected stories dealing with the revolution of the American Negro after he had perfected a way of turning his skin pigmentation white. When Negro scientists succeeded in extracting gold from seawater their plans for world domination come to fruition. This example shows admirably the latitude allowed by Gernsback in his publications.

Astute readers may have noticed several names missing from the twelve listed above, two in particular. Where, oh where, are Murray Leinster and Edmond Hamilton, or for that matter Ray Cummings, Ralph Milne Farley and Clare Winger Harris? All were important science fiction writers of this period. Here we come to an interesting point in connection with the Gernsback magazines. None of these authors was a Gernsback discovery, and with one exception none owes fame to Gernsback. The one exception is female author Clare Winger Harris, who was a favourite contributor to *Amazing Stories* during 1927 and 1928 with such tales as "The Fate of the Poseidonia" and "The Miracle of the Lily", but the fact remains that her real start was in *Weird Tales* for July 1926 with "A Runaway World". Only one other of her stories appeared in that magazine, but nevertheless she was a discovery of Farnsworth Wright.

Ralph Milne Farley's popularity rested on the Venusian adventures related in his series about "The Radio Man" which began in *Argosy* in 1924. Farley (real name Roger Sherman Hoar), was essentially a Munsey author, and never once appeared in Gernsback's *Amazing Stories*. He did not contribute to science fiction magazines until 1930. Much the same applies to Ray Cummings and Murray Leinster. Both were quite at home in the Munsey magazines. Ray Cummings did contribute to Gernsback's *Science & Invention*, but despite his popularity he only appeared in one issue of *Amazing Stories*, with the lead novelette in the October 1927 number, "Around the Universe". Even then *Weird Tales* had the upper hand with two Cummings' serials within months of each other. Murray Leinster soon attracted the eye of Gernsback who reprinted many of his early stories ("The Runaway Skyscraper", "The Mad Planet" and "The Red Dust") in *Amazing's* first year. Yet these stories were six years old. Leinster stuck to *Argosy*, but yet again a science fiction serial, "The Strange People" appeared in *Weird Tales* in 1928.

But Edmond Hamilton was quite another matter. Hamilton began in the August 1926 issue of *Weird Tales* with "The Monster God of Mamurth", and in fact had six other stories in that magazine, including two serials, before he was introduced to *Amazing Stories* readers as a 'new' author in January 1928. Hamilton's output was from the start nothing less than prolific, and *Weird Tales* was initially his major market. All his fiction at that time was sf, and as early as February 1929 he introduced his concept of an interstellar Council of Suns, whose laws were enforced by the Interstellar Patrol. Readers who clung to *Amazing Stories* and pooh-poohed the ghost-stories of *Weird Tales* were missing some historical writing.

There was much toing-and-froing from *Weird Tales* to *Amazing Stories*. Hamilton and Clare Harris went one way, David Keller went the other. One momentous scoop of Gernsback in this period was acquiring "The Colour Out of Space" by *Weird Tales*' major author H. P. Lovecraft. The story rejected by both Wright and Davis of *Argosy* has since become a classic of its kind, and I wonder how many of those who have read it realized it was the first printed in the September 1927 *Amazing Stories*.

From April 1926 to April 1929 Gernsback had the monopoly of science fiction magazine publishing, but quite obviously not the monopoly of science fiction. *Weird Tales* and *Argosy* remained his closest rivals, and although *Argosy* exceeded *Amazing Stories* in circulation, its science fiction content was shrinking. *Weird Tales* on the other hand had a far smaller circulation of dedicated readers. That magazine had slight rivalry from a short-lived magazine, *Tales of Magic & Mystery*, which survived for five issues from December 1927 to April 1928. It succeeded in attracting *Weird Tales*' contributors, notably Lovecraft, Frank Owen and Archie Binns. However it cannot claim *Weird Tales*' success at having been the magazine to carry the first works of Disney writer Robert Spencer Carr ("The Composite Brain", March 1925) and Tennessee Williams ("The Vengeance of Nitocris", August 1928).

More of a rival was the large-size pulp magazine *Ghost Stories*, which had appeared two months after *Amazing Stories* in June 1926, as a monthly publication. *Ghost Stories* made some attempts at publishing so called 'true' ghost tales with fake photographs. It was a moderate success, coming in the wake of its big companion magazines *True Story* and *True Detective Mysteries*. The publisher was Bernarr MacFadden (1868-1955), the health fanatic who had started *Physical Culture* in 1898. That magazine had attained a formidable circulation, and he was duly worried at the likely success of Gernsback's competing titles, notably *Your Body*.

One day Gernsback woke to find bankruptcy proceedings filed against the Experimenter Publishing Company. He was forced to sell the titles to the magazines (*Science & Invention* had folded in 1928, but *Radio News* was still published). It was purchased by Radio-Science Publications Inc. of Jamaica Avenue in New York, and subsequently by Teck Publications Inc. of Dunellen, New Jersey. The editorial offices moved first to 381 Fourth Avenue New York, and then to 222 West 39th Street.

But Gernsback was no longer its editor. Although Miriam Bourne was by now Managing Editor, Arthur Lynch was brought in as Editor-in-Chief. However the main job was done by Sloane. The change came with the May 1929 issue, and by the November 1929 issue Sloane was fully in charge. At the age of 77 he took the magazine into its second era. And what of Gernsback? He was to return later with a vengeance.

3—A GATHERING OF SF

The last issue of *Amazing Stories* that Gernsback edited was the April 1929 number. In June 1929 he was back with the first issue of *Science Wonder Stories*. The new publication was published by the Stellar Publishing Corporation, with editorial offices at 96/98 Park Place, New York—within a stone's throw of the old Experimenter Publishing Company's offices.

Gernsback was not deserted. Many of the people he had discovered followed him, particularly Frank Paul as illustrator. At *Amazing Stories* Sloane had to cast around for a new cover artist. Initially Hugh MacKay and Hans Wessolowski filled a few issues, but from February 1930 onwards the mainstay of the magazine was Peruvian artist Leo Morey. Brickbats and roses have been cast upon the works of both Paul and Morey, although in my opinion neither was spectacular. Paul had to be admired for his versatility—it was claimed that he never once drew the same space ship design twice. Paul's failing however was with people, and continuous studies of his work will soon invoke a disdain for his flat-chested, jodhpur-clad females. Morey on the other hand might not have had the imagination of Paul but was passably the more artistic of the two.

Science Wonder Stories was large-size, 96 pages, and sold for 25 cents. Monthly, its first issue began a serial "The Reign of the Ray" by Fletcher Pratt and Irwin Lester. Readers of the first issue were doubly surprised to find announcements of *another* magazine, *Air Wonder Stories*. The companion title appeared in July 1929, same format, but specializing in aerial and inter-planetary adventures. That first issue led with a reprint novel, "Ark of the Covenant" by Victor MacClure.

Gernsback did not stop there. The success he had had with *Amazing Stories Quarterly* warranted a successor. In October 1929 *Science Wonder Quarterly* appeared, large-size, 144 pages for 50 cents. The lead novel was "The Shot Into Infinity" by German author Otto Willi Gail (1896-1956). To a certain extent in *Amazing Stories* Gernsback had tried to locate good European science fiction. He had started with Brandt's translation of Kurt Siodmak's "The Eggs From Lake Tanganyika". With his new publications Gernsback ploughed this field with avid enthusiasm, and Francis Currier's translation of Gail's interlunar adventure led the way. Coincidentally Currier's translation of Hermann Noordung's "The Problems of Space Flying" was serialized in the first three *Science Wonder Stories* issues.

Three sf magazines were not enough for Gernsback. He also began a series of original paperback pocketbooks, the *Science Fiction Series*. With a special offer of twelve books for one dollar, the series led with "The Girl From Mars" by Jack Williamson and Miles Breuer, and within the next few months twelve titles were available.

To top everything, Gernsback experimented one stage further, Starting in January 1930, readers could buy a fourth magazine. *Scientific Detective Monthly*. Gernsback had a penchant for such stories, having reprinted many of the tales by Edwin Balmer and William MacHarg. Arthur B. Reeve, the author of the Craig Kennedy adventures, was enrolled as Editorial Commissioner, with Gernsback acting as Editor-in-Chief. The donkey work fell on the shoulders of Hector Grey, chiefly because this magazine was so specialist. Strictly speaking it was only borderline science fiction. Although it carried some excellent science fiction, it also carried much that was strictly detective with a smattering of volts. As a result the magazine fell into the chasm between two worlds. After five issues it was retitled *Amazing Detective Tales*. Two issues later Hector Grey was replaced by David Lasser, but too late. After ten issues, in October 1930, the magazine folded, Gernsback's first science fiction failure. It came as no surprise though, since it was neither sought after by science fiction fans nor detective fans, other than the most devoted. Nevertheless its existence adds to the evidence for Gernsback's verve in the publishing field. (By now he had also started *Radio-Craft* and *Short Wave Craft*, and later expanded to *Everyday Science & Mechanics, Sexology,* and even *Pirate Stories*).

Once again, as Gernsback had left the menial task of editing to Sloane at Experimenter, at Stellar the Managing Editor was David Lasser. Lasser however was some fifty years Sloane's junior. Born in Baltimore, Maryland on March 20th 1902, Lasser had somehow entered the army in July 1918, and was a member of the U.S. expeditionary force. He was discharged as a sergeant in February 1919, still only *sixteen.* Then he became an Engineer at Rosendale, Newark, and afterwards an Insurance Agent and then Technical Writer. Lasser later became the Founder President of the American Rocket Society in March 1930 and wrote the first book on space travel in the English language, "The Conquest of Space" (1931). All this amply entitled him to edit a science fiction magazine, but is consequently all the more surprising when one discovers what became of him later in life.

Air Wonder Stories was chiefly a specialist publication, and attracted fewer readers than its companion title. As a saving grace, Gernsback combined the titles, and the single issue *Wonder Stories* appeared in June 1930. One reason for the name change was that it was felt that "the word 'Science' has tended to retard the progress of the magazine, because many people had the impression that it is a sort of scientific periodical rather than a fiction magazine."[8] This seemed rather a meagre explanation however since the word 'Science' was printed in minute, pale print, and 'Stories' was always in bolder lettering. After all it had been Gernsback's intention to teach through science fiction, so one would have thought he would have rather attracted those people interested in science.

Be that as it may, *Wonder Stories* appeared in June 1930, in direct opposition to *Amazing Stories.* But lo! Besides the *Quarterlies,* bookstall hunters discovered a third title, *Astounding Stories.* Was this yet another Gernsback title? No, it could not be, since the small flag in the top right corner proclaimed, 'A Clayton Magazine'. What's more it sold for 20 cents, five cents cheaper than the other magazines. And above all, it was a pulp magazine. Gernsback's monopoly of the field was now at an end. The pulp publishers at had last decided to enter the science fiction field.

The new magazine was called *Astounding Stories of Super Science*, of standard pulp size with 144 pages. It was published by William L. Clayton who at one period had Harold Hersey as his head editor. Hersey recalls that he had "discussed plans with Clayton to launch a pseudo-science fantasy sheet".[9] But obviously Clayton needed more time to think. Some two years after Hersey had left Clayton for MacFadden, and Harry Bates was now one of the lead editors, it appeared Clayton had a bee in his bonnet about having a new magazine. It was Bates who suggested a science fiction magazine, and who created the name *Astounding Stories of Super Science*.

Its first issue was dated January 1930, and its list of contributors was formidable· Victor Rousseau, Ray Cummings, S. P. Meek, and Murray Leinster amongst them. Apart from Meek, all were straight Munsey authors. The intent was obvious from the outset—*Astounding Stories* was to be an adventure magazine with just enough science fiction to warrant the title 'super-science'. The cover, by 47 year old Hans Waldemar Wessolowski (known as Wesso), illustrated a scene from Rousseau's serial, "The Beetle Horde", showing our hero having a punch-up with a rather oversized, pugilistic bug. Wesso would be the Paul of the Clayton magazines, being the cover artist on all issues, and illustrative artist in most.

Astounding Stories did not always print science fiction. Occasionally the straight weird story filtered into its pages, but these appeared less and less. *Astounding* soon became very popular, particularly through the appearances of Ray Cummings —who had four serials and three other stories in the first two years of the magazine, and new favourites Charles W. Diffin and Anthony Gilmore. After two lesser stories, Gilmore shot to fame with his novelette "Hawk Carse" in the November 1931 issue. Here was science fiction in the manner of E. E. Smith, with the courageous Hawk Carse chasing the evil pirate Dr. Ku Sui throughout the Solar System. This novelette and its four sequels is fondly remembered as the essence of the Clayton issues. It was not known for a long time that the real authors behind the pen-name Anthony Gilmore were none other than Editor Harry Bates and his assistant editor, Desmond Hall.

Harry Bates was not solely responsible for *Astounding*. He

already had a clutch of adventure magazines, to which *Jungle Stories* was later added, and from September 1931 *Strange Tales*. This magazine was set up in competition with *Weird Tales*, and it published some excellent fiction by that publication's big names, Robert Howard, Clark Ashton Smith and Edmond Hamilton, as well as attracting many weird-scientific stories from *Astounding's* authors Charles W. Diffin, S. P. Meek and Ray Cummings. Many of its stories were pure science fiction of the monster-in-the-laboratory type, but perhaps its most famous story was Jack Williamson's "Wolves of Darkness" with his fourth-dimensional treatment of werewolves.

Weird Tales also had a companion magazine. Farnsworth Wright was partial to oriental fiction, pioneered in his magazine by Frank Owen. Later authors, particularly E. Hoffman Price, had chosen the East as the locale for their bizarre mysteries. Finally, in October 1930, a magazine appeared devoted to the sub-genre, *Oriental Stories*. Every other month, pulp-sized, 144 pages and costing 25 cents, it is of borderline interest to science fiction fans. It carried the occasional science fiction story, particularly when, reborn as *Magic Carpet Magazine* in 1933, it published Edmond Hamilton's adventures of Stuart Merrick on the far-off world of Kaldar, with its mysterious spider people.

Of science fiction magazines, however, 1931 dawned with five major titles, *Amazing Stories, Wonder Stories*, their attendant *Quarterlies* and *Astounding Stories* (the suffix *of Super Science* was dropped with the February 1931 issue). April 1931 saw the birth of another, *Miracle Science and Fantasy Stories*.

Harold Hersey had left Clayton Publications in 1927 for MacFadden, where as Supervising Editor he had a hand in most publications, particular *True Strange Stories* and *Ghost Stories*. But within two years he had established his own Good Story Publishing company, where he specialized in gangster magazines. Elliott Dold was an artist in the company, and he encouraged Hersey to begin his own science fiction magazine. Elliott Dold was drafted as editor, since he commissioned the fiction, although Harold Hersey had a hand in most of the decision-making. This was one of Elliott Dold's rare attempts at editing. His elder brother, Douglas Dold, had been a competent editor at Clayton Magazines with an adventure magazine, *Danger Trail*. The remarkable fact about Douglas Dold however was that as a result of an accident in the First World War, he was blind. An assistant was hired to read manuscripts. This must be one of the rare cases of a blind editor.

Miracle Stories was not exactly top quality. The standard 144 pulp pages, this magazine is today one of the rarest science fiction finds, but only the true collector is likely to search it out. The fiction was not exceptional, although the first issue included such names as Ray Cummings, Victor Rousseau and Arthur Burks. By all accounts Dold was attempting to imitate *Astounding*, even to the extent of including weird fiction. The lead novel to the first issue was his brother's "Valley of Sin", a lost race tale.

The magazine was scheduled to appear every other month, and true enough a second issue appeared in June 1931. But then no more. In all likelihood *Miracle* was too much an imitation of *Astounding* to survive in those Depression days, when twenty cents was at stake. According to Hersey however, "serious illness prevented his (Dold's) continuing services as editor-artist-writer and I decided to put the magazine aside temporarily".[10] It was never revived.

By 1931 however, science fiction was becoming a force to be reckoned with in the publishing field. But not the *scientific* fiction of Gernsback. It was the adventure romance of Munsey that caused the biggest thrill, and obviously here *Astounding Stories* had much influence. The first ripplings that science fiction characters were saleable commodities had come with the transition of Buck Rogers from story to comic-strip. Buck Rogers had been created by Philip Francis Nowlan, and first appeared in "Armageddon 2419" in the August 1928 *Amazing Stories*, followed by "The Airlords of Han" in the March 1929 issue. Nowlan transcribed the adventures to be syndicated in comic-strip format in many hundreds of newspapers, as "Buck Rogers in the 21st Century". The plot outline of super-hero versus arch-criminal was scarcely new, but it took on a different outlook. Here was a theme the pulp adventure magazines could not overlook, and before long titles appeared with whole issues devoted to adventure fiction with a long lead story about some heroic or evil character. In April 1931 came *The Shadow*, and by mid-1932 was appearing twice monthly. The first science fiction character to appear in such a magazine was *Doc Savage*, first issue March 1933. Doctor Clark Savage, Jr. had a fabulous combination of scientific skill, mental wizardry and physical prowess, and made a business of helping people out of any strange or bizarre troubles. Every adventure was scripted by Kennth Robeson, a pseudonym for a variety of authors. But virtually all the Doc Savage adventures were the work of Lester Dent. The magazine appeared regularly every month for the next fourteen years, when issues became less regular. In the early 1940's a 'Doc Savage' comic-book also appeared, but that's another story.

Doc Savage was published by the ubiquitous Street & Smith Publishing Company. One might say that this was their first science fiction magazine if you discount *The Thrill Book*, but strictly speaking *Doc Savage* was not such a publication. Usually only the lead-novel was science fiction—the remainder of the issue filled out by the usual adventure stories. It was aimed at a juvenile audience, and was probably the most popular of the character-adventure magazines. As the 1930's progressed the pulp field became overcrowded with such periodicals. *The Spider* began in October 1933, *Operator* 5 in April 1934, *Secret* 6 in October 1934, and so on.

Further specialization went on in the horror fiction field. *Weird Tales* by now had become a prestige publication. It was an honour to appear in its pages, at least among fellow authors. Nevertheless Farnsworth Wright was never quite satisfied with the knife-edge economics of his magazine, and always had an eye on his rival publications to keep up with trends.

The competition really began with *Dime Mystery Magazine*, put out from the newly established Popular Publications of Chicago. Harry Steeger was the President of the Company, and Managing Editor Rogers Terrill. *Dime Mystery* concentrated on the weird story, and from its first issue in December 1932 proved very popular, and attracted a great deal of *Weird Tales'* authors, such as Arthur Burks, Paul Ernst and Hugh Cave. *Dime Mystery* was certainly not aimed at a juvenile audience, there was a definite slant towards more sexy and sadistic fiction. Popular Publications soon began to expand in this field, with *Terror Tales* (September 1934) and *Horror Stories* (January 1935), and before long many imitations sprang up: *Spicy Mystery Stories* (July 1934), and *Mystery Adventure Magazine* (January 1935) amongst them.

All this influenced Farnsworth Wright into incorporating sex and sadism into *Weird Tales*, with the result that apart from the continued appearance of Edmond Hamilton, less and less science fiction appeared in its pages. This period denotes the start of *Weird's* decline. Under Wright its heyday lasted from 1928 to 1936. Then, with the deaths of H. P. Lovecraft and Robert E. Howard, the retirement of Clark Ashton Smith, and virtual retirement of Otis Kline, and a move towards sadistic fiction, *Weird Tales* was no longer considered a regular market for science fiction. In this survey we therefore bid it a fond farewell. (*Weird Tales* was edited by Wright until 1940, when the magazine changed hands, and Dorothy McIlwraith the editor of *Short Stories*, took it over until its demise in September 1954, after 279 issues).

All this goes to show the sprouting of specialization in the pulp adventure field in the early 1930's. Science fiction was but one branch on a tree, but a fairly profitable one nevertheless. However, times were hard. The Wall Street Crash of 1929 had heralded the American Depression, and by 1933 it had reached its nadir.

Such would naturally affect the science fiction magazines, and sure enough the first to suffer were the bulky quarterlies which at fifty cents were too expensive for the public. The last two issues of *Amazing Stories Quarterly* were reprints. Dated Winter 1933 and Winter 1934, the magazine was not immediately cut. There is no doubt it would have survived the depression years if it had not been for the aged Editor Sloane, for whom things were becoming too much. In answer to one readers remarks in "Discussions" he said: "The Quarterly will be somewhat irregular in dates of publication. We have sometimes felt like discontinuing it definitely".[11] That was written in May 1935. Obviously, the feelings became insurmountable, as no more appeared.

Wonder Stories Quarterly died in January 1933 with its fourteenth issue, and in the middle of that year *Wonder Stories* found itself missing issues. It regained its monthly status by the end of the year, but not without several changes. The early 1930's had really seen *Wonder Stories* at the top of the popularity tree, and *Astounding* an aspiring joint second with *Amazing*, which was gradually declining. *Amazing* kept its head above water by virtue of two authors, E. E. "Doc" Smith, and John W. Campbell, who had first appeared in the January 1930 issue. *Amazing Stories* however remained large size right up until October 1933 when it at last succumbed to the standard pulp format. Teck had moved their publishing offices to Chicago, although the editorial offices remained in New York.

Wonder Stories had experimented earlier with pulp size. Starting in November 1930, *Wonder* soon followed *Astounding* as the second *pulp* science fiction magazine, but twelve issues later it returned to large size. This remained until October 1933, and then from November it reverted to pulp size.

Strange that these two dates should coincide in the closing months of 1933. But even stranger that *Astounding Stories* also underwent changes in those months.

Under Clayton, *Astounding* had built a formidable following, and Bates was about to instigate some revolutionary new ideas. Already he had bought E. E. Smith's latest novel. But alas, this was not to be. Clayton bought out his partner in the firm, but the cost of raising the money in those dark days was too much. *Astounding* went first every other month, and then Harry Bates was forced to pay on publication. This was a blow to science fiction authors, since *Astounding* had been a profitable market. Gernsback's publications (both early and current) had paid only half-a-cent per word on publication. *Astounding* however paid *two* cents a word on acceptance.

March 1933 saw the end of the Clayton *Astounding Stories*, at a time when the magazine was growing. A regular scientific department, "Science Forum" had just begun. This corresponded to Gernsback's "Science Questions and Answers". But there was no promised "Doc" Smith serial.

But that was not the end of *Astounding Stories*. October 1933 and the magazine was back on the stands, not as a Clayton Magazine, but—'A Street & Smith Publication'. If any publishers deserved an sf magazine after much trying, this firm certainly did. The magazine differed little in format and price, but the cover was certainly not by Wesso. It was the work of veteran Howard V. Brown, who replaced Wesso as the *Astounding* cover artist.

The issue was not all sf either, but included many weird stories, such as "Don Mackinder's Model" by F. S. Howard-Burleigh. But the old names were there too; Paul Ernst, Donald Wandrei, Anthony Gilmore and Nat Schachner, and obviously the magazine attracted its followers. The issue contained no editorial, nor clue as to its editor. This was not disclosed until its December issue, and eyebrows were raised at the name of F. Orlin Tremaine.

Frederick Orlin Tremaine was born on January 7th 1899 at Harrisville, New York, and became the editor of *Torch* in 1920. He was involved with MacFadden's *True Story Magazine* in 1924, and then until 1926 edited *Smart Set*. In 1929 he entered the employ of William Clayton where he stayed until 1933, with a break in 1930 when he edited *Everybody's Magazine*. He then passed to Street & Smith, where among other magazines he edited *Top-Notch*, and inherited *Astounding Stories*. (Tremaine was also responsible for *Bill Barnes*, a magazine of air stories which had some sf issues later in rivalry with *Dusty Ayres And His Battle Birds* edited by Edythe Seims).

Even though Tremaine had had much editorial experience he was virtually unknown to most sf fans. Nevertheless it was he who transformed science fiction in the 1930's, and thus captured the monopoly of the field from Gernsback.

And he did it from the word go. Tremaine's policy was for stories completely original in idea, treatment and scope. Stories that would catch the imagination. He termed them 'thought variant'. The first such appeared in the December 1933 issue: "Ancestral Voices" by Nathan Schachner. It told of a man who travels back in time and kills a Hun who would otherwise have been a distant ancestor. As a result he and thousands of other people disappear. This was followed in the January issue by Donald Wandrei's "Colossus", with a theme that actually harked back to Wertenbaker's "The Man From the Atom", but with a far *wilder* treatment.

During 1934 *Astounding Stories* published brilliant story after brilliant story. There was "Sidewise in Time" by Murray Leinster, "Bright Illusion" by C. L. Moore, "The Man Who Stopped the Dust" by John Russell Fearn. There was Jack Williamson's "Born of the Sun", a story which claimed the planets and satellites were but eggs containing embryo entities. Then there were the classic serials of that year: "Rebirth" by Thomas Calvert McClary, wherein universal amnesia plunged mankind back into savagery; "The Legion of Space", Jack Williamson's extravaganza into the cosmos; "The Skylark of Valeron", E. E. Smith's climactic finale to the Skylark series; and to end the year John Campbell's super science epic "The Mightiest Machine". Add to that the birth of the Don A. Stuart stories, starting with "Twilight", and you have one of the most powerful years in any magazine's history. Then one must not forget that in March 1934 the page count increased from 144 to 160 pages, and from August the print size was reduced to allow more wordage. All this and the price remained at twenty cents, plus excellent fiction by stalwarts Harl Vincent, Raymond Gallun, Nathan Schachner, John Russell Fearn, Donald Wandrei, and Arthur Leo Zagat, and how could the magazine possibly fail! Of course it didn't. By the end of 1934 *Astounding* was the undisputed leader of the field. Throughout 1935, Tremaine continued to present excellent fiction, spearheaded by the mood stories of Don A. Stuart and Raymond Gallun. Stuart was an alternative pen name for John W. Campbell, and it was he, above all other authors, that altered the sf of the mid-thirties. He even forced himself to change. This was exemplified by Tremaine's rejection of Campbell's sequels to "The Mightiest Machine". Such super-science was now a thing of the past. Tremaine had succeeded in building up *Astounding's* circulation by leaning heavily on the giants of super science, Smith, Campbell and Williamson. But the time was now ready for a change. As Don A. Stuart, with such stories as "Twilight", and its sequel "Night", Campbell wrought this change. It was soon copied by Raymond Gallun in such stories as "Old Faithful" and its sequels.

And then 1935 was the year of Stanley G. Weinbaum. But although Weinbaum presented excellent fiction in *Astounding* in 1935, he was not a discovery of Tremaine. Weinbaum had first appeared in *Wonder Stories*, and if you had been wondering what Gernsback had been doing while Tremaine was laying the foundations of modern science fiction, then now's the time to settle your mind.

4—GERNSBACK AND FANDOM

As I've already mentioned, Gernsback discovered when he issued *Amazing Stories* that there was a vast army of ready-made fans just waiting for such a publication. When Gernsback introduced "Discussions" into the magazine, it allowed fans to discover one another, and by and by science fiction fandom was born. Now is not the time nor place to go into a history of science fiction fandom, this has been done completely and far better than I could elsewhere.* But it is essential to an understanding of the science fiction magazines to at least cover some of the amateur magazines, or 'fanzines' of the sf fans.

Fans were particularly vociferous in the magazines' letter departments, notably *Wonder's* "The Reader Speaks". Here would regularly be seen the names of active fans, such as Forrest J. Ackerman, Donald Wollheim, Raymond Palmer, Bob Tucker, and the slightly less active Jack Darrow.

Fans discovered that other fans lived in their neighbourhood, and consequently groups were formed. One of the earliest groups was the Science Correspondence Club, formed in Chicago by Walter Dennis and Raymond Palmer. Naturally the club issued a bulletin, *The Comet*, a mimeographed, 8-page edition dated May 1930. This dealt mostly with science however, and not

* "The Immortal Storm" by Sam Moskowitz. "All Our Yesterdays" by Harry Warner, Jnr.

sf, but it lasted through to 1933 with seventeen variously titled issues.

Walter Dennis struck up correspondence with New York fan Allen Glasser, and Glasser formed his own club The Scienceers, and issued *The Planet*, another mimeographed organ, but with only some three to five pages. *The Planet* concentrated more on science fiction, making it the first science fiction fan magazine. Glasser edited it, and Mort Weisinger was associate editor. Glasser was determined to seek publicity for the organization, and what better place than in a pro-magazine's letter column. Thus we find in the May 1930 *Science Wonder Stories* a letter from Glasser informing readers of the formation of the Scienceers, with editorial recommendation from Gernsback. Furthermore the June 1930 *Wonder Stories* carried another Glasser letter where he informs Gernsback that the Scienceers all voted in favour of the magazine's change of name. Coincidental with the Scienceers, David Lasser (the Managing Editor of *Wonder Stories*) had formed the American Interplanetary Society. Its secretary was C. P. Mason, an associate editor of *Wonder Stories*, and, not to be outdone by the Scienceers, the June 1930 issue carried a letter from that group informing readers of its intentions. (Incidently, besides Lasser and Mason, Laurence Manning was treasurer, and Fletcher Pratt librarian). Lasser impressed upon Glasser the need for their two groups to merge. Only the President, Warren Fitzgerald, joined, and the Scienceers fell apart after just seven months.

Glasser thereupon started *The Time Traveller* from January 1932, which lasted for nine issues during that year. In the meantime Oklahoman Fan Dan McPhail had started the first science fiction information sheet, *Science Fiction News*, which lasted from June 1931 to December 1936.

Gernsback was keen to discover the extent of this fanaticism. In strict competition manner he set a $500·00 prize contest in the Spring 1930 *Science Wonder Quarterly:* "What I Have Done to Spread Science Fiction". Glasser won third prize, by describing the Scienceers club. The first prize was won by Ray Palmer, but of more importance was the second prize, awarded to Indiana printer Conrad H. Ruppert for his suggestion of a Science Fiction Week. Gernsback took the idea to heart and devoted the May 1930 *Science Wonder Stories* editorial to such a venture, from March 31st to April 7th. Gernsback's notion that science fiction was instructional was evident: "If every man, woman, boy and girl, could be induced to read science fiction

right along, there would certainly be a great resulting benefit
to the community, in that the educational standards of its people
would be raised tremendously."[12] The promotional qualities of
a week devoted to the furtherance of science fiction could not
easily be measured, but it does seem evident that chiefly through
Wonder Stories, fan activities began to snowball. Fanzines began
to appear in abundance.

Conrad Ruppert offered his printing facilities and printed
Glasser's *The Time Traveller* from its third issue. This gave the
fanzines a professional appearance. Then in September 1932
came *Science Fiction Digest*, edited by Maurice Ingher, printed
by Ruppert, and assisted generally by Mort Weisinger, Julius
Schwartz and Forrest Ackerman. *Science Fiction Digest* (which
became *Fantasy Magazine* after 1933), was a semi-professional
magazine which constituted a virtual encyclopaedia of sf, not
only with fiction, but with biography, indices, news items and
criticism. It became the voice of fandom right up to its death
in 1937.

A memorable achievement of *Science Fiction Digest* was its
round-robin serial, "Cosmos" which began in the July 1933
issue with an episode by Ralph Milne Farley and lasted for
seventeen instalments until Edmond Hamilton wound it up in
December 1934. All the big names of sf contributed including
David Keller, Francis Flagg, John Campbell, Otis A. Kline,
A. Merritt, E. E. Smith, P. S. Miller and Lloyd Eshbach. (In
its later issues other round robin stories would appear, indeed
one weird fiction story included H. P. Lovecraft and Robert E.
Howard as contributors, but none had the flair or originality of
this prototype).

The peak of semi-professional magazines came when Los
Angeles fan William Crawford issued *Unusual Stories* and *Marvel
Tales* in 1934. Crawford attempted to solicit fiction from
professional authors by offering as payment a lifetime subscription
to the magazine. It worked admirably well, particularly since its
few issues included the works of H. P. Lovecraft, David Keller,
Robert E. Howard, Miles Breuer, Clifford Simak, Robert Bloch
and P. Schuyler Miller. Several of these stories, such as Miller's
"The Titan", Simak's "The Creator" and Howard's "Garden of
Fear" are now acknowledged classics.

Unusual Stories never really got launched, three staggered
issues appearing. *Marvel Tales* had moderately more success.
Both were pocket-book sized, *Marvel Tales* increasing in page
count from its first issue (May 1934) of 40 pages up to the

king-size 108 pages of its fourth (March 1935) issue. Only five issues appeared in all, the magazine dying in Summer 1935. All this time Crawford tried in vain to sell the magazine from the news-stands, but alas it was not to be.

In September 1933 Charles Hornig, a seventeen year old fan from New Jersey started his own fanzine *The Fantasy Fan*. He sent a copy to each prozine (professional sf magazine) editor, and by one of those strange twists of fate it reached Gernsback at a time when his Managing Editor David Lasser had just been fired. Lasser, despite his presidency of the American Interplanetary Society, was all for waving the banner to help the unemployed worker, and he left Gernsback's employ to become the Chairman of the Workers Unemployed Union, a cause that he would support thereafter.

Gernsback decided that Hornig was the man to edit the magazine from now on, and with the November 1933 issue Hornig was in charge. This meteoric rise from fan to professional would never be equalled, especially by one so young.

Why November 1933 should be so chosen as the turning point for science fiction is conjectural. Yet in the same month that Hornig assumed editorship, Tremaine was announcing his plans for *Astounding Stories*. Obviously, Tremaine was ahead of *Wonder Stories* in planning and scope, and yet Hornig would not let this be so. In rivalry to Tremaine Hornig established his 'New' Policy. Hornig was adamant that it was *Wonder Stories* that instituted the policy ahead of *Astounding*. In a special announcement in the December 1935 issue, Hornig said:

> "In fact, this *new* policy was such a good idea that one of our respected rivals, obeying the maxim that 'imitation is the sincerest form of flattery', came along with what they called 'thought-variants'. We are deriving great satisfaction from the belief that *Wonder Stories* started this new, glamorous era of science-fiction, so different from the old days of rehashed themes and stereotyped characters."[13]

Obviously Hornig had not had time to institute a New Policy, but Gernsback had. It is quite probable that Lasser would not altogether concur with Gernsback's views to this end, but that Hornig was fully in favour. Only this explanation would cover Hornig's insistence that *Wonder Stories* was first.

Whatever the explanation there is no denying that both magazines published excellent fiction in 1934 and 1935. It was in *Wonder Stories* that Stanley G. Weinbaum first appeared with

"A Martian Odyssey" in the July 1934 issue. That, and its sequel "Valley of Dreams" in November, took the reader through the bizarre landscape of Mars with its legion of amazingly diverse creatures. Weinbaum had a broad streak of humour running through his fiction, and he was one of the first authors to make his aliens alien-yet-human. Besides Weinbaum, *Wonder* cornered worthy fiction by David Keller, Edmond Hamilton, Alan Connell, M. M. Kaplan, David Daniels and Laurence Manning. 1934 could also be classed as *Wonder's* top year.

The popularity of *Wonder Stories* had been proved early in 1934 when Raymond Palmer, chairman for the Jules Verne Prize, awarded it to the best story for 1933—Edmond Hamilton's "The Island of Unreason", which had appeared in the May 1933 *Wonder*. Since the magazine had carried several excellent stories during the year by no less than Nathan Schachner with his "Technocracy" series and Laurence Manning's "The Man Who Awoke" stories, it was a sign of how popular Hamilton was. *Wonder* had also beaten *Amazing*, *Weird* and *Astounding*, even though those magazines had carried such memorable stories as "Shambleau" by C. L. Moore (*Weird*, November), "Unto Us A Child Is Born" by David Keller (*Amazing*, July) or Donald Wandrei's "A Race Through Time" (*Astounding*, October).

But the major event of 1934 in *Wonder* was not its fiction. In February 1934 Gernsback instituted the Science Fiction League to enhance the popularity of sf. Within months it became quite a force in fandom. *Wonder* published a regular monthly feature devoted to news and suggestions, and together with league buttons, letterheads and a Certificate, one felt that fandom had never been so organized. For science fiction *fans* the fiction became secondary in *Wonder Stories*. As Robert Lowndes recalled "From the days of Charles D. Hornig in *Wonder Stories* . . . I've been a sucker for the personal magazine or the magazine that presents a distinct personality. That was why I looked forward to the next issue of *Wonder* more regularly than *Astounding* in those days. . . ."[14]

Astounding presented a fairly lively letter column, "Brass Tacks", but this was not a patch on *Wonder* with its League and "The Reader Speaks". Like wildfire various Chapters of the League were formed throughout the United States, and even in England (Maurice Hanson formed a Nuneaton Chapter, Douglas Mayer the Leeds Chapter. There was a Belfast chapter with Hugh Carswell, and even one in Sydney, Australia formed by W. J. J. Osland).

By all accounts the League was doing great stuff, but that was only on the surface. The September 1935 issue carried the announcement that three league members had been expelled for working against the League. They were Donald Wollheim, John Michel and William Sykora. Wollheim had been instrumental in forming the International Scientific Association which opposed the Science Fiction League. Their stand was that only an independent organization could develop fandom to maturity and greatness, because a professional club, by its very nature, must be commercial and would hamper the free flow of criticism.

Thus the feud was born. It lasted for two years and as a result fandom grew and grew beyond anyone's wildest imagining. New clubs, new fanzines and above all new fans. The outcome of the battle was eventually decided when *Wonder Stories* found itself on the rocks.

Remember that Street & Smith at *Astounding Stories* paid two cents a word whereas Gernsback rarely varied from his half- or three-quarter cent a word. Obviously if writers could sell to *Astounding* they would. *Amazing Stories* paid no better, and writers were further discouraged to submit manuscripts to Sloane because he held on to them for so long. Since payment was on publication this was just not viable. By August 1935 *Amazing Stories* came out every other month. In November 1935 *Wonder Stories* also began to appear alternate months. *Astounding* on the other hand had begun monthly in October 1933, and by 1934 there was talk of it appearing twice monthly. This never materialized, but *Astounding* has never failed to appear each and every month from that day to this.

Another factor is the further specialization of other pulps. *Doc Savage* was a second Street & Smith winner, and with only so much money around obviously readers would go for the most value for their twenty cents. In an attempt to reach the market *Wonder Stories* cut their cover price down to *fifteen* cents in 1935 (the equivalent of about 9d), but this did not work, and in fact lowered their income drastically. Ten years after *Amazing Stories* had exploded onto the sf scene, Gernsback was for the first time facing difficulties.

Then came the March-April 1936 issue of *Wonder Stories*, and for the first time the public learnt the facts. In his editorial "Wonders of Distribution" Gernsback explained how racketeering in the magazine business had grown out of all proportion. Major distributors were removing the magazine covers, and then selling them as imperfect copies at a cheaper rate to the public, keeping all the revenue themselves. Gernsback decided that the only way to avoid this was to cut out the distributor, and do the distributing himself.

Thus was devised his postal plan. In a special announcement in the issue Gernsback reveals that whereas sf was "tops" in 1926, it is now in decline, whereas detective and western fiction were the best sellers. His plan was for subscription in reverse. A special printed coupon was supplied in that issue. Readers were asked to clip this out and mail it to Gernsback. They would then receive the next issue of *Wonder Stories* with a bill for fifteen cents, plus a return envelope. There was no extra expense for the reader since all postage was prepaid. He would receive his magazine and pay the money afterwards.

Gernsback concluded his announcement by saying,

"And let me thank all of you in advance for making the new movement possible. I know that you will not fail me in this great experiment!"[15]

He was to be bitterly disappointed. Just two thousand replies were received, far from enough to make his scheme practicable. Gernsback sold *Wonder Stories* to Standard Magazines, and retired from the sf field, to continue with his far more profitable *Sexology* publication.

Since by then *Amazing Stories* was less than a shadow of its former self, *Astounding Stories* was left supreme in the field. Tremaine's policy of new ideas by big names had succeeded. A thought must be spared for Gernsback's excuse of distribution problems. This has always been a major problem for magazines, especially science fiction, and one must realise that Street & Smith, as the bigger publisher of the two, had far better distributors and thus more ability to bring *Astounding* to the eyes of likely customers.

March 1936 and the United States had seen ten years of science fiction magazines. 115 issues of *Amazing Stories*, 79 *Wonder Stories* and 64 *Astoundings*, and yet as they say, the last shall be first.

And what of Britain all this time? There is no denying that American publishers were always more willing to take a chance than British firms. True that if an American publisher had a British branch they would bring out a British edition, exactly the same as the American. Street & Smith, who had offices at Covent Garden in London had brought out such an edition of *The Thrill Book*, identical in every detail to the U.S. version.

Obviously what Britain wanted was an indigenous publisher

ready to gamble on an all sf magazine. The hybrids were plentiful. Ever since *Strand* and *Pearson's*, many British magazines had carried science fiction in their pages, such as *Grand Magazine*, *Red Magazine*, and *Royal*. The only complete science fiction series that had appeared were the British reprints of Frank Reade 'dime novels' put out by the Aldine Publishing Company of Crown Court off Chancery Lane in London. Described as the "Invention, Travel and Adventure" Library this series of paperbound pocket books ran for several years, one per week, in the mid-1890's. There was also Aldine's *The Cheerful Library*, and *O'er Land And Sea Library*. They all pandered to junvenile audiences, but were still fun to read.

The import of American pulp adventure magazines seemed to convince British publishers that there was already more than enough to go round and any attempts at a British science fiction magazine would be superfluous. It is not as if there was any shortage of British authors. Gernsback's readers saw plenty of their fiction; George C. Wallis, John Beynon (Wyndham) Harris, Festus Pragnell, J. M. Walsh, Benson Herbert, W. P. Cockcroft *et al.*

Various fan groups had formed in Britain, one of the earliest at Hayes had issued the prototype British fanzine, *Fantasia*. At this same time Walter Gillings (born 1912) who was destined to change the shape of British science fiction was forming his Ilford Science Literary Circle. Efforts to convince British publishers that a British sf magazine was essential were fruitless. The negative response was hard to bear at a time when detective magazines were quite regular, and Fleetway House had brough out a twopenny weekly called *The Thriller*, which featured mystery stories by people like Edgar Wallace, Sax Rohmer, Anthony Skene and Sydney Horler.

So it came as a great surprise when Pearsons brought out their 2d weekly *Scoops*. It was more of a newspaper than a magazine, with thirty-two small-type covered large-size pages. Its first issue was dated February 10th, and was anonymously edited by *Scout* editor Haydn Dimmock. All its contributors were anonymous too, and all the reader had to go on were such titles as "Master of the Moon", "The Striding Terror", "The Rebel Robots", "Rocket of Doom", "The Mystery of the Blue Mist", "Voice From the Void" and "The Soundless Hour". Three of these were serials.

With its second issue it slanted even further towards a young audience, and a further serial began. This was the only story in the early issues to carry an author credit, Professor A. M. Low. The novel "Space" was eventually brought out in hardback as "Adrift in the Stratosphere". [This was the first science fiction book apart from Verne that I was to read. I can still remember the thrill when I read it in the 50's as the three intrepid lads who had accidently launched themselves into space tried to avoid menaces from Mars and found themselves in a strange corridor of flame. As it was this book that launched me as far as science fiction was concerned, I cannot be harsh towards it. In the same way I feel it must certainly have instilled considerable interest in the youth of 1934 as they waited for each successive episode.]

It also appealed to many adults, but not to the die-hard fans who had been initiated on American pulp science fiction. When in later issues *Scoops* attempts to grow up, it fell in between the two markets and after twenty issues it died, last issue June 23rd 1934. By that time it was crediting authors, and here one would find John Russell Fearn, Maurice Hugi, W. P. Cockcroft, a serial by George E. Rochester, plus a reprint of Conan Doyle's "The Poison Belt".

The failure of *Scoops* was to give British publishers the impression that a native sf magazine could not support itself. And not only British publishers. Nottingham fan James Dudley appeared in the March 1936 *Wonder* with a letter proclaiming that:

"for the man or men with courage and the capital to start with, this little land of ours would be a 'verdant pasture' for science-fiction, and prove a gold-mine to him or them."

To which editor Hornig replied:

"You do not seem to be acquainted with the fact that a British science-fiction magazine was published for twenty weekly issues, after which it 'went under'. This proved to us and other British publishers that your country is not yet prepared to support a professional science-fiction magazine enough to make it pay for itself."[16]

And so the case rested. British science fiction had virtually died before it began, and despite a strange publication called *Breezy Science Stories* that had its only appearance some time in 1934, British fans had to resort to searching back through general magazines, although their best bet now was Odham's *Passing Show*, which had already reprinted some Edgar Rice

Burroughs' novels, and in July 1935 began to serialize John Beynon Harris' "The Secret People", his novel of a lost race under the Sahara desert.

* * *

Ten years from the birth of the sf magazine: the Gernsback era, which gave way in 1934 to the Tremaine period, that itself gave way in 1938 to the Campbell era.

Revel for a while in the glory of something special, something new. In the days between 1926 and 1936 science fiction was a very personal subject. Fans, although growing in number, were far apart. They had no one with which to share their new found joy until Gernsback's letter columns allowed them the chance to locate others. As you read these stories remember the fans of yesteryear, and see if you too can escape into that dream world of tomorrow which is now but a phantom hope of the past. After 1936 science fiction would never be the same again.

Mike Ashley
February 1974

SOURCES OF QUOTATIONS

¹ From a Guest Editorial by Hugo Gernsback in *Amazing Stories* for April 1961, published by Ziff-Davis Pub. Co., Chicago. (Page 7).

² From the "For Your Information" column by Willy Ley in *Galaxy* for February 1963, published by Galaxy Publishing Corporation, New York. (Page 91).

³ From "Pulpwood Editor" by Harold B. Hersey, published by F. A. Stokes Co., New York (1937). From Chapter 10, "Take Your Choice". (Page 188).

⁴ From Hugo Gernsback's editorial "Editorially Speaking" in the September 1926 *Amazing Stories*, published by Experimenter Publishing Co., New York.

⁵ From Hugo Gernsback's editorial in the April 1926 *Amazing Stories*. Transcribed from the reprint published in *Amazing Stories* for April 1966, published by Ultimate Publishing Co., New York. (Pages 188/9).

⁶ From the obituary to Wilbur C. Whithead in *Amazing Stories* for September 1931, published by the Teck Pub. Corp., New York. (Page 484). Probably written by Hugo Gernsback.

⁷ From Hugo Gernsback's editorial in the June 1926 *Amazing Stories*. Transcribed from the quotation in the chapter "Hugo Gernsback" in *Explorers Of The Infinite* by Sam Moskowitz (World Pub. Co. Ohio, 1963). (Page 236).

⁸ From an Accouncement in *Science Wonder Stories* for May 1930, published by Stellar Pub. Corp. New York. (Page 1099).

⁹ and ¹⁰ Same as ³ above.

¹¹ From an editorial comment by T. O'Conor Sloane in the letter column "Discussions" of the May 1935 *Amazing Stories*. (Page 140).

¹² From Hugo Gernsback's editorial "Science Fiction Week" in the May 1930 *Science Wonder Stories*. (Page 1061).

¹³ From an announcement, "New Policy Still 'New' " in the December 1935 *Wonder Stories* published by Continental Publications Inc. (Page 748). Probably written by Charles Hornig.

[14] From a letter by Robert A. W. Lowndes published in the ". . . Or So You Say" column in the January 1973 *Amazing Stories*. (Page 121).

[15] From a special announcement by Gernsback in the March-April 1936 *Wonder Stories*. (Page 923).

[16] From a letter by James Dudley and comment by Charles Hornig in "The Reader Speaks" column of the March-April 1936 *Wonder Stories*. (Pages 1017/8).

The Coming of the Ice
by G. Peyton Wertenbaker

from AMAZING STORIES, June 1926

There is no denying that the science fiction field attracts young
and old alike. T. O'Conor Sloane, who was no doubt the first to
read the above submission, was 74, the author was 19, and he had
already been a science fiction writer for three years.

Green Peyton Wertenbaker's writings first appeared in the
special science fiction issue of *Science & Invention* in August 1923
when he was only 16 years old, with his story "The Man From
the Atom". Despite many scientific crudities, the story was handled with the maturity of an author many years his senior. "The
Man From the Atom" told of a youth who tests a professor's
invention to make objects larger or smaller. With complete dis-
regard for any of Newton's laws, the narrator finds himself
growing and growing until the Earth is but a marble. Continuing to grow, he eventually leaves the universe, and enters a
macrocosm, a universe in which our Earth is but an electron.
When he tries to return to the Earth, he finds it a dead world
extinct for millions of years. The feeling of desolation imparted
by this 16 year old is phenomenal.

The knack was not a one-shot. "The Coming of the Ice" was
the first *new* story to appear in *Amazing Stories*, in its third
issue. Here again you will find that same feeling of loneliness,
but this time of an immortal man.

Wertenbaker was the son of William Wertenbaker and Imogen
Peyton, and was the younger brother of novelist Charles Christian
Wertenbaker. He was born in Virginia in 1907, and deserted the
science fiction field after but five stories, all competently written
and deserving of further reprinting. (Although one must grant
the licence of some rickety science). Subsequently he became an

editor of *Fortune* magazine, and he went on to write many regional volumes on the American south west.

Wertenbaker was not the youngest author to write in science fiction magazines. For instance Charles Cloukey made his first sale, "Sub-Satellite" to Gernsback when he was only fifteen. Within a few years this genius would be dead. The record however is held by Kenneth Sterling whose humorous story "The Brain Eaters of Pluto" was sold to *Wonder Stories* when he was thirteen! No big name author can equal these early beginnings in the sf field. Isaac Asimov was eighteen when "Marooned Off Vesta" was sold to Ray Palmer, whereas Robert Heinlein was *thirty-one* when John Campbell bought "Life Line". This is just added emphasis to the early achievement of G. Peyton Wertenbaker.

It is strange to be alone, and so cold. To be the last man on earth...

The snow drives silently about me, ceaselessly, drearily. And I am isolated in this tiny white, indistinguishable corner of a blurred world, surely the loneliest creature in the universe. How many thousands of years is it since I last knew the true companionship? For a long time I have been lonely, but there *were* people, creatures of flesh and blood. Now they are gone. Now I have not even the stars to keep me company, for they are all lost in an infinity of snow and twilight here below.

If only I could know how long it has been since first I was imprisoned upon the earth. It cannot matter now. And yet some vague dissatisfaction, some faint instinct, asks over and over in my throbbing ears: What year? What year?

It was in the year 1930 that the great thing began in my life. There was then a very great man who performed operations on his fellows to compose their vitals— we called such men surgeons. John Granden wore the title "Sir" before his name, in indication of nobility by birth according to the prevailing standards in England. But surgery was only a hobby of Sir John's, if I must be precise, for, while he had achieved an enormous reputation as a surgeon, he always felt that his real work lay in the experimental end of his profession. He was, in a way a dreamer, but a dreamer who could make his dreams come true.

I was a very close friend of Sir John's. In fact, we shared the same apartments in London. I have never forgotten that day when he first mentioned to me his momentous discovery. I had just come in from a long sleighride in the country with Alice, and I was seated drowsily in the window-seat, writing idly in my mind a description of the wind and the snow and the grey twilight of the evening. It is strange, is it not, that my tale should begin and end with the snow and the twilight.

Sir John opened suddenly a door at one end of the room and came hurrying across to another door. He looked at me, grinning rather like a triumphant maniac.

"It's coming!" he cried, without pausing, "I've almost got it!" I smiled at him: he looked very ludicrous at that moment.

"What have you got?" I asked.

"Good Lord, man, the Secret—the Secret!" And then he was gone again, the door closing upon his victorious cry, "The Secret!"

I was, of course, amused. But I was also very much interested. I knew Sir John well enough to realize that, however amazing his appearance might be, there would be nothing absurd about his "Secret"—whatever it was. But it was useless to speculate. I could only hope for enlightenment at dinner. So I immersed myself in one of the surgeon's volumes from his fine Library of Imagination, and waited.

I think the book was one of Mr. H. G. Wells's, probably "The Sleeper Awakes," or some other of his brilliant fantasies and predictions, for I was in a mood conducive to belief in almost anything when, later, we sat down together across the table. I only wish I could give some idea of the atmosphere that permeated our apartments, the reality it lent to whatever was vast and amazing and strange. You could then, whoever you are, understand a little the ease with which I accepted Sir John's new discovery.

He began to explain it to me at once, as though he could keep it to himself no longer.

"Did you think I had gone mad, Dennell?" he asked. "I quite wonder that I haven't. Why, I have been studying for many years —for most of my life—on this problem. And, suddenly, I have solved it! Or, rather, I am afraid I have solved another one much greater."

"Tell me about it, but for God's sake don't be technical."

"Right," he said. Then he paused. "Dennell, it's *magnificent*! It will change everything that is in the world." His eyes held mine suddenly with the fatality of a hypnotist's. "Dennell, it is the Secret of Eternal Life," he said.

"Good Lord, Sir John!" I cried, half inclined to laugh.

"I mean it," he said. "You know I have spent most of my life studying the processes of birth, trying to find out precisely what went on in the whole history of conception."

"You have found out?"

"No, that is just what amuses me. I have discovered something else without knowing yet what causes either process.

"I don't want to be technical, and I know very little of what actually takes place myself. But I can try to give you some idea of it."

It is thousands, perhaps millions of years since Sir John explained to me. What little I understood at the time I may have forgotten, yet I try to reproduce what I can of his theory.

"In my study of the processes of birth," he began, "I discovered the rudiments of an action which takes place in the bodies of both men and women. There are certain properties in the foods we eat that remain in the body for the reproduction of life, two distinct Essences, so to speak, of which one is retained by the woman, another by the man. It is the union of these two properties that, of course, creates the child.

"Now, I made a slight mistake one day in experimenting with a guinea-pig, and I re-arranged certain organs which I need not describe so that I thought I had completely messed up the poor creature's abdomen. It lived, however, and I laid it aside. It was some years later that I happened to notice it again. It had not given birth to any young, but I was amazed to note that it had apparently grown no older: it seemed precisely in the same state of growth in which I had left it.

"From that I built up. I re-examined the guinea-pig, and observed it carefully. I need not detail my studies. But in the end I found that my 'mistake' had in reality been a momentous discovery. I found that I had only to close certain organs, to rearrange certain ducts, and to open certain dormant organs, and, *mirabile dictu*, the whole process of reproduction was changed.

"You have heard, of course, that our bodies are continually changing, hour by hour, minute by minute, so that every few years we have been literally reborn. Some such principle as this seems to operate in reproduction, except that, instead of the old body being replaced by the new, and in its form, approximately, the new body is created apart from it. It is the creation of children that causes us to die, it would seem, because if this activity is, so to speak, dammed up or turned aside into new channels, the reproduction operates on the old body, renewing it continually. It is very obscure and very absurd, is it not? But the most absurd part of it is that it is true. Whatever the true explanation may be the fact remains that the operation can be done, that it actually prolongs life indefinitely, and that I alone know the secret."

Sir John told me a very great deal more, but, after all, I think it amounted to little more than this. It would be impossible for me to express the great hold his discovery took upon my mind the moment he recounted it. From the very first, under the spell of his personality, I believed, and I knew he was speaking the truth. And it opened up before me new vistas. I began to see myself become suddenly eternal, never again to know the fear of death. I could see myself storing up, century after century, an amplitude of wisdom and experience that would make me truly a god.

"Sir John!" I cried, long before he was finished, "You must perform that operation on me!"

"But Dennell, you are too hasty. You must not put yourself so rashly into my hands."

"You have perfected the operation, haven't you?"

"That is true," he said.

"You must try it out on somebody, must you not?"

"Yes, of course. And yet—somehow, Dennell, I am afraid. I cannot help feeling that man is not yet prepared for such a vast thing. There are sacrifices. One must give up love and all sensual pleasure. This operation not only takes away the mere fact of reproduction, but it deprives one of all the things that go with sex, all love, all sense of beauty, all feeling for poetry and the arts. It leaves only the few emotions, selfish emotions, that are necessary to self-preservation. Do you not see? One becomes an intellect, nothing more—a cold apotheosis of reason. And I, for one, cannot face such a thing calmly."

"But, Sir John, like many fears, it is largely horrible in the foresight. After you have changed your nature you cannot regret it. What you are would be as horrible an idea to you afterwards as the thought of what you will be seems now."

"True, true. I know it. But it is hard to face, nevertheless."

"I am not afraid to face it."

"You do not understand it, Dennell, I am afraid. And I wonder whether you or I or any of us on this earth are ready for such a step. After all, to make a race deathless, one should be sure it is a perfect race."

"Sir John," I said, "it is not you who have to face this, nor any one else in the world till you are ready. But I am firmly resolved, and I demand it of you as my friend."

Well, we argued much further, but in the end I won. Sir John promised to perform the operation three days later.

. . . But do you perceive now what I had forgotten during all that discussion, the one thing I had thought I could never forget so long as I lived, not even for an instant? It was my love for Alice—I had forgotten that!

I cannot write here all the infinity of emotions I experienced later, when, with Alice in my arms, it suddenly came upon me what I had done. Ages ago—I have forgotten now to feel. I could name now a thousand feelings I used to have, but I can no longer even understand them. For only the heart can understand the heart, and the intellect only the intellect.

With Alice in my arms, I told the whole story. It was she who, with her quick instinct, grasped what I had never noticed.

"But Carl!" she cried, "Don't you see?—It will mean that we can never be married!" And, for the first time, I understood. If only I could re-capture some conception of that love! I have always known, since the last shred of comprehension slipped from me, that I lost something very wonderful when I lost love. But what does it matter? I lost Alice too, and I could not have known love again without her.

We were very sad and very tragic that night. For hours and hours we argued the question over. But I felt somewhat that I was inextricably caught in my fate, that I could not retreat now from my resolve. I was perhaps, very school-boyish, but I felt that it would be cowardice to back out now. But it was Alice again who perceived a final aspect of the matter.

"Carl," she said to me, her lips very close to mine, "it need not come between our love. After all, ours would be a poor sort of love if it were not more of the mind than of the flesh. We shall remain lovers, but we shall forget mere carnal desire. I shall submit to that operation too!"

And I could not shake her from her resolve. I would speak of danger that I could not let her face. But, after the fashion of women, she disarmed me with the accusation that I did not love her, that I did not want her love, that I was trying to escape from love. What answer had I for that, but that I loved her and would do anything in the world not to lose her?

I have wondered sometimes since whether we might have known the love of the mind. Is love something entirely of the flesh, something created by an ironic God merely to propagate His race? Or can there be love without emotion, love without passion—love between two cold intellects? I do not know. I did not ask then. I accepted anything that would make our way more easy.

There is no need to draw out the tale. Already my hand wavers, and my time grows short. Soon there will be no more of me, no more of my tale—no more of Mankind. There will be only the snow, and the ice, and the cold . . .

Three days later I entered John's Hospital with Alice on my arm. All my affairs—and they were few enough—were in order. I had insisted that Alice wait until I had come safely through the operation, before she submitted to it. I had been carefully starved for two days, and I was lost in an unreal world of white walls and white clothes and white lights, drunk with my dreams of the future. When I was wheeled into the operating room on the long, hard table, for a moment it shone with brilliant distinctness, a neat, methodical white chamber, tall and more or less circular. Then I was beneath the glare of soft white lights, and the room faded into a misty vagueness from which little steel rays flashed and quivered from silvery cold instruments. For a moment our hands, Sir John's and mine, gripped and we were saying good-bye —for a little while—in the way men say these things. Then I felt the warm touch of Alice's lips upon mine, and I felt sudden painful things I cannot describe, that I could not have described then. For a moment I felt that I must rise and cry out that I could not do it. But the feeling passed, and I was passive.

Something was pressed about my mouth and nose, something with an etherial smell. Staring eyes swam about me from behind their white masks. I struggled instinctively, but in vain—I was held securely. Infinitesimal points of light began to wave back and forth on a pitch-black background; a great hollow buzzing echoed in my head. My head seemed suddenly to have become all throat, a great, cavernous, empty throat in which sounds and lights were mingled together, in a swift rhythm, approaching, receding eternally. Then, I think, there were dreams. But I have forgotten them. . . .

I began to emerge from the effect of the ether. Everything was dim, but I could perceive Alice beside me, and Sir John.

"Bravely done!" Sir John was saying, and Alice, too was say-something, but I cannot remember what. For a long while we talked, I speaking the nonsense of those who are coming out from under ether, they teasing me a little solemnly. But after a little while I became aware of the fact that they were about to leave. Suddenly, God knows why, I knew that they must not leave. Something cried in the back of my head that they *must* stay —one cannot explain these things, except by after events. I began to press them to remain, but they smiled and said they must get their dinner. I commanded them not to go; but they spoke kindly and said they would be back before long. I think I even wept a little, like a child, but Sir John said something to the nurse, who began to reason with me firmly, and then they were gone, and somehow I was asleep. . . .

When I awoke again, my head was fairly clear, but there was an abominable reek of ether all about me. The moment I opened my eyes, I felt that something had happened. I asked for Sir John and for Alice. I saw a swift, curious look that I could not interpret come over the face of the nurse, then she was calm again, her countenance impassive. She reassured me in quick meaningless phrases, and told me to sleep. But I could not sleep: I was absolutely sure that something had happened to them, to my friend and to the woman I loved. Yet all my insistence profited me nothing, for the nurses were a silent lot. Finally, I think, they must have given me a sleeping potion of some sort, for I fell asleep again.

For two endless, chaotic days, I saw nothing of either of them, Alice or Sir John. I became more and more agitated, the nurse more and more taciturn. She would only say that they had gone away for a day or two.

And then, on the third day, I found out. They thought I was asleep. The night nurse had just come in to relieve the other.

"Has he been asking about them again?" she asked.

"Yes, poor fellow. I have hardly managed to keep him quiet."

"We will have to keep it from him until he is recovered fully." There was a long pause, and I could hardly control my labored breathing.

"How sudden it was!" one of them said. "To be killed like that—" I heard no more, for I leapt suddenly up in bed, crying out.

"Quick! For God's sake, tell me what has happened!" I jumped to the floor and seized one of them by the collar. She was horrified. I shook her with a superhuman strength.

"Tell me!" I shouted, "Tell me—Or, I'll—!" She told me— what else could she do.

"They were killed in an accident," she gasped, "in a taxi—a collision—the Strand—!" And at that moment a crowd of nurses and attendants arrived, called by the other frantic woman, and they put me to bed again.

I have no memory of the next few days. I was in delirium, and

I was never told what I said during my ravings. Nor can I express the feelings I was saturated with when at last I regained my mind. Between my old emotions and any attempt to put them into words, or even to remember them, lies always that insurmountable wall of my Change. I cannot understand what I must have felt, I cannot express it.

I only know that for weeks I was sunk in a misery beyond any misery I had ever imagined before. The only two friends I had on earth were gone to me. I was left alone. And, for the first time, I began to see before me all these endless years that would be the same, dull, lonely.

Yet I recovered. I could feel each day the growth of a strange new vigor in my limbs, a vast force that was something tangibily expressive to eternal life. Slowly my anguish began to die. After a week more, I began to understand how my emotions were leaving me, how love and beauty and everything of which poetry was made—how all this was going. I could not bear the thought at first. I would look at the golden sunlight and the blue shadow of the wind, and I would say,

"God! How beautiful!" And the words would echo meaninglessly in my ears. Or I would remember Alice's face, that face I had once loved so inextinguishably, and I would weep and clutch my forehead, and clench my fists, crying.

"O God, how can I live without her!" Yet there would be a little strange fancy in my head at the same moment, saying,

"Who is this Alice? You know no such person." And truly I would wonder whether she had ever existed.

So, slowly the old emotions were shed away from me, and I began to joy in a corresponding growth of my mental perceptions. I began to toy idly with mathematical formulae I had forgotten years ago, in the same fashion that a poet toys with a word and its shades of meaning. I would look at everything with new, seeing eyes, new perception, and I would understand things I had never understood before, because formerly my emotions had always occupied me more than my thoughts.

And so the weeks went by, until, one day, I was well.

. . . What, after all, is the use of this chronicle? Surely there will never be men to read it. I have them say that the snow will never go, I will be buried, it will be buried with me; and it will be the end of us both. Yet, somehow, it eases my weary soul a little to write. . . .

Need I say that I lived, thereafter, many thousands of thousands of years, until this day? I cannot detail that life. It is a long round of new, fantastic impressions, coming dream-like, one after another, melting into each other. In looking back, as in looking back upon dreams, I seem to recall only a few isolated periods clearly; and it seems that my imagination must have filled in the swift movement between episodes. I think now, of necessity, in terms of centuries and millenniums, rather than days and months. . . . The snow blows terribly about my little fire, and I know it will soon gather courage to quench us both . . .

Years passed, at first with a sort of clear wonder. I watched things that took place everywhere in the world. I studied. The other students were much amazed to see me, a man of thirty odd, coming back to college.

"But Judas, Dennell, you've already got your Ph.D! What more do you want?" So they would all ask me. And I would reply;

"I want an M.D. and an F.R.C.S." I didn't tell them that I wanted degrees in Law, too and in Biology and Chemistry, in Architecture and Engineering, in Psychology and Philosophy. Even so, I believe they thought me mad. But poor fools! I would think. They can hardly realize that I have all of eternity before me to study.

"I went to school for many decades. I would pass from University to University, leisurely gathering all the fruits of every subject I took up, revelling in study as no student revelled ever before. There was no need of hurry in my life, no fear of death too soon. There was a magnificence of vigor in my body, and a magnificence of vision and clarity in my brain. I felt myself a super-man. I had only to go on storing up wisdom until the day should come when all knowledge of the world was mine, and then I could command the world. I had no need for hurry. O vast life! How I gloried in my eternity! And how little good it has ever done me, by the irony of God.

For several centuries, changing my name and passing from place to place, I continued my studies. I had no consciousness of monotony, for to the intellect, monotony cannot exist: it was one of those emotions I had left behind. One day, however, in the year 2132, a great discovery was made by a man called Zarentzov. It had to do with the curvature of space, quite changing the conceptions that we had all followed since Einstein. I had long ago mastered the last detail of Einstein's theory, as had, in time, the rest of the world. I threw myself immediately into the study of this new, epoch-making conception.

To my amazement, it all seemed to me curiously dim and

elusive. I could not quite grasp what Zarentzov was trying to formulate.

"Why," I cried, "the thing is a monstrous fraud!" I went to the professor of Physics in the University I then attended, and I told him it was a fraud, a huge book of mere nonsense. He looked at me rather pityingly.

"I am afraid, Modevski," he said, addressing me by the name I was at the time using, "I am afraid you do not understand it, that is all. When your mind has broadened, you will. You should apply yourself more carefully to your Physics." But that angered me, for I had mastered my Physics before he was ever born. I challenged him to explain the theory. And he did! He put it obviously, in the clearest language he could. Yet I understood nothing. I stared at him dumbly, until he shook his head impatiently, saying that it was useless, that if I could not grasp it I would simply have to keep on studying. I was stunned. I wandered away in a daze.

For do you see what happened? During all those years I had studied ceaselessly, and my mind had been clear and quick as the day I first had left the hospital. But all that time I had been able only to remain what I was—an extraordinarily intelligent man of the twentieth century. And the rest of the race had been progressing! It had been swiftly gathering knowledge and power and ability all that time, faster and faster, while I had been only remaining still. And now here was Zarentzov and the teachers of the Universities, and, probably, a hundred intelligent men, who had all outstripped me! I was being left behind.

And that is what happened. I need not dilate further upon it. By the end of that century I had been left behind by all the students of the world, and I never did understand Zarentzov. Other men came with other theories, and these theories were accepted by the world. But I could not understand them. My intellectual life was at an end. I had nothing more to understand. I knew everything I was capable of knowing, and, thenceforth, I could only play wearily with the old ideas.

Many things happened in the world. A time came when the East and West, two mighty unified hemispheres, rose up in arms: the civil war of a planet. I recall only chaotic visions of fire and thunder and hell. It was all incomprehensible to me: like a bizarre dream, things happened, people rushed about, but I never knew what they were doing. I lurked all that time in a tiny shuddering hole under the city of Yokohama, and by a miracle I survived.

And the East won. But it seems to have mattered little who did win, for all the world had become, in all except its few remaining prejudices, a single race, and nothing was changed when it was all rebuilt again, under a single government.

I saw the first of the strange creatures who appeared among us in the year 6371, men who were later known to be from the planet Venus. But they were repulsed, for they were savages compared with the Earthmen, although they were about equal to the people of my own century, 1900. Those of them who did not perish of the cold after the intense warmth of their world, and those who were not killed by our hands, those few returned silently home again. And I have always regretted that I had not the courage to go with them.

I watched a time when the world reached perfection in mechanics, when men could accomplish anything with a touch of the finger. Strange men, these creatures of the hundredth century, men with huge brains and tiny shriveled bodies, atrophied limbs, and slow ponderous movements on their little conveyances. It was I, with my ancient compunctions, who shuddered when at last they put to death all the perverts, the criminals, and the insane, ridding the world of the scum for which they had no more need. It was then that I was forced to produce my tattered old papers, proving my identity and my story. They knew it was true, in some strange fashion of theirs, and, thereafter, I was kept on exhibition as an archaic survival.

I saw the world made immortal through the new invention of a man called Kathol, who used somewhat the same method "legend" decreed had been used upon me. I observed the end of speech, of all perceptions except one, when men learned to communicate directly by thought, and to receive directly into the brain all the myriad vibrations of the universe.

All these things I saw, and more, until that time when there was no more discovery, but a Perfect World in which there was on need for anything but memory, Men ceased to count time at last. Several hundred years after the 154th Dynasty from the Last War, or, as we would have counted in my time, about 200,000 A.D., official records of time were no longer kept carefully. They fell into disuse. Men began to forget years, to forget time at all. Of what significance was time when one was immortal?

After long, long uncounted centuries, a time came when the days grew noticeably colder. Slowly the winters became longer, and the summers diminished to but a month or two. Fierce storms raged endlessly in winter, and in summmer sometimes there was severe frost, sometimes there was only frost. In the high places and in the north and the sub-equatorial south, the snow came and would not go.

Men died by the thousands in the higher latitudes. New York became, after a while, the furthest habitable city north, an arctic city, where warmth seldom penetrated. And great fields of ice began to make their way southward, grinding before them the brittle remains of civilizations, covering over relentlessly all of man's proud work.

Snow appeared in Florida and Italy one summer. In the end, snow was there always. Men left New York, Chicago, Paris, Yokohama, and everywhere they traveled by the millions southward, perishing as they went, pursued by the snow and the cold, and that inevitable field of ice. They were feeble creatures when the Cold first came upon them, but I speak in terms of thousands of years; and they turned every weapon of science to the recovery of their physical power, for they foresaw that the only chance of survival lay in a hard, strong body. As for me, at last I had found a use for my few powers, for my physique was the finest in that world. It was but little comfort, however, for we were all united in our awful fear of that Cold and that grinding field of Ice. All the great cities were deserted. We would catch silent, fearful glimpses of them as we sped on in our machines over the snow—great hungry, haggard skeletons of cities, shrouded in banks of snow, snow that the wind rustled through desolate streets where the cream of human life once had passed in calm security. Yet still the Ice pursued. For men had forgotten about that Last Ice Age when they ceased to reckon time, when they lost sight of the future and steeped themselves in memories. They had not remembered that a time must come when Ice would lie white and smooth over all the earth, when the sun would shine bleakly between unending intervals of dim, twilight snow and sleet.

Slowly the Ice pursued us down the earth, until all the feeble remains of civilization were gathered in Egypt and India and South America. The deserts flowered again, but the frost would come always to bite the tiny crops. For still the Ice came. All the world now, but for a narrow strip about the equator, was one great silent desolate vista of stark ice-plains, ice that brooded above the hidden ruins of cities that had endured for hundreds of thousands of years. It was terrible to imagine the awful solitude and the endless twilight that lay on these places, and the grim snow, sailing in silence over all. . . .

It surrounded us on all sides, until life remained only in a few scattered clearings all about that equator of the globe, with an eternal fire going to hold away the hungry Ice. Perpetual winter reigned now; and we were becoming terror-stricken beasts that preyed on each other for a life already doomed. Ah, but I, I the archaic survival, I had my revenge then, with my great physique and strong jaws—God! Let me think of something else. Those men who lived upon each other—it was horrible. And I was one.

So inevitably the Ice closed in. . . . One day the men of our tiny clearing were but a score. We huddled about our dying fire of bones and stray logs. We said nothing. We just sat, in deep, wordless, thoughtless silence. We were the last outpost of Mankind.

I think suddenly something very noble must have transformed these creatures to a semblance of what they had been of old. I saw, in their eyes, the question they sent from one to another and in every eye I saw that the answer was, Yes. With one accord they rose before my eyes and, ignoring me as a baser creature, they stripped away their load of tattered rags and, one by one they stalked with their tiny shrivelled limbs into the shivering gale of swirling, gusting snow, and disappeared. And I was alone. . . .

So am I alone now. I have written this last fantastic history of myself and of Mankind upon a substance that will, I know, outlast even the snow and the Ice—as it has outlasted Mankind that made it. It is the only thing with which I have never parted. For is it not irony that I should be the historian of this race—I, a savage, an 'archaic survival?' Why do I write? God knows, but some instinct prompts me, although there will never be men to read.

I have been sitting here, waiting, and I have thought often of Sir John and Alice, whom I loved. Can it be that I am feeling again, after all these ages, some tiny portion of that emotion, that great passion I once knew? I see her face before me, the face I have lost from my thoughts for eons, and something is in it that stirs my blood again. Her eyes are half-closed and deep, her lips are parted as though I could crush them with an infinity of wonder and discovery. O God! It is love again, love that I thought was lost! They have often smiled upon me when I spoke of God, and muttered about my foolish, primitive superstitions. But they are gone, and I am left who believe in God, and surely there is purpose in it.

I am cold, I have written. Ah, I am frozen. My breath freezes as it mingles with the air, and I can hardly move my numbed fingers. The Ice is closing over me, and I cannot break it any longer. The storm cries weirdly all about me in the twilight, and I know this is the end. The end of the world. And I—I, the last man. . . .

The last man. . . .

. . . I am cold—cold. . . .

But is it you, Alice, Is it you?

The Machine Man of Ardathia
by Francis Flagg

from AMAZING STORIES, November 1927

Francis Flagg was the pseudonym used by George Henry Weiss, but since all his fiction appeared under this one pen name It has usurped his given name in readers' memories. "The Machine Man of Ardathia" marked Flagg's debut in the science fiction field, and he arrived with a bang. Always a popular author, he was also the first to drift from Gernsback to *Weird Tales*, which he did with his fourth story, "The Chemical Brain". There is every possibility that these were stories that Gernsback rejected, since their elements of bizarrerie lent themselves more to the editorial policy of *Weird Tales*. Whatever the reason Flagg, became a frequent contributor to *Weird Tales*, which in fact carried some of his best fiction, particularly "The Distortion Out of Space", one of his last pieces, which appeared in the August 1934 issue.

Flagg ranks as one of the few authors who had their initial story illustrated on the cover of the magazine (although it was not credited visually until you peered closely at the base of the contents' column). However, on deeper research, it is not so surprising since the rest of that particular issue of *Amazing Stories* was not of such quality as Flagg's story. To begin with it was the only other new story. The second belonged to A. Hyatt Verrill, archaeologist and naturalist, and this was a mere humorous, spot-the-error story, "The Astounding Discoveries of Dr. Mentiroso". The remainder of the issue was reprint, including H. G. Wells's "A Story of the Stone Age", hardly his most scientific story, and the conclusion of Garrett Smith's praiseworthy novel, "Treasures of Tantalus".

What is notable about Flagg is his attitude towards characters.

Science fiction could be split into two spheres, the Verne school complete with gadgetry and invention, and the Wells school, with the emphasis on humanity and society. Flagg was without doubt a Wellsian, and it is this that helps keep his fiction alive today, when so much of his period is now outdated and archaic.

After "The Distortion Out of Space", Flagg virtually disappeared from the science fiction magazine scene, apart from two collaborations with Forrest J. Ackerman. He died in 1946 when he was only 48. A novel, "The Night People" was published posthumously by the Fantasy Publishing Corp. Inc., in 1947 and is now a rare collector's item.

I do not know what to believe. Sometimes, I am positive I dreamed it all. But, then, there is the matter of the heavy rocking-chair. That, undeniably, did disappear. Perhaps someone played a trick on me; but who would stoop to a deception so bizarre, merely for the purpose of befuddling the wits of an old man? Perhaps someone stole the rocking-chair; but why should anyone want to steal it? It was, it is true, a sturdy piece of furniture, but hardly valuable enough to excite the cupidity of a thief. Besides, it was in its place when I sat down in the easy-chair.

Of course, I may be lying. Peters, to whom I was misguided enough to tell everything on the night of its occurrence, wrote the story for his paper, and the editor says as much in his editorial when he remarks: "Mr. Matthews seems to possess an imagination equal to that of an H. G. Wells." And, considering the nature of my story I am quite ready to forgive him for doubting my veracity.

However, the few friends who know me better think that I had dined a little too wisely or too well, and was visited with a nightmare. Hodge suggested that the Jap who cleans my rooms had, for some reason, removed the rocking chair from its place, and that I merely took its presence for granted when I sat down in the other; but the Jap strenuously denies having done so.

I must explain that I have two rooms and a bath on the third floor of a modern apartment house fronting the Lake. Since my wife's death three years ago, I have lived thus, taking my breakfast and lunch at a restaurant, and my dinners, generally, at the club. I also have a room in a down-town office building where I spend a few hours every day working on my book, which is intended to be a critical analysis of the fallacies inherent in the Marxian theory of economics, embracing at the same time a thorough refutation of Lewis Morgan's *Ancient Society*. A rather ambitious undertaking, you will admit, and one not apt to engage the interest of a person given to inventing wild yards for the purpose of amazing his friends.

No; I emphatically deny having invented the story. However, the future will speak for itself. I will merely proceed to put the details of my strange experience on paper—justice to myself demands that I should do so, so many garbled accounts have appeared in the press—and leave the reader to draw his own conclusions.

Contrary to my usual custom, I had dined that evening with Hodge at the Hotel Oaks. Let me emphatically state that, while it is well-known among his intimates that Hodge has a decided taste for liquor, I had absolutely nothing of an intoxicating nature to drink, and Hodge will verify this. About eight-thirty, I refused an invitation to attend the theatre with him, and went to my rooms. There I changed into smoking-jacket and slippers, and lit a mild Havana.

The rocking-chair was occupying its accustomed place near the centre of the sitting-room floor. I remember that clearly because, as usual, I had either to push it aside or step around it, wondering for the thousandth time, as I did so, why that idiotic Jap persisted in placing it in such an inconvenient spot, and resolving, also for the thousandth time to speak to him about it. With a note-book and pencil placed on the stand beside me, and a copy of Frederick Engels' *Origin of The Family, Private Property and The State*, I turned on the light in my green-shaded reading lamp, switched off all the others, and sank with a sigh of relief into the easy-chair.

It was my intention to make a few notes from Engels' work relative to plural marriages, showing that he contradicted certain conclusions of Morgan's, but after a few minutes' work, I leaned back in my chair and closed my eyes. I did not doze; I am positive of that. My mind was actively engaged in trying to piece together a sentence that would clearly express my thoughts.

I can best describe what happened, then, by saying there was an explosion. It wasn't that, exactly; but, at the time, it seemed to me there must have been an explosion. A blinding flash of light registered with appalling vividness, through the closed lids, on the retina of my eyes. My first thought was that someone had dynamited the building; my second, that the electric

fuses had blown out. It was some time before I could see clearly.
When I could:

"Good Lord!" I whispered weakly. "What's that?"

Occupying the space where the rocking-chair had stood
(though I did not notice its absence at the time) was a cylinder
of what appeared to be glass, standing, I should judge, above
five feet high. Encased in this cylinder was what seemed to be a
caricature of a man—or a child. I say caricature because, while
the cylinder was all of five feet in height, the being inside of it
was hardly three; and you can imagine my amazement while I
stared at this apparition. After a while, I got up and switched
on all the lights, to better observe it.

You may wonder why I did not try to call someone in, but that
never occurred to me. In spite of my age—I am sixty—my nerves
are steady, and I am not easily frightened. I walked very carefully around the cylinder, and viewed the creature inside from all
angles. It was sustained in the centre, midway between top and
bottom, by what appeared to be an intricate arrangement of
glass and metal tubes. These tubes seemed to run at places into
the body; and I noticed some sort of dark fluid circulating
through the glass tubes.

The head was very large and hairless; it had bulging brows,
and no ears. The eyes were large and winkless, the nose well
defined; but the lower part of the face and mouth ran into the
small, round body with no sign of a chin. Its legs hung down,
skinny, flabby; and the arms were more like short tentacles
reaching down from where the head and body joined. The thing
was, of course, naked.

I drew the easy-chair up to the cylinder, and sat down facing it.
Several times I stretched out my hand in an effort to touch
its surface, but some force prevented my fingers from making
contact, which was very curious. Also, I could detect no movement of the body or limbs of the weird thing inside the glass.

"What I would like to know," I muttered, "is what you are
and where you come from; are you alive, and am I dreaming
or am I awake?"

Suddenly, the creature came to life. One of its tentacle-like
hands, holding a metal tube, darted to its mouth. From the tube
shot a white streak, which fastened itself to the cylinder.

"Ah!" came a clear, metallic voice. "English, Primitive;
probably of the twentieth century." The words were uttered
with an indescribable intonation, much as if a foreigner were
speaking our language. Yet, more than that, as if he were speaking

a language long dead. I don't know why that thought should have occurred to me, then. Perhaps . . .

"So you can talk!" I exclaimed.

The creature gave a metallic chuckle. "As you say, I can talk."

"Then tell me what you are."

"I am an Ardathian—a Machine-Man of Ardathia. And you . . . ? Tell me, is that really hair on your head?"

"Yes," I replied.

"And those coverings you wear on your body, are they clothes?'

I answered in the affirmative.

"How odd! Then you really are a Primitive; a Prehistoric Man," The eyes behind the glass shield regarded me intently.

"A prehistoric man!" I exclaimed. "What do you mean?"

"I mean that you are one of that race of early men whose skeletons we have dug up, here and there, and reconstructed for our Schools of Biology. Marvellous how our scientists have copied you from some fragments of bone! The small head covered with hair, the beast-like jaw, the abnormally large body and legs, the artificial coverings made of cloth . . . even your language!"

For the first time, I began to suspect that I was the victim of a hoax. I got up again and walked carefully around the cylinder, but could detect no outside agency controlling the contraption. Besides, it was absurd to think that anyone would go to the trouble of constructing such a complicated apparatus as this appeared to be, merely for the sake of a practical joke. Nevertheless, I looked out on the landing. Seeing nobody, I came back and resumed my seat in front of the cylinder.

"Pardon me," I said, "but you referred to me as belonging to a period much more remote than yours."

"That is correct. If I am not mistaken in my calculations, you are thirty thousand years in the past. What date is this?"

"June 5th, 1939," I replied, feebly. The creature went through some contortions, sorted a few metal tubes with its hands, and then announced in its metallic voice:

"Computed in terms of your method of reckoning, I have travelled back through time exactly twenty-eight thousand years, nine months, three weeks, two days, seven hours, and a certain number of minutes and seconds which it is useless for me to enumerate exactly."

It was at this point that I endeavoured to make sure I was

wide awake and in full possession of my faculties. I got up, selected a fresh cigar from the humidor, struck a light, and began puffing away. After a few puffs, I laid it beside the one I had been smoking earlier in the evening. I found it there, later. Incontestable proof. . . . .

I said that I am a man of steady nerves. Once more I sat down in front of the cylinder, determined this time to find out what I could about the incredible creature within.

"You say you have travelled back through time thousands of years. How is that possible?" I demanded.

"By verifying time as a fourth dimension, and perfecting devices for travelling in it."

"In what manner?"

"I do not know whether I can explain it exactly, in your language, and you are too primitive and unevolved to understand mine. However, I shall try. Know, then, that space is as much a relative thing as time. In itself, aside from its relation to matter, it has no existence. You can neither see nor touch it, yet you move freely in space. Is that clear?"

"It sounds like Einstein's theory."

"Einstein?"

"One of our great scientists and mathematicians," I explained.

"So you have scientists and mathematicians? Wonderful! That bears out what Hoomi says. I must remember to tell . . . However, to resume my explanation. Time is apprehended in the same manner as is space—that is, in its relation to matter. When you measure space, you do so by letting your measuring rod leap from point to point of matter; or, in the case of spanning the void, let us say, from the Earth to Venus, you start and end with matter, remarking that between lies so many miles of space.

"But it is clear that you see and touch no space, merely spanning the distance between two points of matter with the vision or the measuring rod. You do the same when you compute time with the Sun, or by means of the clock which I see hanging on the wall there, Time, then, is no more of an abstraction than is space. If it is possible for man to move freely in space, it is possible for him to move freely in time, and we Ardathians are beginning to do so."

"But how?"

"I am afraid your limited intelligence could not grasp that. You must realise that compared with us, you are hardly as much as human. When I look at you, I perceive that your body is enormously larger than your head. This means that you are dominated by animal passions, and that your mental capacity is not very high."

That this weirdly humorous thing inside a glass cylinder should come to such a conclusion regarding me, made me smile.

"If any of my fellow citizens should see you," I replied, "they would consider you—well, absurd."

"That is because they would judge me by the only standard they know—themselves. In Ardathia, you would be regarded as bestial; in fact, that is exactly how your reconstructed skeletons are regarded. Tell me, is it true that you nourish your bodies by taking food through your mouths into your stomachs?"

"Yes."

"And are still at that stage of bodily evolution when you eliminate the waste products through the alimentary canal?"

I lowered my head.

"How revolting."

The unwinking eyes regarded me intently. Then something happened which startled me greatly. The creature raised a glass tube to its face, and from the end of the tube leaped a purple ray which came through the glass casing and played over the room.

"There is no need to be alarmed," said the metallic voice. "I was merely viewing your habitat, and making some deductions. Correct me if I am wrong, please. You are an English-speaking man of the twentieth century. You and your kind live in cities and houses. You eat, digest, and reproduce your young, much as do the animals from which you have sprung. You use crude machines, and have an elementary understanding of physics and chemistry. Correct me if I am wrong, please."

"You are right, to a certain extent," I replied. "But I am not interested in having you tell me what I am; I know that. I wish to know what you are. You claim to have come from thirty thousand years in the future, but you advance no evidence to support the claim. How do I know you are not a trick, a fake, an hallucination of mine? You say you can move freely in time. Then how is it you have never come this way before? Tell me something about yourself; I am curious."

"Your questions are well put," replied the voice, "and I shall seek to answer them. It is true that we Machine-Men of Ardathia are beginning to move in time as well as in space, but note that I say beginning. Our Time Machines are very crude, as yet, and I am the first Ardathian to penetrate the past beyond a period of six thousand years. You must realise that a time traveller runs certain hazards. At any place on the road, he may materialise inside of a solid of some sort. In that case, he is almost certain to be destroyed.

"Such was the constant danger until I perfected my enveloping ray. I cannot name or describe it in your tongue, but if you approach me too closely, you will feel its resistance. This ray has the effect of disintegrating and dispersing any body of matter inside which a time traveller may materialise. Perhaps you were aware of a great light when I appeared in your room? I probably took shape within a body of matter, and the ray destroyed it."

"The rocking-chair!" I exclaimed. "It was standing on the spot you now occupy."

"Then it has been reduced to its original atoms. This is a wonderful moment for me! My ray has proved an unqualified success, for the second time. It not only removes any hindering matter from about the time-traveller, but also creates a void within which he is perfectly safe from harm. But to resume . . .

"It is hard to believe that we Ardathians evolved from such creatures as you. Our written history does not go back to a time when men nourished themselves by taking food into their stomachs through their mouths, or reproduced their young in the animal-like fashion in which you do. The earliest men of whom we have any records were the Bi-Chanics. They lived about fifteen thousand years before our era, and were already well along the road of mechanical evolution when their civilisation fell.

"The Bi-Chanics vaporised their food substances and breathed them through the nostril, excreting the waste products of the body through the pores of the skin. Their children were brought to the point of birth in ecto-genetic incubators. There is enough authentic evidence to prove that the Bi-Chanics had perfected the use of mechanical hearts, and were crudely able to make . . .

"I cannot find the words to explain what they made, but it does not matter. The point is that, while they had only partly subordinated machinery to their use, they are the earliest race of human beings of whom we possess any real knowledge, and it was their period of time that I was seeking when I inadvertently came too far and landed in yours."

The metallic voice ceased for a moment, and I took advantage of the pause to speak.

"I do not know a thing about the Bi-Chanics, or whatever it

is you call them," I remarked, "but they were certainly not the first to make mechanical hearts. I remember reading about a Russian scientist who kept a dog alive four hours by means of a motor which pumped the blood through the dog's body."

"You mean the motor was used as a heart?"

"Exactly."

The Ardathian made a quick motion with one of its hands.

"I have made a note of your information; it is very interesting."

"Furthermore," I pursued, "I recall reading of how, some years ago, one of our surgeons was hatching out rabbits and guinea pigs in ecto-genetic incubators."

The Ardathian made another quick gesture with its hand. I could see that my remarks excited it.

"Perhaps," I said, not without a feeling of satisfaction (for the casual allusion to myself as hardly human had irked my pride), "perhaps you will find it as interesting to visit the people of five hundred years from now, let us say, as you would to visit the Bi-Chanics."

"I assure you," replied the metallic voice, "that if I succeed in returning to my native Ardathia, those periods will be thoroughly explored. I can only express surprise at your having advanced as far as you have, and wonder why it is you have made no practical use of your knowledge."

"Sometimes I wonder myself," I returned. "But I am very much interested in learning more about yourself and your times. If you would resume your story . . . ?"

"With pleasure," replied the Ardathian. "In Ardathia, we do not live in houses or in cities; neither do we nourish ourselves as do you, or as did the Bi-Chanics. The chemical fluid you see circulating through these tubes which run into and through my body, has taken the place of blood. The fluid is produced by the action of a light-ray on certain life-giving elements in the air. It is constantly being produced in those tubes under my feet, and driven through my body be a mechanism too intricate for me to describe.

"The same fluid circulates through my body only once, nourishing it and gathering all impurities as it goes. Having completed its revolution, it is dissipated by means of another ray which carries it back into the surrounding air. Have you noticed the transparent substance enclosing me?"

"The cylinder of glass, you mean?"

"Glass! What do you mean by glass?"

"Why, that there," I said, pointing to the window. The

Ardathian directed a metal tube at the spot indicated. A purple streak flashed out, hovered a moment on a pane, and then withdrew.

"No," came the metallic voice; "not that. The cylinder, as you call it, is made of a transparent substance, very strong and practically unbreakable. Nothing can penetrate it but the rays which you see, and the two whose action I have just described, which are invisible.

"We Ardathians, you must understand, are not delivered of the flesh; nor are we introduced into incubators as ova taken from female bodies, as were the Bi-Chanics. Among the Ardathians, there are no males or females. The cell from which we are to develop is created synthetically. It is fertilised by means of a ray, and then put into a cylinder such as you observe surrounding me. As the embryo develops, the various tubes and mechanical devices are introduced into the body by our mechanics, and become an integral part of it.

"When the young Ardathian is born, he does not leave the case in which he has developed. That case—or cylinder, as you call it—protects him from the action of a hostile environment. If it were to break and expose him to the elements, he would perish miserably. Do you follow me?"

Not quite," I confessed. "You say that you have evolved from men like us, and then go on to state that you are synthetically conceived and machine made. I do not see how this evolution was possible."

"And you may never understand! Nevertheless, I shall try to explain. Did you not tell me you had wise ones among you who experiment with mechanical hearts and ecto-genetic incubators? Tell me, have you not others engaged in tests tending to show that it is the action of environment, and not the passing of time, which accounts for the ageing of organisms?"

"Well," I said, hesitatingly, "I have heard tell of chicken's hearts being kept alive in special containers which protect them from their normal environment."

"Ah!" exclaimed the metallic voice. "But Hoomi will be astounded when he learns that such experiments were carried on by prehistoric men fifteen thousand years before the Bi-Chanics! Listen closely, for what you have told me provides a starting-point from which you may be able to follow my explanation of man's evolution from your time to mine.

"Of the thousands of years separating your day from that of

the Bi-Chanics, I have no authentic knowledge. My exact
knowledge begins with the Bi-chanics. They were the first to
realise that man's bodily advancement lay in, and through,
the machine. They perceived that man only became human
when he fashioned tools; that the tools increased the length of
his arms, the grip of his hands, the strength of his muscles.
They observed that, with the aid of the machine, man could
circle the Earth, speak to the planets, gaze intimately at the stars.
We will increase our span of life on Earth, said the Bi-Chanics,
by throwing the protection of the machine, the thing that the
machine produces, around and into our bodies.

"This they did, to the best of their ability, and increased their
longevity to an average of about two hundred years. Then
came the Tri-Namics. More advanced than the Bi-Chanics,
they reasoned that old age was caused, not by the passage of
time, but by the action of environment on the matter of which
men were composed. It is this reasoning which causes the men
of your time to experiment with chicken's hearts. The Tri-Namics
sought to perfect devices for safeguarding the flesh against the
wear and tear of its environment. They made envelopes—
cylinders—in which they attempted to bring embryos to birth,
and to rear children; but they met with only partial success."

"You speak of the Bi-Chanics and of the Tri-Namics," I
said, "as if they were two distinct races of people. Yet you imply
that the latter evolved from the former. If the Bi-Chanics'
civilisation fell, did any period of time elapse between that fall
and the rise of the Tri-Namics? And how did the latter inherit
from their predecessors?"

"It is because of your language, which I find very crude and
inadequate, that I have not already made that clear," answered
the Ardathian. "The Tri-Namics were really a more progressive
part of the Bi-Chanics. When I said the civilisation of the latter
fell, I did not mean what that implies in your language.

"You must realise that, fifteen thousand years in your future,
the race of man was, scientifically speaking, making rapid strides.
But it was not always possible for backward or conservative
minds to adjust themselves to new discoveries. Minority groups,
composed mostly of the young, forged ahead, proposed radical
changes, entertained new ideas, and finally culminated in what
I have alluded to as the Tri-Namics. Inevitably, in the course
of time, the Bi-Chanics died off, and conservative methods
with them. That is what I meant when I said their civilisation fell.

"In the same fashion did we follow the Tri-Namics. When

the latter succeeded in raising children inside the cylinder, they destroyed themselves. Soon, all children were born in this manner; and in time, the fate of the Bi-Chanics became that of the Tri-Namics leaving behind them the Machine-Men of Ardathia, who differed radically from them in bodily structure, yet were none the less their direct descendants."

At last, I began to get an inkling of what the Ardathian meant when it alluded to itself as a Machine-Man. The appalling story of man's final evolution into a controlling centre that directed a mechanical body, awoke something akin to fear in my heart. If it were true, what of the soul, the spirit . . . ? The metallic voice went on.

"You must not imagine that the early Ardathians possessed a cylinder as invulnerable as the one which protects me. The first envelopes of this nature were made of a pliable substance, which wore out within three centuries. But the substance composing the envelope has gradually been improved, perfected, until now it is immune for fifteen hundred years to anything save a powerful explosion or some other major catastrophe."

"Fifteen hundred years!" I exclaimed.

"Barring accident, that is the length of time an Ardathian lives. But to us, fifteen hundred years is no longer than a hundred would be to you. Remember, please, that time is relative: twelve hours of your time is a second of ours, and a year . . . But suffice it to say that very few Ardathians live out their allotted span. Since we are constantly engaged in hazardous experiments and dangerous expeditions, accidents are many. Thousands of our brave explorers have plunged into the past and never returned. They probably materialised inside solids, and were annihilated; but I believe I have finally overcome this danger with my disintegrating ray."

"And how old are you?"

"As you count time, five hundred and seventy years. You must understand that there has been no change in my body since birth. If the cylinder were everlasting, or proof against accident, I should live for ever. It is the wearing out, or breaking up, of the envelope, which exposes us to the dangerous forces of nature and causes death. Some of our scientists are trying to perfect means for building up the cylinder as fast as the wear and tear of environment breaks it down; others are seeking to rear embryos to birth with nothing but rays for covering—rays incapable of harming the organism, yet immune to dissipation by environment and incapable of destruction by explosion. So far, they have been unsuccessful; but I have every confidence in their ultimate triumph. Then we shall be as immortal as the planet on which we live."

I stared at the cylinder, at the creature inside the cylinder, at the ceiling, the four walls of the room, and then back again at the cylinder, I pinched the soft flesh of my thigh with my fingers. I was awake, all right; there could be no doubt about that.

"Are there any questions you would like to ask?" came the metallic voice.

"Yes," I said at last, half-fearfully. "What joy can there be in existence for you? You have no sex; you cannot mate. It seems to me—" I hesitated. "It seems to me that no hell could be worse than centuries of being caged alive inside that thing you call an envelope. Now, I have full command of my limbs and can go where I please. I can—".

I came to a breathless stop, awed by the lurid light which suddenly gleamed in the winkless eyes.

"Poor prehistoric mammal," came the answer, "how could you, groping in the dawn of human existence, comprehend what is beyond your lowly environment! Compared to you, we are as gods. No longer are our loves and hates the reactions of viscera. Our thoughts, out thinking, our emotions, are conditioned, moulded to the extent that we control our immediate environment. There is no such thing as—

"But it is impossible to continue. Your mentality—it is not the word I like to use but, as I have repeatedly said, your language is woefully inadequate—has a restricted range of but a few thousand words: therefore, I cannot explain further. Only the same lack—in a different fashion, of course, and with objects instead of words—hinders the free movement of your limbs. You have command of them, you say. Poor primitive, do you realise how shackled you are with nothing but your hands and feet? You augment them, of course, with a few machines, but they are crude and cumbersome. It is you who are caged alive, and not I. I have broken through the walls of your cage, have shaken off its shackles—have gone free. Behold the command I have of my limbs!"

From an extended tube shot a streak of white, like a funnel, whose radius was great enough to encircle my seated body. I was conscious of being scooped up, and drawn forward, with inconceivable speed. For one breathless moment, I hung suspended against the cylinder itself, the winkless eyes not an inch from my own. In that moment, I had the sensation of being probed, handled. Several times I was revolved, as a man might twirl a stick. Then I was back in the easy-chair again, white and shaken.

"It is true that I never leave the envelope in which I am encased," continued the metallic voice, "but I have at my command rays which can bring me anything I desire. In Ardathia are machines—it would be useless for me to describe them to you—with which I can walk, fly, move mountains, delve in the earth, investigate the stars, and loose forces of which you have no conception. Those machines are mechanical parts of my body, extensions of my limbs. I take them off and put them on at will. With their help, I can view one continent while busily employed in another, I can make time machines, harness rays, and plunge for thirty thousand years into the past. Let me again illustrate."

The tentacle-like hand of the Ardathian waved a tube. The five-foot cylinder glowed with an intense light, spun like a top, and so spinning, dissolved into space. Even as I gaped, like one petrified, the cylinder reappeared with the same rapidity. The metallic voice announced:

"I have just been five years into your future."

"My future!" I exclaimed. "How can that be when I have not lived it yet?"

"But of course you have lived it!"

I stared, bewildered.

"Could I visit my past if you had not lived your future?" the creature persisted.

"I do not understand," I said, feebly. "It doesn't seem possible that while I am here, actually in this room, you should be able to travel ahead in time and find out what I shall be doing in a future I haven't reached yet."

"That is because you are unable to grasp intelligently what time is. Think of it as a dimension—a fourth dimension—which stretches like a road ahead and behind you."

"But even then," I protested, "I could only be at one place at a given time, on that road, and not where I am and somewhere else in the same second."

"You are never anywhere at any time," replied the metallic voice, "save always in the past or the future. But it is useless trying to acquaint you with a simple truth, thirty thousand years ahead of your ability to understand it. As I said, I travelled five years into your future. Men were wrecking this building."

"Tearing down this place? Nonsense! It was only erected two years ago."

"Nevertheless, they were tearing it down. I sent forth my visual-ray to locate you. You were in a great room with numerous other men. They were all doing a variety of odd things. There was—"

At that moment came a heavy knock on the door of my room.

"What's the matter, Matthews?" called a loud voice. "What are you talking about, all this time? Are you sick?"

I uttered an exclamation of annoyance, because I recognised the voice of John Peters, a newspaperman who occupied the apartment next to mine. My first impulse was to tell him I was busy, but the next moment I had a better idea. Here was someone to whom I could show the cylinder, and the creature inside it; someone to bear witness to having seen it, besides myself! I hurried to the door and threw it open.

"Quick!" I said, grasping Peters by the arm and hauling him into the room. "What do you think of that?"

"Think of what?" he demanded.

"Why of that, there," I began, pointing with my finger, and then stopping short with my mouth wide open; for on the spot where, a few seconds before, the cylinder had stood, there was nothing. The envelope and the Ardathian had disappeared.

*   *   *

AUTHOR'S NOTE

The material for this manuscript came into my hands in an odd fashion. About a year after the Press had ceased to print garbled versions of Matthews' experience, I made the acquaintance of his friend, Hodge, with whom he had dined on that evening. I asked him about Matthews, He said:

"Did you know they've put him in an asylum? You didn't? Well, they have. He's crazy enough now, poor devil; though he was always a little queer, I thought. I went to visit him the other day, and it gave me quite a shock to see him in a ward with a lot of other men, all doing something queer.

"By the way, Peters told me the other day that the apartment house where Matthews lived is to be torn down. They are going to demolish several houses along the Lake Shore, to widen the boulevard; but he says they won't wreck them for three or four years yet. Funny, eh? Would you like to see what Matthews wrote about the affair himself?"

Out of the Sub-Universe
by R. F. Starzl

from AMAZING STORIES QUARTERLY, Summer 1928

Nineteen-twenty-eight was the boom year for *Amazing Stories*.
Whereas reprints had held sway during most of its first eighteen
months of existence, in 1928 a whole army of new authors
swamped the field, amongst them David H. Keller, Jack
Williamson, Stanton Coblentz and R. F. Starzl.

Starzl took as the theme for his first story the sub-microscopic
world. It was far from new. Fitz-James O'Brien had more or less
invented it with his lengthy story "The Diamond Lens" which
had appeared in *Atlantic Monthly* for January 1858. This story is
marred however by O'Brien's lapses into spiritualism. Coming
more up-to date, the theme was really taken into hand by Ray
Cummings, whose own first story. "The Girl in the Golden
Atom" appeared in *All-Story* for March 15th 1919. His hero man-
ages to enter the miniature world, where his adventures were not
unlike imitation Burroughs. Nevertheless Cummings returned
again and again to the mini-world theme, but he never expanded
on his original concept.

Starzl in all probability had read the Cummings story. He
would have been nineteen at the time. But it is quite likely he
was inspired by Wertenbaker's story "The Man in the Atom",
which, if he had not read it when it originally appeared, he would
have doubtless found when Gernsback reprinted it in the first
issue of *Amazing Stories*. Wertenbaker was intrigued with the
mechanics of sub-universes, something Cummings avoided. But
whereas Wertenbaker approached the theme from within, Starzl
approached it from without. Hence with "Out of the Sub-
Universe" we have a unique view of a world within a world.

Sub-Universes was a popular theme in the first decade of

sf magazines. It was being used so often that in the end it became monotonous. Stories in the Cummings school were the more common, unfortunately, although some were more adventurous, such as S.P. Meek's "Submicroscopic" and its sequel "Awlo of Ulm" which appeared in *Amazing Stories* in 1931. Fiction of the Starzl shcool is echoed in such capable gems as Edmond Hamilton's "The Cosmic Pantograph" (*Wonder Stories* October 1935). So common was the theme, that it even recurs in this anthology, but only as a device within the story. But I shall let that story come as a surprise.

Starzl was a reporter whose fiction was always competent and literate. Born in 1899 he would feature prominently in Gernsback's magazines, but also appeared in *Argosy* in the 1930's. He is strictly an author of this period, since, apart from reprints, his last sf magazine appearance was "Dimension of the Conquered" in the October 1934 *Astounding Stories*.

"If you really are so anxious to go, I won't keep you from going any more," said Professor Halley with a sigh, to the young man who sat opposite to him in his laboratory. "Eventually it will become necessary for a human being to make the journey, and no better qualified than you to make an accurate report."

"Indeed, I should think not," smiled Hale McLaren, his friend and pupil, "as long as I've been your assistant, and, you might say, co-discoverer. But—" his eyes clouded, "I don't know about Shirley. She wants to go along."

"I think you should let her go along if she wants to," said Halley slowly. "You know that I love my daughter even more than she loves you, but I realize that if you failed to come back, as our experimental rabbits failed to come back, she could never be happy again. She would rather be with you, no matter how inhospitable the little world to which you are going."

"But I will come back!" insisted Hale McLaren urgently. "We know why our experimental animals did not return. As soon as they arrived on the surface of whatever little planet they happened to land on, they did not bother to wonder where they might be. They simply wandered on, and of course, it was impossible for our apparatus to find them again. You may be sure that I won't leave the landing spot."

"Nevertheless, it is possible you may fail to return. Shirley is almost a grown woman. We will explain the dangers to her, and if she still wants to go, she shall go."

He stepped to the telephone and called the number of his home, only a short distance from the little inland college where he was head of the physics department. In a few minutes Shirley came into the presence of the two men and regarded their soberness amusedly.

"Whose funeral are you holding today?" she asked.

"Don't talk of funerals at a time like this," said McLaren, a little crossly. "We called you over here to explain to you again the danger of the trip you want to make with me. Frankly, I don't want you along ,but your father says you can come if you want to."

"Of course I'm going!" she retorted with mock defiance. "Do you think I want to lose you to some atomic vamp?"

"This is serious," he persisted, refusing for once to yield to her rallying. He led the way to the corner of the big, bare room, where he moved aside a denim curtain sliding on a wire, which hid a maze of enigmatic apparatus, evidently electrical in its nature. In the center of a large helix, on a base of peculiar translucent green material, stood a great glass bell, large enough for two or three persons to stand inside. A bank of high-voltage vacuum tubes against one wall was connected by means of heavy copper tubing to various points on the helix. The translucent green base was supported on a number of cylinders, which formed a hydraulic hoist so that the heavy green disc could be lowered in order to permit the introduction of objects under the independently supported bell.

"I'm going to start in a few minutes," McLaren informed Shirley, and despite his assumed brusqueness, his voice betrayed a tremor of tenderness. "Your father is going to explain the danger to you, and if you still want to go, we start together."

"You know, Shirley" began Professor Halley in his best class-room manner, "that Hale and I have been engaging extensively in research work to discover the ultimate composition of matter. I will admit that we are as much in the dark regarding our primary quest as ever, but in our researches we have opened new vistas that are fully as beautiful and as interesting as the truths we first sought.

"By utilizing the newly discovered cosmic ray, which has a wave-length infinitely shorter than any other known kind of light, we have been able to get circumstantial evidence that electrons do not consist solely of a negative electric charge, as physicists have thought before, but that this charge is actually held by a real particle of matter, so infinitely small that we would never get direct evidence ot its existence by the older methods.

"While pursuing these studies, we stumbled upon another property of the cosmic ray. We found that certain harmonics of the ray, when enormously amplified, have the property of reducing or increasing the mass and volume of all matter, without changing its form. We have discovered no limit to this power. We believe it is infinite.

"Now this suggests a possible solution of the problem of the constitution of the universe. Could we prove that the atom, with its central nucleus and its satellites, called electrons, is really only a miniature universe, in fact and not by analogy only, we could safely assume that the constituents of the infra-universe beneath us and the super-universe above us are only links of a chain that stretches into infinity!"

Professor Halley paused. His assistant was flushed and enthusiasic, and his daughter's cheeks glowed brightly and her eyes sparkled. But she was not looking at the apparatus; she was looking at the smooth, dark hair of her fiancé.

"We have sent things into that sub-universe," he continued, "chairs, coins, glasses, bricks and things like that. And we have brought some of them back. But when we sent guinea pigs or rabbits, or a stray dog into the world of mystery, we could not bring them back. Hale thinks the animals may have wandered away, out of focus of our rays. I don't know. He may be right, or they may have met some terrible unknown fate. Now he offers himself for the experiment. It is dangerous. It may be ghastly. But if you wish to go with him, you may. Your mother is dead. You may leave me lonely in my old age; but you may go—for science!"

A solemn hush followed the simple words. Then Shirley said clearly: "I will go."

The physicist turned his head for a moment. When he faced them again, there was no sign of his mental struggle. Firmly, he threw a lever, and the green base silently lowered to the floor. McLaren and the girl stepped upon it, and when it rose again it carried them into the glass bell. The professor turned to the raised platform where the control board was located.

"Good-bye!" he called. "I'll bring you back when an hour has passed."

"Good-bye!" they returned, their voices muffled.

A powerful generator sprang into action, filling the laboratory with its high-pitched whine. The vacuum tubes glowed dully, and a powerful odor of ozone permeated the air. With a loud crash, the high-tension electricity discharged between adjacent turns of the helix. The professor hastened to adjust a condenser, and again the silence was broken only by the whine of the generator and a low humming.

As the professor continued to adjust the controls, the bell gradually filled with a deep violet light that swayed and swirled tenuously like the drapes of an aurora borealis. The light swirled around the man and the girl, at times almost hiding them from view. It gradually concentrated toward the bottom of the bell, seeming to cling to the green base, intertwining the two living forms until it almost hid them from view. Yet they continued to smile and wave encouragement.

And now it was evident that they were growing smaller. Already they were less than four feet tall, and as the apparatus was brought more and more into perfect resonance, their rate of shrinkage accelerated. Soon they were but a foot high, standing in a sea of violet light, then six inches, then hardly an inch. The professor turned off the generator.

The girl and the man now walked the few inches necessary to bring them to the exact center of the base. Here, in a slight depression in the smooth material, was a tiny granule of carbon, one of the atoms of which they were to explore. It was so tiny that it could hardly be seen under the microscope, ordinarily, yet to McLaren, it must already have become plainly visible, for he soon spoke to the girl and she joined him, standing with him very closely near a spot on the floor which he indicated.

Again the mysterious harmonics of the cosmic ray were brought into action, and the two tiny figures vanished from sight. The professor stayed at the controls, his eyes fixed anxiously on his watch until the proper time had elapsed, as indicated by his calculations. He stopped the dynamo again and laid his watch on the table. He marked the time when he should recall them, 10 minutes after four, and paced nervously up and down the room in which he was now alone. Moisture beading his brow, he stopped and stared at the slight depression in which lay a million universes, each one as complete and as perfect as his own, and in one of those universes was a whirling speck on which he had deposited his daughter and best-loved assistant.

He started as the telephone whirred and disposed of a student who wanted to make a trifling inquiry. Then he went back to his watch again, listened to see if his watch might have stopped. It was very still in the laboratory, and when a small rill of water suddenly cascaded out of the cooling jacket of one of the heavy duty vacuum tubes, the noise seemed loud and strident.

A new thought was now harassing Professor Halley. Suppose that in that unthinkably small world, there were dangerous creatures, with whom Hale and Shirley might be battling for their lives even at that moment. Perhaps this world might happen to be a blazing sun; suppose they had gasped their lives out on a sterile and airless moon? He looked at his watch again. The half-hour was almost up. A few more minutes, and they'd be ready and waiting to come back—wouldn't do to turn on the ray while they might be a short distance away, out of focus.—A few more seconds—now!

With a fierce sweep, he threw the switch and the violet light filled the glass bell again, Quickly he reversed the current— then crept to the base of the glass dome so that he might see the returned wanderers as soon as they grew into visibility.

Within a few minutes a small cloudy patch appeared in the glassy depression where the microscopic granule of carbon lay. Before the physicist's eyes this spot resolved itself into hundreds of tiny dots—dots that grew rapidly until they resembled minute upright pegs—pegs that presently grew large enough to show arms and legs. Small human-like creatures that were plainly men and women by the time they were half an inch tall. Men and women that grew and walked about, and were evidently greatly perturbed.

Halley watched them with amazement until they were a few inches tall. He did not move until they began to be so crowded that there was danger of smothering some of them. Then he leaped to the switch to stop their growth, and lowered the green disc until it was at the same level as the table, to which some of the more venturesome now jumped for the sake of more room. As he watched them in stupefaction, looking vainly for McLaren and Shirley, a man separated himself from the crowd, walked to the edge of the table, made a deep obeisance, and called:

"Where are we?"

His voice was thin and reedy, like the chirp of an insect, and his accent was slurred and difficult to understand. Yet he spoke recognizable English.

"You are on earth, " said Halley automatically.

This remark created the most profound impression. A thin, sighing cry arose from the little people, and many of them prostrated themselves. They wore filmy, short robes that came to their knees, held to their bodies by girdles. Men and women were dressed pretty nearly alike, but there was a well defined plan of ornamentation which distinguished the sexes.

The leader turned on them and cried.

"Hark! Hark! Is it not as we, your priests, have told you! To the faithful shall it be granted to be carried from our vale of tears to the Earth, with its portals of gold, where the milk and honey flow. You have heard the voice of the Angel. In a voice of thunder he has told you, you are at the gateway of the Earth, while those who believe not shall be cast into the outer darkness, where there is wailing and gnashing of teeth!

Someone in the background began a hymn. The mass of pygmy humanity joined, and the faint insect-like chorus filled the room.

Halley addressed the priest again.

"Where do you come from?"

"We are citizens of Elektron, so named by our illustrious ancestors, Haël, the Man, and Shuërrely, the Woman, who came to our planet in its youth, aeons and aeons ago—so many millions of years ago that they are to be reckoned only in geological epochs."

"How did you know the name of our earth?"

"It was handed down to us from generation to generation. It is preserved in our monuments and temples and in the records of our wise men. We knew for many ages that it is the elysium of perfection—the place of infinite happiness. For did not our illustrious forebears, Haël and Shuërrely, pine for the Earth, though they came to our Elektron when it was a young planet with a soft climate, and rich in luscious fruits?"

"You say Hale and Shirley came to your planet many ages ago? Wasn't your planet peopled then?"

"There were animals, some of terrifying size and frightful armament. But our Earth-sent ancestors, through superior cunning, overcame them, and their children gradually conquered all of Elektron. We are their descendants, but we have preserved their language, and their traditions, and their religion, and we treasured the Great Promise?"

"The Great Promise?"

"The Great Promise," the Elektronite intoned, almost sonorously, despite his small size, "was given us by Haël and Shuërrely. They declared that a great wizard, an Angel of superlative power and understanding, would some day penetrate the vast empty Earth. On the spot where they first appeared, they commanded that their children reside and await the coming of the Angel, which they called Cosmicray. Many were there who fell from that true religion, but we have builded ourselves a temple on that sacred spot, and The Great Promise has been kept!"

Halley said to them dully, pain in his heart, "I am Shirley's father and Hale's friend, and it is not an hour since I sent them to your Elektron!"

But his grandchildren a thousand generations removed, again prostrated themselves and burst into song anew.

Professor Halley was in a decidedly awkward position, He narrowly escaped being indicted for murder. The disappearance of his daughter and his assistant naturally provoked inquiry, and the ugly suspicion was current that he had done away with them and consumed the bodies in his formidable looking Cosmic Ray machine.

Curiously enough, the proof which finally cleared him of the murder suspicion got him into trouble with the immigration authorities, who did not know what to do with several hundred lilliputian peole who couldn't be deported to anywhere. Professor Halley positively refused to send them back to Elektron unless they agreed to go of their own free will, and none of them wanted to go back. Finally the immigration authorities consented to admit the Elektonites under bond, after they had been increased to normal size. Friends were found who assisted them in adjusting themselves to a new type of civilization, and according to latest reports, most of them are getting along very well.

The writer, after many attempts, finally obtained from Professor Halley a first-hand account of his experience and a detailed explanation of the operation of his invention. Skipping the technical details, which have nothing to do with this story, it is only necessary to give here the professor's own explanation of the remarkable fast life-cycle as lived on Elektron.

"I blame myself," said Professor Halley sadly, "for overlooking this important point. While it is true that the sub-universe resembles our own; while it is true that the electrons follow their orbits in a manner analogous to the planets around the suns; yet I overlooked the fact that due to the great difference in size there is also an enormous difference in time. It takes the earth a year to go around the sun; an electron circles its positive nucleus millions of times a second. Yet every time it completes its orbit it is like a year to the inhabitants.

"Before I had time to even blink an eye, Shirley and Hale had lived, loved, died, and many generations of their children had gone through their life cycles. It was normal to them—to us it was unthinkably brief."

He turned his patient face wearily towards the window, staring over the broad campus with unseeing eyes. They say his scientific apparatus is dusty from disuse, but the college board has decided to keep him on the faculty as long as he lives. He is a gentle, pathetic old man who will not live long.

The Eternal Man
by D. D. Sharp

from SCIENCE WONDER STORIES,
August 1929

Sharp was not really one of Gernsback's discoveries, since he had already sold two stories to *Weird Tales*, one of which, "The Goddess of the Painted Priests" had appeared when "The Eternal Man" made him an instant success with the readers of the new *Science Wonder Stories*. Thereafter Sharp left *Weird Tales* and concentrated on the Gernsback magazines. A sequel, "The Eternal Man Revives" appeared in the Summer 1930 *Wonder Stories Quarterly*. Meanwhile, the May 1930 *Science Wonder Stories* carried "The Day of the Beast", a run-of-the mill plot wherein a scientist succeeds in perfecting a process to increase the size of living objects, and soon finds himself battling a giant spider. A spark of originality in the ending appears when we find that for once the scientist does not destroy his notes so that no one else will discover his terrible secret—he merely locks them away in a steel safe. In an age when dread discoveries were usually doomed to instant destruction by fire or acid, such an ending was refreshing.

Sharp appeared with slow regularity during this period, five more stories appeared in *Wonder Stories*, amongst them "The Satellite of Doom", in the January 1931 issue, which introduces the idea of a rocket postal system (and since editor Lasser was the President of the American Rocket Society its acceptance must have been inevitable), and "Captive of the Crater", wherein the protagonist finds himself swinging like a pendulum from one side of the Moon to the other, linked by a hollow crater.

But "The Eternal Man" remains as one of his most memorable stories, if only for that striking observation with which the story closes. We have already had one immortality story in this book,

Wertenbaker's "The Coming of the Ice". However, it is a sign of a good author that he can inject strains of originality. All the Wertenbaker and Sharp stories have in common is the one theme, immortality. Thereafter they are as divergent as the tributaries of the Amazon.

Sharp faded away from the sf field during World War II, his last appearance was "Children of the Gods" in the June 1943 *Thrilling Wonder Stories.*

Herbert Zulerich was a big, heavy-framed man with a tangled mop of shaggy hair which lay back from his sloping forehead and clustered about the collar of his dark coat. His nose was big and prominent, swelling like a huge peak upon his face, and his mouth was a deep-lined canyon between the peak of his nose and the bulge of his chin.

Zulerich's habits were as strange as his face, and ponderous as his big body. How he lived no one knew, and no one knew either how he managed to maintain the formidable array of test tubes, and retorts. In his laboratory was every conceivable kind of peculiar glass, holding liquids of all colors.

Zulerich had, at one time, been a chemist of somewhat more than local fame, but of late years he had become a recluse, staying alone most of the time in his big stone house just back of the highway where the constant stream of autos seemed to disturb him but little.

In truth they disturbed him a great deal. Some days he would watch them in their hurry as they drove furiously along the straight line of paved roadway, and into his face would come gloom and melancholy. And into his large blue eyes would come a hurt look; a feeling of sympathy for those who seemed so full of life, so fey, so thoughtless.

"Death! Death!" the old man would whisper. "Man goes through long years of preparation for the few days of accomplishment before the conqueror destroys all."

"So much preparation," he would whisper as he shook his big head. "So many brilliant minds polished and blazing for an hour, like roses grown and tended to be cut for an evening's bloom; hands so skillfully trained, and so soon folded quietly at rest."

That he was in quest of some great secret, everyone who knew him had long ago suspected. But what that secret was, no one knew and few could even guess.

The truth was that Zulerich's mind was obsessed by a single thought—the appalling waste of death. And since science and invention were conquering the other enemies of man's existence, Zulerich set out after the example of Ponce de Leon to discover the elements which might be combined to give eternal life.

Strange as it may seem, Zulerich was making some progress. He had found out some things which had astonished him. Some of his experiments had awed and stupefied him and then he made a discovery which gave him a decided fright.

He had been experimenting with unicellular organisms, and had found that they did not behave as inorganic chemicals did. He knew that the reaction of those animalcules as distinctly physiological and not merely physical organic and not purely chemical. They did not resemble any known chemicals, for they reacted as individuals and not as mere materials. This discovery, he found, was confirmed by Jennings in his book, *Behavior of Unicellular Organisms.*

Old Zulerich had studied the intricate processes of cellular division and multiplication, hoping to penetrate the law of the organism and discover what it was that, at the peak of growth, prevented further cleavage of the cells. In short, he wanted to find the principle which confined the limits of size and growth. Find what it was that caused the cells of a living body to increase and multiply until maturity and then cease growing except when incited by a cut or other accident to the tissue. Why should a cell become active to replace wounded flesh, yet balk at rebuilding vital tissues, such as the lungs; or refuse to replace a lost tooth more than once?

He experimented in numerous ways to provoke cell growth, trying to divine whether they had individualities of their own or whether they were bounded by the individuality of the whole. He wanted to find whether cells had an intelligence which caused them to do the remarkable things necessary to their co-ordination in the body.

Zulerich found out many things; stupendous, mystifying things, which no amount of scientific theory could possibly explain. He perfected chemicals which applied to a rabbit's head caused its hair to grow so long as to make it necessary for him to gather it into a bag. And even then the weight of it grew so great the rabbit could no longer drag its load and he killed the animal out of mercy. But still its hair grew and grew. His high-walled backyard soon held some monstrous freaks from his chemicals; dogs with heads as big as water barrels and bodies of normal size, and rats with bodies as big as cows and small peanut-sized heads. And one day he applied a chemical to a horse's eyes and the eyes grew out of their sockets like long ropes of white sinew with great knobs of gelatine-like iris—limp flabby canes which dragged upon the ground. The effect of this last experiment so cut the kind soul of Zulerich that he killed the monstrosities and wished to abandon the whole business. Then he would look again from his window over the wide world where death laid waste, and he would sigh and tighten his lips to plunge ahead again.

Growth was not what Zulerich wanted. He was quite content that man should retain his present stature. What he desired was to increase man's years.

And then he discovered it. He did not need to prove the experiment by waiting and watching until the end of time to find out whether the cells would eventually die. He knew they would not die. A few drops of pale green fluid in the graduating glass in his hand would permit any man to live eternally. He knew this was possible for he had at last found the combination he sought; the chemical which continued life without the necessity of decay.

After a year of experiments upon his cells he tried a drop upon a rat. He caught the rat in one hand and held his medicine dropper with its pale green fluid in the other. But, as the dropper released its globule, the rat moved its head and the drop hit the side of its face and spread about its throat. It left a scar upon the hair, a peculiar scar like a question mark. Zulerich tried again with a second drop with better success. The rat swallowed it.

Zulerich watched carefully. The animal's heart seemed to cease beating. The lungs became motionless, and yet the rat lived, with a fire in its pink eyes. It lived on, day by day, week after week, month on month, without the slightest loss of weight or sign of hunger or thirst. It lived with its tiny soul imprisoned in it.

Yet even then Zulerich dared not drink his elixir, though his work was exhausting his strength and his heart was very weak and with its flutterings gave him frights at times. There was a flaw in his experiment. The animal lived without breath, food or water, but it was entirely *unable to move*! To see it one would presume it dead except for the fire in its fierce little eyes and its lack of decay.

So Zulerich set out to mend the flaw. He worked feverishly now, for he was a very old man and his heart threatened to fail. He did not want to die with success just within his reach. He did not want to come so near offering mankind the one boon it craved and then to fail.

Two years passed before Zulerich found the ingredient lacking in his pale greenish drops. The thing was so simple he had overlooked it altogether. He discovered it quite by accident.

One day he had a pail containing a solution of washing soda near the window and was washing down the dusty glass so that he might see out over the blighted world and gain strength from its curse to continue his work. He would allow no one else in his laboratory and washed the windows himself.

A few spattering drops fell into the motionless upturned mouth of the rat where it stood upon the deep casement. Its mouth was open in the same position Zulerich had left it when he had forced it to receive the life-preserving drops. It had stood a tiny, paralysed, living statue in that same attitude for two long years. Zulerich had really thought to remove the animal from the window before beginning to wash them. But as he grew older he had grown more absent minded. He was unable to use the same care and forethought he once had; but this time his carelessness resulted in a great discovery.

Immediately when the soda dropped into the rat's mouth it squealed and scurried for cover. But it soon came out to nibble a crust of cracker the parrot had dropped on the floor.

Zulerich had been overjoyed at the rat regaining the use of its muscles, but now he became worried and anxious because it developed hunger—this might forebode decay which meant death.

Even as he pondered he trembled, for he knew he was very old and had not much time to watch and wait. And then as the result of his suspense and relief over the new discovery of the soda drops, his heart began fluttering alarmingly. It acted as it had never done before. He thought his time had come to die, and his precious experiment was almost completed, perfected, but not yet given to a life-hungry world.

All the legends he had ever read of the discovery of elixirs of life had had their fruits frosted just before the eating. And so it was to be with him. This was the end. Then he thought of his drops! He would drink them and there would be ample time to conclude his experiment.

He prepared a glass of soda water, then went over to the table and sat upon his high stool. Then picking up the vial of pale green, which had become dusty with its long idleness upon its shelf, he measured his drops. But his hand trembled so that the vial dropped to the floor and spilt its precious fluid. He drank the drops in the measuring glass, then he reached for the soda water sitting just at a touch of his hand.

He would not move! He had forgotten he would be unable to hand the soda to his mouth. For the moment he was too upset and frightened to think clearly. He had overlooked a very vital thing. There was nothing to do but sit and wait for a neighbor to pass. He was as immovable as though cut in stone. He could not move an eyelid. He was very frightened.

A week went by.

During that week the rat played all over the room. One time it came out mockingly upon the table before him. Zulerich regarded it closely. It was not breathing.

Another week passed before anyone came into the house. During this time the rat became bolder and Zulerich had much time to observe it. He knew his experiment had been a success. The rat only consumed food to replace its physical energy. It needed fuel for running about the room, which of course was a method of decay. The rat needed no food to support its life. Zulerich knew he had discovered a great secret. He had accomplished life perpetual which only needed food for its physical energies.

Then a neighbor peeped in. His look of uneasiness gave way to one of pained sorrow. The neighbor's face became melancholy as he saw old Zulerich sitting stiffly upon his stool beside his chemicals. Zulerich tried to cry out, but his voice like his limbs was paralysed. He tried to croak, even to whisper, but there was no noise at all. He put his appeal into the fierce, cold fire of his living eyes which were turned straight toward the door. The man saw the eyes, bright and living. He slammed the door and fled the room.

Zulerich created quite a sensation after that. No one knew what had happened to him. They thought he was dead, and surmised that he had spilled some mysterious compound over him which had embalmed him with the look of life in his eyes.

Undertakers came from long distances to study him as he sat in his laboratory. They pried and tested among the fluids in the bottles, and years passed, and still old Zulerich was not buried because they believed he had found some marvelous embalming fluid and he was kept for observation.

Old Zulerich, growing no older, knew all this for he sat there, in a glass case now, and heard all they said and saw before his eyes all that was done.

And in the dead of night the rat with its selfishness and its eternal life, and the unselfish chemist in his glass case, would meet again. The rat would scamper lively across the top of the glass case, in which Zulerich sat as stiffly as though sculptured in stone. It would sit upon the table before him and stare at him with red spiteful eyes, and then scamper away. And Zulerich always knew it by the peculiar scar upon its neck. The rat knew what he lacked. For two long years it had been frozen, as he was now, before he had given it movement as well as life. But it was too mean to do so great a deed to a man. It hated him. It never brought him the few drops of alkali he craved.

One day they packed Zulerich carefully in a case and moved him, and when the case was opened he found himself in a lofty building with the mummy of a Pharaoh on one side of him and musty relics of other ages all around him. He recognized the old building, for in the other days he had loved to potter around there and let his fancies wander and his thoughts seek something tangible in these fragments of a vanished age.

As he sat there upon his stool, protected within his glass case, the unalterable line of his vision vaulted the narrow aisles below him and gazed through the great glass of a tall window in the opposite wall.

Out there he watched the throngs that passed. People of a day. Men who yesterday were babes in mothers' arms, today fighting up the long and difficult ladder for their fragment of success, to leap tomorrow into oblivion at their allotted rung.

Customs changed, women scrambled with the male, and there became even less time or inclination to enjoy the fruits of preparation. The years of training lengthened.

In all their years upon Earth, it was bound to happen that the two should meet again: the rat with its selfish greediness and the chemist with his unselfish dream. The rat had been seeking him so that it might gloat over him as it used to do. So that it might scamper upon his case and deride him with its motion. But the keeper of the museum saw the rat and beat it with his broom and mangled it with his leather-shod heel. This happened in the night and he left the rat upon the floor until morning so that the cleaners might take it away.

Before the cleaners came the next morning one of the scientists who were studying Zulerich saw the rat lying there upon the floor before the case with its mangled body and its eyes were so bright and full of pain. He stooped to examine it, and his interest became intense, for its heart and lungs were quiet and it seemed quite dead; and yet its eyes had the same living look of the man Zulerich in the glass case.

So the rat, too, was placed under observation and set in a tiny case upon a perch just before the case in which sat old Zulerich looking out upon the great world through the big window. The rat in its case cut off part of the vision of the chemist so that in seeing the world beyond the window he must look straight into the eyes of the creature to whom he had given eternal life, and which had been mangled until it was given eternal pain.

The years passed on, long years, all the longer that there should be no end of them. It was all the sadder that, instead of viewing the misery and waste of eighty years, he must watch it for eight hundred years, and even then not be done.

Life streamed by under his gaze, burning up with decay. Yet he held the secret they so much desired. Between them and eternal life was a connecting link, a few drops of alkaline water. The wires of communication were down and none had the wisdom nor the wit to raise them up. He had the secret, they had the power, if they only knew.

Eager, anxious, weary, discouraged and broken, the people of the world tramped by; torrents of wasted motion. For long years he envied them, of all that waste, the power to say one small word for freedom. For long years the undying man and the undying rat stared hatefully at each other. For long years he studied and contrived within his mind some means for breaking the paralysis of his body so that he might give eternal life to humanity. Then he learned a great lesson from a small child.

The child had discovered the mangled rat and had seen the pain and desire of death in its eyes. She begged her father to kill the little rat as he had killed her little dog after a car had mangled it.

That night Zulerich's eyes softened as he regarded the rat under the bright glow of the electric lights, and in his heart felt remorse. For the first time he was glad that he had not been able to give man his magic formula. He discovered that he should need to improve life before trying to lengthen it.

The Power and the Glory
by Charles Willard Diffin

from ASTOUNDING STORIES, July 1930

At a time when the emphasis was on long stories it was surprising to find how expertly the shorter ones, when attempted, were handled. After 'The Eternal Man" here is another short piece with a similar treatment, although an entirely different theme. Note in particular the sardonic closing lines.

Charles Willard Diffin had a knack at closing stories. "The Dog That Laughed" was a long story published in the first issue of *Astounding's* companion magazine *Strange Tales*, dated September 1931. *Strange Tales* was an attempt to rival *Weird Tales*, and carried as many weird-scientific stories as straight horror. "The Dog That Laughed" was a menace-in-the-laboratory type of story but has one of the most chilling final lines of any story I can remember.*

Diffin's skill at writing was evident from the beginning, and his short-lived appearance in the science fiction field seems to imply that he was probably a staff-writer for Clayton's magazines, especially since only three of his eighteen published ventures into the field appeared outside the two Clayton sf publications, and these appeared in *Astounding Stories* shortly after its revival by Street & Smith. A number of his stories were also featured in a companion adventure magazine *Top-Notch*.

"Spawn of the Stars" in the second issue of *Astounding Stories of Super Science*, February 1930, marked his debut in the field. This was followed by two stories in the June 1930 issue, one under his pseudonym of C. D. Willard. "The Power and the Glory" came in the next issue, and was therefore his fourth sf story,

*Those interested in this story are recommended to acquire MAGAZINE OF HORROR No. 16 (Summer 1967) in which it was reprinted.

and the start of his popularity. His real success came with "Dark Moon" in the May 1931 issue. This was the first of a series of stories relating the adventures of Walt Harkness and Herr Schwartzmann cn this mysterious heavenly unreflective body. Interest soared with the announcement of a novel-length sequel, "Brood of the Dark Moon" starting in August. A third story, "The Finding of Haldgren" tied up all the loose ends.

Why Diffin's output suddenly ceased in 1935 remains obscure, but after the publication of the last episode of his novel, "Blue Magic" in February 1936, Diffin disappeared from the sf field for ever.

There were papers on the desk, a litter of papers scrawled over, in the careless writing of indifferent students, with the symbols of chemistry and long mathematical computations. The man at the desk pushed them aside to rest his lean, lined face on one thin hand. The other arm, ending at the wrist, was on the desk before him.

Students of a great university had long since ceased to speculate about the missing hand. The result of an experiment, they knew—a hand that was a mass of lifeless cells, amputated quickly that the living arm might be saved—but that was some several years ago, ancient history to those who came and went through Professor Eddinger's classroom.

And now Professor Eddinger was weary—weary and old, he told himself—as he closed his eyes to shut out the sight of the interminable papers and the stubby wrist that had ended forever his experiments and the delicate manipulations which only he could do.

He reached slowly for a buzzing phone, but his eyes brightened at the voice that came to him.

"I've got it—I've got it!" The words were almost incoherent. "This is Avery, Professor—Avery! You must come at once. You will share in it; I owe it all to you . . . you will be the first to see . . . I am sending a taxi for you—"

Professor Eddinger's tired eyes crinkled to a smile. Enthusiasm like this was rare among his youngsters. But Avery—with the face of a poet, a dreamer's eyes and the mind of a scientist—good boy, Avery!—a long time since he had seen him—had him in his own laboratory for two years . . . .

"What's this all about?" he asked.

"No—no!" said a voice; "I can't tell you—it is too big—

greater than the induction motor—greater than the electric light
—it is the greatest thing in the world. The taxi should be there
now—you must come—"

A knock at the office door where a voice said, "Car for
Professor Eddinger," confirmed the excited words.

"I'll come," said the Professor, "right away."

He pondered, as the car whirled him across the city, on what
this greatest thing in the world might be. And he hoped with
gentle skepticism that the enthusiasm was warranted. A young
man opened the car door as they stopped. His face was flushed,
Eddinger noted, hair pushed back in disarray, his shirt torn
open at the throat.

"Wait here," he told the driver and took the Professor by the
arm to hurry him into a dilapidated building.

"Not much of a laboratory," he said, "but we'll have better,
you and I; we'll have better—"

The room seemed bare with its meagre equipment, but it was
neat, as became the best student of Professor Eddinger. Rows of
reagent bottles stood on the shelves, but the tables were a litter
of misplaced instruments and broken glassware where trembling
hands had fumbled in heedless excitement.

"Glad to see you again, Avery." The gentle voice of Professor
Eddinger had lost its tired tone. "It's been two years you've been
working, I judge. Now what is this great discovery, boy? What
have you found?"

The younger man, in whose face the color came and went, and
whose eyes were shining from dark hollows that marked long
days and sleepless nights, still clung to the other's arm.

"It's real," he said; "it's great! It means fortune and fame, and
you're in on that, Professor. The old master," he said and
clapped a hand affectionately upon a thin shoulder; "I owe it
all to you. And now I have—I have learned. . . . No, you shall
see for yourself. Wait—"

He crossed quickly to a table. On it was an apparatus; the eyes
of the older man widened as he saw it. It was intricate—a maze
of tubing. There was a glass bulb above—the generator of a
cathode ray, obviously and electro-magnets below and on each
side. Beneath was a crude sphere of heavy lead—a retort, it
might be—and from this there passed two massive, insulated
cables. The understanding eyes of the Professor followed them,
one to a terminal on a great insulating block upon the floor,
the other to a similarly protected terminal of carbon some feet
above it in the air.

The trembling fingers of the young man made some few adjustments, then he left the instrument to take his place by an electric switch. "Stand back," he warned, and closed the switch.

There was a gentle hissing from within glass tubes, the faint glow of a blue-green light. And that was all, until—with a crash like the ripping crackle of lightning, a white flame arced between the terminals of the heavy cables. It hissed ceaselessly through the air where now the tang of ozone was apparent. The carbon blocks glowed with a brilliant incandescence when the flame ceased with the motion of a hand where Avery pulled a switch.

The man's voice was quiet now. "You do not know yet, what you have seen, but there was a tremendous potential there—an amperage I can't measure with my limited facilities." He waved a deprecating hand about the ill-furnished laboratory. "But you have seen—" His voice trembled and failed at the forming of the words.

"—The disintegration of the atom," said Professor Eddinger quietly, "and the release of power unlimited. Did you use thorium?" he inquired.

The other looked at him in amazement. Then: "I should have known you would understand," he said humbly. "And you know what it means"—again his voice rose—"power without end to do the work of the world—great vessels driven a lifetime on a mere ounce of matter—a revolution in transportation—in living. . . ." He paused. "The liberation of mankind," he added, and his voice was reverent. "This will do the work of the world; It will make a new heaven and a new earth! Oh, I have dreamed dreams," he exclaimed, "I have seen visions. And it has been given to me—me!—to liberate man from the curse of Adam . . . the sweat of his brow. . . . I can't realize it even yet. I—I am not worthy. . . ."

He raised his eyes slowly in the silence to gaze in wondering astonishment at the older man. There was no answering light, no exaltation on the lined face. Only sadness in the tired eyes that looked at him and through him as if focused upon something in a dim future—or past.

"Don't you see?" asked the wondering man. "The freedom of men—the liberation of a race. No more poverty, no endless, grinding labor." His young eyes, too, were looking into the future, a future of blinding light, "Culture," he said, "instead of heart-breaking toil, a chance to grow mentally, spiritually; it is another world, a new life—" And again he asked: "Surely, you see?"

"I see," said the other; "I see—plainly."

"The new world," said Avery. "It—it dazzles me; it rings like music in my hears."

"I see no new world," was the slow response.

The young face was plainly perplexed. "Don't you believe?" he stammered. "After you have seen . . . I thought *you* would have the vision, would help me emancipate the world, save it—" His voice failed.

"Men have a way of crucifying their saviors," said the tired voice.

The inventor was suddenly indignant. "You are blind," he said harshly; "it is too big for you. And I would have had you stand beside me in the great work. . . . I shall announce it alone. . . . There will be laboratories—enormous!—and factories. My invention will be perfected, simplified, compressed. A generator will be made—thousands of horsepower to do the work of a city, free thousands of men —made so small you can hold it in one hand."

The sensitive face was proudly alight, proud and a trifle arrogant. The exaltation of his coming power was strong upon him.

"Yes," said Professor Eddinger, "in one hand." And he raised his right arm that he might see where the end of a sleeve was empty.

"I am sorry," said the inventor abruptly; "I didn't mean . . . But you will excuse me now; there is so much to be done—" But the thin figure of Professor Eddinger had crossed to the far table to examine the apparatus there.

"Crude," he said beneath his breath, "crude—but efficient!"

In the silence a rat had appeared in the distant corner. The Professor nodded as he saw it. The animal stopped as the man's eyes came upon it; then sat squirrel-like on one of the shelves as it ate a crumb of food. Some morsel from a hurried lunch of Avery's, the Professor reflected—poor Avery! Yes, there was much to be done. He spoke as much to himself as to the man who was now beside him. "It enters here," he said and peered downward toward the lead bulb. He placed a finger on the side of the metal. "About here, I should think. . . . Have you a drill? And a bit of quartz?"

The inventor's eyes were puzzled, but the assurance of his old instructor claimed obedience. He produced a small drill and a fragment like broken glass. And he started visibly as the one hand worked awkwardly to make a small hole in the side of the lead. But he withdrew his own restraining hand, and he watched in mystified silence while the quartz was fitted to make a tiny window and a thin figure stooped to sight as if aiming the opening toward a far corner where a brown rat sat upright in earnest munching of a dry crust.

The Professor drew Avery with him as he retreated noiselessly from the instrument. "Will you close the switch," he whispered.

The young man hesitated, bewildered, at this unexpected demonstration, and the Professor himself reached with his one hand for the black lever. Again the arc crashed into life, to hold for a brief instant until Professor Eddinger opened the switch.

"Well," demanded Avery, "what's all the show? Do you think you are teaching me anything—about my own instrument?" There was hurt pride and jealous resentment in his voice.

"See," said Professor Eddinger quietly. And his one thin hand pointed to a far shelf, where, in the shadow, was a huddle of brown fur and bit of crust. It fell as they watched, and the "plop" of the soft body upon the floor sounded loud in the silent room.

"The law of compensation," said Professor Eddinger. "Two sides to the medal! Darkness and light—good and evil—life . . . and death!"

The young man was stammering. "What do you mean?—a death ray evolved?" And: "What of it?" he demanded; "what of it? What's that got to do with it?"

"A death ray," the other agreed. "You have dreamed, Avery— one must in order to create—but it is only a dream. You dreamed of life—a fuller life—for the world, but you would have given them, as you have just seen, death."

The face of Avery was white as wax; his eyes glared savagely from dark hollows.

"A rat!" he protested. "You have killed a rat . . . and you say —you say—" He raised one trembling hand to his lips to hold them from forming the unspeakable words.

"A rat," said the Professor—"or a man . . . or a million men."

"We will control it."

"All men will have it—the best and the worst . . . and there is no defence."

"It will free the world—"

"It will destroy it."

"No!"—and the white-faced man was shouting now—"you don't understand—you can't see—"

The lean figure of the scientist straightened to its full height. His eyes met those of the younger man, silent now before him, but Avery knew the eyes never saw him; they were looking far off, following the wings of thought. In the stillness the man's words came harsh and commanding—

"Do you see the cities," he said, "crumbling to ruins under the cold stars? The fields? They are rank with wild growth, torn and gullied by the waters; a desolate land where animals prowl. And the people—the people!—wandering bands, lower, as the years drag on, than the beasts themselves; the children dying, forgotten, in the forgotten lands; a people to whom the progress of our civilization is one with the ages past, for whom there is again the slow, toiling road toward the light.

"And somewhere, perhaps, a conquering race, the most brutal and callous of mankind, rioting in their sense of power dragging themselves down to oblivion. . . ."

His gaze came slowly back to the loom and the figure of the man still fighting for his dream.

"They would not," said Avery hoarsely; "they'd use it for good."

"Would they?" asked Professor Eddinger. He spoke simply as one stating simple facts. "I love my fellow men," he said, "and I killed them in thousands in the last war—I, and my science, and my poison gas."

The figure of Avery slumped suddenly upon a chair; his face was buried in his hands. "And I would have been," he groaned, "the greatest man in the world."

"You shall be greater," said the Professor, "though only we shall know it—you and I. . . . You will save the world—from itself."

The figure, bowed and sunken in the chair, made no move; the man was heedless of the kindly hand upon his shoulder. His voice, when he spoke, was that of one afar off, speaking out of a great loneliness. "You don't understand," he said dully; "you can't—"

But Professor Eddinger, a cog in the wheels of a great educational machine, glanced at the watch on his wrist. Again his thin shoulders were stooped, his voice tired. "My classes!" he said. "I must be going. . . ."

In the gathering dusk Professor Eddinger locked carefully the door of his office. He crossed beyond his desk and fumbled with his one hand for his keys.

There was a cabinet to be opened, and he stared long in the

dim light at the object he withdrew. He looked approvingly at the exquisite workmanship of an instrument where a generator of the cathode ray and an intricate maze of tubing surmounted electro-magnets and a round lead bulb. There were terminals for attaching heavy cables; it was a beautiful thing . . . His useless arm moved to bring an imaginary hand before the window of quartz in the lead sphere.

"Power," he whispered and repeated Avery's words; power to build a city—or destroy a civilization . . . and I hold it in one hand."

He replaced the apparatus in the safety of its case. "The saviors of mankind!" he said, and his tone was harsh and bitter.

But a smile, whimsical, kindly, crinkled his tired eyes as he turned to his desk and its usual litter of examination papers.

"It is something, Avery," he whispered to that distant man, "to belong in so distinguished a group."

The Voice from the Ether
by Lloyd Arthur Eshbach

from AMAZING STORIES, May 1931

Readers of *Amazing Stories* were used to the aged whims of octogenarian editor T. O'Conor Sloane, but they were nevertheless often put to unnecessary anxiety. Fans and followers of Lloyd Arthur Eshbach were obviously thrilled upon receiving the March 1931 *Amazing Stories* to find his latest story, "The Valley of the Titans" illustrated on the cover.

As was the policy of most magazines at that time, beneath the author's by-line under the story title, a little further identification was given by describing the author as "Author of . . . ." and giving the name of a previous successful story. Naturally that story would have appeared in that magazine, or a sister title, but obviously no story from a rival publication would be advertised. But Eshbach up until that time had not appeared in *Amazing Stories*. Readers must therefore have had a double take when the credits under "The Valley of the Titans" announced 'By the Author of "The Voice From the Ether" '. Had they missed something? Where had "The Voice From the Ether" appeared?

A quick look through their collections would have revealed to fans that it had appeared nowhere. Only three stories had seen print up to that time. Two were in Gernsback's magazines, *Scientific Detective Monthly* and *Air Wonder Stories*, and the third in Clayton's *Astounding Stories*.

It was two months before baffled readers discovered "The Voice From the Ether", but their wait was worthwhile. Obviously Eshbach had submitted the two stories together and Sloane had overlooked the fact that he had not yet printed one of them. But in the May 1931 issue, in its correct sequence, the story was billed as by the 'Author of "The Valley of the Titans" '.

Eshbach was born in 1910, and was a frequent correspondent in the magazines' letter columns. In the late 1940's Eshbach established the Fantasy Press which was responsible for bringing out in hardback some of the greats of early magazine sf, notably E. E. Smith and John Campbell. A collection of his own fiction appeared in 1955 under the title "The Tyrant of Time". A non-fiction item of special interest was "Of Worlds Beyond: The Science of Science-Fiction Writing" (1947) edited by Eshbach in which top authors outlined the various ways in which they approached sf writing.

On August 22nd, 1924, the planet Mars was in opposition to the earth. That is to say, the two planets in their perpetual journeying had assumed such a position as to be in one straight line with the sun, the earth eclipsing the superior planet Mars. A superior planet is one whose orbit is of greater diameter than that of the earth. At the same time, the distance separating Mars from the earth was less than it had been for more than one hundred years. Only 34,640,000 miles lay between the two heavenly bodies.

The night of the 22nd was remarkably clear, an ideal night for astronomical observation. Innumerable telescopes, large and small, were focused upon the red planet. Ingenious devices of various kinds were striving to communicate with the inhabitants of Mars. And, in a little cabin high up in the Adirondack Mountains, I sat before my radio. Far away from any "interference," I strove to make the greatest radio pick-up ever attempted.

I had made rather elaborate preparations for the recording of any interplanetary communication I might receive, securing for that purpose a device working on the same principle as the dictaphone. It differed from that instrument, however, in that it could record words continually for a period of ten hours. This device, the invention of an obscure mechanical engineer, stood within a few feet of the loudspeaker.

With practised fingers I twirled the dials. One pick-up after another rewarded my efforts. A voice raised in song, the wail of a saxophone, the sonorous voice of an announcer—the usual radio programs. Little cared I for these, however, for they were commonplace; I was after bigger game. But Mars continued in that silence which it had maintained for countless ages.

Slowly the hours passed. Midnight came—one o'clock. A fine radio night, I thought, rather hazily—I dozed.

The time signal from the station to which I had last been

listening, called me back to consciousness. One—two! I heard
the strokes faintly, as from a great distance. Then, suddenly I
raised my nodding head erect; I was fully awake.

A discordant shriek of static assailed my ears. A frightful
howl, like that of a tortured imp, filled the room. Then, as
suddenly as the coming of the static, silence, oppressive, heavy,
fell like a mantle over the radio.

And then I heard the—Voice. Clear and loud it came, un-
marred by any interfering static. It was a shrill, piping voice,
which, in the course of its narrative, traversed the entire gamut
of emotion.

I was spellbound. A feeling of triumph pervaded my being,
triumph intermingled with awe. I had succeeded! Victory! I
was certain that I had received a message from Mars. I trembled
with excitement. Hesitantly I reached toward the dials—and
drew my hand away before it touched the radio. I was held
back by the thought that perhaps I might break the tenuous
thread which held that distant station in communication with
the earth. At that, there was no need of adjusting the dials,
for the reception was well-nigh perfect.

Eventually, the excitement of the first few moments passed,
and I paid more attention to the words coming from the loudspeaker. As I listened, a note of excitement crept into the Voice.
Excitement, then anger, cold and terrible. And quickly on the
heels of that anger came hate, an insane hate that somehow
filled me with dread.

Through the balance of the night I listened. Although the
words spoken by the Voice were so much meaningless gibberish
to me, each passing hour saw me seated there, motionless, held
by the power of that strange, high-pitched voice.

A gray pencil of light pierced the gloom; the darkness gave
way to the radiance of a new day; and suddenly the Voice—
broke. There was a moment of utter silence, and then a shrill
shriek of fear and terrible agony. The last notes of the shriek
were strangely, horribly muffled! And there followed that dead,
unbroken silence——.

Outside in the long grass a cricket chirped. The spell was
broken. Slowly, I rose upon my trembling limbs; slowly, I
raised my hand and brushed the beads of cold perspiration
from my forehead. The experience had been so strange, those
last moments so terrible! It was with great difficulty that I
regained my mental equilibrium.

Questions leaped to my mind. Had I really tuned in on

Mars? If I had, what was the nature of the message I had received? What manner of creature had done the broadcasting? And—what had caused that shriek?

Not until four years later did I learn the answers to those questions. Four long years during which Millard labored tirelessly on the translation of that message from another world.

Millard? Yes, Phineas J. Millard, antiquarian and archeologist He, in all probability, is the only man living today who is able to translate a record consisting only of phonetics. And even he required four years for the accomplishment of that task.

Little more remains to be said by way of introduction. For the sake of convenience, I have taken advantage of natural breaks in the action of the narrative and divided it into chapters. Also, I have taken the liberty of substituting the English names of scientific apparatus for the incomprehensible names used by the Voice. Aside from that, the narrative is unchanged. And now you may read this amazing tale as it is related by Tuol Oro, scientist of another planet.

CHAPTER I

In this vast Universe, teeming with its myriad forms of life, there is surely one race of beings who will hear and understand this, my warning, And understanding, perhaps they may heed. It is with that hope in mind that I am telling my story.

When I began my life upon this planet, I was called Tuol Oro. Through the brilliancy of my intellect and the power of my mind, I made that name a name that was respected throughout the world. Yet, through the stupidity of one man, and in spite of all I had done, I became an outcast. I was scorned, derided, and openly shunned by those who had respected me. They referred to me as Tuol the Madman, or Tuol the Fool, as it suited their fancy.

Revenge became the one purpose of my life. I loved only that I might destroy the race of fools that ruled over Kotar. And I've done it! Failures were they; who thought themselves perfect; but they are gone. And I, who alone survive, was thought to be the only failure of their civilization. Tuol, the Fool? No, Tuol, the Conqueror, am I.

There are others, now, that have taken the place of man, others that, eventually, I shall also rule. Those others, that I loosed upon the world to do my will, shall feel the power of my might, and I will reign supreme over all Kotar. Soon I will go out and claim that which is rightfully mine; then, indeed, will I be conqueror.

But, before that occurs, I will tell the story of man's downfall and destruction; the story of Tuol Oro's revenge. And that tale heard, perhaps, on some other world, may be a warning, so that men who advance strange and unusual facts may receive audience, and be respected as they deserve.

I remember well those events which were the cause of my banishment. The meeting of the Council; my report about the wonderful discovery I had made; the incredulity of the Council; my taking of that oath——

The Supreme Council, that august body of Searchers-after-the-Truth, had called a meeting of all the scientists upon the planet. Report was to be made as to what had been accomplished for the advancement of civilization in each field of research.

The gigantic hall, the Hall of the Council, was filled to overflowing. Thousands of scientists representing a vast accumulation of knowledge, occupied the countless compartments which made up the hall. They, however, were unimportant; only upon very rare occasions did they learn anything that was of real value.

The really worth-while discoveries of the age had been made by a small, insignificant group of six men who occupied one large compartment at the front of the hall. Six men, the greatest minds in all Kotar. Six men, and I was one of them!

I remember them well; even now I can see, in my mind's eye, those men of knowledge. Each was an expert in his chosen field, the accepted authority on his special branch of science.

There was Bor Akon, the historian. No important occurrence of any past age, no matter how remote, was unknown to him. Then there was Sarig Om, the astronomer, who had plumbed the depths of space with his instruments, and who knew the innermost secrets of innumerable heavenly bodies. Great was his knowledge.

I mention these two particularly because of the important part they play at a later date.

The others in the group are Dees Oeb, specialist in the study of matter; Stol Verta, lover of things mechanical the greatest inventor in Kotar's history; Gano Tor, whose strange concoctions could well nigh bring the dead back to life; and Tuol Oro, delver into the infinitely minute. Truly a remarkable concentration of wisdom. Yet everyone in that group, and all those minor intellectuals were failures. All were blotted out—erased, by the children of my mind, their great intellects rendered helpless. All—save one. I, Tuol, the Mighty, survive! But I digress.

On a platform raised high above our heads sat the Council. Twenty venerable men were they, the ruling body of Kotar. Each one of the Twenty, from the time of his birth, had been trained in just the correct environment, to prepare him for the position he was now holding. They were the judges, the judicial minds of our planet.

As they, the Council, had been trained, so had we, the scientists, been prepared, with the thought of our future place in life, in mind.

Bor Akon, the historian, said at one time, that in former ages there had been no such specialization, that each man and woman decided his or her field of endeavor upon reaching maturity. Utterly rdiculous! Our destinies were predetermined in our infancy by the Sub-Council of each residential district. In this way there was no neglect of one occupation and over-crowding of another. But to return to the gathering in the Council Hall——

Each individual booth was equipped with an instrument employing the mysterious "Power of the Spheres," that power which I am using in giving broadcast this narrative of warning. It was with this instrument that we, the scientists, not only communicated with the Twenty, but, through the use of a large amplifying disc, made our reports audible to every man in the hall.

The members of the Council, by the way, required no such aid in making their thoughts known; through the combined power of their well trained minds, they could impress upon us their every desire. And, because they had a complete knowledge of who occupied each of those many compartments, they had no difficulty in having the scientists speak in the order that they, the Council, wished.

Suddenly the hall became quiet; every sound was hushed. A mental command for silence had come from the Twenty. And then Stol Verta, the inventor, arose. Speaking in a dreamy monotone, he addressed the Council.

Stol's report had to do with his most recent invention, a machine which he claimed would traverse the great void between the planets. How this was to be accomplished, I do not remember. Indeed, little of what he said made an impression upon my memory. The so-called mechanical marvels of the age held little interest for me; and Stol Verta, himself, is an uninteresting individual at best.

His statements, however, seemed to meet with the approval of the Council, for they sent a thought-wave of praise and commendation broadcast through the hall. Smiling slightly, Stol seated himself.

Sarig Om was the second scientist called upon by the Twenty. As he arose to make his report, I decided to pay more attention than I had before. The science of Sarig Om was of interest to me because of the similarity it bore to my own study. His was the study of largeness unfathomable; mine, of the infinitely minute.

Sarig gave a detailed report about the various occurrences in the heavens before he reached the really important feature of his discourse. At the time I was not impressed with the importance of the statement; later I had reason to recall it.

He spoke of the coming opposition of our world with Santel, our nearest inferior planetary neighbor. He stated that the two planets would be closer to each other than they had been for almost fifty mallahs.* It would be an excellent opportunity, he informed us, for us to take steps toward establishing communication with the Santellians. His report also, was approved by the Council.

As Sarig seated himself, I felt a curious tingling at the base of my brain. Then a strangely silent voice in my mind bade me rise. It was the command. I rose to my feet; swept the hall with my eyes, and then faced the Twenty. A command came from me to proceed with my report. After a moment's pause. I began.

"To the Supreme Council, the judicial body of Kotar, I, Tuol Oro, delver into the infinitely minute, make report." This was the customary beginning, and each scientist used it, with variations, of course. I continued:

"My labors of the past mallah, Venerable Twenty, have not been fruitless; indeed, it was my great fortune to make a discovery that is unequalled in the history of microscopy.

"The Council is doubtless aware of the construction of the

---

*We have no possible way of determining what the Kotarian words for periods of time would mean in English. From the action of the narrative, however, we can be fairly certain that the Mallah is equivalent to our year, the Stallo, to our month, the Stal, to our week, and the Tron to our minute. Tuol does not mention anything equal to our day, hour, or second, although it is probable that other time divisions than the former ones exist.
—L.A.E.

atom and its marked similarity to the solar system, with its central body, the sun, or in the atom, the nucleus, and its revolving satellites—planets or planetary electrons. The conception of the atom, of course is not, or I should say, was not accepted as fact, but was thought to be only a plausible theory.

"Five stallos ago, working on a principle different than any ever used before, K constructed a microscope so powerful that it enabled me to see the component parts of an atom. The planetary electrons, themselves, were invisible because of the great speed with which they revolved; but the protons could clearly be seen as rapidly rotating, faintly glowing spheres.

"Very naturally, I was elated with my invention and discovery; still, I wasn't satisfied. I felt that I had only begun, and that the possibilities brought into being by my discovery were practically limitless. So, without delay, I began constructing a microscope far more powerful and efficient than my first instrument. After four stallos of intense effort, I succeeded.

"This latter instrument surpassed all my expectations; with it I discovered something so amazing and incredible that I had difficulty in believing the testimony of my eyes.

"When the microscope was complete to the last minute detail, I trained the lenses upon a particle of sodium. My heart beat more rapidly as I peered into the eye-piece for the first time. What might be revealed to my gaze? A host of impossible conjectures flashed through my mind, yet not in my wildest imaginings did I conceive of such a sight as met my eyes.

"I was looking into a wide, shallow valley, covered with a brilliant, vari-colored vegetation. For some moments I gazed at it unbelievingly; then the scene was gone, replaced by a rounded hill-top. Like the valley, this, too, was covered with the brilliant colorful plant life. And as I watched, the hill followed in the wake of the valley, moving slowly across the line of my vision. Another valley took the place of the hill, a valley far larger than the first.

"As I gazed at it, I became aware of a peculiar phenomenon that had escaped my notice before. The vegetation in the valley was in motion, was constantly shifting and changing position. I changed the focus of the microscope, concentrating its magnifying power on a small portion of the scene. The valley seemed to leap up toward my eyes. No longer could I see a great field of moving plant life; only three plants were now within the range of my vision.

"And what strange growths they were! Nothing like them ever existed on Kotar. In form, and size they were alike, though each was of a different color. When I first saw them, they were small, almost perfect spheres covered with a shiny, scaly skin. As I watched them, they grew larger; indeed, their growth was so rapid that I could actually see it! As they grew, their skins became tighter and tighter, and suddenly they burst, scattering great clouds of brightly colored dust through the air. Much of the dust was blown away, but some of it settled to the ground. Where the spheres had been, were now three pools of slime; it was into this that the dust fell.

"That which followed was perhaps the most amazing thing that I saw during all my observations. Briefly, this is what occurred: the dust, evidently the plants' seeds, upon falling into the slime, sprouted, grew, and reached maturity, and a moment later, burst in turn, casting forth their seeds—all this with such rapidity that it seemed to be one continuous movement.

"In my interest in the valley and its life, I had forgotten the strangeness of the conditions under which I was viewing the land. Deciding to discover the location of this world, I began slowly decreasing the magnifying power of the microscope, focusing the instrument in such manner as to move the world further and further away. Again I saw the panoramic view of the valley and mountains. Then the scene assumed a peculiarly convex appearance. This convexity increased until, finally, all details of the view were lost, and the microscope revealed a huge globe turning slowly on its axis. As this decreased in size, and other globes made their appearance, the truth dawned upon me. I had discovered life on a proton of the nucleus of an atom of sodium!"

Thus did I end my report to the Council

After I had finished. I remained standing, awaiting the commendation of the Twenty. But their approval was never given. Instead, two things occurred which were unprecedented in the history of Kotar. Never had one of the Twenty spoken while the Council was in session; and never had one of the six Masters been publicly condemned by the Twenty. Both occurred then.

San Nober, Head of the Council, arose, an expression of stern disapproval on his face. Then he spoke, uttering the words that spelled doom for Kotar's ruling race.

"Men of Knowledge," he said, "never in all the history of the Council have we had to deal with a problem like the present one. Always have out members spoken truth. But that is no longer so. You, Tuol Oro," addressing me, "have broken all precedence. You have lied! Your report was naught but a series of falsehoods. Your statements are preposterous, ridiculous; nothing of truth is in them.

"We are taught that it is impossible for a normal individual to lie. Obviously, then, you are insane. Even though insanity is almost an unknown malady at present, you are mad. Were it not for the records of your great discoveries in the past, you would be put to death. Because of them, you shall live. But you will be an outcast from society. You may mingle with your fellows, but they will know of your infirmity. For your lies or insanity, whichever it may be, you will be an object of pity and an outcast.

"And now you must go; the Hall of the Council shall know you no more."

While San Nober was speaking, I stood like one stunned. His disapproval and condemnation were so unexpected and so unjust that I could not believe that I had heard aright. Lies! A series of falsehoods! Insane! Mad! By Sklow, mad was I? Fool and son of a fool! An object of pity, eh? An outcast! Suddenly something seemed to snap within my brain, and a red haze came before my eyes. Then all the hatred and rebellion in my being sought outlet.

What I said then, I do not know. Perhaps I acted like a man deprived of his sanity. But I was justified. Condemned, cast out, called a liar and a madman, without an opportunity to prove the truth of my statements! One thing that I said, though, I do remember. That was the oath I took ere leaving the Council Hall.

"By Sklow, by Taw, by Maca, by all the gods that ever lived, I swear that every vestige of this civilisation shall be removed; that all men save Tuol Oro shall be destroyed! I swear it and it shall be so!"

Aye, and it is so! I have destroyed them all. They deserved it, every one of them. Oh, how I hate them, even though they are gone! I hate, loathe, despise them—

After taking that oath of vengeance, I left the Council Hall, followed by thousands of pairs of pitying or derisive eyes. I walked to my boat moored in the Great Waterway, seething with anger. Even then plans for revenge were forming in my mind. By the time I reached my home in the twenty-seventh division of the ninth Minor Waterway, I had decided on a definite plan. It was this plan, conceived on my homeward journey, that brought about the destruction of a world.

CHAPTER II

With as little delay as possible, I began making preparations for the carrying out of my plans, for I knew that many stallos of research would go by ere I accomplished that which I proposed doing. Indeed, the goal I had set before me seemed to be beyond the reach of human ability. I desired to increase the size of those inconceivably minute plants on the diminutive world I had discovered, until I could take them from their protonic birthplace and bring them to the surface of Kotar. With them I intended gaining my revenge.

The first two stallos of effort were fruitless. Often, during that time, I was tempted to abandon my apparently impossible project, and might have done so, had I not been spurred on by my desire for vengeance. However, I continued, and at the beginning of the third stallo I saw the first sign of reward for my tireless efforts.

From the very first, I had had one basic idea on which to work. That was this: since every particle of matter, regardless of its size, could, theoretically, at least, be divided in half forever, it certainly must be possible to reverse the process, and double the size of any particle, even of an electron or proton. Pursuing this line of reasoning, it naturally followed that eventually I would have increased the size of my proton to such an extent as to make it visible to the naked eye, and even larger. The difficulty lay in the actual accomplishment of that enlarging process. Two stallos were spent in vain conjecturing and theorizing along this line.

At the beginning of the third stallo I decided to begin working with the electrons and protons themselves. Taking a portion of chemically pure sodium from the supply I possessed, I placed a minute quantity beneath the lenses of my ultra-microscope. Then I focused the instrument so as to enable me to view the entire atom. Similar to my first observations of the sodium containing the life supporting proton, I now saw twenty-two small, dully glowing protons, and eleven, almost transparent nuclear electrons in a compact group, each rapidly rotating on its axis. About them, at various distances, revolved what seemed to be a tangled maze of gleaming cords. These, I knew, were the glowing paths of the planetary electrons, which moved at such great speed as to be invisible. As long as the atom remained in that condition, I knew that I could do nothing with it.

Consequently, I decided that, in some way, I'd have to decrease the speed of the electrons' rotation until I could observe each one individually. With this purpose in mind, I began a series of experiments. All that I did, by the way, had to be done beneath the lenses of my microscope. Thus handicapped, it seemed that I had a difficult task before me. I was aided materially, however, by a device recently invented by Stol Verta. This machine, far too complex to explain, enabled its user to focus a beam of inconceivable cold or intense heat upon a microscopically fine point. Because of an idea I had in mind, I was certain that Stol's invention would be of great value.

And so it proved to be. Use of the device revealed that heat increased the speed of the electrons, widening their orbits, and causing some of them to whirl outside the field of the microscope. Cold, on the contrary, caused the speed of the electrons' rotation to diminish. The lower the degree of heat, in simpler phrase, the more intense the cold, the slower became the motion, until at absolute zero, both protons and electrons were devoid of all movement. I had taken one big step to ward my goal.

Without loss of time, I continued my research, following out a theory that had come to my mind during my first experiments. For this idea I had gone back to the time of my early training when I had been taught the rudiments of elementary chemistry. My theory involved the lack of symmetry of some atoms, sodium among them, and the mechanism of chemical action.

An atom of sodium, I had been taught, has eleven electrons, negatively charged, revolving in orbits around the nucleus. One of these electrons revolves in an orbit with a much larger axis than those of the other electrons. Because of this, it is not held very firmly by the nucleus. Further, the lack of symmetry in the atom creates unbalanced forces. Consequently, the sodium atom will have a tendency to lose this electron during the collision with other atoms, and leave the atom more symmetrical and balanced. To summarize, atoms having one or more electrons beyond what corresponds to symmetrical forms, have a tendency to give off those electrons.

Similarly, I had learned that some atoms require one or more electrons to complete a symmetrical structure. The chlorine atom is an atom of this type. It has seventeen electrons, needing only one more to make the balanced, symmetrical structure of eighteen electrons.

Consequently, when an atom of sodium is brought in contact with an atom of chlorine, the transfer of an electron from one atom to the other takes place. Both atoms pay for their newly found symmetry with the loss of neutrality. The removal of one negatively charged electron from the sodium atom leaves it with an excess of one unit of positive charge. The addition of the electron to the chlorine atom gives the latter an excess of one unit of negative charge. The two, then, being oppositively charged, join and form sodium chloride.

But sodium chloride held no interest for me; the laws of chemistry involved, alone concerned me. With these recollections of the mechanism of chemical action in mind, I felt I had something definite with which to work.

Before I could begin carrying out my idea, however, I decided that I'd have to leave the privacy of my residence and mingle with the race I despised, long enough to secure the chlorine for my experiment. Immediately upon arriving at this conclusion, I ventured out into the street. If I had needed any additional stimulus to spur me on, I received it in the covert sneers and thinly veiled contempt which greeted me. I returned to my home a short time after securing the chlorine, in the grip of a rekindled anger.

Fully prepared, then, I set to work. First I placed a minute particule of sodium beneath the ultra-microscope's lenses, focusing them so that, as on former occasions, I could see the separate units of a complete atom. Then I put the cold projector in position, in order to be able to stop the atomic action whenever I wanted to. And finally, I liberated some of the chlorine, doing it in such a way that it completely covered the sodium. Then, through the eyepiece of the microscope I watched the atom, waiting for the change that would take place when chemical action began.

At first glance I could detect no difference, but as I watched I saw the electron which was outside the symmetrical structure of the atom, slow down perceptibly and leave its orbit, disappearing entirely. While the atom was in this condition, deprived of one electron, I directed a beam of intense cold upon the sodium and stopped all atomic action, thus preventing the sodium from joining the chlorine. I now had a free atom of sodium with an excess of one positive charge, or one proton more than it could possibly have had in nature. I had taken a second step toward my goal.

It was with a feeling of trepidation that I approached the third part of my task; the success or failure of this phase of the experiment would decide the result of the entire project.

Leaving the sodium and microscope our of my thoughts for the moment, I gave detailed consideration to a recent discovery of Dees Oeb. This was a new ray, the ray of the fifty-fourth octave of the electro-magnetic spectrum. This ray had a peculiar property: it caused anything upon which it was directed to increase in size. How it did this, I do not know, but the fact of its doing so remains. I proposed directing this ray upon the surplus proton in the atom beneath the microscope and increasing its size until it left the atom behind.

A short period of time spent in experimenting with a second cold projector that I possessed enabled me to adapt it to the growth ray. I was prepared to continue.

Returning to the microscope, I peered through the eyepiece, and singled out one of the protons more centrally located than the others. Focusing the projector, I directed a beam of growth ray upon that proton.

There was an immediate change in the appearance of the sphere. Its size increased perceptibly. In a short time it began crowding the other atomic bodies, moving them from their customary positions. As the proton grew in size, it became less solid, even nebulous, until, finally, when there seemed to be no more room for it to occupy, there was a sudden flash—and the atom had disappeared. In its place was a small, dully-glowing sphere, no longer nebulous in appearance, but as solid as it had ever been before. The proton had grown until it had encompassed the entire atom.

I allowed that growth to continue until the sodium had been surrounded by the sphere, now, a comparative giant. While this went on, by the way, it was necessary for me to change the focus of the microscope repeatedly, in order to watch the proton's increase in size.

Up to this time, I had had the cold directed upon the sodium to prevent it from uniting with the chlorine. This was no longer necessary, as there was no further possibility of that union taking place. So, after removing most of the chlorine, I shut off the beam of absolute zero.

I had then, as the result of my endeavors, a small, almost perfect sphere, barely visible to the naked eye. My goal was in sight! I needed only to duplicate my experiment, using the proton supporting the plant life, and vengeance would be within my reach.

Accordingly, I took from its place of safety the sodium

1   AMAZING STORIES, December 1926. Frank R. Paul's
mysterious cover set the ball rolling for story competitions.
The first prize of $250.00 was won by Canadian writer Cyril
G. Wates with "The Visitation", published in AMAZING
June 1927.

2   AMAZING STORIES, November 1927. Francis Flagg's
first sale was "The Machine Man of Ardathia", included in
this collection. Here is Frank R. Paul's interpretation of a
scene from the story.

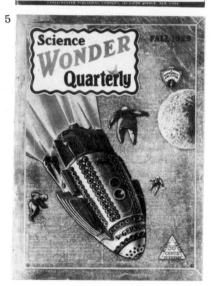

3   AMAZING STORIES, September 1928. Gernsback's flair for competitions often produced remarkable results, in this case the symbol for scientifiction: Paul's version of the prizewinning design by A. A. Kaufman of Brooklyn.

4   AMAZING STORIES QUARTERLY, Winter 1928. Never before or since was there such a bumper feast of science fiction than the QUARTERLIES from Gernsback, and here is Paul's cover for the first of them all.

5   SCIENCE WONDER QUARTERLY, Fall 1929. After Gernsback lost control at AMAZING he came back with a vengeance, and a new QUARTERLY was a must, with Frank Paul still wielding his brush.

6   ASTOUNDING STORIES, January 1930. Gernsback's first competitor was William Clayton's ASTOUNDING. This first issue sported the cover artwork of Hans Wessolowski, illustrating Victor Rousseau's "The Beetle Horde".

10

7   WONDER STORIES, May 1931. Jack Williamson's stories contain a wealth of descriptive and colourful scenes. This made many of them ideal for cover illustration. Such was "Through the Purple Cloud", again by Paul.

8   AMAZING STORIES, August 1932. When Gernsback took Paul with him to Stellar, Leo Morey became the mainstay for AMAZING. Here is his cover for Edwin K. Sloat's "Beyond the Planetoids".

9   WONDER STORIES, May 1933. Clark Ashton Smith is best remembered today for his weird fantasies, but he wrote several science fiction stories. Here is Paul's cover to his "The Visitors from Mlok".

10   SCOOPS, April 14th 1934. Compared to the startling American covers, those adorning Britain's SCOOPS appear to be dull in comparison. The best of the bunch illustrates "Creation's Doom" by Desiderius Papp.

11 ASTOUNDING STORIES, November 1935. Stanley G. Weinbaum's brief but memorable career produced some remarkable science fiction, only now being recognised. This cover illustrates his controversial story "The Red Peri".

containing the protonic world, and treated it as I had the other, centering my attention, of course, upon the proton inhabited by the rapidly moving, strangely formed vegetation. After I had increased the size of the minute sphere until it had taken up nearly all of the sodium, the thought occurred to me that I had neglected to provide a place in which to put the enlarged proton while I strove to secure some of the seed dust from it. In a moment I had turned off the growth ray, directed the cold upon the sodium and left it to its own devices.

I had little difficulty in constructing the apparatus to hold the sphere; in a short time it was completed. It was a simple device, consisting of two tall metal uprights upon whose grooved tops rested a strong, heavy metal bar. This bar or rod turned slowly when power was applied to the small motor with which it was connected by a series of cogwheels and chains. After the machine was complete, I returned to the microscope and enlarging process.

As the proton grew and consumed the sodium of which it was a part, I added more and more of the element, until it had reached a size where there was no further need of the microscope. Taking it from beneath the instrument, I increased its size, without adding sodium to it, until it was a large, wraith-like bubble. Then, taking the cross-bar from the machine I had prepared, I thrust it through the center of the sphere. There was a flash —and the former proton had a metal axis on which to revolve. After returning the rod to its place in the device, I added sodium to the sphere until it had again become solid. I continued the enlarging as long as space remained on the rod, then stopped.

I had taken the third step toward my goal.

I had in my laboratory at that time, a great, box-like room, the walls, floor and ceiling of which were glass. A number of stallos before, I had had it built with the intention of using it as a storage room for numerous bacteria and germ cultures which I had intended studying. Through my interest in my new ultra-microscope, the room had not been used. I was glad of it. Because of the danger involved in the next part of my project, I decided to make use of that room, inasmuch as I could hermetically seal it if that became necessary.

After removing the few articles that had somehow found their way into the big glass box, I covered the floor with a heavy layer of soil. Then, placing rollers beneath the device which held the giant proton, I moved the machine into the room. Directly opposite the sphere I placed a projector with which to throw a fan-shaped flood of cold upon it, and beside it, the growth apparatus. After focusing the growth ray projector so that only a small part of the proton's surface would be affected, I applied power to both machines, as well as to the apparatus holding the proton, and hastily left the room, closing and locking the door behind me.

Looking through the glass wall, I saw that the action of the growth ray must have been instantaneous. Eight different-colored, flesh-like plants were rising from the proton. They were ugly, shapeless masses of cells whose very existence was unnatural. While I watched, they grew from small, insignificant organisms to great, repulsive vegetable monstrosities. As they grew, their skins became increasingly tighter, until, when they had reached the size of the world from which they sprang, they burst, casting their seed dust to all parts of the room.

The dust, as it settled grew in turn, with the result that in a short time, the floor of the room was covered with an ever increasing mass of slime in which grew a repulsive, waving, constantly changing heap of plants. At frequent intervals, the growth ray added other plants, vari-colored and strangely formed, to those upon the floor.

Every metal device in the room became covered with a misty, gray film, The glass walls grew clouded, rendering my view of the room's contents blurred and indistinct. When the seed dust settled upon this film, it took root and grew. In a very few moments, the machines had become grotesque, vegetable caricatures of their former selves.

The plants continued their growth, one layer of either growing or decaying organisms upon another, until the mass had reached a depth of one quarter the height of a man; then my view of the room's interior was shut off. I had no means of determining how long that growth continued, but that was of little consequence.

Another thing remained for me to do before I liberated my servants upon the world to do my bidding. I had yet to learn just what would control the monstrous plants, and what steps I would have to take for my own protection.

In this I encountered no difficulty; the application of heat that was just beyond the limits of human endurance caused the growths to shrivel up, and fall, shrunken, shapeless masses, into the fetid slime beneath them. When the heat was directed against the glass, by the way, that slime began to steam, and a foul, nauseating odor in some way escaped from the glass cube. Heat, then, I decided, was obviously the agency with which to destroy them.

And heat, I felt sure, would protect me from the plants. I'd have men build numerous wide-mouthed nozzles, and have them placed at carefully selected positions on the walls and roof of the outside of my home. Steam pipes connected with these nozzles would cover the building with a protective blanket of heat.

Because of this one rather large remaining task, and several minor ones, and the time necessary for their accomplishment, I decided that I had better conceal the room from the prying eyes of inquisitive neighbors or chance callers, until I was ready to make use of its contents. I had just arrived at this conclusion, when a persistent buzzing in the vicinity of the door told of visitors seeking entrance. Turning to a small screen in the corner of the laboratory, I saw thereon the familiar faces of Bor Akon and Sarig Om.

As I moved toward the door to let them in, I realized in a flash that their coming was a gift of Sklow. They were welcome —how very welcome, they'd never know. I opened the door and bade them enter.

CHAPTER III

When the two faced me in the reception room, I could see in their glances the uncertainty they felt. They were in doubt as to the treatment they would receive at my hands. I smiled at them reassuringly, for it did not suit my purpose to arouse distrust in their minds.

The smile evidently renewed their confidence, for Bor Akon, acting as spokesman, cleared his throat and addressed me.

"Brother Tuol," he began—we were all brothers in conversation, "Sarig and I have taken it upon ourselves to investigate your report to the Council. We believe that you have been treated unjustly. Unquestionably, you were either sick or laboring under some great mental weight when you made those ridiculous statements in the Council Hall.

"We, Sarig and I, thought that we'd attempt to persuade you to take steps towards regaining your former position in the scientific world."

So that was their attitude! Perhaps I was sick, or temporarily deranged! Well, I thought it wouldn't take me long to correct that erroneous idea. Repressing my natural anger, lest it be betrayed through my voice, I replied in studiously careless tones.

"Brother Bor, I assure you that you are mistaken. All that I said to the Twenty was absolutely true. I can't help feeling that I have been shabbily treated. Had I been given a fair opportunity, I would have been able to prove my claims so absolutely, that even the most skeptical would have been convinced. As for my trying to regain my former position no! They have made me an outcast; I am satisfied.

"Now that you are here, I'll show you that proof, the microscope itself. If you will excuse me—" They acquiesced, politely, and I left them seated there while I headed toward the laboratory.

Upon arriving there, I drew a large curtain around the glass room, in order to conceal it from my visitors' eyes. Then I returned to the reception room and led my guests back to that part of the laboratory which held the microscope.

As their eyes fell upon the intricate mechanism, with its multitude of lenses and powerful lights, they displayed a reluctant, though rather skeptical interest. Sarig Om turned to me with a question in his eyes. I answered his unspoken query with:

"There would be no use in explaining its construction or means of magnification to you, inasmuch as neither of you could possibly understand. However, there is nothing to prevent you from observing the wonders that may be seen through it. Which of you will be the first to gaze upon an electron?"

As I placed a particle of matter beneath the lenses, and focused the microscope, Sarig Om expressed his willingness to be first. "I've been looking through lenses all my adult life," he said, "and since one of us must be first, it may as well be I."

While the two alternately gazed through the microscope, crying out in wonder at each new marvel, I excused myself and left the room.

I returned, some moments later, with some articles of food that I had treated with a sleep-inducing drug. As I entered, Sarig Om looked up, and expression of incredulity on his face.

"Brother Tuol," he exclaimed, "we have discovered life on a proton! It's unbelievable!"

"Come, come," I replied. "You've no cause for such great excitement. I have something far more amazing than that to show you. After we have eaten this food, I'll let you see something that is really astounding."

At my invitation, then, my guests seated themselves, and with poorly concealed impatience, ate the food I placed before them. A few moments after they had swallowed the drugged morsels, I saw their eyelids droop. Valiantly they fought the drowsiness that had settled upon them, but the drug was stronger than they and in a moment more they slept.

Securing strong cords, I bound them tightly, and carried them into the room which held the glass box. I placed them against the wall of the room in such a position as to enable them to have an unobstructed view of one of the box's sides, when they awakened.

I waited impatiently for the two scientists to recover from their involuntary slumbers; I was anxious to carry out the experiment I had in mind. At last they stirred, and in a short time were fully conscious.

Any self-possession that they had had, had gone from them. They looked at me with fear filled eyes. In all probability, they thought they were at the mercy of a madman. While I stood there, waiting for any remaining effects of the drug to pass, Bor Akon, in an obvious attempt to bolster his own courage, and perhaps intimidate me, addressed me.

"Tuol, you madman," he exclaimed, "cut these bonds and set us free immediately, or I'll see that you receive the punishment you deserve. You fool! What can you expect to gain by this? And what possible purpose can you have in mind, anyway? Liberate us now, or I'll inform the Council of your insane actions!"

I laughed. I couldn't help it; it was funny. The thought of that brainless fool, bound and helpless as he was, threatening me, bordered on the ridiculous. But my mirth was short-lived; suddenly it turned to anger. These two men were part of the race that had made me an outcast. A fool and a madman, was I?

"Silence!" I roared, as Sarig Om opened his mouth to speak. "Who are you to threaten me? Inform the Council, indeed! Idiots! You'll do just as I bid, and that only.

"What do I expect to gain; what purpose do I have in mind? I'll tell you. When the Council banished me, I swore that I would destroy every vestige of this race of failures, the race of man. I now have the instrument with which to bring about that destruction. For three long stallos I labored tirelessly, striving to achieve the impossible, and I've succeeded!"

While talking, I had moved over toward the glass room. I reached up then, and pulled the curtains aside. Nothing could be seen through the glass, save a grayish-white film on its inside surface, and a vague suggestion of a ceaseless movement within.

"In that glass cube," I continued, "lies the result of my efforts. You remember, of course, that I told the Council about the rapidly growing plant life I had discovered on a proton. Within that room is the proton itself, enormously increased in size. And with it, surrounding it, and I suppose, destroying it, are innumerable plants growing with an insane speed. Plants, they are, that I took from the proton's surface. They grow and grow, one upon another, finding root on any surface. I'll show you how they grow; it's only proper that you know, for you, too, Bor and Sarig, have a part in my plan. It is because of that part which you are to play, that I have bound you."

After testing their bonds, and finding them secure, I turned my back upon the two, closing my ears to their pleas for freedom, and directed a beam of heat upon the door of the glass room. Rapidly the film and the plants growing on the door disappeared, sinking to the floor. Further and further into the noisome, steaming mass the heat cut its way, clearing an ever increasing space. Finally, when I had reduced about half of the room's contents to slime, I shut off the heat ray, and admonished the two pay particular attention.

The plants recovered from the effects of the heat with great rapidity. In a few moments, a red, trinagular head on a long, slender stem, thrust itself up from the mass, and burst, casting its seed dust into the air. The astonished eyes of Bor Akon and Sarig Om saw the dust settle into the slime, spring up, grow to maturity, burst in turn, and die, all in a few moments of time. It was not long before the walls had again assumed their white, translucent covering, and our view was again cut off.

A heavy silence followed this, to them, amazing spectacle. Impatiently I broke that silence.

"Well, how did you enjoy the entertainment?" I asked. "Interesting, wasn't it? There is something still more interesting to follow, but I'll be the only one to see that.

"But consider those plants. Imagine what will happen when I free my pets upon Kotar. Imagine the effects of a little cloud of seed dust settling upon the floor of a boat in one of the great waterways. Curious people gather around, attracted by the peculiar growths. In a moment they are enveloped by a cloud of dust that touches them, and grows, drawing life from their flesh. Imagine a man breathing some of that dust!

"Then picture a strong wind blowing the dust to all parts of the world. News of the menace will cause men to flee. Some will lose their lives in the panic that will ensue. Others, seeking to escape, will perhaps hide in deep pits or cellars. The plants will fill the cracks and crevices of their sanctuaries, and eventually they will die of suffocation.

"Visualize the world after the menace has been at work for a stal. By that time the solid portion of Kotar's surface will have become a flowing, ever changing mass of plant life. The air will be filled with dense clouds of seed-dust of every possible hue. The boats on the waterways will be covered by the plants. Drifting, those boats will force their way through a heavy, viscous scum which will probably cover the water. Plants may be growing in that scum, which, by the way, will be the residue resulting from the decay of the other plants on the shore. Not a sound will break the death-like silence; there will be no more idle chattering coming from the lips of fools. The world will have been cleansed of their presence; all will have been destroyed. All—save one, Tuol Oro. A pretty picture, aye?"

Throughout this rather lengthy recital, both scientists remained motionless, as though frozen, an expression of growing horror and fascination on the face of each. When I ceased talking, Sarig Om attempted to speak, but the words died in his throat; he was dumb with fear, Bor Akon continued to stare fixedly into my face.

Suddenly a thought occurred to me.

"By the way," I exclaimed, "I told you that you, too, have a part in my plans. I've neglected to tell you what that part is, so I'll tell you now. I am not quite certain that those plants will act in just the way that I desire. Perhaps my efforts have been wasted. To avoid taking any chances of my plans going awry, I intend putting you in the glass room, and watching the effects of the plants upon you."

The semi-stupor into which the two had fallen fell from them like a cloak. Scream after scream burst from Bor Akon's lips. Roughly I clapped my hand over his mouth, threatening to gag him if he started screaming again. When I withdrew my hand, he began mumbling and sobbing piteously. His mind had snapped. Fear had dethroned his reason.

Sarig Om was made of sterner stuff. He cursed me in the name of every god that I knew of, and called me everything vile that entered his mind. I was surprised at his fluency.

When his tirade ceased, I picked him up and carried him,

squirming and twisting, over to the glass cube. Depositing him on the floor beside the door, I directed the heat against the glass another time. After burning away about half of the plants I opened the door and thrust Sarig in. Hastily, then, I closed and locked it, and directed the heat all around the edge of the door, in order to destroy any seed dust that might have escaped.

Then I turned my attention to the figure in the room. Sarig seated in a pool of slime, was straining with all his strength at the cords that bound his hands. Suddenly as one of the plants burst above him, he made a supreme effort, and the cords broke.

Slowly the dust settled upon him. As it touched his skin, sending tin rootlets through the pores, into his flesh, and drawing life from his living body, he gave utterance to one piercing shriek.

Strangely formed plants sprang from all parts of Sarig Om's body then. With mad, frenzied haste, the scientist tore them from him, leaving ugly, bloody wounds where the growths had been. But only for a moment was he able to struggle with his vegetable destroyers; several plants, having reached maturity upon him, burst simultaneously, enveloping him in a thick cloud of dust.

He seemed to grow larger before my eyes. Countless plants grew upon him, swelling him to three times his normal size. Grew—and decayed. The figure remained thus for only a moment, then it collapsed and lost itself in the slime and plants upon the floor.

For a fleeting second my resolution to destroy the race was shaken—but only for a second. Although the weapon I possessed was terrible, and the death it meted out, horrible, it wasn't too severe for the fools that ruled over Kotar. They deserved to be obliterated, and I was using the only means of destruction at my command.

I turned to Bor Akon. When last I had noticed him, he had been sobbing and quivering like a frightened infant. Now, he was lying on the floor, unconscious. The sight of Sarig Om's death had been too much for his weakened mind; he had fainted.

I would have spared Bor, then, to wait and be destroyed with his fellows, had it not been for the fact that he was aware of my plans. As it was, he knew too much for my safety; he had to be removed.

Again I burned the plants away; then I thrust the unconscious scientist through the doorway. After all, he was more fortunate than the others, for his death was painless; he never recovered consciousness.

I destroyed all evidence that pointed to the fact that the two had visited me. I took no chances of being implicated if their disappearance was investigated. Any interference at this time would have been fatal to my plans.

But there was no investigation; in all probability, Sarig and Bor had kept their visit secret, for fear of arousing the displeasure of the Council. After about a stal of waiting, I decided that it was safe for me to follow out the rest of my program. I had yet to prepare for my defense, secure a machine to purify the air, and lay in a supply of food tablets, and I would be ready.

Without delay, then, I employed men to make the large, fan-shaped steam nozzles, and fasten them where I directed on the walls and roof of my home. Other men I engaged to cover the building with a network of pipes to carry the steam to the nozzles. This latter crew built the tank that was to form the steam. The water for this, by the way, came through underground pipes from the waterway that flowed before my home. Still others, I hired to fill up every crack and crevice that they could find in the building. In every possible way, I fortified myself against any attacks that the plants might make upon me.

When authorities of the city questioned me about the pipes and nozzles, I told them that they were part of a new device for protection against fire. They believed me, thinking, in all probability, that it was only a fancy of my "disordered" mind. They left me to myself after that; I was glad of it.

During the few trons that preceded the time of my destruction of mankind, I had the oxygen machine installed and operating, and had food tablets enough stored in my bins to last me the rest of my life, if necessary. Likewise, I purchased enough fuel to keep my furnace going full blast for ten mallahs, at the very least.

When darkness fell upon the old, unchanged world of man for the last time, and I retired, I enjoyed the first real rest that had been mine since my banishment. No disturbing spectre of hate or vengeance marred my slumbers, for on the morrow my ultimate goal would be reached.

CHAPTER IV

The six Masters of Science had privileges that were not given to any other individuals on Kotar. One of these was the right to employ the Power of the Spheres in broadcasting on any wavelength we desired. That is, we could command any broadcast station to terminate its program and leave the air, so that we could use its wavelength. Through negligence on the part of the Council, this privilege had not been taken from me.

Shortly after I awakened from my sleep, greatly refreshed, by the way, I made use of that privilege, commanding the International News to cease broadcasting. After the announcer had stated that his station was cutting short its program at the command of one of the Masters, and that the program would continue after the Master had finished talking, his station grew silent.

I closed the switch then, and addressed my unseen audience.

"People of Kotar," I said, "I, Tuol Oro, outcast Master of Science, am taking this opportunity to tell you, in these few moments that will be spared to me ere the Council interferes, some facts about my banishment that have been carefully concealed by those in authority.

"Have you been informed that I was condemned without a trial? That I was given no opportunity to prove my claims? That, just because San Nober could not see the truth of my report, I was called mad, and that, without test being given to my mind? Of course you haven't! All that has been kept secret.

"Immediately after the ringing of the Terai bell, I will prove to those who gather before my home that all that I said in the Council Hall was true, and that San Nober himself should be the one to be condemned, because of his total lack of judgment. If that incompetent individual is listening, I give him a special invitation to be there. He—" There was a sharp, sudden explosion and a blinding flash in the broadcasting apparatus, and my connections with the outside world were broken.

I heard words issuing from the receiving device in another corner of the room. It was San Nober, using the so-called Universal wavelength of the Council, the wavelength that covered every station from the lowest to the highest, thus rendering the speaker's voice audible to every listener on the planet. San's heavy, bass voice quivered with anger.

"Tuol Oro," he growled, "you are a fool. And for your folly you shall die. You will be permitted to offer any proof that you possess, at the time you have set, so that no one may say that there has been a miscarriage of justice.

"I accept your invitation: I'll be there."

With a feeling of satisfaction, I shut off the machine. San Nober would be there! That was what I wanted. What mattered it that he would probably be accompanied by a group of his followers, whose purpose it would be to arrest me? They would be powerless to harm me, for I possessed a weapon more terrible than anything they had ever conceived of.

I occupied myself during the time that I had to wait, with a final survey of all my protective devices. I made sure that everything was in readiness for the great climax. Only the turn of a valve was needed to cover my home with a blanket of steam. A little pressure upon a button would start the oxygen machine. An automatic feeding device would add fuel to that in the furnace whenever it was needed. As far as I could see, there was nothing else to be done along the line of self-protection.

There was one thing, though, that I had not taken into consideration. How was I to free the plants without endangering myself? After some thought I decided upon a method. In a short time I constructed a small, glass box with a tightly fitting lid, which automatically closed at any time I signified on the time-clock within the box.

I burned the plants away again, and set the finished box inside the glass room with the lid timed to close in three trons. Impatiently I waited for the time to go by, dividing my attention between the plants and the clock on a nearby wall.

At last, when the three trons had passed, I managed, by careful application of the heat, to remove the box from the room, filled with plants, seed dust, and slime.

With great care, then, I went over all the space on which seed dust might have found lodgment, with a beam of heat. After I was certain that there was no further possibility of any dust having escaped destruction, I carried the glass box to a window overlooking the Waterway, and there took up my vigil. The time for revenge was almost at hand.

The street below me was filled with a noisy throng of people. Men, women, and children had gathered, for a public statement by one of the Six Masters was far from being commonplace, and was worthy of more than passing notice. Several men in the crowd I recognized as minor scientists who had been in the Council Hall on the day I was banished.

The Waterway was even more crowded than the street. Indeed, the boats were so close to each other that very little water could be seen. And every boat was loaded to capacity with passengers.

Overhead I could hear the low, steady hum of many flying machines. Looking up, I saw small, one-man planes darting here and there, aimlessly. Great helicopters with whirling propellers and whirring wings were suspended above, hanging stationary in mid-air. All were low enough for their passengers to hear anything I had to say.

Suddenly my attention was drawn from the air vehicles by a commotion below. I looked down. In some way, how, I do not know, the boats had been cleared away to form a lane which led directly to the front of my home. At the further end of the lane, I saw the graceful lines of San Nober's stately bark. Its silver trimmings flashed in the sunlight.

As it drew closer, enabling me to distinguish faces, I saw that every member of the Council was there, and that the remaining three Masters were likewise on board. In addition, the International Peace Guard had six representatives present. They, I knew, were there for the purpose of arresting me after I had had my say. But they meant nothing to me.

As the Council boat touched the side of the waterway's banks, I heard a single, deep toned bell note, the Terai bell. The time I had set had come! I flung open the window.

At my appearance, the voice of the throng was stilled. The sound of motors in the air above became less noticeable, as the pilots applied their silencers. And then I spoke.

I described in detail all that had taken place in the Council Hall, I told them of the great discovery I had made, laying stress on the minute plants and their amazingly rapid growth. I spoke of my banishment, and of the oath I had taken—and there I stopped. The bellowing voice of San Nober had interrupted me.

"Have done with this nonsense!" he exclaimed. "This farce must stop! How can your grievances affect these people? You can't expect to gain anything by this additional publicity. You must be mad to expect any benefit to come to you from this.

"If you have any proof to offer, produce it. Stol Verta will begin counting, and if you haven't partially proven your claims by the time he reaches fifty, your liberty will end. You will not be given another opportunity to deceive your fellow men."

"Begin counting, Stol."

While the inventor's hand slowly, mechanically rose and fell, I gave my last message to the world.

"People of Kotar," I said solemnly, "your span of life is almost ended. When San interrupted me, I was about to tell you that the world is doomed, that my oath will be carried out. You are a race of fools, unworthy of the responsibility that has been given you. You are not fitted for the task of controlling a planet's life, so you cannot survive. You——"

I went no further. No one would have heard me if I had. The momentary daze which had held the crowd speechless, vanished. Hoots and jeers, and cries of mingled anger and mirth came from the throng.

Stol Verta stopped counting. San Nober, with a word to his colleagues, stepped from his boat, and, followed by the Guards and Masters, began forcing his way through the crowd. A path opened as though by magic, and the throng grew quiet.

I took advantage of that silence; raising the glass box high above my head, I cried, "This is my proof," and hurled it at the feet of San Nober. Then I banged the window shut, locked it, and turned the valve which started the steam.

San fell back, startled, when the box crashed before him. Then he stared in fascination at the little heap of shattered glass and pulpy matter that lay at his feet. It was growing, and he could see the growth! He leaned forward to observe the strange organisms more carefully—and a plant burst.

A small cloud of dust arose into the air and settled upon San's head and shoulders. For a moment he beat at the vegetation that sprang from his flesh, his arms waving futilely, helplessly; then he fell to the pavement.

Those who saw his death, shrank back, while those further away strove to get closer. But when the seed dust began dropping upon them, only one impulse actuated them, and that was to escape.

Escape, however, was impossible, now; they had delayed too long. Where one plant had been, had grown a thousand; the thousand had become a million; and every moment more and more seed dust was being cast into the air. In little more time than is required for the telling, no human life was left where the crowd had been.

At the very beginning of the destruction, there had been wrecks on the Waterway, caused by boats crashing into each other when their pilots had become heaps of plants and slime. Similarly, there had been accidents in the air, planes darting around erratically, pilotless, with propellers clogged by slime and plants, either crashing into each other, or falling to the ground. But that was all over in a short time.

Some planes and boats had made good their escape, and had wasted no time, I was sure, but rather made haste to tell the world of the horror that menaced civilization. This caused me no concern, however, for I knew that the plants were too firmly established to be affected by anything the puny world of man might do. Kotar's ruling race was unquestionably doomed.

Soon after the last man in sight had been destroyed, and the last plane had disappeared, I turned away from the window. I had taken my revenge; I was satisfied. I had seen San Nober die a horrible death. Before my eyes the members of the Council had been destroyed. And I was the only survivor of the six Masters of Science; they had scorned me, but they had felt the might of my hand.

While walking across the room with the intention of starting the oxygen machine, I spied the broadcasting apparatus. A thought occurred to me. Why not tell the Universe of the things I had done? Why not warn them, so that they, if ever similar circumstances arose, would not make the mistake that the people of Kotar had made. I had one of the most powerful broadcasting machines on Kotar, and it would be a simple matter to increase that that power so that my message would travel to the farthest corner of the Universe. I made a decision: I'd tell the story.

And then I remembered Sarig Om's report to the Council. He had said that Santel would be closer to Kotar on a certain date than it had been for many mallahs. If there were intelligent, reasoning beings on Santel—Sarig had always maintained that there were—they, at least, might be able to hear my warning. At any rate, I decided to wait for that date and broadcast my story then.

I spent the interim between the time I made my decision, and the time of opposition, in studying the plants I could see from my window, enjoying long periods of interesting observation, in spite of the steam that persisted in cutting off my view. I also spent some time in preparing notes for my story, for I wanted nothing to be left from the narrative.

Finally, after stalls of waiting, the time of opposition has arrived. Now, as I am talking, Santel should be at its closest proximity to Kotar.

My story is almost ended. From my place here before the broadcasting apparatus, I can look out through the window. A vast sea of amazingly brilliant plants meets my eye. There are plants that are thick and round, plants tall and angular, plants of every conceivable shape and color. It is a scene of dazzling brilliancy, a scene that has an unnatural, alien beauty. And the impossible speed of the plants' development does much toward creating that sense of the unreal, the fantastic.

There is no strife or discord, no petty quarrelling; the plants seem to be the embodiment of unity. A vast, all-engulfing silence has superseded the noise and bustle of man's civilization. The only sound that breaks the silence is the hiss of escaping steam. That steam, to me, is symbolic of the civilization that has gone, existing for a moment, noisy and purposeless, then vanishing. Of the two forms of life, mankind and the plants, the latter is by far the better.

Still, it is only proper that I, the creator of this vegetable world, should be the ruler thereof. Consequently, in a short time, I shall attempt to gain complete control of those plants, and be supreme ruler over all. I have a plan——

Good Maca! What was that! One of the walls of the glass room has fallen out! the plants are escaping! The heat projector! MACA! OH——

Tuol Oro's tale ended in a shrill scream of horror and pain, a scream that was cut short abruptly, and ended in a strangely muffled sob. One can picture with some degree of accuracy the scene within his room. In some way, the glass square that had held the original plants had collapsed, letting the deadly organisms escape.

The resulting death of the mad scientist can well be imagined.

And on Kotar, or Mars, if it is the red planet, a species of fungus, growing with incredible rapidity, holds uncontested sway.

The Asteroid of Gold
by Clifford D. Simak

from WONDER STORIES, November 1932

Towards the end of the 1930's many readers wondered if Simak would ever appear again. He had contributed only five stories to the professional magazines, and rumour had it he had written a masterpiece for one of those fan publications. . . . what was it? . . . *Marvel Tales* or something.

Indeed Clifford Simak was comfortably making his way up the promotion ladder in newspaper circles. The lack of reliable markets had caused him to give up writing science fiction, and it was only when John Campbell became editor of *Astounding Stories* that he was coaxed back to the field. In hindsight we can all sigh with relief that Simak made that decision otherwise the field would be without a great deal of wealth in the form of Simakian gems.

The last story to appear from Simak in those early days was "The Asteroid of Gold". Here you have a chance to compare a story written by a twenty-seven year old Simak, with his latest science fantasy novels, written in his late sixties. In essence Simak has turned full circle in his writings, but has never lost that basic appeal. His first professional appearance, "World of the Red Sun", in the December 1931 *Wonder Stories* tells of adventurers who travel in time to the future and discover a gigantic brain which controls the remnants of mankind. The story of how they defeat the brain is adeptly related, and the final weapon was not one of the atomic weapons so glibly used in 1930's sf, but simply psychology.

One of his more recent stories, "Construction Shack" in the January 1973 *Galaxy* reveals how explorers of Pluto discover plans for the building of the solar system, and how each planet was given up in turn as a failure. In between these stories Simak has turned out well over one hundred beautiful science fiction stories, such as the "City" series, where old Earth is left to be civilized by intelligent dogs under the careful eye of Jenkins the robot. "City" went on to win the International Fansasy Award, and Simak later scooped the double when "The Big Front Yard" received the Hugo Award in 1959, and a second Hugo for "Way Station".

Simak is noted for the generally optimistic tone of his work, wherin his characters are more saints than sinners, and good generally wins out against evil.

"After this charge we'll knock off for eats and sleep," Vince Drake suggested to his brother.

Vernon Drake nodded.

"I've got the jitters from wearing the suit for such a long stretch," he said. "I'm afraid we're overdoing the work a bit, Vince."

"It's a tough racket," his brother agreed, "but the sooner we get this load to earth, the quicker we can buy *Space Pup II*."

The two moved over the rocky surface of the asteroid in apparently effortless leaps, heading toward the *Space Pup*, which squatted like a silver monster against the drab monotony of the little world. Here the gravity was slight, so slight, in fact, that the brothers wore ropes about their waists while at work, with the other ends fastened to the *Space Pup*. The ship was securely anchored to the planetoid with magnetic plates. Otherwise some slight disturbance might have sent it off into space.

A man, putting his full strength into a leap, could easily have torn himself from the face of the rocky little world and hurled himself beyond its attraction. Thus the ropes attached to the man and the ship. It would have been no joke to inadvertently hop off the tiny slab of rock and be unable to return. They had at first experimented with weighted shoes and then with magnetic plates attached to the soles, but both of these devices has proved cumbersome and awkward.

Overhead the stars moved steadily in the velvety blackness of absolute space. The asteroid, nothing more than a slab of rock some five miles in length, half as wide and approximately four miles thick, was tumbling rapidly end over end through space. Here one was afforded the astounding spectacle of observing the constellations march in orderly procession against the curtain of blackness which enveloped the airless little world.

Descending over the sunward horizon could be seen the Twin, only a matter of some fifteen miles distant. The two tiny slabs of rock, revolving about each other, made up a part of the asteroid belt, all that remained of a mythical planet between Mars and Jupiter (which must have disrupted into the thousands of tiny fragments many millions of years before).

Here and there in the blackness loomed dark splotches, some shining faintly with reflected light from the distant sun—other members of the belt. At times wandering chunks of rock hurtled across space, some passing close to the asteriod upon which the two brothers were located. At times showers of tiny meteors, travelling at bullet-like speeds, bombarded the little island of space. There was danger in plenty, but the stakes were high and the brothers braved the dangers.

Two slabs of rock revolving about one another, true twins of space . . . . but the Twin was only rock, while the one upon which Vince and Vernon Drake were conducting their mining operations was shot through and through with yellow veins of gold. The ore was rich, unbelievably rich, so rich that it practically crumbled under one's fingers. The price of one cargo alone would run into six figures. A treasure house in space! A treasure hoard of the void!

The brothers reached the ship and Vince knelt to connect the wires to the detonator. The nitro was planted in shallow holes, with care taken that the charge was not excessive. With the slight gravity, too large a charge would simply blast a portion of the ore-bearing slab into space, possibly to be lost forever. This had happened several times before they had learned just how much nitro to use.

"Hang on!" cautioned Vince.

Vernon grasped a rung set in the side of the *Space Pup*. Vince slid his arm through a similar rung and with his free hand shot down the plunger of the detonator.

There was no noise, only a slight flush where the charges were planted. The planetoid trembled violently beneath their feet. The *Space Pup* quivered and tugged at its magnetic moorings as the rock beneath it shook to the charge of the explosive. About a half mile away, where the charge had been set, a shower of small rock fragments sailed upward, but they did not drop. Out and out they sailed until they were lost to view, each becoming a separate unit in the mass of debris which formed the asteroid belt.

"Now into the *Pup*," exclaimed Vince, "for some eats and a good long sleep. We've done a lot this shift."

"The thing I look forward to is getting out of this suit." declared Vernon.

He turned toward the door and as he did so he cast a glance. upward. He stopped short in astonishment.

"Vince, look!" he cried.

Looming out of the void, blotting out a portion of the sky, a huge, black ship hung almost directly above them. There had been nothing to apprise them of its coming. It had simply slipped out of the blackness of space and suddenly was there, hanging above the tiny world. They had seen no rocket blasts.

Their earphones rang as an imperative tone cut in upon their receiving sets.

"Stay where you are. Don't move. We are going to land and we have guns on you."

The ship was speaking to them.

"Who the hell are you?" demanded Vernon.

"Max Robinson, of the Space Ship *Star Wanderer*, speaking."

Max Robinson, of the *Star Wanderer*! The faces of the two brothers paled under their helmets. The most notorious raider of the space lines! Plunderer extraordinary. Cut-throat bandit of the void. How had he learned of the wondrous treasure on the little asteroid?

There was nothing to say. The two young miners at first did not realize the true significance of this visit from Robinson. It all came so suddenly that it was impossible to think clearly, impossible to grasp the true possibilities of the situation.

"You damned robber!" said Vernon bitterly.

He felt his brother's hand upon his arm, squeezing with a vice-like grip.

"Men don't talk like that to Max Robinson," the voice came coolly, unflustered, "and get away with it."

Warned by the pressure on his arm, Vernon did not reply.

The two stood silently, watching the great craft settle slowly to a berth only a short distance from where the *Space Pup* lay. Through the lighted ports they could see men in the ship, while here and there heads were outlined against the circles of light, men off duty looking out upon the tiny world where they had landed.

Smoothly a gangplank came down and the outer door of an air chamber swiftly unscrewed and swung free.

"Come into my ship," said the voice of Robinson, " and come peaceably."

There was a horrible threat in the words. The two knew there never would be a moment, except perhaps when they were actually in the air chamber, that they would not be under the guns of the vessel.

In long hops they moved forward and set foot on the gang-plank of the pirate ship. There they halted to unfasten the ropes about their waists.

"What are you stopping for?" growled Robinson.

"To unfasten our safety cables," Vince explained. "The gravity is so low here we anchored ourselves to our ship."

Robinson chuckled.

"Bright idea," he applauded. "I'll never forget the time one of my men jumped off one of these lousy little worlds. We scouted around for hours before we picked him up. He was dead."

They could hear the raider chuckle again, deep in his throat.

"Scared to death," he explained.

The brothers did not answer; neither of them at the moment could find anything particularly funny about a man being frightened to a point where death claimed him. With their ropes free they stepped up the gangplank into the air chamber. Noiselessly the door swung against the port, spinning into the threads. There was a sharp hissing, continuing for several minutes, then the inner door slipped its threads and swung open.

Vernon again felt the warning pressure of his brother's hand as they stepped out of the air chamber into the interior of the ship. Several members of the crew sprang toward them, ran swift hands over their inflated suits.

"That's all right," said Vernon, "we have no guns."

The men dropped back and the brothers unfastened their helmets and swung them back on their rear hinges. They closed the air tank valves and the suits went limp, hanging loosely about them.

Their eyes, roving over the ship, saw that it was extremely modern, equipped with many of the new inventions for comfort and safe space travel.

Six members of the crew stood in the room with them. They were a hardfaced lot; scum drafted from all the infamous space ports of the worlds; perhaps many of them criminals hiding from justice.

"The captain wants to see you immediately," said one of them.

"Mind if we take off our suits?" asked Vernon. "They aren't comfortable after you've worn them for a while."

"Don't see that would hurt any," grunted the man. "Hurry about it, though."

Quickly they unfastened the suits and stepped from them, leaving them on the floor.

"The captain ain't one to be kept waiting," the man explained.

The two followed the man along a central corridor to the forward end of the ship. Before a door their guide stopped and knocked.

"Come in," commanded the voice they had heard over their receiving scts.

The guide swung open the door and motioned the others to step forward. As they did so, the door closed behind them and they stood alone, face to face with Max Robinson, cruelest, and most hunted space raider of the system.

They saw a man attired in a colorful uniform of powder blue, adorned with gold buttons, and with a red circle as a breast insignia. His forehead was high and his chin square, but not over-emphasized. A squat nose hulked above the slighest suggestion of a mustache and the lips were full and well formed. It was such a face as might have belonged to an ordinary, everyday business man of the Earth . . . . . until one looked at the eyes, and there the brothers saw cold calculation and insane cruelty.

He sat behind a large desk of beautiful carved stone, which was at once recognized as Martian art. Perhaps the desk had been part of the loot taken from some flaming homestead upon which Robinson and his crew of vandals descended to obtain a cargo of food. Upon the walls of the room hung paintings, specimens of the best art of the world. Held in wall brackets were other works of art, vases and statues. A heavy rug carpeted the floor.

"You like my office?" queried Robinson.

"It is appointed more tastefully than I would have imagined," replied Vince and the implication of his words was not lost upon the man behind the desk.

"When you become more thoroughly acquainted with me," he purred, "you will receive many surprises."

"Doubtless," said Vince.

Robinson's eyes narrowed. He seemed on the point of speaking sharply, then appeared to change his mind.

"Doing some mining?" he asked.

"No exploring," lied Vince.

"Find anything?"

"A little lead."

Robinson clucked with mock sympathy.

"Too bad," he said, "too bad. Funny you would stay on one asteroid so long when all you found was a little lead. We saw you here 20 days ago when we passed by. When we picked you up again this time we thought you might have found something, so we dropped down."

Vince said nothing. There was nothing to say.

"Been doing a lot of blasting, too," observed the pirate. "In one place. That's funny. Seems to me you would blast a lot of test pits if you were just exploring."

"We were hopeful of finding something really worthwhile," explained Vernon. "Had just decided to quit. If we find nothing from this last shot we won't do any more exploring here. We've wasted too much time here as it is."

"You're right," said Robinson and his voice was silky. "You won't do any more exploring . . . . . here or on any other asteroid."

"What do you mean?" asked Vernon.

Robinson did not seem to hear the question. He leaned forward over the desk and beat a clenched fist on its polished top.

"What did you find?" he bellowed.

"Lead," declared Vince.

The pirate picked up a small hammer and tapped a gong which squatted on his desk. The door opened and the man who had escorted the brothers to his captain stepped into the room.

"Make these gentlemen comfortable," commanded Robinson, "I am going out to have a look at their lead mine."

With an evil grin the man beckoned to the two, led the way out of the door and down the corridor. Far in the rear of the ship he halted and with a key opened a heavy door.

"In you go," he said.

The brothers stepped inside and the door creaked to, behind them. A moment later the key grated in the lock.

The room was bare of furniture except for four steel beds bolted to the floor. They were in the prison room of the *Star Wanderer*.

Vernon sat down heavily on one of the beds.

"What do we do now?" he asked.

"We have to wait and watch our chance," said Vince. "Maybe a chance will never come, but if it does, we'll make the most of it. We have to try not to antagonize Robinson, but we must stand upon our dignity. We must not let him believe for a moment we are afraid of him or afraid of what he might do to us. We have told our story and we are going to stick to it. We explored and we found lead. No matter if he takes tons of gold out of the place, it will always be lead to us."

Vernon grinned. The course suggested by his brother struck a chord of grim humour in him.

Vince seated himself on the bed and threw an arm over Vernon's shoulder.

"It's a tough break, kid," he said. "We are in the hands of the system's worst outlaw. We . . . . . "

He stopped, groping for words.

"Yes, I know," said Vernon and the two of them sat, staring straight at the grey wall in front of them.

Vince broke the silence.

"No use kidding ourselves," he said.

"None at all," agreed Vernon and his voice matched his brother's in tenseness.

"But we must always remember, kid," went on Vince, "that this isn't the first time a Drake has been in a tight spot. Some of them have gotten out of it and some of them haven't. But they always were Drakes. Not a snivelling coward among them. Not a single whimper for mercy. They've never forgotten their *savoir faire*. We've got something that Robinson never had and never can have and maybe we can beat him yet. He'll get small satisfaction out of this deal, no matter what happens."

They sat in silence again.

"Let's get some sleep," suggested Vernon, and Vince nodded.

"Good idea," he said and almost crunched the bones in his brother's shoulder with the grip of an understanding hand.

Dog-tired after hours in space suits, with the labor of wresting the golden fortune from the isolated little asteroid, they slept long and when they awoke a table bearing food stood in the room.

Vernon went to the single port-hole opening out of the prison room. Staring through it he could see feverish activity outside. Several cranes had been rigged up on the surface of the little world and the entire crew of the *Star Wanderer* seemed to be engaged in looting the planetoid of its golden hoard. It was a weird picture. Huge floodlights hastily erected lit up the surface and made the place a plain of light and shadow. Space armor glistened and shone and sudden flashes spurted against the utter blackness of space as charges of explosives were fired. As each charge exploded the *Star Wanderer* vibrated from end to end.

Men with heavy loads of ore toiled up the gangplank and into the airlock.

"What are they doing?" asked Vince sleepily from his bed.

"Come and see," invited Vernon.

Together the two brothers gazed out upon the scene.

"Our mine," said Vernon.   Vince nodded bitterly.

The two turned from the window and gave their attention to the food on the table.

"Poison," suggested Vernon, but Vince shook his head.

"Not Robinson's way of doing things," he declared. "Not bloody enough. No entertainment just sending two poor souls into eternity with a dose of strychnine. Robinson demands dramatics."

"I hope you're right," said Vernon.

"What does it matter if I am or not?" demanded Vince. "We have to eat, don't we? I'd rather eat poison every time in preference to starvation."

The food was good and the brothers, not having eaten for twenty-four hours, did justice to it.

An hour later the same man who had conducted them to their cell appeared and took away the food.

"The captain says to tell you that he's found gold," he stated.

"Tell the captain that he's found lead," corrected Vince.

Hours passed. Ten times the Twin circled its mate in space. Still the work of mining the gold went on without a stop. Apparently Robinson had divided his crew into shifts and was working every minute. Greats pits were being gouged in the surface of the planetoid. It was plain that the pirate would not halt mining operations until either the ore pinched out or until his ship was loaded to capacity.

Food was served the prisoners at regular intervals and they slept when they felt sleepy. Part of the time they spent at the port watching the activity outside. They requested a deck of cards from their keeper and whiled away hours playing for immense imaginary stakes. Neither of them mentioned what lay in store for them. Neither was there talk of escape. They knew there was no escape.

Escape from the ship without space suits meant death of the most horrible kind on the airless surface of the asteroid. Escape even with space suits would have to be made in the face of the pirates swarming outside. Even if they were able to safely reach the *Space Pup*, they knew that the *Star Wanderer* carried weapons which could blast the little ship out of existence.

The Twin had circled its companion eighteen times when they were summoned out of their prison to face Robinson again. As they walked up the corridor with their keeper stalking in their wake, Vernon's hand reached out and grasped his brother's for just an instant in a bonecrushing clasp. They were walking the road to death. Not for a moment was there a doubt in their mind of that. It was not after the manner of Max Robinson to allow men he had plundered to live. It was not well for him to have too many men in the system hating him with that fierce hate which can only come through personal injury.

But they walked with their shoulders square, with their chins up and in their swinging stride there was no hint of condemned men on their way to the scaffold.

Reaching the door of Robinson's office they did not wait for the guard to announce them. Vince beat a tattoo upon the metal.

"Come in, " said the pirate, and once more they stood before the beautifully carved desk behind which sat the most feared, most hated man of the solar system.

Robinson regarded them with narrowed eyes, but his throat gurgled with cruel laughter.

"This asteroid of yours," he said, "is very precious. It is rich beyond dreams. It is full of gold."

"It is full of lead and, at present, cluttered up with damned robbers," said Vince softly.

Robinson seemed not to hear him, but Vernon, watching closely, knew that his brother's words had flicked him on the raw.

"It is regrettable," purred the pirate, "that having discovered such a vast deposit of gold, it should be lost to you. Under the circumstances your fortitude has been truly amazing. You have earned something better than the fate which I generally mete out to my . . . . my . . . . . "

"Victims," suggested Vernon.

"That's it," beamed Robinson. "How did you think of the word?"

"I am way ahead of you all of the time," Vernon told him.

Robinson, however, was determined not to lose face by losing his temper. He had deliberately set out to taunt these men in an attempt to break them. He forced himself to maintain his light tone.

He wagged his head.

"I have taken all I want," he said. "More, perhaps, than I was rightly entitled to, after all it was your mine. You discovered it. Still there is plenty more. I don't plan on returning, for there are many other such treasures in the system and the treasure itself means nothing to Max Robinson, rather the satisfaction of acquiring it."

"I hope," said Vince, "that you have derived considerable satisfaction from our explorations."

Robinson bowed, mocking them.

"Exactly," he said, "So I have decided not to kill you. I will leave you here with your mine. I have done enough wrong in my life. I am sorely in need of a few acts of mercy to counterbalance my sins."

Vernon stirred at Vince's side, but his brother reached out with a hand and gripped him. He steadied . . . . waiting for the joker in Robinson's proposal.

"It is regrettable, however," stated the pirate, "that I am short on oxygen tanks. All I shall be able to give you will be three tanks. One for each of you and one to be divided between you as you see fit."

He stared solemnly at them.

"I am sorry to say, too, that I shall be obliged to take your ship out of your reach temporarily. If I left it where you could use it immediately, I fear that you might hasten to Mars and report my presence in this part of the solar system and it does not suit my plans to have my presence known for some time."

"Canny," declared Vince, "always the old fox."

Robinson grinned.

"I am going to take your ship and anchor it just a few miles away, on the Twin, where you can see it. One of my crew, a reputable instructor of mathematics in an Earth college before he committed a certain indiscretion and sought my protection, informs me that in the matter of a few thousands years the revolutions of the two asteroids will slow down and their orbits will close in, until they finally come together, joining one another. When that occurs you can reach your ship and return to Earth or Mars without harming me in the least."

"If the oxygen holds out," suggested Vince.

"I never thought of that," declared the pirate. "Maybe the oxygen wouldn't last that long."

"I'm afraid it wouldn't," said Vince.

"At least," pointed out the other, "you will have the satisfaction of always having your ship in sight when the Twin is in view."

As he spoke Vince leaped. His body, striking against the desk, shoved it backward and toppled the pirate out of his chair. The chair thudded against the carpeted floor. A vase tottered and fell from a shallow wall bracket, smashing to a thousand bits as it struck against a piece of statuary standing beneath it.

Vince, his body bruised by the force of its impact against the heavy desk, scrambled to his feet.

Vernon was vaulting the desk, and disappeared behind it. With a single effort, Vince followed. Vernon and Robinson were locked on the floor in a tangle of flying arms and legs.

Vince flung himself into the struggle. His hands found and closed with a vice-like grip upon a massive throat.

There was a hammering of feet in the corridor.

"Quick," screamed Vince, "The trick Kan taught us."

Like a flash Vernon was on his feet. With a thud he placed his left knee into the small of Robinson's back, bearing down with his entire weight. Up and back Vince forced the upper part of the body and then, with his fingers still wrapped like tentacles of steel about the pirate's throat, put his full strength into a final thrust. There was a sharp snap as the vertebrae slipped out of place.

Vince released his grip and the body slumped to the floor.

The door burst inward. The brothers vaulted the desk as one man and were in the center of the dozen members of the crew before a gun could be used. With fists working like driving pistons the two went to the attack. Back and forth the fight surged across the room, with the pirates afraid to use their guns at such close quarters.

Vince accounted for his first opponent with a clean smash to the temple, but fumbled the second blow when his fist slid off the granite chin of the second man. Someone hit him hard over the heart and he retaliated with a blow that lifted the man off his feet and sent him staggering. A monstrous fist lashed at his head and almost floored him. Groggy as he was, he failed to duck another fist that smashed him against the wall. A face appeared in front of him and he flailed at it. A red smear appeared on the face as it slumped out of his line of vision. Then there were other fists hitting him . . . hitting hard.

He caught sight of Vernon in the center of the mêlée in the middle of the room; saw a man wilt as his brother drove his fist into his throat; saw his brother topple as someone struck him from behind. Then a fist he could not duck, hard as he tried . . . . .

a moment of dull pain, of flashing lights within his head and then . . . . . nothing.

He awoke with the glare of electric bulbs in his eyes and a throbbing pain in his head. Weakly he gained a sitting position and glanced about him.

Members of the crew thronged the room, all of them clutching weapons. A short distance away Vernon was struggling to his feet.

Walking unsteadily, his brother advanced toward him. Vince forced his aching body to rise and faced Vernon.

"It was a good fight," said Vernon, "while it lasted."

He grinned, wryly. Vince noted that one of his front teeth was missing and that bloodstains were about his mouth.

"Our last good fight, kid," said Vince.

The pirates rimmed them in a tight circle, watching them warily.

"Why don't they polish us off, kid?" asked Vince.

"Orders from Robinson," Vernon explained, "he is still alive."

"What's that!"

"Robinson is still alive."

"The hell you say," exclaimed Vince. "He's the first man I ever knew who could outlive old Kan's trick."

"Too tough to kill. Born to hang," said Vernon.

There was a stir at the edge of the circle which hemmed them in. It parted to let two men pass through. The two cradled a broken man in their arms.

Robinson glared at the brothers out of haggard eyes. His legs dangled grotesquely, seeming to reach despairingly toward the floor. His face was a twisted mask of pain and anger.

"You thought to kill me," he boomed.

"I am sorry," said Vince.

"Sorry!"

"Sorry I didn't succeed."

Robinson was muttering to himself.

"Delirious," said Vernon and Vince nodded.

But they were mistaken.

"Hard men to break," mumbled the pirate, "but loneliness on an asteroid, with a space ship just out of reach, will break you. Too bad I won't be here to see you fight over the third oxygen tank. Too bad I can't hear you scream when you watch the ship, so near . . . . yet just too far. Yes, it is too bad I can't wait to see you break."

Vince, his fists clenched hard at his side, took a step toward the man.

"Listen, Robinson, you won't be anywhere again. You are just a twisted cripple. You'll never walk again. There isn't a man in God's creation who can mend that back of yours. Your spinal column is shattered . . . . and you are hanging on by a thread. You will live, knowing every minute that just one little twist, one wrong move may send you to eternity. I hope to God you live a hundred years and fear every moment you will die.

"You are a broken man . . . . a useless worn-out shell. These hands broke you . . . . broke you, do you hear . . . . and I am damn glad we were able to do it . . . . you sneering, low-lived swine!"

"Take him out," commanded Robinson.

Men sprang forward, and pinioned their arms behind them, forcing them to the door.

The Twin was rising over the rim of the tumbling world.

Two men, seated on a rocky ridge, arms thrown over one another's shoulders, stared up at it. Against its dull lustre could be seen a speck of silver, etched in familiar outline, the *Space Pup*.

"We'll see it just once more," said Vince, "Our oxygen won't last more than another revolution of the asteroids."

"What are we going to do with this?" Vernon touched the extra tank with the toe of his boot.

"You know what we are going to do with it."

Vernon nodded.

"We'll furnish a great newspaper story some day," he said, "if we ever are found. Two dead men in space suits with a tank full of oxygen at their feet. Mystery—why didn't one of them use the oxygen?"

"I have something I want to say, "said Vince. "Hard to word it. Would think a fellow could say things to his brother . . . but you know how it is."

"Sure. Better not sy it. I feel the same way."

"You've been regular," declared Vince.

"Not so bad yourself," replied Vernon.

"It's not hard to die with you, kid. I always pictured us going out differently. Maybe with guns flaming in some out of way station or with the old *Space Pup* busted wide open somewhere out in space . . . . but not like this. Doesn't matter after all . . . . . "

"Why should it?" demanded Vernon.

They sat silently, watching the Twin climb rapidly toward the zenith. Dust spurted in the mine pits as a few tiny meteors plunged down on the asteroid.

"If one of those hit us, it would be over in a minute," observed Vernon.

"Look!" screamed Vince. "The Twin is falling!"

Vernon jerked his head upward.

The Twin was falling! Falling with a rotary motion around the axis of its length. Even as he watched it seemed to draw closer!

"A meteor," exclaimed Vince, his voice tense, "a large meteor. Struck it and threw it out of its orbit! That's the only thing that can account for it."

"It is bringing the *Space Pup* back to us!" said his brother.

"It will crush the *Space Pup*," declared Vince. "Likely smash us, too. It will land smack on top of us."

"It won't hurt the *Space Pup*," argued Vernon. See, it is rotating. The top will be turned toward us when it strikes. The ship will be on top. It will be safe!"

"By God, you're right," yelled Vince. "Here kid, we're getting out of here! Grab a handful of rocks and jump as you've never jumped before! At an angle to carry you out over the edge."

He stooped and scooped up handfuls of rubble.

"Get going!" he screamed at his brother.

Vernon was running. Running with long leaps toward the nearer edge of the planetoid, gaining speed at every leap. Then he shot upward, as if he had been catapulted from a gigantic sling shot. Up and up he went, out and out, until he was a speck against the blackness.

Bouncing along over the surface, Vince put all of his strength into a tremendous leap as he struck the rock beneath with both feet planted firmly. He seemed to be rushing out, away from the asteroid, at an express train speed. Rapidly the bloated space suit encasing his brother seemed to leap to meet him. Then he was floating free in space, looking back at the Twin rushing downward upon the slab of rock he had so recently quit. He could see that the rotary motion of the Twin, probably imparted to it when a meteor had struck with force enough, not only to knock it out of its orbit, but to also reverse its directional spin, had brought the *Space Pup* to the upper side. The two planetoids were so close now that the ship could not possibly be crushed between them. They were due to crash any moment now and the *Space Pup* was on top!

He clawed with his hands at empty space, swinging his body around until his back was toward the asteroid. Then with all his strength he heaved a rock straight away from him. With a rush his body moved backwards, slowed down, glided. Another thrown rock and another leap . . . another . . . another. Over his shoulder he could see out of the tail of his eye that he was proceeding in the right direction.

A short distance away he could see Vernon also heaving rocks. Another rock . . . . but this time his body did not slow to a glide. It kept on moving. He realized that he was falling, that he was influenced by gravity!

Sudden fear assailed him. Had he miscalculated? Had he been captured again by the first asteroid before the Twin had struck? Or had the Twin already struck?

Desperately he attempted to twist about. He succeeded and glimpsed jagged rock surface beneath him. The matter of landing without ripping his suit or cracking his helmets ports took all of his attention during the next few seconds.

He struck on his two feet, tumbled and rolled, his arms shielding his helmet. The ground seemed to be pitching and rocking. He could feel it quivering and moving beneath him. Like an earthquake. He gained his feet, but lost his balance again.

As he fell he caught sight of a familiar silvery shape looming large before him, swaying and rocking as the surface of the asteroid swayed and rocked. He was on the Twin, which must have already struck the first asteroid . . . . and the *Space Pup* was only a few rods away!

He spread his body flat on the surface to keep from being tossed about as the two slabs of rock, suddenly thrown together with terrific force, danced a jig in space.

Where was Vernon? Had he landed? Or was he miles behind? As soon as the Twin struck, the first asteroid also must have been knocked out of its orbit. Both must now be rushing through space. If Vernon had not been close enough to be captured by the gravity of the two, he would now be somewhere out there in the darkness alone, and perhaps helpless.

A wave of illness swept over Vince at that thought. Would he be able to find him in time? Or would he only pick up a corpse, a man floating in space, dead from lack of air?

He raised his head to stare at the *Space Pup* and a cry of gladness welled up into his throat. A man was crawling toward him over the weaving surface. Vernon! His brother . . . . safe!

Words beat in upon him.

"Vince, are you all right? Vince! Vince, you're all right, aren't you?"

"Sure, I'm all right, kid."

The two crawled together and locked arms.

"We took an awful chance, kid," said Vince.

"It was the only thing to do, "replied Vernon. "We couldn't stay and be smashed in the collision."

Arm in arm, they crawled over the buckling, gyrating world toward the *Space Pup*.

The Island of Unreason
by Edmond Hamilton

from WONDER STORIES, May 1933

Edmond Hamilton's writing career is as old as science fiction magazines themselves. His first appearance with "The Monster-God of Mamurth" was in *Weird Tales* for August 1926 when *Amazing Stories* was but five issues old. Over forty years later the May 1969 *Amazing Stories* carried his latest piece, "The Horror From the Magellanic". In between those two dates Hamilton has turned out a virtual library-full of short stories and novels running the entire gamut of imaginative fiction: from detective to horror, from super science fiction to mood sf.

And in each case it was nearly always Hamilton who started the trend. His first sale to *Weird Tales* was a novel "Across Space", the tale of a Martian colony on Easter Island that tries to draw Mars towards Earth so that the dying civilization can transfer planets. Out of such tales grew Hamilton's tendency to subject the Earth to imminent doom only to be saved at the eleventh hour by our hero. These tales, which were born in *Weird Tales* and later transferred to *Amazing Stories*, earned Hamilton the nickname of "World-destroyer".

Hamilton was born in Ohio on October 21st 1904, just two months after Clifford Simak who was some 500 miles away. Hamilton was twenty-one when Farnsworth Wright bought his first fiction, and his writing career was born. *Weird Tales* remained a major market for several years, and he never forsook it. His last original appearance in that magazine was with "The Watcher of the Ages" in the September 1948 issue. In 1930 Hamilton burst into sf magazines in a big way, and immediately his style began to alter, and new plots appeared. "The Man Who Saw The Future" (*Amazing*, October 1930) was a radical change, telling of a fifteenth century apothecary who is sentenced to death for his sorcery, when for no reason of his own he is temporarily transferred to the future. When Hornig's "New Policy" began at *Wonder Stories*, Hamilton experimented further and "The Island of Unreason" is proof of his popularity, whatever the style. In these pre-Hugo award days, a spasmodic Jules Verne Award was given to popular stories. The first winner was Hamilton, and the story was the one you are about to read.

The Director of City 72, North American Division 16, looked up enquiringly from his desk at his assistant.

"The next case is Allan Mann, Serial Number 2473R6," said the First Assistant Director. "The charge is breach of reason."

"The prisoner is ready?" asked the Director, and when his subordinate nodded he ordered, "Send him in."

The First Assistant Director went out and re-entered in a moment, followed by two guards who had the prisoner between them. He was a young man dressed in the regulation sleeveless white shirt and white shorts, with the blue square of the Mechanical Department on his shoulder.

He looked a little uncertainly around the big office, at the keyboards of the big calculating and predicting machines, at the televisor disks through which could be seen cities half around the world, and at the broad windows that looked out across the huge cubical metal buildings of City 72.

The Director read from a sheet on his desk. "Allan Mann, Serial Number 2473R6, was apprehended two days ago on a charge of breach of reason.

"The specific charge is that Allan Mann, who had been working two years on development of a new atomic motor, refused to turn over his work to Michael Russ, Serial Number 1877R6, when ordered to do so by a superior. He could give no reasonable cause for his refusal but stated only that he had developed the new motor for two years and wanted to finish it himself. As this was a plain breach of reason, officers were called."

The Director looked up at the prisoner. "Have you any defense, Allan Mann?"

The young man flushed. "No, sir, I have not. I wish only to say that I realize now I was wrong."

"Why did you rebel against your superior's order? Did he not tell you that Michael Russ was better fitted than you to finish development of your motor?"

"He did, yes," Allan Mann answered. "But I had worked on the motor so long I wanted very much to finish it myself, even though it took longer—I realize it was unreasonable of me—"

The Director laid down the sheet and bent earnestly forward. "You are right, Allan Mann, it was unreasonable of you. It was a breach of reason and as such, it was a blow at the very foundation of our modern world-civilization!"

He raised a lean finger in emphasis. "What is it, Allan Mann, that has built up the present world-state out of a mass of warring nations? What has eliminated conflict, fear, poverty, hardship from the world? What but reason?

"Reason has raised man from the beast-like level he formerly occupied to his present status. Why, in the old days of unreason the very ground on which this city now stands was occupied by a city called New York where men struggled and strove with each other blindly and without cooperation and with infinite waste and toil.

"All that has been changed by reason. The old emotions which twisted and warped men's minds have been overruled and we listen now only to the calm dictates of reason. Reason has brought us up from the barbarism of the twentieth century and to commit a breach of reason has become a serious crime. For it is a crime that aims directly at the demolition of our world-order."

Beneath the Director's calm statement, Allan Mann wilted. "I realize that that is so, sir," he said. "It is my hope that my breach of reason will be regarded only as a temporary aberration."

"I do so regard it," the Director said. "I am sure that by now you realize the wrongness of unreasonable conduct.

"But," he continued, "this explanation of your act does not excuse it. The fact remains that you have committed a breach of reason and that you must be corrected in the way specified by law."

"What is this way of correction?" asked Allan Mann.

The Director considered him. "You are not the first one to commit a breach of reason, Allan Mann. In the past more than one person has let irrational emotions sway him. These atavastic returns to unreason are becoming rarer but they still occur.

"Long ago we devised a plan for the correction of these *unreasonables*, as we call them. We do not punish them, of course, for to inflict punishment on anyone for wrong-doing would be itself unreasonable. We try instead to cure them. We send them to what we call the island of unreason.

"That is a small island a few hundred miles out at sea from this coast. There are taken all the unreasonables and there they are left. There is no form of government on the island and only unreasonables live there. They are not given any of the comforts of life which human reason has devised but instead must live there as best they may in primitive fashion."

"If they fight or attack each other, it is nothing to us. If they steal from each other, we care not. For living like that, in a place where there is no rule of reason, they soon come to see what society would be like without reason. They see and never forget and most of them when their sentence is finished and they are brought back are only too glad for the rest of their lives to live in reasonable fashion. Though a few incorrigible unreasonables must stay on the island all their lives.

"It is to this island that all guilty of breach of reason must be sent. And so as provided by law, I must sentence you to go there."

"To the island of unreason?" Allan Mann said, dismay plain on his face. "But for how long?"

"We never tell those sent there how long their sentence is to be," the Director told him. "We want them to feel that they have a lifetime ahead of them on the island and this brings the lesson further home to them. When your sentence is finished, the guard-flier that takes you there will go there to bring you back."

He stood up. "Have you any complaint to make against this sentence?"

Allan Mann was silent, then spoke in subdued voice. "No, sir, it is but reasonable that I be corrected according to custom."

The Director smiled. "I am glad to see that you are already recovering. When your sentence has expired I hope to see you completely cured."

The guard-flier split the air like a slim metal torpedo as it hurtled eastward over the gray ocean. Long minutes before the coastline had faded from sight behind, and now beneath the noonday sun there extended to the horizons only the gray wastes of the empty ocean.

Allan Mann regarded it from the flier's window with deepening dismay. Reared in the great cities like every other member of civilized humanity, he had an inborn dislike of this solitude. He sought to evade it temporarily by conversing with the two guards who, with a pilot, were the flier's other occupants. But Allan found that they disliked to talk much to unreasonables.

"It'll be in sight in a few minutes," one of them said in answer to his question. "Soon enough for you, I guess."

"Where do you land me there?" Allan asked. "There's some kind of city there?"

"A city on the island of unreason?" The guard shook his head. "Of course not. Those unreasonables couldn't cooperate long enough on anything to build any kind of a city."

"But there's some sort of a place for us to live, isn't there?" asked Allan Mann anxiously.

"No place but what you find for yourself," said the guard unsympathetically. "Some of the unreasonables do have a kind of village of huts but some of them just run wild."

"But even those must sleep and eat *somewhere*," insisted Allan with all the firm faith of his kind in the omnipresence of bed and food and hygienic amusements provided by a paternal government.

"They sleep in the best places they can find, I suppose," said the guard. "They eat fruits and berries and kill small animals and eat them—"

"Eat animals?" Allan Mann, of the world's fiftieth generation of vegetarians, was so shocked by the revolting thought that he sat silent until the pilot droned over his shoulder, "Island ahead!"

He looked anxiously down with the guards as the flier circled and came back and dropped in a spiral toward the island.

It was not a large island, just an oblong bit of land that lay on the great ocean like a sleeping sea-monster. Dense green forest covered its low hills and shallow ravines and extended down to the shelving sandy beaches.

To Allan Mann it looked savage, wild, forbidding.

He could see smoke rising in several thin curls from the island's western end but this evidence of man's presence repelled rather than reassured him. Those smokes came from crude fires where men were perhaps scorching and eating the flesh of lately-living things—

The guard-flier dipped lower, shot along the beach and came to rest with its vertical air-jets spuming up sand.

"Out with you," said the chief guard as he opened the door. "Can stay here but a moment."

Allan Mann, stepping down onto the hot sand, clung to the

flier's door as a last link to civilization. "You'll come back for
me when my sentence is up?" he cried. "You'll know where to
find me?"

"We'll find you if you're on the island but don't worry about
that—maybe your sentence was life," grinned the chief guard.
"If it wasn't, we'll get you unless some unreasonable has killed
you."

"Killed me?" said Allan, aghast. "Do you mean to say that
they kill each other?"

"They do, and with pleasure," said the guard. "Better get
off this beach before you're seen. Remember, you're not living
with reasonable people now!"

With the slam of its door the guard-flier's jets roared and it
shot upward. Allan Mann watched stupefiedly as it rose, circled
in the sunshine like a gleaming gull, and then headed back
westward. Sickly, he watched it vanish, westward toward the
land where people were reasonable and life went safely and
smoothly without the dangers that threatened him here.

With a start Allan Mann realized that he was increasing his
danger by remaining out on the open beach where he might
easily be seen by anyone in the woods. He could not conceive
why any of the unreasonables might want to kill him but he
feared the worst. Allan Mann started on a run up the beach
toward the woods.

His feet slipped in the hot sands and though Allan was
physically perfect like all other citizens of the modern world, he
found progress difficult. Each moment he expected to see a horde
of yelling unreasonables appear along the beach. He quite
forgot that he was a condemned unreasonable himself, and saw
himself as a lone representative of civilization marooned on this
savage island.

He reached the woods and plumped down behind a bush,
panting for breath and looking this way and that. The forest
was very hot and silent, a place of green gloom pillared by bars
of golden sunlight that struck down through chinks in the leafy
canopy above. Allan heard birds chittering around him.

He considered his predicament. He must live on this island
for an unguessable length of time. It might be a month, a year,
even many years. He saw now how true was the fact that the
prisoner's ignorance of his sentence's length made it all the more
felt. Why, he might, as the guard had said, have to spend all
his life on the island!

He tried to tell himself that this was improbable and that his sentence could not be so severe. But no matter what its length, he must prepare to live here. The essentials were shelter and food, and escape from the other unreasonables. He decided that he would first find some secluded spot for a shelter, construct one, and then try to find berries or fruits such as the guard had mentioned. Meat was not to be thought of without revulsion.

Cautiously Allan Mann got to his feet and looked about. The green forest seemed still and peaceful but he peopled it with a myriad dangers. From behind every bush menacing eyes might be spying on him. Nevertheless, he must win to a more hidden spot and so he started in through the woods, determining to keep away from the island's western end where he had seen the smokes.

Allan Mann had gone but a dozen fearful steps when he stopped short, whirled. Through the brush someone was crashing toward him.

His panic-stricken mind had not the time to think of flight before the running figure emerged from the brush beside him, then at sight of him recoiled.

It was a girl clad in a stained, ragged tunic. Her limbs showed brown below its tattered hem, her black hair was cut very short, and as she threw herself back from him in alarm a short spear in her right hand flashed up ready to dart toward him.

Had he made a move toward her the spear would have been driven at him; but he stood as quivering and startled as she. Gradually as they confronted each other, the fact that he was harmless became apparent to the girl and some of the terror left her eyes.

Yet with her gaze still upon him she backed cautiously away until just behind her were some dense bushes. With a quick escape thus assured her, she surveyed him.

"You're new?" she said. "I saw the flier come."

"New?" said Allan mystified.

"New to the island, I mean," she said quickly. "They just left you, didn't they?"

Allan nodded. He was still trembling slightly. "Yes, they just left me. It was breach of reason—"

"Of course," she said. "That's what we're all here for, we unreasonables. Those old fogies of directors send someone here every few days or so."

At this heretical description of the executives of the reasonable world, Allan Mann stared. "Why shouldn't they send them?" he demanded. "It's only fair they should correct unreasonables."

Her bright black eyes widened. "*You* don't talk like an unreasonable," she accused.

"I should hope not," he returned. "I committed a breach of reason but I realize it and I'm sorry I did it."

"Oh," she said, and seemed disappointed. "What's your name? Mine's Lita."

"Mine is Allan Mann. My serial number—" He stopped.

A bird had called loudly back in the woods and the sound had seemed to recall something to the girl and bring fear back into her eyes.

"We'd better get out of here," she said quickly. "Hara will be along here after me—he was chasing me."

"Chasing you?" Allan remembered with a cold feeling the guard's warning. "Who is Hara?"

"Hara's boss of the island—he's a lifer they just brought a few weeks ago but he's beaten all the strongest men here."

"You mean that they *fight* here to see who is to be the leader?" Allan asked incredulously. Lita nodded.

"Of course they do. This isn't back in civilization where the best mind ranks highest, you know. And Hara's after me."

"He wants to kill you?"

"Of course not! He wants me for his woman and I won't consent. I never will, either." The black eyes flashed.

Allan Mann felt that he had strayed into some mystifiying new world. "His woman?" he said with knitted brows.

Lita nodded impatiently. "When people here mate there's no Eugenic Board to assign them to each other so they simply fight for mates.

"Hara has been after me and I won't have him. He got angry today and said he'd make me but I fled the village and when he and some of the others started after me I was—*listen!*"

Lita stopped with the tense command and Allan, listening with her, heard from somewhere in the woods distant trampling and crashing, a hoarse voice calling and others answering.

"They're coming!" Lita cried. "Come on, quick!"

"But they can't—" Allan started vainly to say, and then was cut off as he found himself running with the girl through the woods.

Branches tore at his shorts and briars pricked his legs savagely as they forced through the brush. Lita led inward toward the island's center and Allan struggled to keep beside her.

His muscles were in the pink of condition but he now found

that running from danger through a forest was oddly different from running beneath the sunlamps of one of the great city gymnasiums. There was a tightness across his chest, a cold at his spine, as he heard the hoarse voices behind.

Lita looked back, her face white through its brown, as she and Allan ran. Allan Mann told himself that there was no reason why he should follow this girl into trouble. Before he could formulate the thought further they emerged into a small clearing just as from one side of it there crashed another man.

A bull-like roar of triumph went up and Allan Mann saw that the man was a barrel-bodied, stocky individual with flaming red hair on his head and chest, his hard face alight. He grasped Lita's arm as the girl swiftly shrank back beside Allan.

"Hara!" she panted, trying in vain to break free.

"Ran away, eh?" he said savagely, and then his eyes took in Allan Mann. "And with this white-faced sheep!"

"Well, we'll see whether he's good enough to take a girl away from Hara!" he added. "You've no spear or club so we'll make it fists!"

He tossed his own club and spear to the ground and advanced with balled firsts on Allan. "What do you mean?" asked Allan dazedly.

"Fight, of course!" bellowed Hara. "You wanted this girl and you can fight me for her!"

Allan Mann thought swiftly. Against this brutal fighter he would have small chance—now, if ever, he must use the reason that is man's advantage over the brute. "But I don't want her!" he said. "I don't want to fight for her!"

Hara stopped in sheer surprise and Allan saw Lita's dark eyes stare at him. "Don't want to fight?" cried the other. "Then run, rat!" And as he snarled it in contempt he turned to grasp the girl.

As he turned Allan stooped swiftly, scooped up his heavy club and slammed it against the back of Hara's neck. The red-head went down like a sack of meal.

"Come on!" cried Allan tensely to Lita. "Before he comes to we can get away—quick!"

They rushed in to the brush. Soon they heard the calling voices become suddenly noisy, then die away. They stopped, panting.

"That was brain-work," said Allan Mann exultantly. "He won't come to for an hour."

Lita looked scornfully at him. "That wasn't fair fighting," she accused.

Allan Mann was aghast. "Fair fighting?" he repeated. "But

surely when you wanted to get away from him—you didn't expect me to fight him with my fists—"

"It wasn't fair," she repeated. "You hit him when he wasn't looking and that's cowardly."

If Allan Mann had not been super-civilized he would have sworn.

"But what's wrong about it?" he asked bewilderedly. "Surely it's only reasonable for me to use cunning against his strength?"

"We don't care much on this island about being reasonable—you ought to know that," she told him. "But we do believe in fighting fair."

"In that case you can get away from him the next time yourself," he said furiously. "You unreasonables—"

A thought struck him. "How did you come to be sent to this island anyway?"

Lita smiled. "I'm a lifer. So are Hara and most of the others at the village."

"A lifer? What did you do to get a life-sentence in this horrible place?"

"Well, six months ago the Eugenic Board in my city assigned me a mate. I refused to have him. The Board had me charged with breach of reason and when I persisted in my refusal I was sentenced here for life."

"No wonder," breathed Allan Mann. "To refuse the mate the Board assigned—I never heard of such a thing! Why did you do it?"

"I didn't like the way he looked at me," said Lita, as though that explained everything.

Allan Mann shook his head helplessly. He could not understand the thought-processes of these unreasonables.

"We'd better get on into the island," Lita was saying. "Hara will come to in a little while and he will be very angry with you and will want to catch you."

At that thought Allan's blood ran cold. He could picture the big Hara in bull-like rage and the thought of himself in the grip of those hairy hands was terrifying. He stood up with Lita and looked apprehensively around.

"Which way?" he asked in a whisper.

She nodded toward the island's center. "The woods in there will be best. We'll have to avoid the village."

They started through the woods. Lita went first, her spear ready at all times. Allan followed, and after a few minutes he picked up a heavy section of hard wood that would make an effective club at need He held the weapon awkwardly as they went on.

They were penetrating into deeper woods, and it was all a strange world to Allan. He knew forests only as seen from a flier, green masses that lay between the great cities. Now he was down in one, part of it. The birds and insects, the small animals in the brush, all of these were new to him. More than once Lita had to caution him as he made a noise in stepping on dry sticks. The girl went as quietly through the woods as a cat.

They climbed a slope and went over its ridge. On the ridge Lita halted to point out to him the clearing at the island's west end that held the village, a score or more of solid log cabins. Smoke curled from their chimneys and Allan Mann saw men standing about and children playing in the sunlit clearing. He was deeply interested by this village But Lita led onward.

The woods about them were now so dense that Allan felt more safe. He had acquired a certain confidence of step. Then he was suddenly startled out of it. As a rabbit dashed by under their feet, bolting for cover, Lita's short spear flashed like a streak of light. The rabbit rolled over and over and then lay still.

The girl ran and picked it up, turned and held up the furry thing with her face exultant. It would be their supper, she told him. Allan stared at her incredulously. He felt as revolted by her act as his ancestors of generations before would have been by a murder. He tried not to show Lita how he regarded her.

When they reached a tiny gully deep in the woods, Lita stopped. The sun was sinking and already darkness was invading the forest. They would spend the night there, Lita told him, and she began construction of two tiny branch-shelters.

Under her orders Allan tore branches from the trees and stacked them. More than once she had to correct him and he felt ridiculously incompetent. When they had finished, before them stood two fairly tight little huts. Allan, looking at these shelters that had been brought out of nothing, for the first time felt a certain respect for the girl.

He watched her, as slowly with stone and steel she took from a pouch at her belt, she constructed a fire. He found the business of eliciting and nursing the sparks intensely engrossing. Soon she had a tiny little blaze, too small to show smoke above the darkening woods or to be seen for far.

She calmly cleaned the rabbit then. Allan watched her in entranced horror. When she had finished she began to roast it.

She offered him a red bit on a stick, to roast for himself. "I can't eat that!" he said sickly.

Lita looked at him, then smiled. "I was the same way when I came to the island," she said. "All of us are but we get to like it." "Like eating the flesh of another living creature?" Allan said. "I'll never like that."

"You will when you're hungry enough," she said calmly, and went on roasting the rest of the rabbit.

Allan, watching her eat the browned meat, became aware that he was already very hungry. He had not eaten since that morning.

He contrasted that morning meal in the Nutrition Dispensary, with its automatic service and mushy predigested foods, with this place.

It was too dark for him to look for berries. He sat watching the girl eat. The smell of the scorched flesh, which at first he had found revolting, did not now seem so bad.

"Go ahead, eat it," Lita told him, handing him one of the roasted bits. "No matter how bad it is, it's only reasonable to eat anything that will keep you living, isn't it?"

Allan's face cleared and he nodded troubledly. It certainly was only reasonable to eat what was at hand in necessity. "I don't think I can do it, though," he said, eyeing the browned bit.

He bit gingerly into it. At the thought that he had in his mouth the flesh of another once-living creature, his stomach almost revolted. But with an effort he swallowed the bit.

It was hot and did not seem unpleasant. There were certain juices—quite unlike the foods of the Nutrition Dispensary, he thought. He reached doubtfully for another piece.

From behind her lashes with a secret smile Lita watched him eat another piece and then another of the rabbit. His jaws ached with the unaccustomed labor of chewing but his stomach sent up messages of gladness. He did not stop until all of the rabbit was gone and then he went back to some of the bones he had already discarded and polished them off more thoroughly.

He looked up at last, greasy of hands, to meet Lita's enigmatic expression. Allan flushed.

"It was only reasonable to eat all of it, since it had to be eaten," he defended.

"Did you like it?" she said.

"What has liking got to do with the nutritive qualities of food?" he countered. Lita laughed.

They put out the fire and retired to the two huts. Lita kept her spear but he retained his club. She showed him how to close up his hut once he was inside.

For a time Allan Mann lay awake in the darkness on the branch-bed she had built. It was very uncomfortable, he found.

He could not but contrast it with his neat bed back in the dormitory that was his home in City 72. Now long would it be before he was again in it, he wondered. How long—

Allan sat up, rubbing his eyes, to find bright sunlight filtering through the interstices of his leafy shelter. He had slept on the branches after all, and soundly. Yet he felt stiff and sore as he got to his feet and went out.

It was still early morning though the sunlight was bright. The other hut was empty and Lita was not anywhere in sight.

Allan felt a sudden sense of alarm. Had anything happened to his companion?

He was about to risk calling aloud when bushes rustled behind him and as he spun about she emerged from them. Her hands were full of bright red little berries.

"Breakfast," she smiled at him. "It's all there is."

They ate them. "What are we going to do now?" asked Allan.

Lita's brows knit. "I don't dare to go back to the village yet for Hara might be there. Neither can you go now after what you did."

"I don't want to go there," Allan protested quickly. He had no desire to face any more unreasonables like the one he had met.

"We'd better keep moving on into the island," she said. "We can live for a while in the woods, anyway."

They started on, the girl with her spear and Allan bringing his rude club.

The soreness and stiffness quickly left Allan's muscles as they moved on. He found a certain pleasure in this tramp through the sun-dappled woods.

They heard no sign of pursuit and relaxed their cautiousness of progress a little. It was a mistake, as Allan Mann found when something struck him a numbing blow on the left arm and he spun to find two ragged men charging fiercely from a clump of brush.

One of them had flung his club to stun Allan. The other now rushed forward with bludgeon upraised to do what his companion had failed to do. There was no possible chance to flee or to use strategy and with the blind desperate terror of a cornered animal

Allan Mann struck wildly out with his own club at the onrushing attacker.

He knocked the club spinning from the other's hand by his first wild blow. He heard Lita cry out but he was now gone amuck with terror, was showering crazy blows upon his opponent. Then Allan became suddenly aware that the other was no longer standing before him but lay stunned at his feet. The second man was running to pick up his club.

Lita's spear flashed at the running man and missed. But as the man bent for his weapon Allan swung his club in a mighty blow.

It missed the stooping man by a foot but the terrific swing seemed to unnerve him for he abandoned his weapon and took to his heels, running back into the woods.

"Hara!" he yelled hoarsely as he ran. "Hara, here they are!"

Lita ran to the side of the panting Allan. 'You're not hurt?" she cried. "You beat them both—it was wonderful!"

But Allan Mann's sudden insanity had left him and he felt only terror. "He'll bring Hara and the rest here! he cried. "We've got to flee—"

The girl picked up her spear and they hastened on into the forest. They heard other calling voices behind them now.

"You needn't be so afraid when you can fight like that!" Lita exclaimed as they hurried on, but Allan shook his head.

"I didn't know what I was doing! This terrible place with its fighting and turmoil and craziness—It's even got me acting as unreasonably as the others! If I ever get away from here—"

The calling voices were louder and closer behind them as the two ran on. There seemed a dozen or more of them.

Allan thought he could distinguish the bull-like voice of Hara. At thought of that red-haired giant his body went taut.

He and the girl stumbled down still another wooded slope and emerged suddenly onto an open beach, the blue sea beyond it.

"They've driven us clear to the eastern end of the island!" Allan cried. "We can't go any further and we can't hope to slip back through them!"

Lita halted, seemed to make sudden decision. "Yes, you can get back through them!" she told him. "I'll stay out here on the beach and they'll rush out toward me when they see me. It'll give you a chance to get back through the woods!"

"But I can't go like that and leave you here for Hara to capture!" said Allan in dismay.

"Why not? It wouldn't be reasonable for you to stay here and meet Hara, would it? You know what he would do to you!"

Allan shook his head troubled. "No, that wouldn't be reasonable for it wouldn't do you any good. But even though it's unreasonable I don't like to go—"

"Go and go quickly!" Lita urged, pushing him back toward the dense woods. "They'll be here in a moment!"

Allan Mann stepped reluctantly toward the woods, entered the concealing brush. He stopped, looked back to where Lita stood on the beach. He could now hear a tramping of brush as the pursuers approached.

He felt somehow that there was a defect in his reasoning, something wrong. Yet search as he might he could find nothing unreasonable in his conduct. He had never seen this girl before the preceding day, she was a life-term unreasonable, and altogether it would be completely irrational for him to imperil himself further with the atavistic Hara for her sake. This was indisputable yet—

A big form crashed through the brush close beside the hiding Allan and a triumphant bellow went up from Hara as he merged onto the beach and saw Lita. Before she could turn on him Hara had grasped her arm, tossed her spear aside. The next instant all of Allan's faculty of reason was forgotten as with a crazy red tide of fury running through his veins he leapt out onto the beach.

"Let her go!" he yelled and charged on Hara with uplifted club.

The red-haired giant spun about, released the girl and as Allan swung in a mad blow struck out with his own club, shattering Allan's weapon with stunning force and knocking him back onto the sand.

"So it's you!" gritted Hara. He dropped his own club, clenched his huge fists. "All right, get up and take what's coming to you this time!"

Allan felt as though some resistless outside force was bringing him to his feet and hurling him toward Hara.

He saw the hard, scowling face through a red mist and then it shifted and as his clenched hand suddenly hurt him he was aware that he had struck Hara a stinging blow in the face.

Hara roared, swung furiously. Allan felt a dazing impact and then was aware that he was scrambling up again from the sand and that something warm was running over his cheek.

He flung in upon Hara and this time raised both clenched hands and hammered with them at the red-head's face.

Something hard hit his chest with stunning force, and the world, the beach, the blue sea and sky rocked wildly.

His vision cleared momentarily and he saw Hara's raging face and flailing fists, glimpsed beyond him other ragged men who were yelling as they watched, and then again the feel of hot sand on his back made him aware that he was on the ground and made him struggle up and forward.

He jabbed blindly with his fists into the red haze in which Hara's face seemed dancing. There was something running in his eyes that kept him from seeing well but it seemed to him that Hara's face was bloody.

Something colliding with his head forced him to his knees but he swayed up and struck again with both fists. Now Hara's eyes held astonishment as much as anger. He was backing away as Allan swung crazily.

Allan felt his strength fast running away, hunched himself and then drove forward both fists waist-high with all the weight of his body behind them. He felt smashing blows on mouth and ear as he struck, but in the next instant heard a gasp and glimpsed Hara with face gray toppling over on his side.

Then Allan was conscious of the bright sand of the beach running up to meet his face. There were men yelling and Lita's voice crying something.

He was aware of Lita's arms supporting him, her hands wiping something from his face—her hands—

Her hands became suddenly big and rough. He opened his eyes and it was not Lita at all but a white-clad guard who stood over him.

Allan stared beyond him and saw not beach and sea but the metal-walled interior of a small flier. He could see the back of a pilot sitting in the nose of the craft and could hear the roar of air outside.

"Conscious at last, eh?" said the guard. "You've been out for half an hour."

"But where—how—" Allan struggled to say.

"You don't remember?" the guard said. "I'm not surprised—you were just passing out when we got there. You see, your sentence on the island was only one day. We came to get you and found you'd apparently been having trouble with one of the other unreasonables, but we picked you up and started back. We're almost back to City 72 now."

Allan Mann sat up, utterly dismayed. "But Lita! Where's Lita?"

The guard stared. "You mean the girl unreasonable who was there? Why, she's still there, of course. She's a lifer. She made quite a fuss when we dropped down and got you."

"But I don't want to leave Lita there!" cried Allan. "I tell you, I don't want to leave her!"

"Don't want to leave her?" repeated the astonished guard. "Listen, you're being unreasonable again. If you keep it up you'll get another sentence to the island and it'll be more than a day!"

Allan looked keenly at him. "You mean that if I'm unreasonable enough they'd send me back to the island—for life?"

"They sure would!" the guard declared. "You're mighty lucky to get off with one day there this time."

Allan Mann did not answer nor did he speak again until their destination was reached and he faced the Director once more.

The Director looked at his bruised face and smiled. "Well, it seems that even one day on the island has taught you what it is to live without reason," he said.

"Yes, it's taught me that," Allan answered.

"I am glad of that," the Director told him. "You realize now that my only motive in sending you there was to cure you of unreasonable tendencies."

Allan nodded quietly. "It would be about the most unreasonable thing possible for me to resent your efforts to cure and help me, wouldn't it?"

The Director smiled complacently. "Yes, my boy, that would certainly be the height of unreason."

"I thought it would," said Allan Mann in the same quiet voice.

His fist came back—

The guard were wholly unsympathetic as their flier sped with Allan Mann for a second time toward the island.

"It's your own fault you got a life-sentence on the island," the chief guard said. "Whoever heard of anyone doing such a crazy thing as knocking down a Director?"

But Allan, unlistening, was gazing eagerly ahead. "There it is!" he bawled joyfully. "There's the island!"

"And you're glad to get back?" The chief guard gave up in disgust. "Of all the unreasonables we ever carried, you're the worst."

The flier sank down through the warm afternoon sunlight and poised again above the sandy beach.

Allan leapt out and started up the beach. He did not hear

what the guard shouted as the flier rose and departed.

Nor did he look after it as it vanished this time. He pressed along the beach and then through the woods toward the island's western end.

He came into the clearing where was the village of cabins. There were people in the clearing and one of them saw Allan Mann, ran toward him with a glad cry. It was a girl—it was Lita!

They met and somehow Allan found it natural to be holding her in the curve of his arm as she clung to him.

"They took you away this morning!" she was crying. "I thought you'd never come back—"

"I've come back to stay," Allan told her. "I'm a lifer now, too." He said it almost proudly.

"You a lifer?" Rapidly he told her what he had done.

"I didn't want to stay back there. I like it better here!" he finished.

"So you're back, are you?" It was Hara's bull-voice that sounded close beside them and Allan spun with a snarl on his lips.

But Hara was grinning across all his battered face as he came forward and extended his hand to Allan. "I'm glad that you're back! You're the first man ever to knock me out and I like you!"

Allan stared dazedly. "But you surely don't like me because I did that? It's not reasonable—"

A chorus of laughs from the men and women gathered around cut him short. "Remember that you're living on the island of unreason, lad!" cried Hara.

"But Lita?" exclaimed Allan. "You can't have her—you—"

"Calm yourself," advised Hara with a grin. He beckoned and a pert blond girl came out of the others to him. "Look what was left by a flier while you were gone, and with a life-sentence too. I forgot all about Lita when I saw her, didn't I, darling?"

"You'd better," she advised him, and then smiled at Allan. "We're getting married this evening."

"Married?" he repeated, and Hara nodded.

"Sure, by the old ceremonies like we use here. We've a religious preacher here that was sent here because religion's unreasonable too, and he performs them."

Allan Mann turned to the girl in his arm, a great new idea dawning across his brain. "Then Lita, you and I—"

That evening after the double marriage had been performed and those in the village were engaged in noisy and completely irrational merrymaking, Allan and Lita sat with Hara and his bride on a bluff at the island's western end, looking toward the last glow of sunset's red embers in the darkening sky.

"Some day," said Hara, "when there's a lot more of us unreasonables we'll go back there and take the world and make it all unreasonable and inefficient and human again."

"Some day—" Allan murmured.

One Prehistoric Night
by Philip Barshofsky

from WONDER STORIES, November 1934

Sometimes in sf a writer will appear with a captivating story, and readers will wait impatiently for his next attempt to see if he can possibly beat his maiden tale. And yet one more story would eventually appear and then nothing. The author would disappear into oblivion. Such occurrences are common, and are often puzzling.

Philip Barshofsky was such a case. "One Prehistoric Night" marked his debut and caught the cover of the November 1934 *Wonder Stories*. It was overshadowed in that issue by the appearance of Stanley G. Weinbaum's "The Valley of Dreams", his sequel to "A Martian Odyssey". But even with that competition, Barshofsky's story received much favourable comment. And yet the name Barshofsky only appeared once again, in the last Gernsback *Wonder Stories*, in March 1936 with "The Imperfect Guess", a humorous story satirizing sf writers. An amusing tale but not memorable.

One assumption could be that Barshofsky was a pen name for a better known author. It was later discovered that whoever had written the Barshofsky stories had also written stories under the name of Philip Jacques Bartel. Bartel had appeared for the first time in that same November 1934 *Wonder Stories* with the intriguing "Twenty Five Centuries Late", and had had several other stories in both *Wonder* and *Amazing*.

But who was the real author? When it was finally revealed that the man behind the pseudonyms was a certain M. M. Kaplan, many shoulders were shrugged. Kaplan is definitely the mystery man of this collection. As Bartel he would last appear in the first issue of Hornig's *Future Fiction* in November

1939 with "The Infinite Eye", and since then nothing.

Such mysteries are what make science fiction fascinating. Who was M. M. Kaplan? What made him choose such Muscovian and Gallic pen names? Did he write other sf under even more obscure pseudonyms? I hope to find answers to these questions one day. In the meantime we have stories like "One Prehistoric Night" to remember him by.

With a reverberating roar, a huge torpedo-shaped body leaped up out of the dim steam-laden horizon and came rushing towards a large and rugged island, followed by a fiery tail and leaving behind a trail of falling sparks. The piercing rays of the noonday sun picked up bright reflections from the surface of the hurtling metal monster. They also showed that the strange visitor bore orange and green markings. The noisy arrival had four rounded, metal "fins" that made it appear like some great arrow afire. The fins all began at the blunt prow ending in a slope against the side of the craft, and appeared to be used as observatories with perfectly transparent ends.

The rear part of the rocket-ship sprouted many propulsion tubes. These now rocked the quiet waters with a thunderous concussion. From the center of the blunt nose and the under and side parts, there also extended short tubes to be used in maneuvering the space craft.

The island, its destination, which was surrounded by almost a world of water, (being about the only piece of habitable land on the planet) bore gigantic growths that towered toward the large, blazing red sun. Its surface shook to the heavy footfalls of frightfully crude creatures, that seemed to be some grim experiment of Nature.

Amid heartbeats of thunderous noises, the rocket-ship shot down toward the foliage-covered ground and skimmed over the green tops. Upon reaching an open space where trees and ferns had surrendered the ground to a wide patch of sand, it landed in a burst of fire that somewhat softened its earthward plunge.

At the immediate silence of the ship's propulsion tubes, other noises quickly became perceptible. Strange noises that having been drowned out at the ship's arrival, now rose vigorously into the humid air. From far and near came the hissing and shrieking of monstrous reptiles—reptiles that infested and reigned supreme on this world millions of years ago. Millions of years ago, in the Jurassic period, they lived—a span of years which took up about six per cent of the life of the earth.

The heavy landing of the space-ship shook the ground, and before long a group of tall trees hid the approach of an inquisitive allosaurus, that behind the outermost fringe of trees came to rest. With its comparatively small but strong forelegs, which rarely, if ever touched the earth, it grasped a tall, thin tree to balance itself, while it gazed hesitantly upon this strange being.

The reptile carnivore seemed to pay not the slightest notice to a large rent in its side, from which blood freely flowed. Now and then it turned its head sidewise like a bird to eye the uneven ground, as if it awaited the earth to betray, by its involuntary tremors, the approach of some creature that the cold-blooded reptile could better understand than that large egg-like thing. Overhead a shrilling archaeopteryx, partly hidden by the fogs that rose from the warm earth, attracted the momentary gaze of the huge sentinel. Not knowing whether to brave the sudden terrific heat, which the fires of the rocket-ship had created, or to abandon the glittering, quiet thing before it and hunt elsewhere, the monster stood for a moment perplexed.

Suddenly, in its dilemma, the hungry allosaurus felt the ground vibrate to the dancing feet of some prehistoric combatants that fought for life and food. That signal decided the question. Instantly the short-witted reptile forgot the metal arrival as it turned and made off in the directions of the battle. A sole breeze wafted to its nostrils the enticing odor of blood that had already been carelessly spilt.

With its powerful hind legs, which were almost as long as its body, allosaurus leaped in tremendous bounds, covering ground with amazing speed as a frothy, white foam fell from its long, hissing jaws. Already the dying screams of one of the combatants pierced the air.

The ground heaved and trembled as from all over creatures hurried toward the scene of the battle. Soon the foggy air was filled with the shrilling and screaming of the hungry monsters of an infant planet.

Animals mostly of a smaller type crowded and soon filled a small clearing that was made by the careless fighters in their efforts. Many small individuals were crushed to death beneath the ponderous feet of their larger brothers in the rush for food, and provided another mouthful or so. Here an angry reptile tore into bits a small scavenger that stole a piece of meat from its possession, and in doing so added to its meal. From above, powerful jaws snapped off its head in turn. Thus more meat was provided.

Usually the smaller creatures grabbed a bit of meat and dashed off with it, fearful of losing it to some larger animal while the larger creatures remained, surer of their ground. As the noises increased in volume, hungry mouths fed and empty bellies became filled.

Slowly the blood-red sun set, leaving the steaming forests solely in the possession of the noisy dinosaurs that were the inhabitants. The metal alien lay beneath the subdued glare of the stately moon. With the parting of day, a round door, close to the ground, slid aside and an amazingly small creature stepped out, the door closing immediately behind it. The four-foot arrival, without any noticeable form of physical defence, could hardly have been any more than a mouthful for any of the giant preying carnivora.

An orange skull-cap covered a large head from two beady eyes set under a high forehead, to the back of a short, thick neck. Two pairs of arms and one pair of legs betrayed the fact that this creature had probably evolved from some six-legged creation. A thin green metal tunic covered the remainder of the short body. From a thick black belt, two blunt hooks supported a like number of small, round tubes, and one of the thin arms always hung near them. The little being seemed ready for any form of attack as its watchfulness plainly showed.

The strange creature whistled a few notes which, explained, would read as, "Come out. It is cooler than when the sun shone."

As the door again opened, another and a third of the like species stepped out slowly, hesitantly. They formed a silent group not far from the space-craft, while they gazed up at the planet Mars hanging like a crimson jewel in the sky. One began to whistle, he who had first stepped forth from the ship.

"Our mother planet. See how she looks at us with a burning eye."

"From here we cannot see the misery on the faces of our people," answered he who had first stepped out after the whistle.

"Yet," the first one whistled, "that bright world will soon be uninhabitable and might have been the death of our race had we not discovered this more habitable world.

"Our scientists were right when they explained that this planet wouldn't be too hot for us; and everyone thought we should roast here. Its daylight cannot be much hotter than its night, so as far as heat is concerned, this planet will suit us."

A silence reigned, pierced by reptilic yells from the outside, to which these creatures paid no attention. Each was enveloped in his own thoughts—tremendous thoughts. A world was dying and a desperate race sought a more habitable place, one where their lives would not be endangered. Now a suitable planet was discovered, one that would safely harbor their race. But what form of life existed on this planet?

In a happy frame of mind, the third creature whistled a series of short notes.

"The atmosphere is pure and innocent in composition here, free from any form of contamination which years of needless warfare caused on our world. The ocean water can be utilized by our motors and the ever-rising steam can be caught and condensed to drinkable liquid, being of the same composition that we are used to. The soil is very active, and as for the greater gravity, these specially constructed black belts will take care of that until we become more accustomed to it.

"At the rising of the sun, we will plant the seeds of the wonderful quanghnni tree and some others to see if they bear on this soil the same good, sweet fruit that they bear on Mars. Soon we will fortify ourselves, for who knows what creatures inhabit this world, and at the first hours of dawn, our space-ship will go back to our own planet with the glad tidings, leaving a small colony here to prepare this place for our entire race. This I overheard our Commander tell the chief pilot after we had landed and made the tests."

Having had enough of star-gazing, they looked around them and into the deep, dark forests from which they heard issue loud animal noises, the first being again whistled, betraying solid confidence.

"What have we to fear of noisy, lowly beasts; we are well armed and can surely defend ourelves against brainless animals," and he touched the tubes that hung from the black gravity-belt. Then he added, "Come, now it is time to awaken the others so they will immediately begin preparing our fortifications."

In the hours of darkness, the machines contained in the sky-flier hummed with vibrant activity. Work went on also on the outside of the alien metal monster.

A wire barrier conducting thousands of volts of electricity had been thrown up and it now encased the sandy landing field. The uppermost wire was suspended about twenty feet above the ground and ran through insulated metal posts that had been taken out of the sky vehicle.

Large circular holes were dug as the preparations for a metal fortress. Gangs of these strange beings worked in orderly confusion within the wire enclosure. A few stiff guards stood nervously listening to the strange, noisy goings-on outside of their electrical protection.

Thick, insulated wires were connected onto the wires on the enclosure and led to large digging and welding tools of various shapes. One of the digging tools threw sand in a steady stream into a large container, while it bored deep into the ground with a group of metal bars, the ends of which resembled a bent shovel. Its actions rivaled those of a dog digging for a buried bone.

But if those within the electrical wall showed extreme activity, so too, creatures on the outside of the wall were active, although the survival of their species did not depend on them, which was not the case with the desperate Martians.

A couple of miles away, two yelling reptiles fought, one for food, the other for life itself. A large, noisy thunder-reptile, a mountain of living flesh, was trying desperately to defend itself from a blood-thirsty, screeching allosaurus. The former, a herbivorous reptile that dwelt mainly in the fresh waters of the island because of its bulky thirty-five tons, was hissing angrily at its agile harasser. Caught away from its favorite haunts, it was almost helpless against the smaller but more energetic carnivore. Because of the construction of its body, the herbivorous reptile was not made for too-active movements on land; therefore it tried to reach water, in which it would be safe from Dinosaur Allosaurus.

With a reptilic scream, as if tired of it all, it suddenly turned, almost bowling over its dancing opponent with its long, muscular tail which was easily a third the length of its entire body, and made off in the direction of a large, muddy lake. Screeching, the tremendous carnivore bounded along after it. The ground shook beneath their weight, as both disappeared noisily into the dank forest.

A lumbering, yet more agile diplodocus, a herbivorous reptile resembling the huge brontosaurus or thunder-reptile, but more slenderly built and with an exceptionally small head, made its way through the forest, accidentally stepping on a small reptile in its path, that was a bit too slow in escaping. A tiny bunch of broken bones, well squashed into the soft ground, was all that remained as the monster passed, as mute evidence of some insignificant tragedy. Quietly the reptile passed on, oblivious to the damage it had wrought. It, too, made its way to an inland body of water. Before it had reached its destination, it stopped to eat some young, luscious growth, wholly forgetful of such a thing as water.

Here and there the beaten underbrush and broken trees attested to some vigorous battle that had reigned. Large insects flew or ran along the forest floor looking for food or prey. Everywhere it was hunt or be hunted, and sometimes both. It was miraculous how any of the creatures managed to grow to maturity.

Near a large swamp, hordes of tiny reptiles that had recently emerged from their eggs played and ate together. These little cold-blooded bodies ran noisily, squeaking as if joyful of being alive. They eagerly devoured ·slow, clumsy insects and small growth. Sometimes a miniature combat arose, in which two small reptiles bit, scratched, and tumbled in the soft, warm ground. At the approach of their larger brothers, they scattered, hiding beneath the plentiful growth, their baby-hissing lost in louder noises. Suddenly a large insect, with snapping mandibles, snatched up a baby reptile and disappeared with it writhing in its iron clutch. Not one of the small reptiles seemed to notice or care about its sudden departure.

Not far from this natural incubator, a fleeing morosaurus dashed into the ocean that washed a loamy shore, to escape from a large flesh-eating monster. Silently it swam along the edge of the water, hoping to lose its pursuer that was afraid of the salty water, persistently following its course on land.

Suddenly the pursued set up a tremendous shrilling; a gigantic shark had bitten its long tail into three pieces, one of which remained in the fish's cavernous mouth, while a second and third floated free, the center of a large and widening red spot. Kicking frantically, the morosaurus fell over on its side, while its long neck remained upright. Its yells rang clear and loud, as with the bloody stump of its tail it was unable to reach the land, and if it did, the hungry carnivore eagerly awaited it.

The dying reptile began to turn and heave as numerous preying fish assailed its body, tearing off huge chunks of meat. Yelling, the disappointed carnivora on the land gobbled up a dead fish that had floated in toward the shore, and disappeared in search of less elusive prey, clumsily stepping on three insect gladiators in its path.

Although morosaurus never swam the dangerous waters of the ocean, instinctively preferring the inland bodies of water, its minute brain had decided to chance the ocean rather than certain death at the jaws of the reptile carnivore. Now, however, at the expense of its life, it learned why it had always shunned the ocean.

Back within the Martian wire protection, the alien preparations still went on. Already large green metal stems, embedded in the large circular holes in the ground, supported a thin metallic platform, upon which stood a sentinel near a thick, stationary electron-gun. Above, the skeleton of the second platform was being erected. In two metal huts reposed concentrated supplies. A third hut was being thrown up. Three great electric lights illumined the amazing scene.

A tall, round structure that was partitioned into many cubicles would serve as housing for the small Martian colony that was going to remain. Three digging machines tore holes deep into the earth, then some Martians, carrying small containers, turned small dials on their black gravity belts and fell slowly into the holes. Chemical tests of the ground were being conducted.

Nearby, a group of these intelligent aliens were cutting small growths and testing them with many forms of apparatus. Small successes brought whistles from the workers. Insects, and even a small reptile were not safe from their prying compounded eyes. After they had made a thorough examination of the creatures external appearance, they cut it open, much to the embarrassment of the writhing reptile.

Everything was as methodical as if it had all been prepared in advance, and every Martian knew exactly what he was to do. Tirelessly the alien horde labored on, struggled to make this planet, yet in its infancy, theirs—plans that thwarted those of Nature.

With surprise, the unearthly being felt a new vibration in the ground, one that didn't come from their machinery. The earthly tremors became more distinct; the creature that was the cause of this new note in the ground was apparently approaching them.

Although the workers labored on, they looked up more frequently and the armed guards became more tense. Their three-fingered hands rested on the heat-ray tubes, ready for instant action.

From the nearby trees, a serpent-like head and neck appeared, and as the forest giants swayed, a large, massy body waded through their midst. The bright electric lights shone on a hill of crude and bumpy flesh. Tiny eyes in a ridiculously small head held some twenty-five feet above the ground, peered down on these aliens of a different world.

Brontosaurus advanced to "meet" these creatures. A machine set on the head of one of the Martians hummed, then stopped at the turn of a switch.

"No thoughts," the wearer whistled.

This was the signal for dozens of heatray tubes to flash into instant action. Brilliant purple lights stung the body of the forty-ton thunder-reptile. Hundreds of black burnt spots appeared on the surface of its body. Hissing angrily, it stepped up to the wire barrier.

Instantly the guard on the metal platform whistled a loud note as he stuffed something soft and fluffy into a crevice in the side of his head. The horde of Martians below did likewise. No sooner had they finished than the stationary gun thundered into action, for the puny heat-rays seemed not to affect the attacking reptile at all, and their wire protection, a vital necessity, was being threatened.

With a stupendous roar that absolutely rocked the surrounding forest and caused hundreds of creatures to fall where they stood, an invisible stream of electrons shot out of the muzzle of the gun, striking the huge brontosaurus, just as it was about to crash the puny wire safety. The reptile halted in its tracks. Its mouth opened to howl in agony, but no sound issued forth from that gigantic throat. Its body began to change visibly to a greenish color. It began to shiver. Then, from a terrible dinosaur, Brontosaurus became a mass of struggling green worms!

At the metamorphosis, the thunder of the electron gun ceased, and the sudden silence seemed unearthly. But then reptilic noises began again to fill the humid air.

A soft plump, and the green mass fell onto the wires and a large, brilliant flare lit the surrounding forest. The hot wires electrocuted the alien mass and transformed them to pieces of blackened cinders. The thunder-reptile had died as a horde of unearthly green worms.

The electron gun, which released a flow of loose electrons, caused in organisms violent molecular metamorphosis that changed completely the organism, often forming, if properly adjusted, from one individual, many living organisms. Inorganic compounds were also transformed, if enough power was applied, by this amazing gun.

The weight of the fallen worms had broken a set of wires that had almost short-circuited the electric current. The mending of the broken wires began at once.

One of the workers began to whistle in a disgusted tone, "And we had to fly three-fourths of this planet to come to all this"; he had cut a great gash in his thin arm by accident. A blue liquid gushed to the surface of the hurt appendage.

On Mars the air was so thin that its inhabitants had to whistle, piercingly and shrilly, to make themselves heard. After ages of shrill whistling, their hearing organs had become permanently attuned to high tones and thus many low, earthly noises went by them unnoticed.

No one answered this sally of the injured Martian, which they knew was brought on by pain. But one creature that stopped its digging machine for a moment felt that if it did not express its opinion, it would most certainly burst.

"Yet it is the best that we could find. We never really expected to find this world habitable for us; and it even has meat in tremendous abundance although the vegetable matter is unfit for food. We are safe from death here, and our young will grow up happily. Is that not better than a lingering death on Mars?"

One who mended a broken wire whistled in gleeful tones, "Yes, it certainly is better, and much more so. Will establish the first colony on this planet, but soon our entire race will be here. Then will come my little family, and all will be well. We'll then be safe from death. Cannot that be worthy of our most desperate efforts?"

A guard who was recharging his heat-ray tube turned the high pitched conversation into a new channel "I wonder how the scouts to the other two planets fared?"

As all the Martians became very busy, no answer greeted his query and the work went on in silence. From nearby, reptiles made the night hideous with their loud yells. Many could not hear, for the electron gun, in tearing loose electrons from special compounds, for the firing charge, had caused such noise as to render them partly or wholly deaf. That, however, wasn't such a serious handicap as most of them could easily detect tremors in the earth to warn them of the approach of any creature, but the animals expressed surprise at the novelty of their new physical condition.

Again the earth announced the approach of some monstrous visitor and the Martians again became tensed. A smaller monster appeared on the fringe of the forest. The thought-transmitter again betrayed the fact that the confronter was of some low order.

The forty-foot morosaurus gazed not on the six-limbed aliens; they were only tiny reptiles to it, reptiles that must stand off reverently at its approach, but the queer, round space-craft held its gaze. Was it some egg? Maybe it was good to eat!

The Martians, not caring to have anything to do with such monsters, hoped that the curious reptile would depart, or at least leave them unmolested. It was not a show of intelligence to waste ammunition on creatures that caused no harm. But the guards kept a steady eye and a tense arm on their heat-tubes, ready, if the morosaurus became too inquisitive.

"See," a Martian whistled, "it has a large head and is itself much smaller than the other one was. Does it also want to investigate our little nest?"

Without warning, two creatures simultaneously appeared on the sandy ground, but from different directions. So engrossed had the Martians been in Morosaurus, that except for the vigilance of a guard, they would not have noticed the approach of the two new visitors. Now all eyes turned toward them, and the trio was carefully inspected for any signs of uncontrollable curiosity in the "nest" of the Martians.

Each visitor had a different purpose in view. The allosaurus had scented the morosaurus and was hungry for meat. The grotesque stegosaurus was hurrying to its favorite grazing grounds and it habitually crossed this particular piece of land.

The reptilic monsters never seemed to rest. The heat at night, coming from the warm earth, kept them awake and, in the daytime, the hot sun kept them especially active. They must have rested, if they ever did, when and where the desire seized them.

With a scream of triumphant hunger, the allosaurus leaped at the morosaurus, which had turned to defend its lengthy carcass. Its head shot out and powerful jaws snapped at the hungry carnivore, biting off a piece of flesh from its chest. Screaming, the two circled warily, each seeking an advantageous hold. Their ponderous steps thumped the soft ground, while the awed Martians gazed on a battle supreme.

Although morosaurus was herbivorous, he did not seem to mind a bit of meat, if it could be obtained. His microscopic brain did not warn him of the danger it took in order to get this titbit, hence it undertook a battle with the reptile carnivore.

Morosaurus' long tail swept and mashed the undergrowth, while its pounding feet broke stems and crushed them into the ground. The bodies of the two prehistoric giants broke trees and pounded the ground unmercifully. The earth reverberated to their dancing, and wherever they were, creatures of every sort knew that a noble battle was going on.

Snapping, biting, tearing, and screeching, the combatants tore the night with their gigantic efforts. They both tumbled on the ground, their bodies breaking trees with loud snaps, in prehistoric clinches. Always they separated, streaming blood, but otherwise unharmed—apparently. The carnivore's powerful legs tore at the herbivorous reptile, while the latter's tail kept the former busy, and sometimes landed stinging blows. The stomach of allosaurus was becoming impatient when his chance came.

While the battle had been raging, the stegosaurus, before any of the Martian guards gould attempt to stop it, had, in sudden fear at the approach of some creature behind it, plunged into the electrical wiring, and with a horrid scream, became a charred mass of flesh and horny plates, while it pulled down a few lines of wiring in its fall.

Shutting off the current, the Martians set immediately about repairing the new break in their wall, while the remainder kept interested eyes on the battling pair, hoping that in their efforts they would keep away from the wire wall.

Not in their wildest dreams had the Martians imagined the existence of such monsters. They knew that against such creatures, if they attacked in unison, their weapons would be useless and they themselves would be slaughtered without the slightest hesitation on the part of their reptilic attackers. Yet their case was desperate, and though they had one electron gun, they had come prepared for emergencies and had brought parts for another one. The electron gun seemed to be their only weapon strong enough to hold off the reptilic monsters of this world.

With this in mind, one of the Martians uttered a series of low whistles and a small body of Martians detached themselves from the group of on-lookers and entered the space-rocket, where there were motors that would aid in assembling another electron gun.

At the scream of the stegosaurus, the morosaurus, in sudden surprise, turned its head. That gave the hungry allosaurus its chance and it leaped to the side of its herbivorous combatant. As morosaurus turned back its head, the allosaurus, with a scream, leaped astride its opponent, almost breaking its back in the fall.

Instantly the herbivorous monster turned its head to bite at the carnivore, which seized the terrifying head in its short fore-legs and held it while its powerful teeth sank into its prey's long neck; at the same time its long legs squashed the sides of its opponent. The jaws of the morosaurus locked in a useless flesh hold on the side of the carnivorous fighter. Allosaurus bit large pieces of living flesh from the desperate morosaurus that released its hold so as to seek a better one. At this, the allosaurus' jaws locked in a death clamp near the head of its prey, where the neck was the thinnest.

The alien horde watched the battle of the giants with bated breath. The ground was torn and scarred; the growth was trampled and demolished, almost as well as their mechanism could have done it. But the most harmful effect the battle had caused was the fact that it had brought ever-hungry carnivora and insects to the scene, which was immediately outside their enclosure.

The earth again began to tremble at the weight of approaching creatures whose bellies craved meat—meat that would be found on the dying body of the morosaurus. The herbivorous giant, in its death agony, carried its victorious opponent and itself, on aimless legs, into the wire enclosure; and the wire, which had not yet been mended, carried no electric current.

Interested in the battle and hence unprepared, the startled Martians had expected to see the morosaurus fall dead at least from loss of blood, instead of the two combatants, as one, rushing into their enclosure and up onto their space-ship, causing it to turn on its side.

The allosaurus, seeing the space-craft and supposing it to be more meat, greedily leaped onto the ship, denting its smooth exterior, and crashing the transparent metal used as glass. For a moment it resembled King Kong atop the Empire State Building.

Nowhere, except on the rocket-tubes, could the victorious carnivora find a tooth hold, and as heat-rays burnt black spots on it, the warning was given and hearing organs were again stopped up as the roaring electron gun went, for the second time that night, into reverberating action.

Excepting the thunder-reptile, never had the electron gun had such a huge organic target. Always its target had been some enemy space-ship, or Martian soil had been changed into some useful metal, but such a mountain of living flesh had never before been touched.

After the allosaurus had been transformed into a wriggling pile of green worms, the heat-rays burned the loathsome results. Then a terrifying horde burst onto the sandy clearing, from all sides of the forest—animals. Almost a solid hundred of them faced a puny wire wall. The element of excitement immediately manifested itself in the Martians. They milled around for a moment, nervously preparing for wholesale slaughter.

Cold-blooded monstrosities of various sizes, with empty bellies, faced the alien horde, as if accusing them of trying to wrest from Nature a world that did not belong to them. Not a second did these hungry creatures waste. With one accord they surged forward.

The noise of the battle had not been the only thing that had caused their appearance. All night a steady rumbling in the earth had aroused their excitement, but they could not locate the source. Therefore, many were hungrier than usual as they had wasted many hours in a vain search. Naturally this battle brought up a larger hungry mob of animals than was usual.

Hissing and yelling, they forced their way to the dead, but unchanged morosaurus. After a timely warning to the Martians, the electron gun went once more into a thunderous activity, at which Hell broke loose. The gun easily drowned out all sounds, so it appeared that reptilic mouths opened in silence.

The wire protection, bearing no current, as it had not been mended, disappeared instantly. Had the hungry stampeding mob more brains and less stomach, they would have fled in panic at the terrific din of the gun, but as it was, they fearlessly came on crushing down their own kind.

Magically there appeared amongst them green, loathsome, crawling worms that were instantly pounced upon by hungry insects that the scent of blood also brought. A Martian guard went down as a large flying beetle sank long mandibles into his neck. A tiny reptile carnivore grasped a Martian by a leg and bit it easily off, as the alien being drew himself away whistling in agony. The lights went out and only the light of the moon and stars showed the turmoil that reigned.

Yells of agony, screams of the dying, alien whistles, and the noise of stamping feet were all lost in the clamoring of the electron gun that chose a large creature for a target and transformed it directly. Luckily for the hungry creatures the second electron gun had not a chance of being constructed, for the space-ship had been turned on its side by the rush of the dying morosaurus and the machinery didn't function properly.

Heat guns shone a steady light, cutting, burning, slicing, and killing; but it wasn't enough. The electron gun suddenly stopped its thundering activity; some insect, escaping the notice of the guard, had investigated its inner works and its dead body now hampered the action of the mechanism which had become jammed. As the voice of the electron gun died out, the noise of the triumphant reptiles rose to shrill heights.

A struggling Martian, lost in the midst of fighting animals, was bitten to pieces, and insects pierced his thin skin very easily. His body was finally a mass of blood that attracted the notice of more creatures. A large pile of loathsome green worms fell and smothered a horde of insects that were busily devouring the body of a writhing, small reptile. The body of a dead Martian jerked in various directions as it was torn apart.

Screams of the beastly and whistles of the intelligent intermingled and pierced the air as one. Thrashing bodies filled what had once been an alien landing field. Reptile fought reptile and Martian.

An attempt, by the aliens, was made to get to their ship, but their venture ended in death, sudden but painlessly merciful. Even the impassive moon gasped in awed surprise.

The last group of Martians made their last stand, surrounded by hungry mountains of living flesh. Crowding together in a defensive bunch and facing the outside, they cut a brilliant wall of heat. From above, by means of a tremendous leap from the backs of the surrounding animals, a blood-mad creature fell amongst the Martians and broke their defense.

With the death of her last scout on Earth, the Martian race was destined to believe the third planet from the sun uninhabitable though they never learned why.

More animals arrived and many battles raged around the body of the strange metal monster of another world. The wounded fled, leaving comparatively few hungry beasts to gorge themselves with a sudden abundance of meat. Over the masses of green, helpless worms swarmed insects of all sizes—earthly insects bent on the extermination of an unearthly species.

As usual, the sun rose and, with its usual dignity, glared majestically down on the warm earth. Where in the night there had been an alien electrical barrier, now lay piles of bones and the bodies of dead animals, attesting to the savageness of the inhabitants of an infant planet. Here and there lay the round skull of a Martian, a skull that denoted intelligence—a skull that was a sort of prediction that seemed to foretell of a species that would, millions of years in the future, rule the earth.

Stupid earthly creatures had preserved the world for earthly intelligence to come aeons later.

Davy Jones' Ambassador
by Raymond Z. Gallun

When F. Orlin Tremaine began to recruit talent for the revived *Astounding Stories* he was able to tempt them with the formidable two cents a word, four times *Wonder's* or *Amazing's* fee. Payment on acceptance was an additional carrot to dangle. Naturally authors would send their stories to *Astounding* first, and let the other titles make do with rejects. But this did not mean that Tremaine was in receipt of hurried, hackneyed manuscripts. Writers respected Tremaine's criteria and immediately responded with original and intriguing fiction.

Up until then Gallun had not been an outstanding author, although his fiction had all been readable and enjoyable. His first two stories were published in concurrent issues of *Air Wonder* and *Science Wonder* in November 1929, but he then lay dormant until 1931 saw two more stories in *Amazing*, "Atomic Fire" and "Lunar Chrysalis" both good stories. The occasional story appeared over the next two years, and then suddenly he found Tremaine, and it was like a fish finding water.

Raymond Zinke Gallun was born in 1911, so had only been eighteen when "The Crystal Ray" marked his debut, and still only twenty-two when Tremaine bought "Space Flotsam". That tale appeared in the February 1934 *Astounding*, and Gallun then appeared almost endlessly in that magazine for the next three years. He shot to the fore with "Old Faithful" in the December 1934 issue, which became one of the most popular stories of the year. Old Faithful was a Martian who made a self-sacrificing attempt to cross space. Its popularity warranted two sequels, and Gallun had now reached his peak. The same sentimental mood occurred in many of his stories thereafter particularly with "Derelict" and "Davy Jones' Ambassador".

Gallun for years would spend his time travelling around the world, cramming his writing into short periods in New York. Nevertheless he maintained a remarkable output during the 1930's and barely ever turned out a bad story.

It didn't look like a jet of water at all. It seemed too rigid, like a rod of glass; and it spattered over the instruments with a brittle, jingling sound, for such was the effect of the pressure behind it: more than four thousand pounds per square inch—the weight of nearly two and a half miles of black ocean.

Cliff Rodney, hunched in the pilot seat, stared at the widening stream. It made him see how good a thing life was, and how empty and drab the alternative was going to be. Cliff Rodney was young; he did not wish to die.

A few seconds ago all had been normal aboard the bathyspheric submarine. The velvet darkness of the depths, visible beyond the massive ports of the craft, had inspired awe in him, as it always would in human hearts; but to Cliff it had become familiar. The same was true of the schools of phosphorescent fish shining foggily through the gloom, and of the swarms of nether-world horrors that had darted in the bright golden path of the search beam.

Clifford Rodney, during his explorations, had grown accustomed to these elements of the deep-sea environment, until they had assumed an aspect that was almost friendly.

But the illusion that it was safe here had been abruptly broken. Sinuous, rusty shadows, which bore a suggestion of menace that was new to him, had surged toward the submarine from out of the surrounding murk and ooze.

Attenuated, spidery crustaceans with long feelers had burrowed into the shelter of the mud beneath them. Little fish, some of them equipped with lamp-like organs, some blind and lightless, all of them at once dreadful and comic with their needle-fanged jaws and grotesque heads, had scattered in terror.

Bulbous medusae, contracting and expanding their umbrella-shaped bodies, had swum hurriedly away. Even the pallid anemones had displayed defensive attitudes in the guarded contraction of their flowerlike crowns.

With canny craft the unknowns had avoided the search beam. Cliff had glimpsed only the swift motion of monstrous, armored limbs, and the baneful glitter of great eyes. Then the blow had fallen, like that of a battering ram. It had struck the forward observation port with a grinding concussion.

A crack, looking like a twisted ribbon of silver, had appeared in the thick, vitreous substance of the pane. From it, water had begun to spurt in a slender, unstanchable shaft that grew ominously as the sea spread the edges of the crevice wider and wider apart.

Automatically Cliff had done what he could. He had set the vertical screws of his craft churning at top speed to raise it toward the surface. But, in a moment, the blades had met with fierce resistance, as though clutched and held. The motors had refused to turn. The submarine had sunk back into the muck of the Atlantic's bed. An SOS was the last resort.

Cliff had sent it out quickly, knowing that though it would be picked up by the *Etruria*, the surface ship that served as his base of operations, nothing could be done to help him. He had reached the end of his resources.

Now, there was a breathless pause. The blackness without was inky. Cliff continued to gaze impotently at that slim cylinder of water. Ricocheting bits of it struck him, stinging fiercely, but he did not heed. It fascinated him, making him forget, almost, how it had all happened. His mind was blurred so that it conceived odd notions.

Pretty, the way that jet of water broke apart when it hit the bright metal of the instruments. You wouldn't think that it was dangerous. Flying droplets scattered here and there like jewels, each of them glinting in the shaded glow of the light bulbs. And the sounds they made resembled the chucklings of elves and fairies.

A small creature of the depths, sucked through the breach, burst, with a dull plop as the pressure of its normal habitat was removed.

He and that creature had much in common, Rodney thought. Both were pawns which chance had elected to annihilate. Only he was a man; men boasted of their control over natural forces. And he himself was a blatant and ironic symbol of that boast: They had sent him here in the belief that even the bed of the Atlantic might soon yield to human dominance!

The submarine gave a gentle lurch. The youth's eyes sharpened to a keener focus. A yard beyond the fractured port a pair of orbs hung suspended. Beneath them was a fleshy beak that opened and closed as the creature sucked water through its gills. Black, whiplike tentacles swarmed around it like the hairs of a

Gorgon beard. And the flesh of the monster was transparent. Cliff could see the throbbing outlines of its vital organs.

Nothing unusual here—just another devil of the depths. So Cliff Rodney would have thought had it not been for certain suggestive impressions that touched lightly on his blurred faculties. That beaked mouth was vacuously empty of expression, but the great limpid orbs were keen. The tentacles clutched a little rod, pointed at one end as a goad would be. The impression was fleeting. With a ripple of finny members the horror disappeared from view.

"That rod," Cliff muttered aloud, "I wonder if that thing made it!"

He felt a cold twinge, that was an expression of many emotions, ripple over his flesh. He moved quickly, his booted feet sloshing in the water that was now six inches deep within the stout hull of the submarine. He turned a switch; the lights winked out. It was best to be concealed in darkness.

Once more the bathyspheric submarine rocked. Then it was whirled completely over. Cliff Rodney tumbled from the pilot chair. Icy fluid cascaded around him as his body struck the hard steel of the craft's interior.

He managed to protect his head with his arms, but contact with the metal sent a numbing, aching shock through his flesh. Electricity; it could not have been anything else. He tried to curse, but the result was only a ragged gasp. Clinging desperately to the sunset edge of oblivion, he fell back among his instruments.

Impressions were very dim after that. The submarine was being towed somewhere by something. Water continued to pour into the hull, making a confused babble of sound. Rodney lay in the growing pool, the briny stuff bitter on his lips. Too near stunned to master his limbs, he rolled about the inundated floor.

With each eccentric motion of the craft, churning water slapped viciously against his face. He choked and coughed. If only he could keep his nose above the flood and breathe!

In some foggy recess of his mind he wondered why he was fighting for life, when the broken port alone was enough to doom him. Was instinct, or some deeper, more reasoned urge responsible? Cliff did not know, but for a fleeting instant the blank look of pain on his face was punctuated by a grim smile.

He was not the mythical iron man; he was a median of strengths and weaknesses as are most humans. And, among humans, courage is almost as cheap as it is glorious.

Cliff could still hear the swish of great flippers shearing the sea beyond the eighteen-inch shell of the submarine. Harsh to his submerged ears, it was the last impression he received when consciousness faded out.

II

Reawakening was slow agony. He had been half-drowned. When his brain was clear enough for him to take stock of his surroundings he did not immediately note any remarkable change.

He was still within the stout little undersea boat that had brought him to the depths. The vessel was nearly two thirds full of brine, but by luck his body had been thrown over a metal brace, and for part of the time his head had been supported above the flood.

No more water was entering the hull through the eroded crevice in the window. In fact there was no motion at all, and except for a distant, pulsating hiss, the stillness was tomblike.

The air was heavy and oppressive. It reeked with a fetid stench that was almost unbearable. Mingled with the odor was a faint pungence of chlorine, doubtless brought about by the electrolysis of sea water where it had penetrated some minor fault in the submarine's electrical equipment. A gray luminescence seeped through the ports, lighting up the interior of the vessel dimly.

Soaked, dazed, battered, and chilled to the bone, Cliff struggled to the fractured window. There was air beyond it, not water. He had not extinguished the searchlight, and it still burned, for the storage cells that supplied current had been well protected against mishap.

There was no need to waste power to produce light here. A faint but adequate radiance seemed to come from the curving walls of the chamber in which the submarine had been docked. Cliff switched off the beam.

Groping down under the water, he found a lever and tugged at it. A valve opened, and the brine began to drain out of the submarine. The gurgling sound it made was harsh to his ears. Evidently the atmospheric pressure here was far above normal.

Next, he unfastened the hatch above his head, and hoisted its ponderous weight. Wearily he clambered through the opening and dropped down beside his craft.

The room was elliptical, domed, and bare of any furnishings. Its largest diameter was perhaps thirty-five feet, twice the length of the submarine. Puddles dotted the floor, and the walls were beaded with moisture which showed plainly that the place had been flooded recently. At opposite points there had been circular openings in the walls, one much larger than the other. Both were blocked now by great plugs of a translucent, amorphous material.

Cliff had two immediate urges: One was to get a better idea of where he was; the other was to find, if possible, a means of allaying his discomfort.

He started his investigations with the larger of the two plugs. It was held in place by a tough, glutinous cement, still sticky to the touch. From beyond it came a distant murmur of the sea. This, then, was the way by which the submarine had entered the chamber.

After the entrance had been sealed the water had been drawn off by some means through the several drains in the floor. The stream from the valve in the side of the submarine still gurgled into them, pumped away, perhaps, by some hidden mechanism, So much was clear.

Cliff's attention wandered to the walls, in quest of some explanation of the phosphorescence that came from them. Their surface was hard and smooth like that of glass, but the substance that composed them was not glass. It had a peculiar, milky opalescent sheen, like mother-of-pearl. Squinting, he tried to peer through the cloudy, semi-transparent material.

At a depth of a few inches little specks of fire flitted. They were tiny, self-luminous marine animals. Beyond the swarming myriads of them was another shell, white and opaque. He understood. The chamber was double-walled. There was water between the walls, and in it those minute light-giving organisms were imprisoned for the purpose of supplying illumination.

It was a simple bit of inventive ingenuity, but not one which men would be likely to make use of. In fact there was nothing about his new surroundings that was not at least subtly different from any similar thing that human beings would produce.

The glass of the domed chamber was not glass. It seemed to be nearer to the substance that composes the inner portion of a mollusk's shell, and yet it had apparently been made in one piece, for there was no visible evidence of joints where separate parts of the dome might have been fastened together. The blocks that sealed the openings in the walls were almost equally strange. Among men they would surely have been made of metal.

Clifford Rodney became more and more aware of the fact that he had come in contact with a civilization and science more fantastic than that of Mars or Venus could ever be. Those planets were worlds of air, as was the Earth he knew, while this was a world of water. Environment here presented handicaps and possibly advantages which might well have turned the sea folk's path of advancement in a direction utterly different from that followed by mankind.

Continuing his investigations, Cliff discovered that the air under the dome was admitted through four pipelike tubes which penetrated the double walls of his prison; but, of course, he could not discover where they originated. The air came through those tubes in rhythmic, hissing puffs, and escaped, he supposed, down the drains through which the water had been drawn, since there was no other outlet in evidence.

He wondered how the rancid stuff had been produced, and how his hosts had even known that he needed gaseous oxygen to breathe. He wondered whether they could have any conception of the place whence he had come. To them a land of sunshine must be as ungraspable as a region of the fourth dimension!

He remembered the electric shock that had almost stunned him at the time of his capture. Electricity was produced here then. But how? As yet he had not so much as glimpsed a scrap of metal in his new surroundings.

Cliff shuddered, nor was the dank, bitter cold alone responsible. He could realize clearer than before that beyond the barriers that protected him was a realm of pressure and darkness and water with which his own normal environment had few things in common.

Belatedly it occurred to him that he was being watched by the curious of Submarinia. Standing now in the center of the slippery floor, he scanned the dome above him for evidence that his logic was correct. It was. Spaced evenly around the arching roof, more than halfway toward its central axis, was a ring of circular areas more transparent than the surrounding texture of the double walls.

Though not easily discernible at a casual glance, they were plain enough to him now. Through each, a pair of huge, glowing eyes and a Gorgon mass of black tentacles was visible. The ovoid bodies of the creatures were silhouetted against a nebulous luminescence originating from some unknown source beyond them.

The gaze of those monsters seemed cool and interested and intense, though Clifford Rodney felt that one could never be sure of what emotions, if any, their vacuous, beaked lips and limpid eyes betrayed. It would be difficult indeed to forget that they were completely inhuman.

Cliff's reaction was a kind of terror; though the only outward evidences of it were the strained hollows that came suddenly into his cheeks; still, the realization of his position thudded with ghastly weight into his mind. To those sea beings he was doubtless like a simple amoeba beneath a microscope, a specimen to be observed and studied!

Then his sense of humor rescued him. He chuckled half-heartedly through chattering teeth. At least no man had ever before been in a situation quite as novel as this. It was one which a scientist, eager to learn new things, should appreciate. Besides, perhaps now he could bring the adventure to a head.

He waved his arms toward the pairs of eyes that gazed steadily at him. "Hello!" he shouted. "What in the name of good manners are you trying to do to me? Get me out of here!"

They couldn't understand him, but anyway they could see by his gestures that he had discovered them, and that he was insisting on some sort of attention. Cliff Rodney was cold, and half-choked by the rancid air.

Things had to happen soon, or his stamina would be worn down and he would no longer be in a position to see them happen. The dank, frigid chill was the worst. The air would not have been so bad if it had not been for the retch-provoking stench that impregnated it. If he only had a dry cigarette and a match, it would help a lot.

That was a funny thought—a cigarette and a match! Had he expected these ovoid beings to supply him with such luxuries?

However, since there was no one else to whom he might appeal for help, he continued to shout epithets and pleas, and to flail his arms until he was nearly spent with the effort.

Yet, the sea people gave no evidence of special response. The vital organs throbbed within their transparent bodies, tympanic membranes beneath their beaked mouths vibrated, perhaps transmitting to the water around them signals of a kind of vocal speech, inaudible to him, of course; and their tentacles scurried over the outer surfaces of the spy windows, producing a noise such as a mouse scampering inside a box might make, but Cliff saw no promise in their evident interest.

Every few minutes, one pair of eyes would turn away from a window, and another pair would take its place. The ovoids were managing the scrutiny of him just as humans would manage a show featuring a freak. He could imagine them out there waiting in line for a chance to see him. It was funny, but it was ghastly too.

Exhausted, he gave up. Probably they couldn't help him anyway. If he only had something dry to keep the chill away from his shivering flesh!

Hopefully he scrambled up the side of the submarine and lowered himself through the hatch. There was a little electric heater there, but a brief examination of it confirmed his well-founded suspicions. Soaked with brine, its coils were shorted and it refused to work. He had no means of drying it out sufficiently, and so he turned on the search beam. If he crouched against the lamp, he might capture a little heat.

He climbed out of the dripping, disordered interior. Before dropping to the floor of the domed chamber he stood on tiptoe on the curved back of the submarine and attempted to peer through one of the spy windows in the rotunda over his head.

Even now the mystery of what lay beyond the glowing walls of the room beneath the sea could fascinate him. But his vantage point was not quite high enough, nor was there any easy means to make it higher. He saw only a flicker of soft, greenish light beyond the motionless, ovoid shape that occupied the window.

He slid weakly off the submarine and pressed his body against the lens of the searchlight. The rays warmed him a little—a very little—enough to tantalize him with the thought that such a thing as warmth really existed.

He thought of exercise as a means to start his sluggish blood circulating faster; he even made an effort to put the thought into execution by shaking his arms and stamping his feet. But he felt too far gone to keep up the exertion. His head slumped against the mounting of the searchlight.

Some minutes later, a throbbing radiance caused him to look up. At one of the spy windows was a creature different from the sea people. Its body was flat, and as pallid as a mushroom. It was shaped curiously like an oak leaf with curled edges. Its mouth was a slit at the anterior extremity of its queer form. On either side of it were pulsing gill openings, and above were beady eyes supported on stalky members. From the thin edges of the creature's body, long, slender filaments projected, glinting like new-drawn copper wire. And the flesh of the thing glowed intermittently like a firefly.

After several seconds this phenomenon ceased, and another far more startling one took its place. The creature turned its dorsal surface toward the window.

Then it was as though some invisible hand and brush were printing a message in letters of fire on the pallid hide of the monster. They were old, familiar letters spelling out English words. One by one they appeared, traced with swift and practised accuracy until the message was complete:

I am far away, man; but I am coming. I wish to write with you. Do not die yet. Wait until I arrive.

The Student

If Clifford Rodney had been himself, his consternation at this odd note and the outlandish means of its transmission would have been greater, and his analysis of the phenomena involved would have been more keen. As matters were, he was still able to discern the shadows of the causes underlying the enigma.

This was the subsea version of wireless. He was too tired to construct a theory of its principle; he only glanced at the fine filaments projecting from the body of the creature that had served as an agent of the miracle, and dismissed the vague germ of an idea that had oozed unbidden into his sluggish mind.

Even though this was a science completely inhuman, still it was self-evident that there were logical explanations. At present Cliff didn't care particularly whether he ever learned them. Nor did he ponder for long the riddle of how this distant spokesman of the ovoids was able to write English. Somewhere there must be a simple answer.

However, the wording of the message, strikingly demonstrating the broad physical and psychological differences between his kind and the unknowns, won somewhat more attention from him. It was "I wish to write with you," instead of "I wish to speak with you." The ovoid tympanums, vibrating in water, could not produce or convey to him the sounds of human speech.

"Do not die yet. Wait until I arrive." Did those two simple commands express naive brutality or—Cliff scarcely knew how to think the thought. No human being would have expressed an idea of that sort with such guileless frankness. The meaning, of course, was perfectly clear; and Cliff knew that he had been afforded a glimpse into a mind differing radically from those of men.

"The Student." That at least had a familiar aspect. Because of the way the message was signed, the anger and depression which it aroused in him subsided.

The lettering vanished from the flat back of the creature which had been the means of conveying to Cliff Rodney the first expression of subsea thought. Another fire-traced message appeared, letter by letter:

We have waited too long for the arrival of one of you, man. We must learn more about your kind before you die. All in our power has been done for you. If you require more, perhaps it is beyond the small sealed exit. Unseal it. Live until I come.

The Student.

Rodney cursed and shook his fist feebly at the messenger. Nevertheless, hope gave him fresh energy. He proceeded to obey the suggestion. Returning to the submarine he procured a heavy knife, extinguished the search beam for economy, and came forth again to attack the smaller door.

The cement here was thoroughly hard, glassy; but tough and elastic rather than brittle. Cliff worked at it fiercely, digging out the gummy stuff with the point of his knife. For a time it seemed that the stubborn block would never yield; but at length, when his expiring energies were all but burned up, and little specks of blackness flitted before his vision, success came.

The plug of amorphous material toppled from the opening and thudded resoundingly to the floor. For a minute young Rodney lay exhausted beside it, a rustle in his ears that he knew was not the distant whisper of the ocean.

Then, rested a bit, he crept through the opening. He was too dazed to be very conscious of the things around him. The character of the chamber was much the same as that of the one he had just quitted, except that it was larger, and the floor was a much more elongated oval. It had the same kind of pearly, phosphorescent dome equipped with spy windows.

Even now the windows were being occupied by the grotesque forms of the sea people, eager to observe the fresh reactions of their strange captive. The air, though, was drier, for the place had not recently been flooded, and it was musty with the odor of ancient decay, like that of a tomb.

The floor was piled high with a numerous assortment of things —every one of them of human origin. Cliff let his eyes wander over the array. There was a generator, part of a ship's turbine, several life preservers, a fire extinguisher, books, tattered and pulped by sea water and pressure, rugs, and so forth. There were even two human figures.

They were propped on a dilapidated divan, and were fully clothed. Whoever had placed them there had apparently made some attempt to arrange them naturally.

Cliff Rodney came closer to examine them. One had been a man, the other a woman. Their flesh was gone, their faces were only skeleton masks. The woman's dress had once been white and beautiful, but it was just a mottled, gray rag now. Yet, the diamond pendant at her throat still gleamed as brightly as ever. The pair clutched each other with a fierceness that was still apparent. Perhaps they had died in each other's arms like that long ago. A grim tragedy of the Atlantic—

Rodney's reactions were not quite normal. He felt sick. "Damn museum!" he grumbled in a sort of inane disgust. "Damn stinky museum of Davy Jones!" He choked and sneezed.

The haze of his numbed faculties was not so dense that it obscured the animal urge to seek comfort, however. He picked up a heavy rug which, though rotted and odorous, was fairly dry.

He stripped off his soaked garments, and wrapped himself in the rug. Tearing up a book and heaping the fragments into a pile with the intention of making a fire, was quite natural and automatic. So was locating his cigarette lighter and attempting to make it work. Here, though, he struck a snag. Sparks flew, but the wick was too wet to burn.

Out of his angry chagrin an inspiration was born. He unscrewed the cap from the fuel container, poured a few drops of benzine onto the paper, and applied the sparks direct. The tinder flared up merrily, and grotesque shadows leaped about the walls of the eerie chamber. Delighted, Cliff huddled down beside the blaze, absorbing its welcome heat.

Only once did he glance at the ovoids watching him. He could not have guessed what wonder his activities provoked in the minds of those strange people of the depths.

"Go to hell!" He called to them in dismissal.

The air didn't smell so bad with the smoke in it. As the embers began to die, Clifford Rodney drew the carpet tighter about him and sprawled on the pavement. Worn out, he was quickly asleep.

III

Through the gloom of the bottoms, seven slim shapes were speeding. They were neither crustaceans nor sharklike elasmobranchs; they bore some of the characteristics of both.

Their bodies were protected by horny armor, and were tapered in such a manner as to suggest the lines of a torpedo, a comparison that was heightened by the waspish air of concentrated power about them. Rows of flippers along their flanks churned the dark water, sending them swiftly on their way. Folded carefully against their bellies were pairs of huge claws resembling the pinchers of a crawfish, though much larger. Projecting like swollen cheeks on either side of their heads were protuberances of modified muscle—their most effective weapons.

These monstrous creations were not entirely the product of nature. The knowledge of a gifted people working on their kind for ages had achieved a miracle, making of them efficient, dependable, fighting machines.

They swam in a military formation. The largest individual of the group formed its center. Above, below, ahead, behind, and on either side—one in each position—the others swam. There was a reason. Every now and then schools of small, devil-fanged fish would glide out of the darkness to attack the cavalcade. The nearest members of the escort would leap to meet them.

For an instant, many fierce little teeth would try to penetrate the tough shells of the fighters. Then the latter would strike back, invisibly, except for a momentary flicker of lavender sparks around their snouts. The attacking fish would stiffen and go drifting limply into the darkness again, dead or stunned.

The fighters were protecting their master, he who had named himself "The Student." He rode the central individual of the formation, suckerlike cups on the ventral surface of his body, clinging to its back. He had flattened himself against his mount to minimize the surge of water that swept past him. His eyes peered ahead with an expectant glitter.

He changed position only to trace queer symbols, with a goad of glassy material, on the flesh of the fragile messenger that clung beside him, and to scan the phosphorescent replies to his queries, that came in return. But within him, dread and eagerness were mingled. He had received the call that he had both hoped for and feared. And he was responding.

Out of the murk and ooze that blanketed the sea floor ahead, an emerald glow arose like some infernal dawn. The cavalcade continued to speed on its way, and the radiance brightened.

A broad depression in the bottoms emerged from the fog of suspended mud, gray like tarnished silver. Above it swarmed myriads of minute, luminous animals, forming an immense canopy of green light, limned against the blackness of the depths. That canopy looked as though it had been placed there for a purpose.

To paint the scene beneath, would have challenged the genius of Gustave Doré. It was as abhorrent as the visions of a mad demon; still it possessed elements of majesty and beauty.

A city was there in the hollow—a city or a colony. The seven fighters were moving close above it now. The valley was pitted by countless small openings, arranged edge to edge after the fashion of the cells of a honeycomb. Into them and from them, ovoids swam, going about whatever business was theirs. Here and there, queer structures of a pearly, translucent material, reared twisted spires that seemed to wriggle with the motion of the water.

Monsters were everywhere, vague in the shifting shadows. Scores of types were represented, each type seemingly stranger than its associates. All of the monsters were busy, guided in their activities by alert ovoids that hung in the water, goads poised, flippers stirring idly.

Some of the monsters wallowed in the muck, digging with broad, spatulate members. Wormlike in form, pallid and smooth, one knew that their purpose in life was to dig, and nothing else.

Others kneaded their bloated, shapless bodies, froming elfin creations around them, seemingly from their substance. Some fanned the water with long, flattened limbs, perhaps performing a function akin to ventilation. Others—they were fighters like The Student's escort—guarded the colony, swimming steadily back and forth.

And so it went. Each of the horrors followed the vocation for which it was intended. Each was a robot, a machine of living flesh, capable of some special function.

A man would have been held spellbound by this teeming, alien activity; but The Student scarcely noticed it at all. Everything—the lights, the motion, the whispering, slithering sounds that found their way to his auditory organs—held the familiarity of life-long experience, of home.

His gaze, though, wandered intently across the valley to the place where the gutted hull of an ocean liner sprawled half over on its side, its form almost obscured by the dusky murk of the depths.

Slim ribbons that had the appearance of vegetation streamed up from it, waving like banners. They were not vegetation, though they were alive. There were no plants here, away from the sunshine; and the fauna of this world was dependent for its sustenance upon organic débris settling from above, where there was sunlight, where clorophyll could act, and where both fauna and flora could exist.

Always the wrecks of upper-world ships had interested The Student, as something from another planet would interest us. He had rummaged through their slimy interiors, examining and exploring this and that.

Of all their wondrous contents, books had fascinated him the most. With a zeal and care and love that an archaeologist would understand, he had made copies of those fragile, water-soaked storehouses of knowledge, tracing the still legible parts of them on a parchment that could withstand the action of the sea.

He had studied the queer symbol groups they bore; he had discovered the value of the dictionary. And as the Rosetta Stone Stone had been the key to Egyptian hieroglyphics, so the dictionary had been his means of solving the riddle of mankind's literature.

There was another thing that won a brief glance from The Student, as he guided his mount and escort toward the concourse of ovoids that had collected around the structures which housed the reason for his coming.

On a low rise a circular vat, filled with living protoplasm, squatted. Above it two crudely hammered bars of iron converged together, Between their adjacent ends blue sparks purred. The apparatus was a recent development which would have startled the wise inventors who had contributed so much to another culture.

With a thrusting motion The Student hurled himself from the back of the fighters. The flippers along his sides took hold of the water with powerful sweeps. The crowd made a lane for him as he approached. Tympanic voices buzzed around him, questioning, demanding; yet, he paid no heed.

IV

The Student reached a spy window in the dome, looked down. The man was there, sprawled motionless amid the relics of his civilization. A piece of ragged fabric wrapped his pallid body.

Revulsion, fear, hope, and anxiety were not beyond The Student's understanding, and he felt them all now.

Was the prisoner dead? Was all that had been promised to end in disappointment? Paradoxically The Student would have been more at ease if such were the case. There is no harm in an enemy whose vital functions have stopped. Yet The Student himself did not live for peace and security alone. The boon of existence had many meanings.

He moved to a window in the smaller dome, and surveyed the bathyspheric submarine, marvelling at the smooth, metal hull, and the precise perfection of each detail. No ovoid could fabricate such wonders.

Patiently he waited until the buzzing tympanic voice of the throng about him impinged on his sense organs, telling him that the time had arrived.

Coolly The Student returned to the window of the museum chamber. The man was awake. He stood unsteadily in the center of the floor, the rug still wrapped around him and his eyes turned upward.

Two peoples, two cultures, two backgrounds, two histories, and two points of view were face to face at last, ready for whatever might come of the meeting. The bizarre stood versus the bizarre from opposite angles. Between them the abyss was wide. Was there—could there be—any sympathy to bridge it?

It was up to The Student to open negotiations, and he did not hesitate, for he had planned well. From a pouch, which was a natural part of him, he removed a stylus of chalky material. Then, concentrating on what he had learned during his years of study he printed a command on the pane of the window: "You made fire, man. Make it again."

He traced the letters in reverse, so that they would appear normally to the being inside the dome.

The prisoner seemed uncertain for a brief spell; then he obeyed. Paper, a daub of liquid from what appeared to be a tiny black box, a swift movement, sparks, and finally—flame! The man held up the blazing paper for his visitor to see.

The Student watched the phenomenon of rapid oxidation, drinking in the marvel of it until the flame was burned out. The water had washed the chalky letters from the window. He traced another message: "Fire gives you metals, machine, power—everything you have?"

If, before it had happened, Clifford Rodney had had an opportunity to construct a mental picture of what this meeting would be like, he would no doubt have expected to be amazed. But he could not have conceived beforehand an adequate idea of his own wonder. Tangible truth was so much more startling than a bare thought could be.

Here was a thing which bore many of the outward charactersistics of the marine animals with which he was acquainted—pulsing gills, stirring flippers—organs used in a medium which must ever be foreign to those forms of life that live in air and sunshine.

There was even in the visage of the thing—if visage it might be called—a deceptive look of vacuity which only the cool glitter of the great eyes denied. And yet, clutched in the being's tentacles was a crayon, with which it was writing in English, words that displayed a considerable knowledge of human attainments!

Cliff almost forgot that he himself was a delver after hidden facts. Then his own calm purpose conquered. His sleep had refreshed him; and though he felt stiff, sore, and uncomfortable, he could still respond to the appeal of an enigma.

He looked about for some means to answer. His attention was drawn to a small area of unencumbered floor, on which a thin layer of sea sand had been deposited. With a finger he traced words in it: "Yes. Fire brought us out of the Stone Age, and kept us going since. You got it right, friend. How?"

And the swift-moving tentacles traced a reply: "I have translated books—men's books. I have read of fire. But we have never produced fire. We might produce fire from electric sparks—soon."

Rodney looked with a quizzical awe at the gleaming orbs of the ovoid. Behind them, he knew, was a brilliant brain, whose brilliance had perhaps been augmented by the very handicaps which it had faced and overcome. The truth concealed behind this intriguing statement was already dimly formulated in his mind. Now he might clear up the matter completely.

He smoothed out the sand and printed another message: "You have electricity, glass and a kind of wireless—still, no fire. It is too wet here for fire; but how did you do it all? And write like a man—how?"

The Student chose to answer the last question first. " I mimic the writing of men," he printed. "I must—so men understand. Glass, electricity, wireless, and other things, come from animals. Nearly everything comes from animals. We have made the animals so. We have developed the useful characteristics of the animals—great care, selection, breeding, crossbreeding—a long time—ages."

It was a confirmation of the vague theory that Cliff had formulated. Handicapped by the impossibility of fire in their normal environment, the sea folk's advancement had followed another path. Controlled evolution was what it amounted to.

Cliff remembered what miracles men such as Luther Burbank had achieved with plants—changing them, improving them. And to a lesser extent, similar marvels had been achieved with animals. Here in the depths of the Atlantic the same science had been used for ages!

Without visible excitement Cliff traced another note in the sand: "Electricity from living flesh, from modified muscle as in the electric eel or the torpedo? Glass from—Tell me!"

And on the spy window the answer appeared: "Yes. Glass from animal—from mollusk—deposited and grown as a mollusks shell is deposited and grown. And it is formed as we wish. Electricity from modified muscle, as in the electric eel or the torpedo. I have read of them. We have animals like them—but larger. The animals fight for us, kill with electricity. And we have—electric batteries—metal from the ships. Rods—protoplasm—"

The Student's black tentacles switched and hesitated uncertainly as he groped for words that would express his thoughts to this strange monstrosity of another realm.

But Clifford Rodney had captured enough of his meaning to make a guess. "You mean," he wrote, "that you have developed a way of producing a steady current of electricity from a form of living protoplasm? A sort of isolated electric organ with metal details and grids to draw off the power?"

"Yes,"

Cliff thought it over, briefly but intensely. Such protoplasm would need only food to keep it active, and it could probably obtain food from the organic dust in the sea water around it.

"Splendid!" he printed. "And the wireless, the radio beast—tell me about it!"

The Student concentrated all his powers on the task of formulating an adequate response. Slowly, hesitantly, now, he began to trace it out; for the was thinking almost in an alien plane, working with words and ideas subtly different from his own. To make the man understand, he had to choose phrases and expressions from the books he had read.

"It is the same," he inscribed. "A characteristic developed to usefulness. Long ago we studied these animals. We discovered that they could—communicate—through—over great distances. We increased—improved this power by—by—"

"By choosing those individuals in which the power was strangest, for breeding purposes, and in turn selecting those of their offspring and the descendants of their offspring in which the characteristics you desired to emphasize were most prominent," Cliff prompted. "Thus the abilities of these messenger creatures were gradually improved. Right?"

"Yes. Right," The Student printed. "Now, we make marks

on the flesh of a messenger creature. The irritation produces stimuli—a sequence of stimuli through nerves of skin, through brain, through—communicating organs. Other creatures, far off, pick up the impulses. Again there is a sequence of stimuli—communicating organs, nerves of skin, luminous cells of skin. The luminous cells which—which—"

Cliff had followed the strange explanation keenly, and now his own quick analytical powers grasped the idea which The Student was trying to express.

"The result is that the luminous cells in the skin of the receiving animals, corresponding in position to the luminous cells in the skin of the transmitting animal, are stimulated so that they emit light. Thus the symbols are made visible on the hide of the receiving messenger, just as they were originally traced. Is that correct?"

"Correct," the ovoid printed.

"There are entomologists who have suggested that certain insects have the power to communicate over distances like that," Cliff answered, "the cockroach, for instance. Their antennae are supposed to be miniature wireless sets, or something."

The Student did not offer to reply to this immediately, and so Rodney scratched one word in the sand. It was "Wait." For a minute or two he was busy piling odds and ends of wreckage beneath the spy window. Then, equipped with a piece of board, and a pencil taken from his discarded clothing, he scrambled to the top.

V

For the first time, he viewed the colony of the ovoids, the green canopy of luminous organisms, the hordes of sea people, the welter of infernal activity, the protoplasmic battery sparking on its isolated knoll, the moving shadows of robot beings, and the alert fighters that patrolled the outskirts of the city, where light and darkness met, like enemies holding each other in deadlock.

And the greatest of these miracles was this devil who called himself The Student, and who had backed off in revulsion at Cliff's approach.

But there were matters still to be investigated more closely. Dimly visible against the outer walls of the dome was a great shapeless mass that expanded and contracted as if it were breathing. Above the thing, and projecting from the dome like a canopy, was a curious curved shell of pearly, vitreous material.

His deductive faculties keyed up Cliff was almost certain that he understood the function of the arrangement. With his pencil he traced two questions on the board he held: "You know chemistry, physics, what oxygen and nitrogen are?"

"Yes. I have learned from research. I have learned from men's books," The Student replied, conquering his revulsion.

"You know that the air bladders of fish are filled with a mixture of oxygen and nitrogen?" Cliff asked. "You know that these gases are derived from the blood through the capillaries that line the air bladders, and that this oxygen and nitrogen is drawn originally from the oxygen and nitrogen dissolved in sea water, by means of the gills?"

"Yes."

"Then," Rodney went on, "the air in this place comes from animals too! That creature out there under that roof arrangement —it has gills which take the gases from the sea water and deliver them into the blood stream.

"Part of the oxygen is used to keep the creature alive, of course; but another part of it, together with the nitrogen, is discharged through the walls of capillaries as an actual, free gas, just as a portion of the oxygen and nitrogen in the blood of a fish is discharged into its hydrostatic organ or air bladder! The roof arrangement probably collects it in some way, and delivers it here to me!"

"That is correct," The Student printed. "Several animals work to give you air. Something new—ages to produce."

"Ages all right," Cliff breathed fervently. "I can well believe it!" He had spoken aloud.

But he was not finished yet. His face was flushed with eagerness, and his pulses were pounding. He had another question to print: "How is the water kept out of here? Nothing of flesh could prevent it from entering when the pressure is so great."

"There our skill failed," The Student responded. "We used the skill of men. We made pumps from parts of ships, and from materials which were our own. Air is pumped into the domes and from the domes—and water, when necessary."

The black tendrils withdrew from the window. Transparent lids flickered over the ovoid's great eyes. The transparent body swayed languorously, reminding Cliff of the first sting ray he had seen in an aquarium when he was a child.

It was clear at last, this alien science. Low down beyond the window, and against the shell of the dome, he glimpsed vague motion, where a monster toiled, swinging the lever of a rusty mechanism back and forth. The machine was a pump. Its operator was forcing to him the air which those other monsters produced. And beyond extended the murky, unbelievable reality of this submarine world.

"It is all glorious," Cliff printed in tribute, "even beautiful, almost—your achievements, your ways of doing things!"

The Student's tentacles stirred uneasily, but he made no reply.

A climax had been reached and passed. Rodney's enthusiasm began to cool a little, leaving him to become more cognizant of his own position. He thought of people and friends that he had known, and experiences he had enjoyed. The thoughts made him feel very cold and lonely.

His pencil scratched in the silence. "What are you going to do with me?" he was demanding.

"Keep you," was the response.

"Until I rot?"

"Until you rot."

It was a simple statement, devoid of either malice or compassion. Yet it was loaded with a dread significance. It meant staying here in this awful place, dying of starvation, perhaps, if the icy dankness didn't get him.

It meant death in any event; probably it meant madness. There would be ovoid eyes watching him, studying him, there would be ovoid beaks opening and closing vacuously—crazy, wonderful things everywhere, but only his submarine, and the depressing relics in the museum, familiar!

They had conversed, The Student and he. They had been almost friends. But beneath their apparently amicable attitudes toward each other had lain mistrust, broadened and deepened by the fact that they had so very little in common. Cliff saw it now.

Fury smoldered within him, but he held it in check.

He tossed aside the board, which was too covered with messages to be of any further use, and selected in its stead the pulped remnants of a book from the stack of things which supported him close to the spy window.

On one of the illegible pages he printed a note and held it up for the ovoid to see: "I know a better way for you to learn about my mind. Why not establish friendly relations with the world above? Certainly we have many things that you could use. And you have many things that we could use."

"No!" The Student's slender, boneless limbs seemed to jerk with emphasis as they traced the word and repeated it. "No!"

"It will happen anyway," Cliff promised. "Soon my people will come in machines of steel. They will make you understand what is best."

"Men coming here will not return," The Student answered.

And Clifford Rodney, remembering his own capture, and seeing now the waspish fighters patrolling the city of the ovoids, had no reason to doubt the weight of the statement. The sea people could protect themselves in their native element.

"You fear us? You mistrust us?" Cliff wanted to know.

The response was frank: "Yes."

"There is no reason."

To this The Student offered nothing.

Cliff tried a new angle, printing swiftly: "What do you know of the place we live in, really—sun, stars, planets, day, night? You have read of such things, no doubt. Wouldn't you like to see them? They are beautiful!"

"Beautiful?" The Student questioned. "Beautiful to you. To me—to us—horrible. The sun, the great dazzling light—it is horrible—and the heat, and the emptiness of air. They make me afraid. But they are wonderful—interesting, very interesting."

Some emotion seemed to stir the nameless soul of the ovoid, making him hesitant and uncertain.

Clifford Rodney thought he glimpsed a shadow of hope. He scarcely understood why he argued; whether he had some dim idea that he might save himself, or whether he was trying to advance the cause of mankind in its demand for expansion into alien realms.

Perhaps he was urging this queer intelligence of the deeps only because it is in the nature of any strong, healthy-minded youth to fight even the most adverse circumstance.

"You are interested, but you are afraid," he wrote. "Why don't you give your interest the chance it deserves? Why don't you—" He hesitated, not knowing quite what he wished to say. "Why don't you try to make contact with my people?"

For a flickering instant The Student paused, in a way that betrayed some hidden process within him. Then his decision seemed to come. "The world of men is the world of men," he printed. "The world of the sea is our world."

Further urgings on Cliff's part met only with flat refusal. He desisted at last, feeling oddly like a salesman, who through a slip in technique, has lost a sale. But that comparison could not be true either. He felt that The Student's obstinacy was too deep-seated to be overcome by mere salesmanship.

Dejectedly he watched the chalky words of the ovoid's last rebuff being washed from the window by the ocean.

Then those black tendrils holding the crayon went to work once more.

"You wish to escape," they printed, "it would be interesting, man, to watch you trying to escape."

Startled, Cliff wondered what bizarre mental process had given birth to these statements. Hope was resurrected.

"I cannot escape," he printed warily. "A glass port of my submarine needs repairing, for one thing. I have no materials."

"We will give you materials," was the astounding assertion.

"Eh?" the man said aloud, before he remembered that the ovoid could not hear his words, or understand them if he had been able to. "I could not get out of these domes anyway," he wrote. "It is useless."

Cliff Rodney was trying to make a subtle suggestion, in the hope that his unfathomable jailer would offer him a chance for freedom.

"Men have many tricks," The Student responded. "Watching you make use of tricks will be very interesting. We will learn much. Men have powerful explosives."

"I have no explosives!" Cliff insisted truthfully. A feeling of exasperation was rising within him.

"Men have many tricks," the ovoid repeated.

It was a tribute, nothing less; a tribute of mingled awe and mistrust, which the people of the depths felt for the people of the upper air. It was an example of other-world minds at work.

"You expect me to escape?" Cliff demanded.

"You will not escape," was the answer. "This is a test of your powers—a test of men's powers—an experiment. If you escape from the domes you shall be recaptured. We understand caution, man."

Thus Rodney's hopes were broken. But before this message had faded from the spy window, he wrote on a page of the tattered book an acceptance of the challenge: "Good! Get the materials you promised, and go to the devil!"

"Materials shall come," was the reply. "Go to the devil."

Breaking off the conversation thus, The Student wheeled in the water. His silvery fins flashed, and he vanished amid the throng of nightmare watchers.

Cliff wondered in a detached way what emotion, if any, had prompted the ovoid to repeat his angry epithet. Was it fury, amusement, some feeling beyond human conception, or just another bit of mimicry? Cliff didn't know; and because he didn't, the skin at the back of his neck tightened unpleasantly.

VI

The Student was out there among his fellows, giving orders in buzzing, tympanic tones, and preparing for the test. None could see the turmoil inside his brain—fear pitted against intense eagerness and interest.

He had made no decisions yet, nor would the decision he had in mind be sanctioned by his people. And it is certain, too, that he had no sympathy for the man who had fallen into his clutches, nor any desire to help him win his way to freedom.

Clifford Rodney did not immediately climb down from his position atop the wreckage he had piled up. Instead he remained by the window, looking out, for no particular reason. The only sound, the gentle, pulsing hiss of air being forced into his prison, had a monotonous effect that was more oppressive than absolute silence.

The weird colony wasn't so very different, though, from the cities at home, if you allowed your eyes to sort of blur out of focus; if you didn't see that sunken liner with the wispy ribbons trailing up from it, or the twisted architecture, or the inhabitants. The moving lights made you think of gay places and of gay music and people. One corner of his mouth drew back thoughtfully.

He could see that his chance of getting out of this mess was practically nil: In the first place, he had not the ghost of an idea how he might escape from the two domes. And if he did manage to break free from them, those armored fighters would bar his way. Their great claws would grip the submarine while they discharged their bolts of electric force. The metal hull would protect him to some extent, but not sufficiently, as he knew from experience.

More conscious than ever of the aches in his body, his loneliness and dejection, he looked down at his feet absently. Under them were books. He toed one. Its gilt title was obliterated, but he still could make it out—Kipling's "Barrack Room Ballads."

There was a friendliness in those dim, familiar words, and he chuckled a bit. Funny to think of an ovoid intellect trying to read and understand the poems in that volume—"Danny Deever," "Mandalay"! "If" was one of Kipling's works too: "If you can keep your head—"

Cliff smiled ruefully. Anyway he couldn't go wrong by attempting to improve matters a little.

He cast a final glance through the spy window. The ovoid crowd was growing thicker, anticipating activity. Behind them the fighters were gathering in the dusky shadows. In their claws some of them clutched massive bars of some material—rams, no doubt. Probably it had been one of those rams that had broken the port of his submarine.

Still garmented in the tattered carpet, he started in by setting his craft in order as best he could; straightening a warped propeller blade, draining water out of machines and instruments, and repairing those that were broken, whenever it was possible. At least, he had cloth and paper from the museum to help him mop up the wetness of everything.

The radio was a tangle, but he had hope of fixing it some way so that, by means of its beam, he could get a word up to the boys aboard the *Etruria*, on the surface. They couldn't help him, of course; they could only watch and wait.

Several hours must have passed without incident. While he worked, Cliff kept a close lookout for some sign of The Student. When it came, it was not delivered by the wizard of the deeps in person, but through the proxy of a messenger beast. The oak-leaf body of the creature wavered before a window, and on its hide luminous words appeared: "Food is coming through an air tube. Eat."

Cliff waited. From one of the air passages that entered the chamber, a mass of albuminous substance was blown, and it plopped to the floor. It looked like white of egg. Cliff touched a finger to it, and tasted the adhering dab.

No doubt it was from the body of some specialized marine animal. Probably it was very nourishing, and though it hardly excited Cliff's appetite, he realized that a man might train himself to relish such fare. At present, however, he preferred the brine-soaked chocolate and other food articles that he had brought with him on his adventure.

The messenger now exhibited another message: "Cement for port of the submarine, through same tube."

Its manner of arrival was similar to that of the food. A great lump of clear, firm jelly, probably also the product of a subsea creature.

Rodney gathered it up. As he carried it, a thin film of the substance hardened to glassy consistency on his hands, as collodion would do. He applied the jelly to the submarine's fractured port, inside and out, pressing it as firmly as he could. It would take some time for the cement to set.

He returned his attention to the radio transmitter, but only for a moment. Out of some inner well of his consciousness, the faint shadow of an idea had appeared.

He clambered from the submarine, and with a knife proceeded to dig the cement from around the huge, glassy plug that kept out the sea, just as he had done with the smaller plug that had sealed the entrance dome from the museum.

He worked entirely around the circular mass, loosening the adhesive substance as deeply as he could probe with his blade. No seepage of sea water appeared. The great block was intended to open outwardly. It was very thick, and beyond it, holding it shut, was the weight of the Atlantic.

But Clifford Rodney's plan was maturing. His efforts were not entirely useless. Undoubtedly that external door was not as firmly placed as it had previously been.

Cliff felt that he might yet demonstrate his ability to get out of the domes, though once beyond them, he could find no glimmer of reason to expect that he could elude the circle of horror that awaited him, even for a few seconds. He could only try to do his best, not so much in the expectation of escape, but to keep his energies busy.

Conscious that his every move was watched with absorbing interest by the ovoid audience at the spy windows, he rummaged in the museum, finding there some wire and strips of metal. These he brought back beside the submarine.

The drinking-water container of his craft was glass-lined. He unfastened it from its mounting, bashed in the top, and added to its contents a small amount of acid from his batteries. Then he carried it up through the hatch and set it on the floor of the chamber.

Into the water, at opposite sides of the container, he placed upright strips of metal to act as electrodes. To each of these he fastened wires, and attached their opposite ends to the powerful storage of the submarine.

Next, with paper and other refuse, he plugged the air tubes and drains of the two domes. Then he closed the switch, sending current through the apparatus he had just constructed.

There was a hiss as of a cauldron boiling as the electricity went through the water in the container, splitting it up into the elemental gases that composed it. Free oxygen and hydrogen bubbled away from the electrodes, mixing with the air of the domes.

This crude process of electrolysis was only the beginning. From the museum Cliff collected all the combustible materials he could find, and carried them into the chamber of the submarine—books, wood, a few scraps of celluloid, hard rubber, and so forth Then, with a little of the glassy cement that remained, he sealed the block that had separated the two domes, back into place.

There was another matter. For a few seconds it puzzled him, but finally a solution came. With wrenches he unbolted the heavy glass lens of the submarine's searchlight. Carefully he tapped the incandescent bulb beneath, beneath it, but leaving the delicate tungsten filaments undamaged. Against them he placed a wad of paper, daubed with the remaining benzine of his cigarette lighter.

So far, so good. He investigated the electrolysis apparatus again, shutting off the current for a moment while he scrape away the interfering bubbles that had collected on the crude electrodes.

Satisfied that his preparations were as complete as they could be made for the present, he shut himself inside the submarine and continued to work on the radio. After perhaps an hour of fussing and tampering, he believed that he might get a code message up to the *Etruria*.

He was almost ready, but there was one thing more. Aboard the craft there were ten flasks of compressed oxygen. Opening the valves of nine of these, he tosssed them through the hatch, retaining only one for breathing purposes.

While their contents soughed away he disconnected the electrolysis wires and closed the heavy steel door over his head. Working the key of the radio, he flashed out his appeal:

Rodney calling S. S. *Etruria*. . . . Rodney calling S. S. *Etruria* . . . .Captured by deep-sea creatures. . . . Trying to escape. . . . Get position and stand by to help. . . .

He repeated the communication several times. If it were received, it would be simple for his confrères to calculate his position from the direction the waves came in. They'd be waiting to pick him up. He even chuckled ruefully at the thought.

Through the ports he could see that the ovoids had moved back from the spy windows of the dome, anticipating danger; but their forms, and the forms of their fighters still hovered tensely in the luminescent haze of the ocean bed. He could not see many from his unfavorable position, but doubtless they were above and all around the dome, waiting for him to make a move!

214 A History of the Science-Fiction Magazine

Cliff forced himself to forget these unnerving thoughts. His hand touched the searchlight switch. His face was grim as he directed his gaze through another port toward the great, circular block that kept out the sea.

"Any one of three things can happen," he muttered: "The force can be insufficient, in which case what I have done won't accomplish anything at all—I'll still be locked in this dome. Or it can be too great, forcing out that plug all at once and letting the water in here all at once, to smash this steel coffin—all at once. Or it can be just right, admitting the ocean gradually enough so that this old tub can stand the strain."

Even the stout steel hull couldn't withstand the sudden thrust of the pressure of the deeps, he knew. Its position would be something like that of a nut under the blow of a hammer.

Cliff didn't want to give himself time to think. He closed the switch. Almost immediately there was a flash of red, as the hot filaments of the searchlight ignited the benzine-soaked paper that was in contact with them.

The flame spread through the dome in a wave of orange, as the hydrogen in the air burned. The sound which penetrated the thick shell of the craft was not the concussion of an explosion. Rather, it was a whispering, soughing roar; for the weight of the sea without was too vast for this feeble beginning of chemical forces to combat.

However, the reserves now came into action. Immersed in a highly oxygenated atmosphere under pressure, the paraphernalia from the museum took fire, and, though damp, rapidly became an inferno of incandescence that threw off enormous volumes of gas, expanding irresistibly with heat.

His heart thumping, Rodney kept his eyes glued to the great block which he hoped to dislodge. Stubbornly it continued to stand its ground, unmoved. He gritted his teeth as if, by sheer force of will, he sought to move the insensate thing that barred his way.

Moments passed. There was a snap like a muffled rifle shot. The block jerked, shuddered. Around its rim a curtain of glass appeared—no—not glass—water, screaming like a concourse of mad devils. The flood rolled over the floor, found the fire, and burst into steam, the pressure of which added to the titanic forces combating the titanic weight of the deeps.

More moments—the chamber was half full of water. Then,

with a sort of majestic resignation, the plug yielded, folding outward like a dying colossus. The ocean was in then, swiftly—so swiftly that a living eye could not capture its movements. The thud of it was heavier than a clap of thunder.

The submarine bobbed in the maelstrom like a bit of flotsam. But its hull held, even though it was flung repeatedly against the walls of the dome.

A minute went by before Clifford Rodney was able to do anything. He picked himself up from the place where he had been hurled, and scrambled to the controls. He could see the opening which led from his prison. The motors throbbed and the submarine turned, heading through the still surging water.

It did get clear of the dome. Cliff almost thought he had a chance. Maybe the confusion produced in the vicinity by the suction when the sea had entered the dome, had unnerved the ovoids momentarily.

He set the vertical screws spinning. Their lift wasn't very good. They had been damaged again. It was hardly remarkable after the way the little ship had been bounced around.

Cliff looked up through a ceiling port. Six fighters were pouncing down upon him, their hinged claws spread wide, their long, armored forms ghostly in the shadows. Others were approaching from all directions, accompanied by a horde of ovoids.

A seventh had joined the six now. Rodney had not seen it dart up from the deep muck of the bottoms, where it had lain, hidden even to the people of the depths. It bore a strange, glassy object of considerable size. Without much attention the man wondered what it might be.

"All right," he muttered, "you win! I hope you enjoyed the show!"

The fighters were upon him. He could hear the scrape of their claws against metal. Clouds of black stuff, like the ink of a squid, surrounded the submarine, hiding everything from view. He was still rising though—rather rapidly, he thought. In a moment the electric bolts would stun him.

Upward and upward he went. Cliff began to be puzzled. He detected scraping noises that he could not interpret. He must have advanced half a mile toward the surface since the start. It was all very odd.

There was a jolt. The climb became halting and erratic. The motors labored doggedly.

The water cleared. Cliff could make out schools of phosphorescent fish, hanging in the darkness like scattered galaxies. He was alone, far above the bottoms. There were no fighters around him, though he thought he glimpsed dim shapes vanishing beneath. They could not endure the reduced pressure that existed here.

Matters were better, far better, than he had dared to expect—mysteriously so. Now if the vertical screws continued to function at all—the submarine appeared to be badly damaged. It seemed clumsy, heavy.

Cliff came into a region of deep bluish light, beautiful as some fairy-peopled realm of infinity. Not long thereafter the bathyspheric craft broke through the sunlit surface of the Atlantic. Cliff opened the valves of a pressure tank, inflating the bellows like water wings which supported the heavy submarine when it was on the surface.

How had this all happened? There was still the mystery. He almost forgot that he must gradually reduce the pressure around him, to avoid the "bends."

At length he opened the hatch and crawled out onto the rounded top of the undersea boat. An egg-shaped object was fastened to the metal shell just behind the hatch. Rodney approached it, unable yet to fathom its nature. Glassy cement, like that with which he had recently become acquainted, held the thing in place.

It was a massive object, six feet through at its greatest diameter. It was made of the same material as the domes, except that this substance was darker, perhaps to shield what it covered from the fierce sun.

Rodney peered into the semi-transparent depths of the object, discerning there a huddled form enveloped in a milky, semi-liquid film. The form was delicate; vital organs pulsed visibly beneath its skin. It had flippers, and masses of black tendrils. Its beaked mouth opened and closed, giving it an air of vacuous solemnity, but its eyes were keen. Its tentacles clutched a white crayon. It was The Student!

Clifford Rodney's mind was a whirl as he sought to solve the riddle. Then, since no other means of printing a message was available, he traced words with a finger on the wet surface of the oval object:

"You helped me—how?"

The Student's tendrils trembled as he printed the answer on the inside of his protecting shell: "I helped you. The six fighters, and the seventh, were mine. They did not attack you. Concealed by the liquid that darkens the sea, they raised your submarine upward.

"They attached me to the submarine. They raised it as far as they could climb. It was a trick to outwit my people. They forbid traffic with the upper world. They are afraid. I was afraid, but at last I chose. While you prepared for the test an idea came. I used it, outwitting my people. I am afraid. But I am glad."

Rodney was lost in the fantastic wonder of it all. "Thank you, my friend!" he printed.

The Student plied his crayon again: "Friend? No. I am not your friend. What I did, I did for myself."

"Then why in reason's name are you here?" Cliff printed. "Men will put you in an aquarium, and stare at and study you!"

"Good," was the response, "I am glad. Men study me. I study them. Good. That is why I came: to see the accomplishments of men, to see the stars, to see the planets. Now I see the sun and sky—dreadful but interesting—very interesting. Good."

"Good if you don't smother before you can be transferred to a suitable aquarium," Rodney traced.

"I am safe here," the ovoid answered with a nervous flurry of tendrils. "The pressure is normal. There is much oxygen in the fluid which surrounds me. But do what you must, man. I am waiting."

Cliff was accustomed enough to the situation by now to grin down at the great dark egg. Mixed with his awe there was a curious inner warmth. Man and ovoid were different in form and mind; perhaps real sympathy between them was impossible. But Cliff had found a tangible similarity.

In this sullen devil of the depths eagerness to know the unknown had battled fear, and had won. The Student had placed himself, without defense, in the power of the unknown. It took guts to do that, courage—

Young Rodney thought of many things as he looked out over the water in search of signs of rescue. A ship was approaching. It was near enough so that he could recognize it as the *Etruria*.

"The boys'll probably call you Davy Jones' ambassador or something," he said banteringly, addressing the ovoid, "I hope you're sport enough to take it, old socks!"

But The Student wouldn't have listened even if he were able. His eyes were drinking in the miracle of the approaching ship.

Appendices

The following appendices are for the use of those whom, I hope, have had their appetite whetted by this anthology and wish to know slightly more about the period. Such detail would fill volumes, and I have tried my best to condense it into assimilable form without losing too much detail.

The appendices are made up as follows:

(a) Checklist of Authors' Works (1926-1935): This details the science fiction and fantasy works of the ten authors represented in this collection, plus ten other authors whose work best reflects this period of sf.

(b) Summary of Magazine Issues (1926-1935): A guide to the number and frequency of issues of the sf and weird magazines covered in this book, professional and amateur alike.

(c) Glossary of Magazine Editors: A Who's Who of sf/fantasy editors during this period with a guide to the number of issues for which they were responsible.

(d) Note on Key Illustrators: A guide to the cover artists of the major magazines at this time.

In the author index it has been necessary to use a certain number of abbreviations. These are standard in the case of the magazine dates (e.g. Feb 30 = February 1930; Fall 28 = Fall (Autumn) 1928). After the story title is an indication as to its length, i.e.

> s = short story (up to 12,000 words)
>
> nt = novelette (up to 20,000 words)
>
> sn = short novel (up to 30,000 words)
>
> n = novel (over 30,000 words). If serialized then n3 = three part serial. (In the case of a serial the date that follows is for the first episode.)

Magazine Titles have been abbreviated as follows:

AD   =   Amazing Detective Tales.
ARG   =   Argosy.
AS   =   Amazing Stories.
ASQ   =   Amazing Stories Quarterly.
ASS   =   Astounding Stories.
AW   =   Air Wonder Stories.
FF   =   The Fantasy Fan.
FM   =   Fantasy Magazine.
GN   =   The Galleon.
MC   =   The Magic Carpet Magazine.
MT   =   Marvel Tales.
OS   =   Oriental Stories.
PN   =   Paris Nights.
S & I =   Science & Invention
SD   =   Scientific Detective Monthly.
SFD   =   Science Fiction Digest.
SFS   =   Science Fiction Series.
ST   =   Strange Tales.
SW   =   Science Wonder Stories.
SWQ   =   Science Wonder Quarterly.
TSB   =   Ten Story Book.
WS   =   Wonder Stories.
WSQ   =   Wonder Stories Quarterly.
WT   =   Weird Tales.

An asterisk (*) after a story title implies the story was published under a pseudonym. Information on this will appear immediately below each author's listing.

A stiletto (†) after a story means it was written in collaboration with another author(s) whose name(s) will appear immediately afterwards.

Letters following a story title means the story forms part of a series. Information on this will appear immediately below each author's listing.

(A) CHECKLIST OF AUTHORS' WORKS, 1926-35

1—CHARLES WILLARD DIFFIN—

1. Spawn of the Stars	s	ASS	Feb 30
2. The Moon Master	nt	ASS	Jun 30
3. Out of the Dreadful Depths*	s	ASS	Jun 30
4. The Power and the Glory	s	ASS	Jul 30
5. The Pirate Planet	n4	ASS	Nov 30
6. The Eye of Allah*	s	ASS	Jan 31
7. When the Mountain Came to Miramar	s	ASS	Mar 31
8. Dark Moon .. (A)	nt	ASS	May 31
9. Holocaust	s	ASS	Jun 31
10. Brood of the Dark Moon (A)	n4	ASS	Aug 31
11. The Dog That Laughed	nt	ST	Sep 31
12. The Hammer of Thor	s	ASS	Mar 32
13. The Finding of Haldgren .. (A)	nt	ASS	Apr 32
14. Two Thousand Miles Below	n4	ASS	Jun 32
15. The Terror By Night	s	ST	Jan 33
16. Land of the Lost	n2	ASS	Dec 33
17. The Long Night	nt	ASS	May 34
18. Blue Magic	n4	ASS	Nov 35

Pseudonyms: *C. D. Willard (stories 3, 6).

Series: A: the 'Dark Moon' trilogy (stories 8, 10, 13).

2—LLOYD ARTHUR ESHBACH—

1. The Man With the Silver Disc	s	SD	Feb 30
2. The Invisible Destroyer	s	AW	May 30
3. The Gray Plague	s	ASS	Nov 30
4. The Valley of Titans	nt	AS	Mar 31
5. A Voice From the Ether	nt	AS	May 31
6. The Light From Infinity	s	AS	Mar 32
7. The Time Conqueror	s	WS	Jul 32
8. The Man With the Hour Glass	s	MT	May 34
9. 'Cosmos' serial (part 15)	s	FM	Sep 34
10. The Brain of Ali Kahn	s	WS	Oct 34
11. The Kingdom of Thought	nt	AS	Aug 35
12. The Meteor Miners	s	AS	Dec 35

Note: Eshbach's name appeared on some stories as Eschbach.

3—FRANCIS FLAGG—

1. The Machine Man of Ardathia (A)	s	AS	Nov 27
2. The Master Ants	nt	AS	May 28
3. The Blue Dimension	s	AS	Jun 28
4. The Chemical Brain	s	WT	Jan 29

5. The Dancer in thr Crystal	.. ..	s	WT	Dec 29
6. The Land of the Bipos	.. ..	s	SW	Feb 30
7. An Adventure in Time	.. ..,	s	SW	Apr 30
8. The Lizard Men of Bu-Lo	.. ..	s	WS	Oct 30
9. The Jelly-Fish	.. ..	s	WT	Oct 30
10. The Seed of the Toc-Toc Birds	.. .. ..	s	ASS	Jan 31
11. The Picture	.. ..	s	WT	Feb 31
12. The Synthetic Monster ..	.. .. .· ..	s	WS	Mar 31
13. The Heads of Apex	.. ..	s	ASS	Oct 31
14. The Superman of Dr. Jukes ..	.. .. ..	s	WS	Nov 31
15. The Smell	.. ..	s	ST	Jan 32
16. The Cities of Ardathia .. (A)	.. .. ..	nt	AS	Mar 32
17. By the Hands of the Dead	.. ..	s	ST	Mar 32
18. The Resistant Ray	.. ..	s	AS	Jul 32
19. After Armageddon	.. ..	s	WS	Sep 32
20. 'Cosmos' serial (part 5) ..	.. ..	s	SFD	Nov 33
21. The Mentanicals ..	.. ..	s	AS	Apr 34
22. The Distortion Out of Space ..	.. .. ..	s	WT	Aug 34
23. Earth's Lucky Day (†Forrest J. Ackerman)..		s	WS	Mar 36

Series: A: Ardathia (stories 1, 16).

4—RAYMOND Z. GALLUN—

1. The Crystal Ray	.. ..	s	AW	Nov 29
2. The Space Dwellers	.. ..	s	SW	Nov 29
3. Atomic Fire	.. .. ..·.	s	AS	Apr 31
4. The Lunar Chrysalis ..	.. ..	s	AS	Sep 31
5. The Revolt of the Star Men ..	.. .. ..	nt	WSQ	Win 32
6. Waves of Compulsion ..	.. ..	s	WS	Mar 32
7. Moon Mistress	.. ..	s	WS	May 32
8. The Menace From Mercury († John B. Michel)	.. ..	s	WSQ	Sum 32
9. The Flight of the RX-1 ..	.. ..	s	AS	Jul 33
10. Moon Plague	.. ..	nt	WS	Jan 34
11. Space Flotsam	.. ..	s	ASS	Feb 34
12. The World Wrecker ..	.. ..	s	ASS	Jun 34
13. The Wand of Creation	.. .. ..	s	ASS	Sep 34
14. The Machine from Ganymede	.. .. ..	s	ASS	Nov 34
15. Old Faithful .. (A) ..	.. .. ..	nt	ASS	Dec 34
16. Mind Over Matter	.. ..	s	ASS	Jan 35
17. Telepathic Piracy	.. ..	s	ASS	Mar 35
18. N'goc	.. ..	s	ASS	May 35
19. Blue Haze on Pluto	.. ..	s	ASS	Jun 35
20. The Son of Old Faithful .. (A)	.. .. ..	nt	ASS	Jul 35
21. Derelict	.. ..	s	ASS	Oct 35
22. Davy Jones' Ambassador	.. ..	ñt	ASS	Dec 35
23. Avalanche*	.. ..	s	ASS	Dec 35
24. Nova Solis**	.. ..	s	ASS	Dec 35

25. Buried Moon	..	..	..	..	..	..	.. s ASS Feb 36
26. Mad Robot	..	..	..	..	..	..	.. s ASS Mar 36

Pseudonyms: *Dow Elstar (story 23); **E. V. Raymond (story 24).

Series: A: Old Faithful (stories 15, 20). As bibliographer's licence, the third story of the trilogy, "Child of the Stars" would be number 27, as it appeared in *Astounding Stories* for April 1936.

5—EDMOND HAMILTON—

1. The Monster-God of Mamurth	s	WT	Aug 26
2. Across Space	n3	WT	Sep 26
3. The Metal Giants	nt	WT	Dec 26
4. The Atomic Conquerors	nt	WT	Feb 27
5. Evolution Island	s	WT	Mar 27
6. The Moon Menace	nt	WT	Sep 27
7. The Time Raider	n4	WT	Oct 27
8. The Comet Doom	nt	AS	Jan 28
9. The Dimension Terror	nt	WT	Jun 28
10. Crashing Suns	n2	WT	Aug 28
11. The Polar Doom	nt	WT	Nov 28
12. The Star-Stealers .. (A)	nt	WT	Feb 29
13. The Sea Horror	nt	WT	Mar 29
14. Locked Worlds	s	ASQ	Spr 29
15. Within the Nebula .. (A)	nt	WT	May 29
16. The Abysmal Invaders	s	WT	Jun 29
17. Outside the Universe .. (A)	n4	WT	Jul 29
18. The Other Side of the Moon	nt	ASQ	Fal 29
19. Hidden World	n	SWQ	Fal 29
20. Cities in the Air	n2	AW	Nov 29
21. The Life Masters	s	WT	Jan 30
22. The Comet-Drivers .. (A)	nt	WT	Feb 30
23. Evans of the Earth Guard	s	AW	Apr 30
24. The Invisible Master	nt	SD	Apr 30
25. The Plant Revolt	s	WT	Apr 30
26. The Space Visitors	s	AW	May 30
27. The Murder in the Clinic	nt	SD	May 30
28. The Sun People.. (A)	s	WT	May 30
29. The Universe Wreckers	n3	AS	May 30
30. The Death Lord	nt	WT	Jul 30
31. World Atavism	s	AS	Aug 30
32. The Second Satellite..	s	ASS	Aug 30
33. Pigmy Island	s	WT	Aug 30
34. The Man Who Saw the Future	s	AS	Oct 30
35. The Mind-Master	s	WT	Oct 30
36. The Cosmic Cloud .. (A)	nt	WT	Nov 30
37. The Horror City .. ..-	s	WT	Feb 31
38. Monsters of Mars	nt	ASS	Apr 31

39. Ten Million Years Ahead	..	..	..	..	nt WT Apr 31
40. The Man Who Evolved ..	..	..	..	..	s WS Apr 31
41. The Earth-Owners ..	..	..	..	..	s WT Aug 31
42. The Sargasso of Space	..	,.	..	..	s ASS Sep 31
43. The Shot From Saturn	..	..	..	..	s WT Oct 31
44. Creatures of the Comet ..	..	..	..	..	s WT Dec 31
45. The Reign of the Robots	..	..	..	..	s WS Dec 31
46. Dead Legs	..	..	..	..	s ST Jan 32
47. The Three from the Tomb	..	..	..	..	s WT Feb 32
48. A Conquest of Two Worlds ..	..	..	..	..	s WS Feb 32
49. The Earth-Brain	..	..	..	..	s WT Apr 32
50. The Terror Planet ..	..	..	..	..	s WT May 32
51. Space Rocket Murders ..	..	..	..	..	nt AS Oct 32
52. The Dogs of Dr. Dwann	..	..	..	..	nt WT Oct 32
53. Vampire Village* ..	..	..	..	..	s WT Nov 32
54. The Man Who Conquered Age	..	..	..	s WT Dec 32
55. Snake-Man* ..	..	..	..	..	s WT Jan 33
56. Kaldar, World of Antares	.. (B)	..	..	s MC Apr 33
57. The Star-Roamers ..	..	..	..	..	s WT Apr 33
58. The Island of Unreason ..	..	..	..	s WS May 33
59. The Fire Creatures ..	..	..	..	..	s WT Jul 33
60. The Horror on the Asteroid ..	..	..	..	s WT Sep 33
61. The Snake-Men of Kaldar	.. (B)	..	..	s MC Oct 33
62. The Vampire Master*	..	..	..	..	n4 WT Oct 33
63. The War of the Sexes	..	..	..	..	s WT Nov 33
64. The Man with X-Ray Eyes	..	..	..	..	s WS Nov 33
65. The Man Who Returned ..	..	..	..	..	s WT Feb 34
66. Thundering Worlds ..	..	..	..	..	s WT Mar 34
67. Corsairs of the Cosmos	.. (A)	..	..	nt WT Apr 34
68. 'Cosmos' serial (part 17)	..	..	..	s FM Dec 34
69. Master of the Genes	..	..	..	..	s WS Jan 35
70. Murder in the Grave	..	..	..	..	s WT Feb 35
71. The Truth Gas ..	..	..	..	..	s WS Feb 35
72. The Eternal Cycle	..	..	..	..	s WS Mar 35
73. The Accursed Galaxy	..	..	..	..	s ASS Jul 35
74. The Avenger From Atlantis ..	..	..	..	s WT Jul 35
75. The Six Sleepers	..	..	..	..	s WT Oct 35
76. The Cosmic Pantograph ..	..	..	..	s WS Oct 35
77. The Great Brain of Kaldar	.. (B)	..	..	nt WT Dec 35
78. In The World's Dusk	..	..	..	..	s WT Mar 36

Pseudonyms: *Hugh Davidson (stories 53, 55, 62).

Series: A: Interstellar Patrol (stories 12, 15, 17, 22, 28, 36, 67).
        B: Stuart Merrick on Kaldar (stories 56, 61, 77).

6—M. M. KAPLAN—

1. One Prehistoric Night* .. .. s WS Nov 34

2. Twenty-Five Centuries Late**	s	WS	Nov 34
3. When Time Stood Still**	s	AS	Feb 35
4. The Elixir of Progress**	s	WS	Apr 35
5. One Hundred Generations**	s	WS	Sep 35
6. The Imperfect Guess*	s	WS	Mar 36

Pseudonyms: *Philip Barshofsky (stories 1, 6); **Philip Jacques Bartel (others).

7—DRURY D. SHARP—

1. The Goddess of the Painted Priests	s	WT	Apr 29
2. The Eternal Man .. (A)	s	SW	Aug 29
3. In the Toils of the Black Kiva	s	WT	Oct 29
4. Thirty Miles Down	nt	SFS	Dec 29
5. The Day of the Beast	s	SW	May 30
6. The Eternal Man Revives .. (A)	s	WSQ	Sum 30
7. Three Worlds of Conquer	s	WSQ	Win 31
8. The Satellite of Doom	s	WS	Jan 31
9. The Messenger From Space	s	WS	Jan 33
10. At Bay in the Void	s	WS	Feb 33
11. Captive of the Crater	s	WS	Jun 33
12. Higher Jurisdiction	s	WS	Dec 34

Series: A: The Eternal Man (stories 2, 6).

8—CLIFFORD D. SIMAK

1. The World of the Red Sun	s	WS	Dec 31
2. Mutiny on Mercury	s	WS	Mar 32
3. The Voice in the Void	s	WSQ	Spr 32
4. Hellhounds of the Cosmos	s	ASS	Jun 32
5. The Asteroid of Gold	s	WS	Nov 32
6. The Creator	s	MT	Mar 35

9—R. F. STARZL—

1. Out of the Sub-Universe	s	ASQ	Sum 28
2. The Eye of Prometheus	s	SD	Jan 30
3. Madness of the Dust	s	AS	May 30
4. The Planet of Dread	s	ASS	Aug 30
5. The King of the Black Bowl	s	WS	Sep 30
6. The Red Gem of Courage	s	ARG	Sep 30
7. The Globoid Terror	s	AS	Nov 30
8. Hornets of Space	s	WS	Nov 30
9. The Terrors of Aryl	s	WS	Mar 31
10. The Earthman's Burden	s	ASS	Jun 31
11. The Man Who Changed the Future	s	WS	Jun 31

Beside these ten authors represented in the anthology I have chosen a further ten most representative of this decade. Choosing was not easy, but I have avoided those authors whose main influence was pre-1926 or post-1935, and also authors such as John Russell Fearn who will appear in future collections in this series. Similarly authors whose main contribution to sf was outside the magazine field have, of necessity, been avoided. Nevertheless this has still left a difficult choice, and I feel honourable mention should be made of such authors as Edgar Rice Burroughs, Ray Cummings, Abraham Merritt, Arthur Burks, Paul Ernst, Ralph Milne Farley, Otis Adelbert Kline, Murray Leinster, Ed Earl Repp, Bob Olsen, Harl Vincent, Clare Winger Harris, John Beynon Harris, Joseph Skidmore and Eando Binder, none of whom is listed here.

The chosen ten are:

Miles J. Breuer   P. Schuyler Miller
John W. Campbell   Nathan Schachner
Stanton Coblentz   Edward E. Smith
David H. Keller   A. Hyatt Verrill
S. P. Meek   Donald Wandrei

1—MILES J. BREUER, M.D. (1889-1947)

4. The Puzzle Duel	s	ASQ	Win 28
5. The Appendix and the Spectacles	s	AS	Dec 28
6. The Captured Cross-Section	s	AS	Feb 29
7. Buried Treasure	s	AS	Apr 29
8. The Book of Worlds	s	AS	Jul 29
9. Rays and Men	nt	ASQ	Sum 29
10. The Girl From Mars (†Jack Williamson)	nt	SFS	Nov 29
11. A Baby on Neptune (†Clare Winger Harris)	s	AS	Dec 29
12. The Hungry Guinea-Pig	s	AS	Jan 30
13. The Fitzgerald Contraction .. (A)	s	SW	Jan 30
14. The Gostak and the Doshes	s	AS	Mar 30
15. The Driving Power	s	AS	Jul 30
16. Paradise and Iron	n	ASQ	Sum 30
17. The Time Valve .. (A)	s	WS	Jul 30
18. Inferiority Complex	s	AS	Sep 30
19. A Problem in Communication	s	ASS	Sep 30
20. The Birth of a New Republic (†Jack Williamson)	n	ASQ	Win 30
21. On Board the Martian Liner	s	AS	Mar 31
22. The Time Flight	s	AS	Jun 31
23. The Demons of Rhadi-Mu	s	ASQ	Fall 31
24. Mechanocracy	s	AS	Apr 32
25. The Einstein See-Saw	s	ASS	Apr 32
26. The Perfect Planet	s	AS	May 32
27. The Finger of the Past	s	AS	Nov 32
28. The Strength of the Weak	s	AS	Dec 33
29. Millions for Defense	s	AS	Mar 35
30. Mars Colonizes	s	MT	Sum 35
31. The Chemistry Murder Case	s	AS	Oct 35

Series: (A) Herman Wendelin (stories 13, 17).

2—JOHN W. CAMPBELL (1910-1971)

1. When the Atoms Failed .. (A)	s	AS	Jan 30
2. The Metal Horde .. (A)	s	AS	Apr 30
3. Piracy Preferred .. (B)	nt	AS	Jun 30
4. The Voice in the Void	s	ASQ	Sum 30
5. The Black Star Passes .. (B)	n	ASQ	Fal 30
6. Solarite .. (B)	nt	AS	Nov 30
7. Islands of Space .. (B)	n	ASQ	Spr 31
8. The Derelicts of Ganymede	s	WS	Jan 32
9. Invaders From The Infinite .. (B)	n	ASQ	Spr 32
10. The Electronic Siege .. (C)	s	WS	Apr 32
11. The Last Evolution	s	AS	Aug 32
12. Space Rays .. (C)	s	WS	Dec 32
13. Beyond the End of Space	n2	AS	Mar 33
14. The Battery of Hate	s	AS	Nov 33
15. 'Cosmos' serial (part 6)	s	SFD	Dec 33

16. Twilight* .. (D)	s	ASS	Nov 34
17. The Irrelevant**	s	ASS	Dec 34
18. Atomic Power* .. .., ..	s	ASS	Dec 34
19. The Mightiest Machine	n5	ASS	Dec 34
20. Mother World	n3	AS	Jan 35
21. The Machine* .. (E)	s	ASS	Feb 35
22. Blindness*	s	ASS	Mar 35
23. The Escape*	nt	ASS	May 35
24. The Invaders* .. (E)	nt	ASS	Jun 35
25. Rebellion* .. (E)	nt	ASS	Jul 35
26. Night* .. (D)	nt	ASS	Oct 35

Pseudonyms: *Don A. Stuart (stories 16, 18, 21, 22, 23, 24, 25, 26).
**Karl Van Kampen (story 17).

Series: A: Steven Waterson (stories 1, 2); B: Arcot, Wade & Morey (stories 3, 5, 6, 7, 9); C: Don Barclay (stories 10, 12); D: Dying Earth (stories 16, 26); E: The Teachers (stories 21, 24, 25).

3—STANTON A. COBLENTZ (born 1896)—

1. The Sunken World	n	ASQ	Sum 28
2. After 12,000 Years	n	ASQ	Spr 29
3. The Gas-Weed	s	AS	May 29
4. The Radio Telescope	s	AS	Jun 29
5. The Making of Misty Isle	s	SW	Jun 29
6. Wand of Creation	s	AS	Aug 29
7. Reclaimers of the Ice	n	ASQ	Spr 30
8. A Circle of Science	s	AS	May 30
9. Missionaries from the Sky	s	AS	Nov 30
10. Into Plutonian Depths	n	WSQ	Spr 31
11. The Blue Barbarians	n	ASQ	Sum 31
12. The Planet of Youth	s	WS	Oct 32
13. The Man From Tomorrow	n	ASQ	Spr 33
14. The Men Without Shadows	s	AS	Oct 13
15. The Confession of Dr. DeKalb	s	ASS	Jan 34
16. Manna From Mars	s	ASS	Mar 34
17. The Green Plague	s	ASS	Apr 34
18. The Radio Mind-Ray	s	ASS	Jul 34
19. In The Footsteps of the Wasp	s	AS	Aug 34
20. The Truth About the Psycho-Tector	s	ASS	Oct 34
21. Beyond the Universe	s	AS	Dec 34
22. Riches For Pluto	s	ASS	Dec 34
23. In Caverns Below	n3	WS	Mar 35
24. Triple-Geared	s	ASS	Apr 35
25. Older Than Methusaleh	s	AS	May 35
26. An Episode In Space	s	ASS	May 35
27. The Golden Planetoid	s	AS	Aug 35

4—DAVID H. KELLER (1880-1966)

1. The Revolt of the Pedestrians	s	AS	Feb	28
2. The Yeast Men	s	AS	Apr	28
3. A Biological Experiment	s	AS	Jun	28
The Menace: .. (A)	n	ASQ	Sum	28
4. (i) The Menace				
5. (ii) The Gold Ship				
6. (iii) The Tainted Flood				
7. (iv) The Insane Avalanche				
8. The Little Husbands	s	WT	Jul	28
9. Unlocking The Past	s	AS	Sep	28
10. The Dogs of Salem ..	s	WT	Sep	28
11. Stenographer's Hands	s	ASQ	Fall	28
12. The Psychophonic Nurse	s	AS	Nov	28
13. The Jelly Fish ..	s	WT	Jan	29
14. The Worm	s	AS	Mar	29
15. The Damsel and Her Cat	s	WT	Apr	29
16. The Threat of the Robot..	s	SW	Jun	29
17. White Collars ..	s	ASQ	Sum	29
18. The Bloodless War ..	s	AW	Jul	29
19. The Flying Fool	s	AS	Jul	29
20. The Boneless Horror	s	SW	Jul	29
21. The Eternal Professors	s	AS	Aug	29
22. The Feminine Metamorphosis .. (A)	s	SW	Aug	29
23. The Human Termites	n3	SW	Sep	29
24. Euthanasia Limited .. (A)	s	ASQ	Fall	29
25. The Battle of the Toads .. (B)	s	WT	Oct	29
26. Tailed Men of Cornwall .. (B)	s	WT	Nov	29
27. Eight, Sixty Seven	s	TSB	Nov	29
28. The Garnet Mine* ..	s	TSB	Nov	29
29. The Conquerors	n2	SW	Dec	29
30. No Other Man .. (B)	s	WT	Dec	29
31. A 1950 Marriage*	s	PN	Dec	29
32. The Thought Projector	nt	SFS	Nov	29
33. Air Lines ..	s	AS	Jan	30
34. Mr. Summer's Adventure*	s	TSB	Jan	30
35. A Twentieth Century Homunculus	s	AS	Feb	30
36. A Scientific Widowhood .. (A)	s	SD	Feb	30
37. The Flying Threat ..	nt	ASQ	Spr	30
38. Creation Unforgiveable ..	s	WT	Apr	30
39. The Evening Star	n2	SW	Apr	30
40. The Ivy War	s	AS	May	30
41. Burning Water .. (A)	s	AD	Jun	30
42. The Moon Rays	s	WSQ	Sum	30
43. Menacing Claws .. (A)	s	AD	Sep	30
44. The Virgin*	s	TSB	Sep	30
45. Boomeranging 'Round the Moon ..	s	ASQ	Fall	30

Pseudonyms: *Amy Worth (non-sf fiction, many horror).

Series: A: Detective Taine of San Francisco (stories 4-7, 22, 24, 36, 41, 43, 53, 81, 84).
B: Overlord of Cornwall (stories 25, 26, 30, 46).

5—STERNER ST. PAUL MEEK (born 1894)

1. The Murgatroyd Experiments		s	ASQ	Win 29
2. Futility		s	AS	Jul 29
3. The Red Peril		s	AS	Sep 29
4. The Cave of Horror	(A)	s	ASF	Jan 30
5. The Perfect Counterfeit	(A)	s	SD	Jan 30
6. The Radio Robbery		s	AS	Feb 30
7. The Thief of Time	(A)	s	ASF	Feb 30
8. Into Space*		s	ASF	Feb 30
9. The Ray of Madness	(A)	s	ASF	Apr 30
10. Cold Light	(A)	s	ASF	May 30
11. The Gland Murders	(A)	s	AD	Jun 30
12. Trapped in the Depths		s	WS	Jun 30
13. Beyond the Heaviside Layer		s	ASF	Jul 30
14. The Last War		nt	AS	Aug 30
15. The Attack From Space		s	ASF	Sep 30
16. The Tragedy of Spider Island		s	WS	Sep 30
17. Stolen Brains		s	ASF	Oct 30
18. Drums of Tapajos		n3	AS	Nov 30
19. The Sea Terror	(A)	s	ASF	Dec 30
20. The Osmotic Theorem		s	WSQ	Win 30
21. The Black Lamp	(A)	s	ASF	Feb 31
22. The Earth's Cancer	(A)	s	AS	Mar 31
23. When Caverns Yawned	(A)	s	ASF	May 31
24. Submicroscopic	(B)	s	AS	Aug 31
25. The Port of Missing Planes	(A)	s	ASF	Aug 31
26. Awlo of Ulm	(B)	s	AS	Sep 31
27. Nasturtia		s	ST	Sep 31
28. The Solar Magnet	(A)	s	ASF	Oct 31
29. The Black Mass		s	ST	Nov 31
30. Giants on the Earth		n2	ASF	Dec 31
31. Troyana		n3	AS	Feb 32
32. Poisoned Air	(A)	s	ASF	Mar 32
33. B.C. 30,000		s	ASF	Apr 32
34. The Great Drought	(A)	s	ASF	May 32
35. Vanishing Gold	(A)	s	WS	May 32
36. The Synthetic Entity		s	WS	Jan 33
37. The Curse of the Valedi		s	WT	Jul 35

Pseudonyms: *Sterner St. Paul (story 8).

Series: A: Dr. Bird & Operative Carnes (stories 4, 5, 7, 9-11, 19, 21-23, 25, 28, 32, 34, 35).
B: Ulm (stories 24, 26).

6—P. SCHUYLER MILLER (born 1912)

1. The Red Plague		s	WS	Jul 30
2. Dust of Destruction		s	WS	Feb 31

Pseudonyms: *Dennis McDermott (used by Miller on story 6, but by Walter Dennis and Paul McDermott on story 9).

7—NATHAN SCHACHNER (1895-1955)

(Note: in this index the symbol ‡ following the story title denotes Schachner collaborated with Arthur Leo Zagat).

26. Redmask of the Outlands .. (B) .. .. .. nt ASS Jan 34
27. The Time Imposter .. .. s ASS Mar 34
28. He From Procyon .. .. n ASS Apr 34
29. The 100th Generation .. .. s ASS May 34
30. Stratosphere Towers .. .. nt ASS Aug 34
31. The Living Equation .. .. s ASS Sep 34
32. The Great Thirst .. .. nt ASS Nov 34
33. The Ultimate Metal .. .. s ASS Feb 35
34. Mind of the World .. .. nt ASS Mar 35
35. When the Sun Dies** .. .. s ASS Mar 35
36. The Orb of Probability .. .. nt ASS Jun 35
37. The Son of Redmask .. (B) .. .. .. nt ASS Aug 35
38. World Gone Mad .. .. s AS Oct 35
39. Intra-Planetary** .. .. s ASS Oct 35
40. I Am Not God .. .. n2 ASS Oct 35
41. The Isotope Men .. .. nt ASS Jan 36
42. Entropy .. .. nt ASS Mar 36

Pseudonyms: *Walter Glamis (story 24); **Chan Corbett (stories 35, 39).
Series: Note—story 3 is the sequel to story 2.
        A: The Scientists Revolt (stories 19, 20, 21).
        B: Redmask (stories 26, 37).

8—EDWARD ELMER SMITH (1890-1965)

1. The Skylark of Space .. (A) .. .. .. n3 AS Aug 28
2. Skylark Three .. (A) .. .. n3 AS Aug 30
3. Spacehounds of IPC .. .. n3 AS Jul 31
4. Triplanetary .. (B) .. .. n4 AS Jan 34
5. 'Cosmos' serial (Part 13) .. .. s FM Jul 34
6. The Skylark of Valeron .. (A) .. .. .. n7 ASS Aug 34

Series: A: Seaton and DuQuesne.
        B: (This would later be rewritten to form part of the Lensman series).

9—A. HYATT VERRILL (1871-1954)

1. Beyond the Pole .. .. n2 AS Oct 26
2. Through the Crater's Rim .. .. s AS Dec 26
3. The Man Who Could Vanish .. .. .. s AS Jan 27
4. The Plague of the Living Dead .. .. .. nt AS Apr 27
5. The Voice From the Inner World .. .. .. s AS Jul 27
6. The Ultra-Elixir of Youth .. .. s AS Aug 27
7. The Astounding Discoveries of Doctor
      Mentiroso.. .. .. s AS Nov 27
8. The Psychological Solution .. .. s AS Jan 28
9. The King of the Monkey Men .. .. .. nt ASQ Spr 28
10. The World of the Giant Ants.. .. .. .. n ASQ Fall 28
11. Into the Green Prism .. .. n2 AS Mar 29

12. The Bridge of Light	n	ASQ	Fall 29
13. Death From the Skies	nt	AS	Oct 29
14. Vampires of the Desert	s	AS	Dec 29
15. The Dirigibles of Death	nt	ASQ	Win 30
16. Beyond the Green Prism	n2	AS	Jan 30
17. The Feathered Detective	s	AS	Apr 30
18. The Non-Gravitational Vortex	nt	AS	Jun 30
19. Monsters of the Ray	nt	ASQ	Sum 30
20. A Visit to Suari	s	AS	Jul 30
21. When the Moon Ran Wild	n	ASQ	Win 31
22. The Exterminator	s	AS	Feb 31
23. The Treasure of the Golden God	n2	AS	Jan 33
24. The Death Drum	nt	AS	May 33
25. Through the Andes	n3	AS	Sep 34
26. The Inner World	n3	AS	Jun 35

10—DONALD WANDREI (Born 1908)

1. The Red Brain	s	WT	Oct 27
2. The Shadow of a Nightmare	s	WT	May 29
3. The Green Flame	s	WT	Jul 30
4. Something From Above	s	WT	Dec 30
5. The Tree-Man of M'Bwa	s	WT	Feb 32
6. Raiders of the Universes	s	ASS	Sep 32
7. The Lives of Alfred Kramar	s	WT	Dec 32
8. The Fire Vampires	s	WT	Feb 33
9. Spawn of the Sea	s	WT	May 33
10. A Race Through Time (A)	nt	ASS	Oct 33
11. Farewell to Earth (A)	nt	ASS	Dec 33
12. The Lady in Gray	s	WT	Dec 33
13. Colossus (B)	nt	ASS	Jan 34
14. The Man Who Never Lived	s	ASS	Mar 34
15. The Atom Smasher	s	ASS	Apr 34
16. Blinding Shadows	s	ASS	May 34
17. The Nerveless Man	s	ASS	Jul 34
18. A Scientist Divides	s	ASS	Sep 34
19. Colossus Eternal (B)	nt	ASS	Dec 34
20. Life Current	s	ASS	Apr 35
21. The Whisperers	s	ASS	May 35
22. Murray's Light	s	ASS	Jun 35
23. The Destroying Horde	s	WT	Jun 35
24. Earth Minus	nt	ASS	Sep 35

Series: A: Daniels and Conning (stories 10, 11); B: Colossus (stories 13, 19).

B—SUMMARY OF MAGAZINE ISSUES, 1926-1935

I—Science Fiction

Magazine	Number of Issues										
	1926*	1927	1928	1929	1930	1931	1932	1933	1934	1935*	Total
AIR WONDER STORIES	—	—	—	9	2	—	—	—	—	—	11
AMAZING STORIES	12	12	12	12	12	12	12	11	12	8	115
AMAZING STORIES ANNUAL	—	1	—	—	—	—	—	—	—	—	1
AMAZING STORIES QUARTERLY	—	1	4	4	4	4	2	2	1	—	22
ASTOUNDING STORIES	—	—	—	3	12	12	7	6	12	12	64
DOC SAVAGE	—	—	—	—	—	—	1	12	12	12	37
(a) MARVEL TALES	—	—	—	—	—	—	—	—	4	1	5
MIRACLE STORIES	—	—	—	—	—	2	—	—	—	—	2
(b) SCIENCE FICTION DIGEST	—	—	—	—	—	—	7	12	9	8	36
(c) SCIENTIFIC DETECTIVE MONTHLY	—	—	—	3	7	—	—	—	—	—	10
(d) SCIENCE WONDER QUARTERLY	—	—	—	2	4	4	4	—	—	—	14
(e) SCIENCE WONDER STORIES	—	—	—	10	12	12	12	10	12	10	78
SCOOPS	—	—	—	—	—	—	—	8	12	—	20
(a) UNUSUAL STORIES	—	—	—	—	—	—	—	1	—	2	3
	12	14	16	43	53	46	45	62	74	53	418

Note*: The year is taken from April to the following March, therefore for 1929 this covers the period, April 1929 to March 1930. This has been adopted because AMAZING STORIES first appeared in April 1926.

Magazine	1926	1927	1928	1929	1930	1931	1932	1933	1934	1935	Total
II—Weird											
DR. DEATH	—	—	—	—	—	—	—	—	2	1	3
GHOST STORIES	9	12	12	12	12	7	—	—	—	—	64
HORROR STORIES	—	—	—	—	—	—	—	—	3	8	11
(f) ORIENTAL STORIES	—	—	—	—	3	4	3	4	—	—	14
STRANGE TALES	—	—	—	—	—	4	3	—	—	—	7
TALES OF MAGIC & MYSTERY	—	4	1	—	—	—	—	—	—	—	5
TERROR TALES	—	—	—	—	—	—	—	—	7	12	19
THRILLING MYSTERY	—	—	—	—	—	—	—	—	—	5	5
(g) WEIRD TALES	12	12	12	12	11	10	12	12	12	12	117
	21	28	25	24	26	25	18	16	24	38	245

Number of Issues

(a) MARVEL TALES and UNUSUAL STORIES were semi-professional titles.

(b) SCIENCE FICTION DIGEST was an amateur magazine (or fanzine), but is included as a guide to its regularity since it was the news magazine of its period, and included the 'Cosmos' round-robin serial by many big-name authors.

(c) Includes issues retitled AMAZING DETECTIVE TALES.

(d) Includes issues retitled WONDER STORIES QUARTERLY.

(e) Includes issues retitled WONDER STORIES.

(f) Includes issues retitled THE MAGIC CARPET MAGAZINE.

(g) Prior to April 1926 thirty issues of WEIRD TALES had appeared.

N.B. SCOOPS is the only British title.

236 *Appendices*

C—GLOSSARY OF MAGAZINE EDITORS

BAIRD, Edwin. Editor WEIRD TALES, March 1923-May 1924 (13 issues).

BATES, Harry. Editor ASTOUNDING STORIES, January 1930-March 1933 (34 issues). Editor STRANGE TALES, (all 7 issues).

BOURNE, Miriam. Associate Editor AMAZING STORIES from October 1928. Later became Managing Editor until Sloane took full control in 1932.

CRAWFORD, William. Editor all issues MARVEL TALES (5) and UNUSUAL STORIES (3)

DAME, M. E. Associate Editor of: SCIENCE WONDER STORIES (all 12 issues).

DIMMOCK, Haydn. Editor all issues (20) of SCOOP.

DOLD, Elliot. Editor all issues (2) of MIRACLE SCIENCE & FANTASY STORIES.

GREY, Hector. Editor SCIENTIFIC DETECTIVE MONTHLY (all issues, 5), Editor AMAZING DETECTIVE TALES, June and July 1930 (2 issues).

GERNSBACK, Hugo. Editor or Editor-in-Chief of: AIR WONDER STORIES (all 11 issues); AMAZING STORIES April 1926-April 1929 (37 issues); AMAZING STORIES ANNUAL 1927 (1 issue); AMAZING STORIES QUARTERLY Winter 1928-Winter 1929 (5 issues); SCIENCE WONDER STORIES (all 12 issues); (SCIENCE) WONDER STORIES QUARTERLY (all 14 issues); SCIENTIFIC DETECTIVE MONTHLY (all 5 issues); AMAZING DETECTIVE TALES (all 5 issues); WONDER STORIES (all 66 issues). Plus many scientific magazines.

HALL, Desmond. Assistant Editor on ASTOUNDING STORIES for all Clayton issues, and initially under Street & Smith.

HORNIG, Charles. Editor WONDER STORIES November 1933-March 1936 (27 issues).

INGHER, Maurice. Editor SCIENCE FICTION DIGEST Sept 1932-March 1933 (7 issues).

LASSER, David. Managing Editor of: AIR WONDER STORIES (all 11 issues); SCIENCE WONDER STORIES (all 12 issues); WONDER STORIES June 1930-October 1933 (first 39 issues); WONDER STORIES QUARTERLY (all 14 issues); AMAZING DETECTIVE TALES August to October 1930 (last 3 issues).

LYNCH, Arthur H. Editor AMAZING STORIES May to October 1929 (6 issues), Editor AMAZING STORIES QUARTERLY, Spring & Summer 1929 (2 issues).

MASON, C. P. Associate Editor of: SCIENCE WONDER STORIES (all 12 issues); AIR WONDER STORIES (all 11 issues); WONDER STORIES (all 66 issues); WONDER STORIES QUARTERLY (all 14 issues).

NAPIER, Robert. Probable editor of GHOST STORIES (all 64 issues).

REEVE, Arthur B. Editorial Commissioner all 10 issues SCIENTIFIC DETECTIVE MONTHLY.

RUPPERT, Conrad H. Editor S. F. DIGEST/FANTASY MAGAZINE April 1933-January 1937 (32 issues).

SLOANE, T. O'Conor. Held the following posts: AMAZING STORIES: Managing Editor April 1926 (1 issue); Associate Editor, May 1926-October 1929 (42 issues); Editor November 1929-April 1938 (85 issues). AMAZING STORIES QUARTERLY: Associate Editor Winter 1928-Summer 1929 (7 issues); Editor Fall 1929 to Fall 1934 (15 issues).

TREMAINE, F. Orlin. Editor ASTOUNDING STORIES October 1933-October 1937 (49 issues).

WRIGHT, Farnsworth. Editor WEIRD TALES November 1924-March 1940 (179 issues); Editor ORIENTAL STORIES October 1930-Summer 1932 (all 9 issues); Editor MAGIC CARPET MAGAZINE January 1933-January 1934 (all 5 issues).

D—NOTE ON KEY ILLUSTRATORS

Naturally to sell on the news-stands a magazine must have an impressive cover, and during this period 1926-1935 each magazine is noted for its major artists, notably Frank R. Paul, Leo Morey, Howard Brown, Hans Wesso and Margaret Brundage. The following shows the proportion of covers each artist did for the magazines.

AIR WONDER STORIES	Frank R. Paul	11	(100%)
AMAZING STORIES	Leo Morey	61	(53%)
	Frank R. Paul	37	(32%)
	A. Sigmond	7	(6%)
	Hans Wesso	5	
	Hugh MacKay	2	
	Unknown	3	
AMAZING STORIES ANNUAL & QUARTERLY	Leo Morey	12	(52%)
	Frank R. Paul	8	(35%)
	Hans Wesso	1	
	Unknown	2	
ASTOUNDING STORIES	Hans Wesso	34	(53%)
	Howard V. Brown	30	(47%)
MIRACLE STORIES	Elliott Dold	2	(100%)
SCIENTIFIC DETECTIVE MONTHLY	Jnr. Rugo	6	(60%)
	Frank Paul	1	
	Unknown	3	
WONDER STORIES	Frank R. Paul	78	(100%)
WONDER STORIES QUARTERLY	Frank R. Paul	14	(100%)
WEIRD TALES	C. C. Senf	45	(39%)
	Margaret Brundage	37	(32%)
	Hugh Rankin	15	(13%)
	J. Allan St. John	7	(6%)
	E. M. Stevenson	5	
	C. Barker Petrie	5	
	Andrew Bensen	1	
	Joseph Doolin	1	
	T. Wyatt Nelson	1	
STRANGE TALES	Hans Wesso	7	(100%)
ORIENTAL STORIES (inc. MAGIC CARPET)	Margaret Brundage	6	(43%)
	Von Gelb	5	(36%)
	J. Allan St. John	2	
	Lucille Holling	1	

ACKNOWLEDGEMENTS

Apart from actual magazine issues, the following books and indices were consulted in whole or in part during the course of compiling this collection.

CARTER, Lin: "Imaginary Worlds", Ballantine Books Inc,. New York (June 1973).

GRUBER, Frank: "The Pulp Jungle", Sherbourne Press, Los Angeles (1967).

HERSEY, Harold: "Pulpwood Editor", F. A. Stokes Co., New York (1937).

MOSKOWITZ, Sam: "Science Fiction by Gaslight", World Pub. Co., Cleveland (1968); "Explorers of the Infinite", World Pub. Co., Cleveland (1963); "Seekers of Tomorrow", World Pub. Co., Cleveland (1966).

ROGERS, Alva: "A Requiem For Astounding", Advent Pub. Inc., Chicago (1964).

WARNER, Harry: "All Our Yesterdays", Advent Pub. Inc., Chicago (April 1969).

HARBOTTLE, Philip: "The Multi-Man: A biographical and Bibliographical study of John Russell Fearn", Wallsend (1968).

GILLINGS, Walter: "The Clamorous Dreamers", a series of personal articles published in VISION OF TOMORROW from issue 1 to 12.

COCKCROFT, T. G. L.: "Index to the Weird Fiction Magazines", Cockcroft, New Zealand (1964).

DAY, Brad M: "The Complete Checklist of Science-Fiction Magazines", Wehman Bros., New York (1961).

DAY, Donald B.: "Index to the Science-Fiction Magazines", Perri Press, Portland (1952).

EVANS, Bill & PAVLAT, Bob: "Fanzine Index", Piser, New York (1965).

In addition certain usage was made of the standard reference books such as "Who's Who" and "Who Was Who", and "Contemporary Authors".